KEN SANCHEZ

Starcrossed (Willowbrook Book Four)

A Tale of Hope and Love

Contents

Author's Acknowledgement

Hi there! Thanks for picking up this book. If you're enjoying my work, you can find more stories like this if you scan the QR code below. While you're there, consider leaving a review once you've finished reading the book – it really helps a writer out!

Prologue

Rowan Elderwood stood before his father, King Oberon, in the grand throne room of the Seelie Court. The air was thick with tension, and Rowan could feel the weight of his father's gaze upon him, appraising and critical.

"Rowan," the king began, his voice a deep, resonant baritone that echoed through the cavernous space. "I have a task for you, one that will prove your worth as a prince of this realm."

Rowan's heart leapt at the words, a flicker of excitement and apprehension washing over him. He had always longed for his father's approval, for some sign that he was more than just a disappointment, a failure in the eyes of the great King Oberon.

"Of course, Father," he said, his voice steady and strong despite the nerves that fluttered in his stomach. "I am ready and willing to serve, to do whatever you ask of me."

The king's lips curved in a smile, but there was no warmth in the gesture, no hint of affection or pride. "Good," he said, his voice cold and calculating. "I need you to gather a rare and powerful artifact hidden deep within the heart of the Willowbrook forest. It is a gem of great beauty and power, one that will help to secure our reign over this realm for generations to come."

Rowan frowned, a flicker of unease washing over him at his father's words. He had heard whispers of the dark magic that lurked within the Willowbrook forest, of the ancient and terrible curses that guarded its secrets. But he pushed those thoughts aside, determined to prove himself worthy of his father's trust.

"I will not fail you, Father," he said, his chin lifted and his eyes blazing with determination. "I will find this gem and bring it back to you, no matter what challenges may lie ahead."

The king's smile widened, but there was something cold and calculating in his gaze, a glimmer of malice that made Rowan's skin crawl. "See that you do, my son," he said, his voice a low, menacing purr. "For the consequences of failure would be… most unpleasant."

Rowan swallowed hard, a shiver of fear running down his spine at the unspoken threat in his father's words. But he refused to let his doubts show, refused to give any hint of the uncertainty that gnawed at his heart.

"I understand, Father," he said, his voice calm and even. "I will not let you down."

And with that, Rowan turned and strode from the throne room, his steps quick and purposeful as he made his way towards the stables, towards the horse that would carry him to his destiny.

As he rode through the lush, verdant forests of the Seelie Court, Rowan's mind raced with thoughts of the task that lay ahead. He had always been a dutiful son, a loyal servant to his father and his realm. But something about this mission felt different, felt wrong in a way that he couldn't quite put into words.

"Stop being so paranoid," he muttered to himself, shaking his head to clear away the nagging doubts that whispered in his mind. "Father knows what he's doing. He wouldn't send you on a fool's errand, not when the fate of the kingdom is at stake."

But even as he spoke the words, Rowan couldn't shake the feeling of unease that settled in the pit of his stomach, the sense that he was walking into a trap of his own making.

As he approached the borders of the Willowbrook forest, Rowan felt a strange sensation wash over him, a tingling, electric hum that seemed to vibrate through his very bones. The air was thick and heavy, charged with an ancient, primal energy that made the hairs on the back of his neck stand on end.

"What is this place?" he whispered, his eyes wide and wary as he scanned the dense, twisting trees that loomed before him. "It feels… alive, somehow. Like it's watching me, waiting for me to make a move."

But Rowan was not one to be easily deterred, not when he had a mission to complete and a father to impress. With a deep, steadying breath, he dismounted from his horse, his hand resting on the hilt of his sword as he took his first steps into the shadowy depths of the forest.

As he walked, Rowan couldn't shake the feeling that he was being watched, that unseen eyes were tracking his every move. The trees seemed to whisper and sigh, their branches creaking and groaning like ancient, arthritic bones. And the shadows… the shadows seemed to dance and flicker with a life of their own, twisting and writhing like serpents in the gloom.

"Get a grip, Rowan," he muttered, his voice tight with tension as he pushed deeper into the forest. "It's just your imagination playing tricks on you. There's nothing to be afraid of."

But even as he spoke the words, he heard a sound that made his blood run cold, a low, menacing growl that seemed to come from everywhere and nowhere all at once.

Rowan froze, his hand tightening on the hilt of his sword as he scanned the shadows, searching for the source of the sound. But there was nothing, only the endless, oppressive gloom of the forest pressing in on him from all sides.

"Who's there?" he called out, his voice ringing with false bravado. "Show yourself, coward!"

But there was no response, only the echo of his own words fading into the silence.

With a shudder, Rowan pressed on, his steps growing more cautious and wary as he delved deeper into the heart of the forest. He knew that he had to find the gem, had to complete the task that his father had set before him. But with every passing moment, he could feel the weight of the forest's dark magic pressing down on him, suffocating him like a heavy, woolen cloak.

Suddenly, he heard another sound, a faint, musical chiming that seemed to dance on the edge of his hearing. It was a sound he recognized, a sound that made his heart leap with sudden, wild hope.

"The gem," he breathed, his eyes widening with excitement as he quickened his pace, following the elusive melody deeper into the shadows. "It has to be close. I can feel it."

As he rounded a bend in the path, Rowan stopped short, his breath catching in his throat at the sight that greeted him. There, in the center of a small, moonlit clearing, was a tree unlike any he had ever seen. Its bark was a shimmering, iridescent silver, its leaves a deep, rich green that seemed to glow with an inner light. And there, nestled in the crook of its branches, was a gem of such breathtaking beauty that it stole the air from his lungs.

"Finally," Rowan whispered, a grin spreading across his face as he stepped forward, his hand outstretched to claim his prize.

But as his fingers closed around the gem, he felt a sudden, searing pain rip through his body, a white-hot agony that brought him to his knees. The world around him began to blur and distort, the colors bleeding together like a kaleidoscope of madness.

And then, through the haze of pain and confusion, Rowan heard a voice, a cold, cruel laugh that made his blood run cold.

"Foolish boy," the voice said, dripping with malice and contempt. "Did you really think it would be so easy? Did you really believe that I would let you claim such power for yourself?"

Rowan's head snapped up, his eyes widening with horror as he saw his father step out from behind the tree, his face twisted into a mask of cruel, mocking triumph.

"Father?" he gasped, his voice raw and ragged with betrayal. "What… what have you done?"

King Oberon chuckled, his eyes glittering with a dark, malevolent glee. "Oh, my naive little prince," he crooned, his voice sickly sweet. "I've simply ensured that you will never be a threat to me, never be more than a pawn in my grand designs."

He raised his hand, and Rowan felt the pain intensify, his body convulsing and twisting as the dark magic of the tree began to seep into his veins.

"You see, Rowan," the king continued, his voice cold and pitiless, "I knew that you would come here, knew that your foolish sense of loyalty and duty would lead you straight into my trap. And now, thanks to your own stubborn pride, you will spend the rest of eternity trapped within this tree, a fitting punishment for a son who dared to dream of surpassing his father."

Rowan tried to scream, tried to beg for mercy, but his voice was silenced, trapped within the wooden prison that was slowly consuming him. He could feel his limbs growing heavy and stiff, his skin hardening into bark as the curse took hold.

And then, with a final, agonized gasp, Prince Rowan Elderwood was gone, his consciousness fading into the endless, dreamless sleep of the enchanted tree.

King Oberon stood over the twisted, gnarled trunk that had once been his son, a cruel smile playing across his lips. "Sleep well, my foolish boy," he whispered, his voice thick with malice. "May your dreams be filled with the knowledge of your own failure, your own pathetic inadequacy."

And with that, he turned and strode from the clearing, his laughter echoing through the shadows as he left his son to his fate.

For centuries, Rowan slumbered within the heart of the tree, his mind trapped in an endless, tortured loop of regret and despair. He dreamed of his brothers, of Aedan and his powerful magic and unshakeable courage. He dreamed of the kingdom he had failed, the people he had let down with his own stubborn pride.

But most of all, he dreamed of love, of the soulmate he had always longed for but never found. In his dreams, he saw a face, a smile that lit up the darkness like a beacon of hope. But always, just as he reached out to take his love's hand, the dream would shatter, leaving him once more alone and lost in the endless void.

And so Rowan waited, trapped within the silver tree, his heart yearning for a love he had never known and a freedom he feared would never come. The world turned and changed around him, but still he remained, a forgotten prince, a lost soul bound by the cruelest of fates.

Until one day, when a gentle hand brushed against the bark of the tree, and a voice like music whispered his name. Until the kiss of true love, given freely and without hesitation, broke the curse at last and set him free.

But that is a story for another time, a tale of love and redemption that has yet to be told. For now, Rowan sleeps on, waiting for the day when his soulmate will find him and bring him back to the world of the living.

Waiting, always waiting, for the love that will finally set him free.

1

Restless Heart

Luca

Luca Wolfheart was in his workshop. It was like his own little world, a place where he could just tune out all the pack drama and lose himself in his craft. The warm, golden light filtering through the high windows made the whole room feel cozy and inviting. And the smell? Man, it was like a mix of wood, metal, and leather all rolled into one - the kind of scent that just filled your lungs and made you feel at home.

So, there he was, standing at his workbench, his hands working like magic on his latest project - this wicked hunting knife. The blade was so shiny and sharp, it could probably cut through anything. And Luca? He was totally in the zone, etching these crazy detailed designs into the handle like it was nothing.

The workshop was like a treasure hunt, with shelves packed full of jars, leather, and all sorts of raw materials. And the forge in the corner? It was glowing like a beacon, casting this warm, orange light that made everything feel a little bit warmer. Everywhere you looked, there were Luca's creations - swords, bows, armor - each one a masterpiece in its

1

own right.

But even as he worked, Luca's mind kept drifting to the upcoming pack run. It was his chance to show his father and brother that he was more than just the spare, the second-best. He wanted their approval so badly, to feel like he belonged. But at the same time, a part of him just wanted to rebel against their expectations.

Just then, he heard footsteps and looked up to see his mother, Emilia, walking into the workshop. She was this tall, classy lady with warm brown eyes and a smile that could melt even the coldest heart.

"Luca, my love," she said, her voice soft and worried. "You've been holed up in here for hours. Everything okay?"

Luca put down his tools and turned to look at her, a small smile tugging at his lips. "I'm good, Mother. Just working on a new project."

His mother stepped closer, checking out the knife on the workbench. "It's gorgeous, Luca. Your father would be so proud."

Luca's smile faltered, and he looked away. "I doubt it. He's never been proud of anything I've done."

She reached out, putting her hand on Luca's shoulder. "That's not true, Luca. Your father loves you, even if he's not always the best at showing it."

Luca sighed, his shoulders sagging under the weight of his doubts. "I just want to prove myself, Mother. To show him that I'm worthy of being his son."

"You don't need to prove anything, Luca," his mother said, her voice firm but kind. "You're a talented craftsman, a loyal member of the pack, and a loving son. That's all that matters."

Luca nodded, his heart full of gratitude for his mother's constant support. "Thanks, Mother. I don't know what I'd do without you."

She smiled, her eyes crinkling at the corners. "You'd be just fine, my love. But I'll always be here for you, no matter what."

They stood there for a moment, just enjoying each other's company.

Then, his mother spoke again, her voice full of genuine curiosity.

"Are you excited for the pack run, Luca? I know how much you love the thrill of the hunt."

"You can say that. It's always been one of my favorite times of the year. Running with the pack, feeling the wind in my fur... there's nothing like it."

She chuckled, her eyes twinkling with amusement. "I remember when you were just a little pup, tripping over your own paws trying to keep up with your father and brother. You've come a long way since then."

Luca grinned, a rare moment of pure joy breaking through his serious exterior. "I may have grown up, but I still feel that same excitement every time we run together."

She nodded, her expression soft and understanding. "I do, Luca. The pack is more than just a bunch of wolves—it's a family, tied together by love and loyalty. And you, my son, are a crucial part of that family, no matter what anyone else may say or think."

Luca's heart swelled with emotion, his mother's words soothing his troubled soul. He knew the road ahead wouldn't be easy—that he'd have to face his own doubts and insecurities, as well as the challenges waiting outside their territory. But with his mother's love and the strength of the pack behind him, he felt a new sense of purpose and determination.

"Thanks, Mother," he said, his voice rough with emotion. "For everything."

Emilia pulled him into a tight hug, her arms wrapping around him with a fierce, protective love. "Always, my son. Always."

After his mother left, Luca turned back to his workbench, feeling a bit better after their chat. His eyes wandered from the shiny weapons to a small, wooden figure tucked away in the corner, almost hidden by all the tools and materials. He reached for it, his fingers wrapping around the smooth, cool surface, and brought it into the light.

The figure was still rough, its features only half-done, but Luca could see the potential in it. He'd been working on it for weeks, ever since the dreams started—these vivid, haunting visions of a young man with golden hair and violet eyes, trapped in an endless sleep. Luca had no idea what the dreams meant, but he felt this weird connection to the figure, like it held the key to unlocking some mystery he hadn't figured out yet.

He turned the figure over in his hands, checking out the delicate lines and curves he'd carved into the wood. The young man's face was peaceful, his eyes closed like he was just resting, but there was this sense of sadness and longing in his expression that tugged at Luca's heart. He wondered what the figure's story was, and why it had chosen to appear to him in his dreams.

As he worked, Luca got lost in the rhythm of his craft, his fingers moving with a sureness and grace that hid the chaos in his heart. He carved and smoothed, shaping the figure with a care and reverence that was almost like worship. The hours flew by without him noticing, the golden light of the workshop fading to a soft, silver glow as the moon climbed high in the sky.

It was only when a distant howl broke the silence that Luca looked up, blinking in surprise as he realized how late it had gotten. He glanced at the figure in his hands, amazed at the progress he'd made. The young man's features were clearer now, more defined, and Luca felt this strange sense of connection to him, like he was a long-lost friend rather than just something he'd imagined.

He set the figure down, his fingers lingering on the smooth wood for a moment longer, before turning towards the door. The call of the wild was strong tonight, and Luca could feel this restless energy humming through his veins, urging him to run, to hunt, to be free.

He stepped outside, the cool night air washing over him like a soothing balm. The moon was full and bright, casting a silver glow over the pack's territory. Luca closed his eyes, feeling the familiar tingle of magic as his body started to shift and change.

Fur rippled over his skin, his bones and muscles rearranging themselves into a new, powerful form. In moments, he was a wolf, his senses sharp and his instincts honed to a razor's edge. He shook out his coat, reveling in the strength and grace of his animal form, before throwing back his head and letting out a long, haunting howl.

The sound echoed through the night, a primal cry of joy and longing that seemed to come from the very depths of his soul. Luca felt a rush of exhilaration as he bounded forward, his paws barely touching the ground as he raced through the forest.

The world was a blur of silver and shadow, the scents and sounds of the night sharp and clear in his heightened senses. Luca ran for the sheer joy of it, his muscles bunching and stretching as he leapt over fallen logs and wove through the undergrowth. He could feel the pulse of the earth beneath his paws, the whisper of the wind in his fur, and for a moment, all his troubles and doubts seemed to fade away.

But even as he ran, his thoughts kept returning to the wooden figure, to the mysterious young man who haunted his dreams. Luca didn't know what the future held, or what role he was meant to play in the unfolding story of his life. But he knew that he would face whatever challenges lay ahead with the same stubborn determination and silent courage that had always been his strength.

Luca's paws carried him through the forest, his heart pounding in rhythm with the steady thrum of the earth beneath him. As he ran, he felt this pull from deep within, like something was guiding him towards an unknown destination. He followed the feeling, his curiosity piqued, until he found himself in this secluded clearing bathed in the soft, silver light of the moon.

He slowed to a walk, his ears twitching as he took in the peaceful surroundings. The clearing was like this small haven, with tall, ancient trees lining the edges, seeming to whisper secrets in the gentle breeze. Luca padded to the center, his nose filled with the scent of wildflowers and damp earth, and settled himself on a soft patch of moss.

As he lay there, his thoughts drifted to the conversation he had overheard between his father and the pack elders. They'd been talking about the possibility of an alliance with a rival pack, a union that would be sealed by Luca's mating with the daughter of the other pack's alpha. Luca's heart had clenched at the thought, a wave of despair washing over him at the idea of being forced into a loveless bond.

He knew that his father only wanted what was best for the pack, but Luca couldn't shake the feeling that there was something more waiting for him, a destiny that went beyond the confines of pack politics and arranged matings.

He closed his eyes, his mind drifting back to a conversation he had had with his grandfather years ago, when he was still a young pup.

"Grandpa, what's a fated mate?" Luca asked, his green eyes wide with curiosity as he looked up at the old wolf.

His grandfather chuckled, a warm, rumbling sound that seemed to come from deep within his chest. "Ah, my boy, that's a question that has been asked by many a wolf over the years."

He settled himself on the ground, his joints creaking with age, and patted the spot beside him. Luca eagerly clambered up, snuggling into his grandfather's side as he waited for the story to begin.

"You see, Luca, a fated mate is a rare and precious thing," his grandfather began, his voice low and filled with reverence. "It's a bond that goes beyond the usual ties of pack and family, a connection that is forged in the very depths of our souls."

Luca frowned, trying to wrap his mind around the concept. "But how do you know when you've found your fated mate?"

His grandfather smiled, his eyes twinkling with a hint of mischief.

"That's the thing, my boy. You don't always know, not at first. It's a feeling that grows over time, a sense of rightness and belonging that cannot be denied."

He paused, his gaze drifting off into the distance as if lost in a memory. "I remember when I first met your grandmother. I was a young wolf then, full of fire and ambition, and I thought I had my whole life planned out. But then I saw her, and it was like the world stopped spinning for a moment."

Luca leaned forward, his eyes wide with wonder. "What happened then, Grandpa?"

His grandfather chuckled, ruffling Luca's fur with a gentle paw. "I made a fool of myself, that's what happened. I stumbled over my words, tripped over my own feet, and generally acted like a love-struck pup. But your grandmother, she just smiled and shook her head, and I knew right then that she was the one for me."

Luca sighed, a wistful expression on his face. "I hope I find my fated mate someday, Grandpa."

His grandfather nodded, his expression turning serious. "You will, my boy. But remember, a fated mate can be anyone, not just another wolf. The moon has a way of bringing together those who are meant to be, regardless of the form they take."

Luca frowned, confused. "But I thought wolves were only supposed to mate with other wolves."

His grandfather shook his head, a knowing smile on his face. "The heart wants what it wants, Luca. And when you find your fated mate, you'll understand that the form they take matters far less than the love you share."

Luca's opened his eyes and his mind lingered on his grandfather's words, the memory as vivid and poignant as the day it had been imparted. He felt a warmth spreading through his chest, a flicker of hope that refused to be extinguished despite the pressures and expectations that weighed upon him.

As he sat in the clearing, lost in thought, a soft breeze began to swirl around him, ruffling his fur with a gentle, almost playful touch. Luca's eyes drifted closed, a shiver running down his spine as the wind seemed to whisper secrets meant only for his ears.

It felt like a caress, a comforting presence that soothed his troubled heart and eased the ache of loneliness that had settled deep within his bones. Luca couldn't help but wonder if this was a sign, a subtle hint from the universe that his fated mate was out there somewhere, waiting to be found.

He inhaled deeply, the scent of the forest filling his lungs and mingling with the faint, elusive aroma carried on the breeze. It was a scent he couldn't quite place, sweet and spicy and altogether enticing, and it seemed to tug at something primal within him, urging him to follow wherever it might lead.

But Luca knew that he couldn't just abandon his responsibilities, couldn't turn his back on the pack that relied on him for guidance and protection. He was the alpha's son, the future leader of their people, and he had duties to uphold and expectations to meet.

Still, as he rose to his feet and began the long trek back to the pack's territory, Luca couldn't shake the feeling that his life was about to change in ways he could never have imagined. The breeze seemed to follow him, dancing around his paws and ruffling his fur with a playful insistence, as if urging him to keep his heart open and his mind ready for the journey ahead.

2

Shadows of the Past

Luca

He stood at the stove, stirring a pot of his favorite stew, the rich aroma of tender meat and fragrant herbs filling the air with a comforting warmth.

As he worked, Luca's mind wandered, drifting back to the days when this kitchen had been the heart of his childhood home, a place where he and his brother Gareth had spent countless hours playing, laughing, and dreaming of the future they would share as leaders of the pack.

But those days were long gone now, lost to the shifting tides of time and the weight of duty and responsibility. Luca sighed, his heart heavy with the memory of all that had changed between them, the once unbreakable bond strained by the expectations and demands of their father and the pack.

Suddenly, the kitchen door swung open with a bang, startling Luca from his thoughts. He looked up to see Gareth striding into the room, his expression hard and his eyes cold as he fixed Luca with a piercing stare.

"What are you doing here?" Gareth demanded, his voice rough with barely contained anger. "Shouldn't you be out patrolling the borders, making sure the pack is safe?"

Luca bristled at the accusation, his own temper flaring to life in the face of his brother's hostility. "I've already completed my patrols for the day," he replied, his voice tight with barely contained frustration. "And I have just as much right to be here as you do."

Gareth scoffed, his lip curling into a sneer as he looked around the kitchen with disdain. "Right," he said, his voice dripping with sarcasm. "Because cooking and cleaning are such important duties for a future alpha."

Luca felt his heart clench at the barb, the words cutting deep into the already raw wound of their fractured relationship. There had been a time when Gareth would have been right there beside him, chopping vegetables and telling jokes as they worked side by side to prepare a meal for the pack.

Luca could still remember the day their father had declared Gareth the next alpha, the pride and triumph that had shone in his brother's eyes as he accepted the mantle of leadership.

At first, Luca had been happy for him, proud to see his brother taking on such an important role in the pack. But as the years passed and Gareth grew more distant, more consumed by the demands of his new position, Luca had begun to feel the sting of betrayal, the sense that he had been left behind and forgotten by the one person who had always been his closest ally and friend.

"Gareth," Luca said, his voice soft and pleading as he looked up at his brother with eyes full of hurt and confusion. "What happened to us? We used to be so close, so inseparable. And now…now it's like I don't even know you anymore."

For a moment, Gareth's expression softened, a flicker of the old warmth and affection shining through the hard mask of the alpha. But then it was gone, replaced by a cold, unyielding determination as he squared his shoulders and fixed Luca with a hard stare.

"Things change, Luca," he said, his voice flat and emotionless. "We're not kids anymore, playing at being warriors and dreaming of the future. I have responsibilities now, duties to the pack that come before everything else. And you…you need to find your own place, your own purpose. Because I can't carry you forever."

Luca felt the words like a blow, the air rushing from his lungs as he stared at his brother in shock and disbelief. He wanted to argue, to protest that he had never asked Gareth to carry him, that he was just as strong and capable as any other member of the pack.

But the words wouldn't come, stuck in his throat like shards of glass as he watched Gareth turn and walk away, his broad shoulders disappearing through the kitchen door and out into the bright sunlight beyond.

For a long moment, Luca simply stood there, his heart aching with the weight of all that had been lost between them. He knew that Gareth was right, that they couldn't go back to the way things had been, to the innocent dreams and unshakable bond of their childhood.

But even so, he couldn't help but cling to the hope that someday, somehow, they would find their way back to each other.

With a heavy sigh, Luca turned back to the stove, his hands moving automatically as he stirred the stew and tried to lose himself once more in the simple, comforting rituals of cooking. He knew that the road ahead would be hard, that there would be challenges and obstacles at every turn.

But he also knew that he would face them with the same stubborn determination and quiet strength that had always been his greatest asset, the unshakable conviction that he would find his own path, his own purpose, no matter how long or difficult the journey might be.

Luca was just about to lose himself in his thoughts when Gareth's voice cut through the silence once more, his tone sharp and impatient. "Father has summoned everyone to the pack house," he said, his eyes narrowing as he looked at Luca with a mixture of annoyance and frustration. "He sent me to fetch you."

Luca felt a surge of irritation at the words, his jaw clenching as he met his brother's gaze with a defiant stare. It was just like his father to send Gareth to do his bidding, to treat Luca like a wayward pup who needed to be brought to heel. He couldn't help but wonder if it was a deliberate slight, a way for his father to remind him of his place in the pack hierarchy.

"And he couldn't come himself?" Luca asked, his voice tight with barely contained anger. "He had to send you, like I'm some kind of errant child who needs to be scolded and corrected?"

Gareth's expression hardened, his eyes flashing with a warning light as he took a step closer to Luca. "Watch your tone, brother," he growled, his voice low and menacing. "Father is the alpha, and his word is law. If he sends me to fetch you, then that's what I'll do. And you'll come, whether you like it or not."

Luca felt a bitter laugh bubbling up in his throat, the sound harsh and humorless as it echoed through the kitchen. He knew that Gareth was right, that he had no choice but to obey his father's summons. But that didn't make it any easier to swallow, didn't ease the sting of rejection and abandonment that he felt every time his father looked at him with those cold, distant eyes.

"Fine," he said at last, his voice flat and emotionless as he turned away from Gareth and back to the stove. "Just let me finish up here, and I'll be right behind you."

Gareth hesitated for a moment, his expression unreadable as he watched Luca work. Then, with a curt nod, he turned and strode out of the kitchen, his footsteps echoing through the empty halls of the house.

He ate quickly, his mind still churning with questions and doubts as he shoveled the stew into his mouth. When he was finished, he washed the bowl and spoon and put them away, his movements mechanical and automatic as he tried to push down the rising tide of anxiety that threatened to overwhelm him.

Then, with a final, deep breath, he squared his shoulders and headed for the door, his steps heavy and reluctant as he made his way out into the bright sunlight.

The walk to the pack house was a familiar one, a path that Luca had trodden countless times over the years. But today, it felt different somehow, weighted with a sense of foreboding that he couldn't quite shake.

As he approached the sprawling, rustic structure that served as the heart of the Wolfheart Pack, Luca felt a pang of nostalgia, a bittersweet longing for the days when things had been simpler, easier. He could still remember the long, hot summers he had spent working alongside his father, learning the skills of carpentry and woodworking as they built the house together.

Luca stepped through the heavy wooden door of the pack house. The rich aroma of burning sage and cedar filled his nostrils, mingling with the earthy musk of wolf and the sweet, floral notes of his mother's favorite perfume.

A pair of strong, slender arms wrapped around him, pulling him into a tight, fierce hug. Luca stiffened for a moment, caught off guard by the sudden display of affection. But then he relaxed into the embrace, breathing in the sweet, comforting scent of his mother as she held him close.

"My boys," she murmured, her voice soft and warm with love as she pulled back to look at them both.

Luca felt a lump rising in his throat as he met his mother's gaze, saw the depth of love and concern shining in her bright, clear eyes. He knew that she could sense the tension between him and Gareth, the unspoken hurt and resentment that had been building for years. But even so, she never took sides, never tried to force them to reconcile or make peace. Instead, she simply loved them both, fiercely and unconditionally, and trusted that they would find their own way back to each other in time.

"Mother," Gareth said, his voice gruff and almost embarrassed as he pulled away from her embrace. "We don't have time for this. Father is waiting for us in the meeting room."

"I know, my love," she said, her voice gentle but firm as she looked at Gareth with a mixture of affection and exasperation. "But a mother's love is never a waste of time. And besides, your father can wait a moment longer. He's not going anywhere."

Gareth looked like he wanted to argue, but something in their mother's expression stopped him. He sighed heavily, his shoulders slumping in resignation as he nodded and stepped back, allowing her to lead them both down the long, winding hallway that led to the heart of the pack house.

Luca couldn't help but marvel at the way his mother seemed to glide through the halls, her steps light and graceful despite the weight of her years. She had always been the heart of their family, the glue that held them together even when everything else seemed to be falling apart. And now, as they made their way towards the meeting room and the unknown challenges that awaited them there, Luca felt a surge of gratitude for her presence, for the way she always seemed to know just what to say or do to ease the tension and soothe the hurt.

As they approached the heavy, iron-bound door that led to the meeting room, Luca felt his heart begin to race, his palms growing damp with sweat as he tried to steady his breathing and calm his racing thoughts. He knew that he needed to be strong, to be the kind of leader that his father, Alpha Wolfheart, expected him to be. But even as he squared his shoulders and lifted his chin, he couldn't shake the feeling that he was walking into a trap, that the ground beneath his feet was about to give way and send him tumbling into an abyss from which there was no escape.

Beside him, Gareth seemed to sense his unease, his eyes narrowing as he glanced over at Luca with a mixture of concern and irritation. "Get a grip, brother," he muttered, his voice low and harsh as he reached for the door handle. "We don't have time for your nerves."

Luca felt a surge of anger at his brother's dismissive tone, but he bit back the sharp retort that rose to his lips, knowing that now was not the time or place for another argument. Instead, he took a deep, steadying breath and nodded, steeling himself for whatever lay beyond that door.

As Gareth pushed the heavy door open and stepped into the room beyond, Luca felt a moment of disorientation, his eyes struggling to adjust to the dim, flickering light of the torches that lined the walls. But as his vision cleared and he took in the scene before him, he felt a jolt of surprise and confusion that nearly knocked him off his feet.

There, seated at the long, wooden table that dominated the center of the room, was his father, his expression grave and his eyes hard as he looked up at his sons with a mixture of expectation and disapproval. But it was the figure seated beside him that caught Luca's attention, the one that made his heart skip a beat and his breath catch in his throat.

Alpha Jensen, the leader of the allied Jensen Pack and one of his father's closest confidants, sat tall and proud in his chair, his piercing blue eyes fixed on Luca with an intensity that made him want to squirm and look away. Luca had never been particularly close to the other alpha, had always felt a sense of unease and mistrust in his presence. But now, as he looked at the man who held the fate of their pack in his hands, he couldn't help but feel a flicker of fear, a cold, creeping sense of dread that threatened to overwhelm him at any moment.

"Father," Gareth said, his voice steady and confident as he inclined his head in a brief, respectful nod. "Alpha Jensen. We came as soon as we received your summons."

Their father grunted in acknowledgment, his eyes never leaving Luca's face as he gestured for them to take their seats at the table. Luca hesitated for a moment, his heart pounding in his chest as he tried to read the expression on his father's face, to glean some hint of what this meeting was about and why Alpha Jensen had been called to attend.

But his father's expression remained inscrutable, his eyes hard and unreadable as he waited for Luca to take his place beside Gareth. With a heavy sigh, Luca sank into his chair, his muscles tense and his nerves thrumming with anticipation as he waited for his father to speak.

"I called you here today because we have important matters to discuss," his father began, his voice deep and resonant as it echoed through the dim, shadowy room. "Matters that concern the future of our pack and the safety of our people."

Luca felt a flicker of unease at his father's words, his mind racing as he tried to understand what could be so important, so urgent that it required the presence of Alpha Jensen and the secrecy of this closed-door meeting. He glanced over at Gareth, hoping to see some hint of understanding or reassurance in his brother's eyes. But Gareth's expression was just as unreadable as their father's, his jaw set and his gaze fixed straight ahead as he waited for their father to continue.

"As you know, the world beyond our borders is changing," their father went on, his voice growing harder and more urgent with each word. "New threats are emerging, old alliances are shifting, and the balance of power is beginning to tilt in ways that could have dire consequences for our pack and our way of life."

"What kind of threats are we talking about, Father?" Gareth asked, his voice steady and even despite the tension that Luca could see in the set of his shoulders and the clench of his jaw. "And what does Alpha Jensen have to do with all of this?"

Their father exchanged a grave look with Alpha Jensen before speaking, his voice heavy with concern. "Some of the wolves from the Jensen Pack have gone missing, and they still haven't been found."

Luca felt a chill run down his spine at the news, his mind racing with the implications of what his father had just said. Missing wolves were always a cause for concern, but for them to have disappeared from an allied pack was even more troubling.

"We suspect that the Silverfang Pack may be responsible," their father continued, his eyes narrowing with suspicion and anger.

Luca's brow furrowed at the accusation, a sense of unease settling in his gut. "Do we have any evidence to support this?" he asked, his voice steady despite the tension that thrummed through his body. "Making accusations against a rival pack like Silverfang could lead to war if we're not careful."

His father was silent for a long moment, his expression unreadable as he studied Luca with a calculating gaze. "There have been reports that some of our own have gone missing as well," he said at last, his voice heavy with the weight of his words.

Luca felt a jolt of shock and disbelief at his father's revelation, his eyes widening as he tried to process what he had just heard. Beside him, Gareth let out a low growl of anger and frustration, his hands clenching into fists as he leaned forward in his chair.

"Why weren't we told about this?" Gareth demanded, his voice tight with barely contained rage. "I'm supposed to be the next Alpha, and yet you've kept this from me?"

Their father's eyes flashed with annoyance at Gareth's outburst, his expression hardening as he fixed his eldest son with a stern glare. "You are not the Alpha yet, Gareth," he said, his voice cold and unyielding. "I will rule this pack as I see fit until the day I step down."

Gareth's jaw clenched at the rebuke, his eyes blazing with anger and defiance as he pushed back from the table and stood up, his chair scraping loudly against the stone floor. "If that's how you want it, then so be it," he snarled, his voice dripping with bitterness and resentment. "But don't expect me to sit back and do nothing while our pack is threatened."

With that, he turned on his heel and stormed out of the room, the heavy wooden door slamming shut behind him with a resounding bang. Luca watched him go, his heart heavy with a sense of helplessness and frustration. He couldn't blame his brother for his anger, couldn't fault him for feeling betrayed and left out of the loop.

But he also knew that losing his temper and lashing out at their father would only make things worse, would only drive a deeper wedge between them at a time when they needed to be united more than ever. With a heavy sigh, Luca pushed back from the table and stood up, his expression apologetic as he met his father's gaze.

"I'll go talk to him," he said, his voice soft but firm. "He's just upset and worried about the pack. I'm sure he didn't mean any disrespect."

His father grunted in acknowledgment, his expression softening slightly as he nodded his head towards the door. "Go on, then," he said, his voice gruff but not unkind. "See if you can talk some sense into that thick skull of his."

Luca nodded, his heart heavy but his resolve unshaken as he turned and headed for the door, his footsteps echoing loudly in the silence of the room. He knew exactly where his brother would have gone, knew the one place where he always retreated when he needed to clear his head and gather his thoughts.

The hidden waterfall in the Willowbrook Woods had been their secret spot since they were pups, a place where they could escape the pressures and expectations of pack life and just be themselves. As Luca made his way through the dense underbrush, his senses attuned to the familiar scents and sounds of the forest, he couldn't help but feel a pang of nostalgia for the simpler times they had shared, the easy camaraderie and unshakable bond that had once defined their relationship.

As Luca emerged into the clearing that housed the waterfall, he caught sight of his brother sitting on a large, flat rock by the water's edge, his shoulders hunched and his head bowed as if under a great weight.

"Gareth," Luca called out, his voice soft and tentative as he approached his brother's side. "I'm sorry about what happened back there. I know how frustrating it must be to feel like you're being kept in the dark."

Gareth snorted, his expression bitter as he glanced up at Luca with hard, unyielding eyes. "Frustrating doesn't even begin to cover it," he said, his voice rough with emotion. "I'm supposed to be the next Alpha, Luca. How am I supposed to lead this pack if I don't even know what's going on?"

Luca sighed, his heart aching with the weight of his brother's pain and anger. He knew that Gareth had always felt the pressure of their father's expectations more keenly than he had, knew that the burden of leadership weighed heavily on his shoulders.

"I know it's not easy," he said, his voice gentle as he settled himself on the rock beside his brother. "But you have to trust that Father knows what he's doing. He's been leading this pack for a long time, and he's always had our best interests at heart."

Gareth let out a bitter laugh, his eyes flashing with a mixture of anger and despair. "Has he, though?" he asked, his voice raw with emotion. "Sometimes I wonder if he even sees us as his sons anymore, or if we're just pawns in some grand game that only he understands."

Luca felt a flicker of unease at his brother's words, a sense of doubt and uncertainty that he had never before allowed himself to acknowledge. He had always trusted in their father's wisdom and guidance, had always believed that he had the pack's best interests at heart.

But now, in the face of Gareth's pain and the growing threats that surrounded them, he couldn't help but wonder if there was more to the story than he had ever realized, if there were secrets and machinations at work that went beyond anything he had ever imagined.

"I don't know, Gareth," he said at last, his voice heavy with the weight of his own doubts and fears. "But what I do know is that we have to stick together, now more than ever. We're stronger as a family, as a pack. And we'll need all of our strength and cunning to face whatever challenges lie ahead."

Gareth was silent for a long moment, his expression unreadable as he stared out over the rushing waters of the waterfall. Then, with a heavy sigh, he pushed himself to his feet, his shoulders squared and his jaw set with a grim determination.

"I hope you're right, Luca," he said, his voice flat and emotionless as he turned to face his brother. "Because if you're not, then we're all in for a world of trouble."

With that, he turned and strode away, his footsteps heavy and purposeful as he disappeared into the dense underbrush of the forest. Luca watched him go, his heart heavy with a sense of loss and regret that he couldn't quite put into words.

3

Whispers in the Pack

Luca

As he walked through the bustling heart of the pack, he couldn't help but notice the small gatherings of his fellow wolves, their voices hushed and their expressions drawn as they huddled together in tense, urgent conversation. Luca's eyes narrowed as he caught snatches of their words, tales of missing packmates and rival packs, of dangers lurking in the shadows that threatened to tear their world apart.

With a sense of growing unease, Luca approached a group of his fellow warriors, their faces grim and their postures tense as they spoke in low, urgent tones. They looked up as he drew near, their eyes wary and guarded as they sized him up with a mixture of respect and suspicion.

"Luca," one of them said, a tall, broad-shouldered wolf with a jagged scar running down the side of his face. "I'm glad you're here. We could use your opinion on what's been going on."

Luca inclined his head in acknowledgment, his expression stoic as he settled himself amongst his packmates. "I've heard the rumors," he said, his voice low and measured. "About the missing wolves and the rival packs. What do you make of it all?"

The scarred wolf shook his head, his expression dark and troubled. "I don't know what to think," he admitted, his voice rough with emotion. "Some say it's the work of the Silverfang Pack, that they're trying to weaken us from within. Others whisper of darker things, of ancient evils stirring in the shadows that we cannot hope to comprehend."

Luca's brow furrowed at the words, a sense of unease settling in the pit of his stomach. He had heard the stories of the ancient evils that lurked beyond the borders of their world, the whispered tales of darkness and madness that had haunted their kind for generations. But he had always dismissed them as nothing more than myths and legends, stories told to frighten pups and keep them in line.

Now, though, in the face of the growing fear and uncertainty that gripped his pack, Luca couldn't help but wonder if there was more to those old tales than he had ever realized. He thought back to the wooden figure that had haunted his dreams, the strange, unsettling sense of familiarity that had washed over him every time he looked upon its carved features.

"We can't afford to give in to fear and speculation," Luca said at last, his voice firm and unwavering as he met the eyes of his packmates. "We need to focus on what we know, on the facts and the evidence that we can gather through our own efforts."

The scarred wolf nodded, his expression grim but determined. "You're right, of course," he said, his voice filled with a grudging respect. "We need to be smart about this, to think with our heads instead of our hearts."

Luca felt a flicker of pride at the words, a sense of purpose and determination that helped to ease the ache of worry and uncertainty that had plagued him for so long. He knew that he had a role to play in all of this, a duty to his pack that went beyond his own selfish desires and fears.

With a final nod to his packmates, Luca pushed himself to his feet and strode off into the heart of the pack's territory, his senses attuned to the subtle shifts in the atmosphere that spoke of danger and unrest. He would not rest until he had unraveled the mystery of the missing wolves, until he had brought peace and security back to the pack that he loved more than life itself.

Luca found himself drifting towards the training grounds, the place where he had spent countless hours honing his skills and pushing himself to be the best warrior he could be. He could hear the sounds of combat drifting on the breeze, the clash of claws and the grunts of exertion that spoke of young wolves pushing themselves to their limits.

And there, in the center of it all, stood Gareth, his posture tall and proud as he led a group of young wolves through a series of drills and exercises. Luca felt a flicker of pride warming his heart as he watched his brother in action, saw the natural leadership and charisma that seemed to radiate from him like a beacon in the darkness.

Despite their differences, despite the resentments and misunderstandings that had grown between them, Luca knew that Gareth was a born leader, a wolf who commanded respect and loyalty from all those who followed him. And in that moment, watching him guide and inspire the next generation of Wolfheart warriors, Luca felt a sudden, fierce surge of love and admiration for his brother, a sense of connection that he had thought lost forever.

Without quite knowing why, Luca found himself moving closer to the training grounds, his steps heavy and purposeful as he approached the group of young wolves. They looked up as he drew near, their eyes wide and curious as they took in the sight of the Alpha's second son, the quiet, stoic warrior who had always seemed to exist in his brother's shadow.

But Luca paid them no mind, his gaze fixed solely on Gareth as he closed the distance between them. For a moment, the two brothers simply stared at each other, a wealth of unspoken emotions passing between them in the space of a heartbeat.

And then, with a small, tentative smile, Luca reached out and clapped his brother on the shoulder, a gesture of support and encouragement that felt like the first step in bridging the gap that had grown between them.

"You're doing a great job with them," he said, his voice low and sincere as he nodded towards the group of young wolves. "They're lucky to have you as their teacher."

Gareth blinked in surprise, his expression softening for a moment before he caught himself and schooled his features back into a mask of stoic professionalism. "Thank you," he said, his voice gruff but not unkind. "I'm just doing my duty to the pack, same as you."

Luca nodded, a flicker of understanding passing between them in that moment. They were both sons of the great Alpha, both burdened with the weight of their father's expectations and the needs of their pack. And though they might have their differences, though they might butt heads and argue and fight, they were still brothers, still bound by a love and loyalty that ran deeper than any petty squabbles or personal ambitions.

"I know we haven't always seen eye to eye," Luca said, his voice low and earnest as he held his brother's gaze. "But I want you to know that I'm here for you, Gareth. No matter what happens, no matter what challenges we face, I will always stand by your side."

Gareth was silent for a long moment, his expression unreadable as he studied Luca's face. And then, with a small, almost imperceptible nod, he reached out and clasped his brother's forearm, a gesture of solidarity and respect that spoke volumes in the space of a single moment.

"I know," he said, his voice rough with emotion.

They stood like that for a moment longer, two brothers united in their love for their pack and their determination to protect it at all costs.

Luca decided to walk away from the training grounds, he couldn't help but feel a little bit of hope and determination burning in his heart, a sense of purpose and resolve that he had thought lost forever. He knew that the road ahead would be hard, that there would be challenges and dangers that would test them all in ways they had never been tested before.

As the day wore on, Luca found himself moving through the pack's territory like a ghost, his presence a silent comfort to those who were struggling to come to terms with the growing unrest and uncertainty that had taken hold of their world. He listened to their fears and their worries, offered what reassurances he could, and tried to be the steady, unwavering presence that they all needed in this time of crisis.

But even as he lent his strength and support to his packmates, Luca couldn't shake the feeling that there was something more going on, something that he hadn't yet been able to put his finger on. The missing wolves, the mysterious visions that had haunted his dreams for so long - they all felt like pieces of a larger puzzle, a tapestry of secrets and lies that he had yet to unravel.

As the sun began to set and the pack prepared for the evening's gatherings, Luca found himself slipping away from the bustle and noise of the main camp, his feet carrying him back to the quiet solitude of his workshop. It was there, among the tools and the half-finished projects, that he felt most at home, most able to sort through the tangled knots of his own thoughts and emotions.

Luca sat at his workbench, the warm glow of the lantern casting flickering shadows across the room. Before him lay the wooden figure, its features still rough and unfinished, yet somehow hauntingly familiar. He picked it up, cradling it gently in his calloused hands, and felt a sudden, inexplicable urge to speak to it, to give voice to the thoughts and feelings that had been swirling inside him for so long.

"I don't know why I'm doing this," he murmured, his voice low and rough in the stillness of the workshop. "Talking to a piece of wood like it's a real person. But somehow, it feels right. Like you're meant to hear the things I can't say to anyone else."

He paused, his thumb tracing the curve of the figure's cheek, the line of its jaw. "I'm scared," he admitted, the words catching in his throat. "Scared for my pack, for the missing wolves, for the future that seems to grow more uncertain with every passing day. I want to be strong for them, to be the leader and protector they need in this time of crisis. But sometimes, I feel like I'm barely holding it together, like I'm just one step away from falling apart completely."

Luca closed his eyes, his breath shuddering in his chest. "And then there's you," he whispered, his voice so soft it was almost lost in the crackling of the lantern's flame. "This strange, mysterious figure that haunts my dreams and my waking thoughts alike. I don't know what you are, or what you mean, but I feel like you're important somehow. Like you're a key to unlocking the secrets that have been plaguing our pack for so long."

He opened his eyes, his gaze searching the figure's face as if looking for answers in the play of light and shadow across its wooden features. "I wish you could talk back to me," he said, a wry smile tugging at the corner of his mouth. "Wish you could give me some kind of sign, some hint of what I'm supposed to do next. But I guess that's not how it works, is it? In the end, it's up to me to figure out the path forward, to find the strength and courage to lead my pack through this darkness and into the light."

Luca set the figure back down on the workbench, his fingers lingering on its surface for a moment longer. "But even if you can't talk back, even if you're just a piece of wood and nothing more, I want you to know that I'm not giving up. I'm going to keep fighting, keep searching for the truth, no matter how hard or painful it might be. Because that's who I am, and that's what I do. I'm a warrior of the Wolfheart Pack, and I will never stop defending the ones I love, no matter what the cost."

As he lay down on his bed and closed his eyes, Luca sent up one last prayer to the moon goddess, asking for her blessing and guidance in the days to come. He prayed for the safety of his pack, for the strength and courage to face whatever challenges lay ahead. And he prayed for the chance to find his fated mate, to know the joy and comfort of a love that would last a lifetime.

And then, with a heart full of hope and a mind at peace, Luca drifted off into a dreamless sleep, ready to face whatever the future might hold with the same stubborn determination and quiet strength that had always been his greatest gift.

For he knew that, no matter what happened, no matter what trials or tribulations might come his way, he would always have the love and support of his pack, the unbreakable bonds of family and friendship that had sustained him through even the darkest of times. And with that knowledge, that unshakable faith in the power of the pack, Luca knew that there was nothing he couldn't overcome, no challenge he couldn't face, no dream he couldn't make real.

4

Elder's Wisdom

Luca

Luca found himself standing in a field of vibrant, colorful flowers that stretched as far as the eye could see. The air was filled with a sweet, intoxicating fragrance that made his head spin and his heart race with a strange, inexplicable longing.

And there, in the middle of the field, was the man from his dreams, his golden hair shimmering in the sunlight and his purple eyes filled with a depth of emotion that took Luca's breath away.

"Who are you?" Luca called out, his voice echoing across the dreamscape. "Why do you keep appearing in my dreams?"

But the man didn't respond, his lips curving into a soft, enigmatic smile as he beckoned Luca closer with a graceful, elegant hand.

Luca hesitated for a moment, his heart pounding with a mixture of fear and anticipation. He had never felt a connection like this before, a pull towards someone that seemed to transcend the boundaries of time and space.

"I don't understand," he said, his voice trembling slightly as he took a step forward, the flowers parting around his feet like a sea of color. "What do you want from me?"

Again, the man remained silent, his eyes filled with a warmth and a tenderness that made Luca's heart ache with a desperate, yearning need.

And then, just as Luca was about to reach out and touch the man, to feel the warmth of his skin beneath his fingertips, the dream began to shift and change, the colors bleeding together in a dizzying, kaleidoscopic swirl.

Symbols and glyphs danced at the edges of his vision, their meanings tantalizingly close but always just out of reach. Luca strained to make sense of them, to unravel the cryptic messages that seemed to hold the key to his destiny.

But even as he struggled to understand, even as he fought to hold onto the fleeting wisps of meaning, he could feel the dream fading away, the colors dimming and the sweet, intoxicating scent of the flowers growing fainter with each passing moment.

"Wait!" he cried out, his hand reaching desperately for the man, for the connection that had filled him with such a profound sense of belonging and purpose. "Please, don't go! I need to know who you are, what you mean to me!"

But it was too late, the dream already slipping away like sand through his fingers. And as Luca felt himself being pulled back to the waking world, back to the cold, harsh reality of his lonely, isolated life, he couldn't shake the feeling that he had just lost something precious, something that he would spend the rest of his days searching for.

Luca woke with a start, his heart pounding and his skin slick with sweat. The dreams had come again, more vivid and intense than ever before. He could still see the wooden figure's face, its carved features twisting and shifting in the flickering light of some unseen flame. And there were symbols too, strange and cryptic, dancing at the edges of his vision like half-remembered fragments of a long-forgotten language.

He sat up in bed, his head spinning and his mind racing. He had always been a practical wolf, a creature of logic and reason. But these dreams, these visions, they defied all explanation. They seemed to come from somewhere deep inside him, some hidden well of knowledge and intuition that he had never before known he possessed.

Luca tried to shake off the lingering unease, to push the dreams back into the depths of his subconscious where they belonged. But even as he went about his daily tasks, as he patrolled the borders and oversaw the training of the pack's young warriors, he could feel the weight of the visions pressing down on him, like a physical burden that he could not escape.

Finally, unable to bear the strain any longer, Luca made a decision. He would seek out the guidance of one of the pack's elders, a wise and respected figure known for their cryptic advice and deep understanding of the mysteries of the world.

He found the Elder sitting beneath a gnarled old tree at the edge of the pack's territory, their eyes closed and their face turned up to the warm sun. Luca approached cautiously, not wanting to disturb the elder's meditation. But as he drew near, the elder's eyes snapped open, fixing him with a piercing gaze that seemed to see straight through to his very soul.

"Luca," the elder said, their voice soft and lilting. "I have been expecting you."

Luca blinked in surprise, taken aback by the elder's words. "You have?" he asked, his brow furrowing in confusion. "But how could you know…"

The elder chuckled, a warm, rich sound that seemed to fill the air around them. "The winds whisper many secrets to those who know how to listen," they said, their eyes twinkling with mischief. "And I have been listening to the winds for a very long time."

Luca nodded slowly, trying to wrap his mind around the elder's cryptic words. He had always known that the elders possessed a deep and mysterious wisdom, a connection to the very fabric of the world that he could scarcely begin to understand. But to hear it spoken of so casually, so matter-of-factly, was still a shock to his system.

"I have been having dreams," he said, his voice low and hesitant. "Dreams of a man, and strange symbols that I cannot decipher. I do not know what they mean, or why they haunt me so. But I feel in my heart that they are important somehow, that they hold the key to some great mystery that I must unravel."

The elder listened intently, their eyes never leaving Luca's face as he spoke. When he had finished, they nodded slowly, as if weighing his words carefully in their mind.

"The dreams are a gift," they said at last, their voice soft and solemn. "A message from the great spirits that watch over us all. They speak to you, Luca, because they have chosen you for a special purpose, a task that only you can fulfill."

Luca felt a shiver run down his spine at the elder's words, a sense of awe and trepidation that he could not quite explain. "What kind of task?" he asked, his voice hoarse with emotion. "What do the spirits want from me?"

The elder shook their head, a small smile playing at the corners of their mouth. "That is for you to discover," they said, their voice gentle but firm. "The path ahead will not be easy, Luca. It will test you in ways you have never been tested before. But you must have faith in yourself, and in the wisdom of the great spirits. They would not have chosen you if they did not believe that you were worthy of the challenge."

Luca swallowed hard, his throat suddenly dry and tight. He wanted to protest, to tell the elder that they had made a mistake, that he was no one special, just an ordinary wolf trying to do right by his pack. But something in the elder's gaze stopped him, a glimmer of understanding and compassion that seemed to see straight through to his very core.

"I am afraid," he admitted, his voice barely more than a whisper. "Afraid of failing, of letting my pack down when they need me most."

The elder reached out, their weathered hand coming to rest on Luca's shoulder in a gesture of comfort and support. "Fear is natural," they said, their voice soft and soothing. "It is a sign that you understand the gravity of the task before you. But you must not let it consume you, Luca. You must learn to master your fear, to use it as a tool to sharpen your mind and strengthen your resolve."

Luca nodded, his jaw clenching with determination. He knew that the elder was right, that he could not afford to let his doubts and insecurities hold him back. Not now, when so much was at stake.

"What must I do?" he asked, his voice steady and strong. "How do I begin to unravel the mystery of these dreams, to fulfill the task that the great spirits have set before me?"

The elder smiled, their eyes crinkling at the corners. "The answers will come to you in time," they said, their voice warm and reassuring. "Trust in yourself, Luca, and in the wisdom of your heart. The path will reveal itself to you, one step at a time."

The elder's words hung in the air between them, heavy with meaning and promise. Luca could feel his heart racing, his mind whirling with the possibilities of what lay ahead. He wanted to know more, to understand the full scope of the task that had been set before him. But he also knew that the elder was right, that the answers would come to him in their own time, when he was ready to receive them.

"There is one more thing," the elder said, their voice low and solemn. "Something that you must understand if you are to fulfill the destiny that the great spirits have laid out for you."

Luca leaned forward, his eyes wide and eager. "What is it?" he asked, his voice barely more than a whisper. "Please, tell me."

The elder smiled, their eyes twinkling with a hint of mischief. "It is about fated mates, Luca," they said, their voice soft and knowing.

Luca's heart skipped a beat, memories of his grandfather's words flooding back to him. He had always been fascinated by the concept of fated mates, the idea that there was someone out there who was destined to be his perfect match, his soulmate in every sense of the word.

"My grandfather used to tell me stories about fated mates," he said, his voice wistful and filled with longing. "He said that they were the key to unlocking great strength and purpose, a bond that goes beyond mere love or attraction."

The elder nodded, their eyes sparkling with approval. "Your grandfather was a wise wolf," they said, their voice warm and affectionate. "He understood the power of the fated mate bond, the way it can transform lives and shape destinies."

Luca felt a flutter of excitement and trepidation in his chest, a sense of anticipation and fear mingling together in a heady mix. "Do you think that my fated mate has something to do with my dreams, with the task that the great spirits have set before me?" he asked, his voice trembling with emotion.

The elder's smile widened, their eyes crinkling with a hint of mischief. "It is possible," they said, their voice coy and teasing. "The ways of the heart are mysterious, even to one as old and wise as I. But I sense that your fated mate will play a crucial role in the journey that lies ahead, that they will be the key to unlocking the full potential of your destiny."

Luca's mind was racing, his thoughts spinning with the possibilities of what the elder's words might mean. He had always dreamed of finding his fated mate, of experiencing the kind of love and connection that his grandfather had spoken of with such reverence and awe. But he had never imagined that his fated mate might be tied to his own destiny, to the greater purpose that he had always sensed was waiting for him out there in the wide, wild world.

"But how will I know?" he asked, his voice hoarse with a mix of excitement and fear. "How will I recognize my fated mate when I find them?"

The elder's expression softened, their eyes filling with a deep, ancient wisdom. "You will know," they said, their voice gentle but firm. "When the time is right, when your hearts are ready to meet, you will feel it in every fiber of your being. It will be like coming home, like finding a piece of yourself that you never even knew was missing."

Luca swallowed hard, his throat suddenly tight with emotion. He wanted to believe the elder's words, wanted to trust in the idea of a love that could transform his life and give him the strength to face whatever challenges lay ahead. But a part of him was still afraid, still unsure of his own worthiness, his own ability to be the kind of mate that someone else might need or want.

"And what if I'm not ready?" he asked, his voice barely more than a whisper. "What if I'm not strong enough, or brave enough, to be the kind of mate that they deserve?"

The elder reached out, their hand coming to rest on Luca's shoulder in a gesture of comfort and support. "You are stronger than you know, Luca," they said, their voice filled with a quiet, unshakable conviction. "And braver than you can even begin to imagine. The great spirits would not have chosen you for this task if they did not believe in your ability to see it through, to be the kind of wolf that your fated mate will need by their side."

Luca took a deep, shuddering breath, feeling a sense of calm and clarity wash over him. He knew that the elder was right, that he had to trust in himself and in the wisdom of the great spirits. Even if the path ahead was uncertain, even if he couldn't see where it would lead, he had to have faith that he was exactly where he was meant to be, doing exactly what he was meant to do.

"Thank you," he said, his voice rough with gratitude. "For your guidance, and for your faith in me. I will do my best to be worthy of it, to follow the path that the great spirits have laid out for me, wherever it may lead."

The elder smiled, their eyes crinkling with warmth and affection. "I have no doubt that you will, Luca," they said, their voice filled with a quiet, unshakable certainty. "Trust in yourself, and in the wisdom of your dreams. They will guide you to where you need to be, to the destiny that awaits you."

With those words, the elder rose to their feet, their movements fluid and graceful despite their advanced age. They placed a hand on Luca's head, their touch warm and comforting, and murmured a quiet blessing in a language that Luca did not understand.

And then they were gone, disappearing into the shadows of the forest like a wisp of smoke on the wind.

Luca stood there for a long moment, his mind whirling with the weight of the elder's words. He knew that the path ahead would be hard, that there would be obstacles and challenges at every turn. But he also knew that he was ready to face them head-on, to trust in the wisdom of his dreams and the guidance of the great spirits.

With a final, determined nod, Luca turned and made his way back to the pack's camp, his heart full of purpose and his mind clear and focused. He would not let his doubts hold him back, would not let his fears cloud his judgment. He was a warrior of the Wolfheart Pack, and he would face whatever lay ahead with the same unwavering courage and loyalty that had always been his greatest strength.

5

Moonlit Revelation

Luca

The sun was just beginning to dip below the horizon, painting the sky in a breathtaking array of oranges and pinks, as Luca made his way towards the edge of the forest. The air was thick with anticipation, the collective energy of the pack thrumming through the air like an electric current.

Despite the underlying tension that had been brewing in the pack for weeks, the evening of the pack run always seemed to bring out a sense of unity and excitement among the wolves. It was a chance to come together, to let go of their human worries and concerns and lose themselves in the primal thrill of the hunt.

As Luca approached the gathering place, he could see his packmates milling about, their wolves restless and eager to run. Some were already shifting, their bodies rippling and changing as they let their animal instincts take over.

Luca felt a flutter of excitement in his own chest, a longing to join his pack in the run and feel the wind whipping through his fur. But he also knew that tonight's run held a deeper significance, a chance to bring the pack together and remind them of the bonds that held them strong.

Luca caught sight of his father standing at the head of the pack, his posture tall and proud. Beside him stood Gareth, his expression serious and focused as he surveyed the gathered wolves.

"My fellow wolves," his father's voice rang out, cutting through the excited chatter of the pack. "We gather here tonight to celebrate the strength and unity of our pack, to come together as one and let our wolves run free."

A chorus of howls and yips rose up from the gathered wolves, a show of solidarity and excitement that made Luca's heart swell with pride.

"Before we begin," his father continued, his eyes scanning the crowd, "I would like to call upon my son, Gareth to say a few words, to carry on the tradition that has been passed down through generations of alphas."

It was rare for Gareth to be called upon to speak in front of the pack, and Luca couldn't help but wonder what he would say.

"Thank you, Alpha," Gareth said, his voice strong and steady as he faced the pack. "I am honored to stand before you tonight, to speak the words that have been passed down through our ancestors."

He paused for a moment, his eyes scanning the crowd as if searching for the right words. Luca could see the tension in his brother's shoulders, the weight of responsibility that seemed to settle over him like a physical burden.

Luca watched with a mixture of pride and apprehension as Gareth stepped forward, his shoulders squared and his head held high. Despite their recent disagreements and the tension that had been simmering between them for weeks, Luca couldn't help but feel a swell of admiration for his brother in that moment.

Gareth's voice rang out clear and strong, his words filling the air with a sense of purpose and determination. "My fellow wolves," he said, his eyes scanning the crowd, "we gather here tonight not just to run and hunt, but to remind ourselves of the bonds that tie us together, the strength that lies within each and every one of us."

Luca felt a shiver run down his spine at his brother's words, a sense of unity and belonging washing over him like a warm breeze. He had always known that the pack was important, that it was the foundation upon which their lives were built. But hearing Gareth speak of it now, with such passion and conviction, made it feel more real than ever before.

"We have faced many challenges in recent days," Gareth continued, his voice growing more intense with each word. "The disappearances of our own, the threats that lurk beyond our borders. But through it all, we have remained strong, united in our love for one another and our determination to protect what is ours."

Luca could see the effect that Gareth's words were having on the pack, the way their eyes shone with pride and their chests swelled with courage. He could feel it in himself too, a renewed sense of purpose and resolve that made him feel as though he could take on anything that the world might throw at him.

"And so, tonight," Gareth said, his voice rising to a crescendo, "we run not just as wolves, but as a family. We run to honor those who came before us, and to pave the way for those who will come after. We run to remind ourselves of the strength that lies within us, and the unbreakable bonds that tie us together."

As Gareth's final words rang out, the pack erupted into a chorus of howls and yips, their voices rising in a symphony of solidarity and determination. Luca could feel his own wolf stirring within him, eager to join in the celebration and let loose the primal energy that had been building inside him for weeks.

With a final rallying cry, Gareth turned and bounded forward, his wolf form rippling and changing as he led the pack into the depths of the forest. Luca felt a thrill of excitement rush through him as he followed suit, his own body shifting and changing as he let his animal instincts take over.

As Luca raced through the forest, his paws pounding against the earth in perfect rhythm with his packmates, he felt a sense of pure, unadulterated joy coursing through his veins. For a moment, all his worries and fears seemed to melt away, replaced by the sheer exhilaration of the hunt, the primal thrill of running with his pack.

He could feel the wind whipping through his fur, the scents of the forest filling his nostrils with each deep, steady breath. The ground beneath his paws was soft and yielding, the undergrowth parting before him like a sea of green and brown.

But then, just as he was about to lose himself completely in the moment, Luca caught a scent that made him skid to a halt, his paws scrabbling against the earth as he fought to keep his balance. It was a scent unlike anything he had ever encountered before, a strange and alluring aroma that seemed to tug at the very edges of his memory, sending a shiver down his spine and making his heart race with a sudden, inexplicable urgency.

Without even realizing what he was doing, Luca found himself veering off from the rest of the pack, his nose pressed close to the ground as he followed the scent deeper into the forest. He could hear the confused and concerned yips of his packmates behind him, but he paid them no heed, his mind focused solely on the strange and compelling aroma that seemed to be drawing him in like a moth to a flame.

As he pushed his way through the undergrowth, Luca's thoughts raced with a thousand questions and uncertainties. What was this scent that had caught his attention so completely? Where was it leading him? And why did it feel so important, so vital to his very existence?

But even as these doubts and fears swirled through his mind, Luca couldn't shake the feeling that he was meant to be here, that this was a path he was destined to follow, no matter where it might lead.

And then, as he burst through a particularly dense thicket of bushes and into a hidden clearing, Luca felt his breath catch in his throat, his eyes widening in awe and wonder at the sight that greeted him.

There, standing in the center of the clearing, was a tree unlike any he had ever seen before. Its trunk was tall and straight, its bark a shimmering silver that seemed to glow with an otherworldly light. Its leaves were a deep, rich green, each one perfectly formed and shimmering with a delicate, almost ethereal beauty.

But it was the scent that really caught Luca's attention, the same strange and alluring aroma that had drawn him here in the first place. It seemed to be coming from the tree itself, a heady, intoxicating fragrance that made his head spin and his heart race with a sudden, inexplicable longing.

For a moment, Luca could only stare, his mind reeling with the implications of what he was seeing. He had heard stories of trees like this before, whispered tales of ancient magic and hidden knowledge that had always seemed like nothing more than myth and legend. But now, standing here in the presence of this majestic silver tree, he couldn't help but wonder if there might be some truth to those old tales after all.

As Luca placed his paw against the shimmering bark of the silver tree, he felt a sudden jolt of energy coursing through him, his mind filled with a rush of images and sensations that left him reeling and breathless. But amidst the swirling chaos of the visions, one image stood out with startling clarity, a face that he had seen countless times in his dreams but never before in waking life.

It was the face of the man in his dreams, a stunningly beautiful man with eyes the color of amethysts, deep and rich and filled with a tenderness that made Luca's heart ache with longing. In the vision, the man was looking directly at Luca, his gaze soft and warm and filled with a love that seemed to transcend time and space itself.

Luca felt his breath catch in his throat, his heart pounding with a mixture of awe and disbelief. He had always known that the man in his dreams was important, that he held the key to unlocking the mysteries that had haunted him for so long. But to see him here, in the heart of the silver tree, was a revelation that left Luca shaken and trembling with emotion.

But before Luca could reach out and touch the man, before he could speak the words that were burning in his heart, the vision began to fade, the colors and shapes blurring and swirling together until all that remained was the shimmering trunk of the silver tree and the dappled sunlight of the clearing.

Luca blinked, his mind still reeling from the intensity of the vision. But before he could make sense of what he had just seen, he heard a voice calling out to him from the edge of the clearing, a familiar sound that jolted him back to reality with a sudden, jarring clarity.

"Luca!" the voice called, urgent and insistent. "The pack run is coming to an end. We need to head back to the den site."

Luca hesitated, his heart torn between his desire to stay and unravel the mysteries of the silver tree and his duty to his pack. But he knew that he could not linger here, that he had to return to his family and his responsibilities, no matter how much he longed to explore the wonders that lay hidden within the heart of the forest.

With a final, reluctant glance back at the shimmering trunk, Luca turned and bounded out of the clearing, his paws carrying him back towards the sound of his packmate's voice. As he ran, he couldn't shake the feeling that something had changed within him, that the vision of the man with the amethyst eyes had awakened a part of himself that he had never even known existed.

6

Deep Slumber

Luca

In the days that followed the pack run, Luca found himself consumed by an inexplicable urgency, a burning desire to return to the silver tree and unravel the secrets that lay hidden within its shimmering bark. It was as if a part of him had been awakened by the visions he had experienced, a dormant power that now thrummed through his veins with every beat of his heart.

He tried to go about his daily routines, to focus on his duties and responsibilities as a member of the pack. But no matter how hard he tried, his thoughts kept drifting back to the clearing in the forest.

Luca knew that he should be cautious, that he should heed the warnings of his rational mind and stay away from the strange and unknown. But there was a part of him, a wild and untamed part, that longed to throw caution to the wind and follow his instincts, no matter where they might lead.

And so, after days of wrestling with his doubts and fears, Luca made a decision. He would return to the silver tree, would seek out the answers that lay hidden within its heart, no matter the cost.

As he set out towards the clearing, his paws moving with a surety and purpose that surprised even himself, Luca couldn't shake the feeling that he was being watched, that some unseen force was guiding his steps and shaping his destiny.

And then, just as he was beginning to doubt himself, just as he was starting to wonder if he had made a terrible mistake, Luca came upon a sight that stopped him dead in his tracks.

There, sitting on a fallen log at the edge of the path, was an old woman, her face lined with age and wisdom, her eyes glinting with a strange and knowing light. She looked up as Luca approached, her lips curving into a smile that was both welcoming and mysterious.

"Ah, Luca of the Wolfheart pack," she said, her voice soft and musical, like the rustling of leaves in the wind. "I have been waiting for you."

Luca blinked, taken aback by the old woman's words. How did she know his name? And what did she mean, she had been waiting for him?

"Who are you?" he asked, his voice rough with suspicion and uncertainty. "How do you know who I am?"

The old woman chuckled, her eyes twinkling with amusement and secrets. "I know many things, young wolf," she said, her voice cryptic and enigmatic. "I know the whispers of the wind and the secrets of the stars. And I know that you are about to embark on a journey that will change your life forever."

Luca felt a chill run down his spine at the old woman's words, a sense of destiny and purpose that made his heart race and his blood sing. But he also felt a flicker of fear, a nagging doubt that whispered in the back of his mind, warning him of the dangers that lay ahead.

"What do you mean?" he asked, his voice hoarse with a mix of excitement and trepidation. "What journey am I about to embark on?"

The old woman smiled, her eyes softening with a strange and tender light. "That is for you to discover, young wolf," she said, her voice gentle but firm. "But know this: the path you are about to walk is not an easy one. It will test you in ways you cannot even imagine, will push you to the very limits of your strength and courage."

The old woman rose from her log and disappeared into the trees, leaving Luca alone with his thoughts.

For a moment, he simply stood there, his mind reeling with the weight of the old woman's words. But then, with a deep breath and a determined nod, Luca squared his shoulders and set off down the path once more, his paws moving with a renewed sense of purpose and resolve.

Luca couldn't shake the feeling that he had been here before, that he had walked this path a thousand times in his dreams and his visions. The trees seemed to whisper to him as he passed, their leaves rustling with secrets and promises that only he could hear.

And then, as he rounded a bend in the path and entered the clearing where the silver tree stood, Luca felt a strange sense of familiarity wash over him, a feeling of coming home that made his heart ache with a bittersweet longing.

Luca approached the silver tree, he could feel his wolf soul stirring within him, a primal force that yearned to connect with the powerful magic emanating from the ancient wood. It was a sensation unlike anything he had ever experienced before, a deep and visceral pull that seemed to resonate with the very core of his being.

He shifted back and moved closer, his hands trembling with a mixture of awe and anticipation. And as he drew nearer, as he reached out to place his hands on the trunk of the tree, Luca felt a surge of energy coursing through his veins, a rush of power and purpose that made his heart race and his blood sing.

"Please," he whispered, his voice hoarse with emotion as he poured his wolf soul and human soul into the tree, focusing all of his energy and intention on the ancient wood. "Show me the way. Help me find the answers I seek."

For a moment, nothing happened. The clearing was silent, the only sound the rustling of leaves in the gentle breeze. But then, slowly at first and then with gathering speed, the tree began to glow, a soft and ethereal light that seemed to emanate from deep within its heart.

He could feel the power of the tree flowing through him, a sensation that was both exhilarating and terrifying, like standing on the edge of a great precipice and knowing that the only way forward was to leap.

And then, as the light reached a blinding crescendo, Luca saw something that made his breath catch in his throat. There, emerging from the trunk of the tree like a figure that resembled the man from his dreams.

Luca watched in awe as the man's features became clearer and more defined, his form taking shape before his very eyes. It was a sight that filled him with a strange and powerful longing, a desire to reach out and touch.

But even as he marveled at the miracle unfolding before him, Luca couldn't shake the feeling that something was wrong. The man's eyes were closed, his breathing steady but shallow, as if he were lost in a deep and enchanted slumber.

But the man did not stir, his form still and silent as the tree that had borne him. And then, with a final pulse of light and a shuddering gasp, he collapsed into Luca's arms, his weight warm and solid against Luca's chest.

For a moment, Luca simply stood there, cradling the man in his arms and marveling at the strange and wondrous turn his life had taken. He had never believed in fate or destiny, had always scoffed at the idea of soulmates and predestined paths. But now, holding this man in his arms and feeling the connection that thrummed between them like a living thing, Luca couldn't deny the truth that had been staring him in the face all along.

"I don't know who you are," he murmured, his voice soft and reverent as he brushed a strand of hair from the man's forehead. "But I feel like I've been waiting for you my whole life."

He knew that he should be afraid, that he should be questioning the strange and inexplicable events that had brought him to this moment. But all Luca could feel was a sense of rightness, a deep and unshakable conviction that this was exactly where he was meant to be.

Luca gathered the man in his arms and began the long journey back to his pack, his steps sure and steady despite the weight of his precious cargo.

Just as Luca was about to take his first step towards home, a chilling howl pierced the air, stopping him dead in his tracks. The hair on the back of his neck stood up, and a sense of dread washed over him as he realized the howl belonged to none other than the Silverfang pack.

Within seconds, a group of wolves burst into the clearing, their eyes glinting with malice and their fangs bared in a snarl. Luca instinctively held the man tighter against his chest, his heart pounding with fear and adrenaline.

"Well, well, well," the leader of the group sneered, his voice dripping with venom. "What do we have here? The second son of the Wolfheart pack, cradling a pretty little treasure in his arms."

Luca growled, his own fangs bared in a warning. "Stay back," he snarled, his voice low and threatening. "I don't want to fight you, but I will if I have to."

The Silverfang wolves laughed, a cruel and mocking sound that made Luca's blood boil with rage. "You think you can take us all on, pup?" the leader taunted, his eyes narrowing with a predatory gleam. "You're outnumbered and outmatched. Hand over the man, and we might just let you live."

Luca's grip on the man tightened, his resolve hardening like steel. He knew he was in a desperate situation, but he would rather die than let these wolves lay a single claw on the man in his arms.

Just as he was about to launch himself at the Silverfang wolves, a fierce howl echoed through the clearing, and Luca's heart leapt with hope. He knew that howl anywhere - it was his brother, Gareth.

In a flash of fur and fangs, Gareth burst into the clearing, flanked by his two betas. They immediately engaged the Silverfang wolves, their snarls and growls filling the air as they fought with a ferocity that made Luca's heart swell with pride.

"Luca, run!" Gareth shouted over the chaos of the battle, his voice strained with effort as he grappled with a particularly vicious Silverfang wolf. "Take the man and go! We'll hold them off!"

Luca hesitated, his heart torn between his desire to fight alongside his brother and the need to protect the man in his arms. He knew Gareth was right - he had to prioritize the man's safety above all else.

"But Gareth-" he started, his voice choked with emotion.

"Go, Luca!" Gareth roared, his eyes flashing with a fierce intensity. "This is your destiny, your path to walk. Don't let anything stand in your way, not even me."

With a heavy heart, Luca nodded, his eyes stinging with unshed tears. He knew he might never see his brother again, but he also knew that Gareth was giving him the greatest gift of all - the chance to fulfill his destiny and protect the man he loved.

"Thank you, brother," he whispered, his voice hoarse with gratitude and sorrow. "I won't forget this."

And with that, Luca turned and fled, cradling the slumbering man in his arms as he raced through the forest, his heart pounding with fear and determination.

7

A Cursed Fate

Luca

Luca's heart pounded in his chest as he raced through the forest, his breath coming in sharp, ragged gasps. The sound of his footsteps echoed through the trees, mingling with the distant howls and snarls of the ongoing battle behind him. Every fiber of his being screamed at him to turn back, to stand beside his brother and betas as they bravely fought against the Silverfang pack. But he knew he couldn't, not with the precious cargo he held in his arms.

As he ran, Luca's mind raced with questions and worries. What could have motivated the Silverfang pack to launch such a bold and calculated attack? He knew there had been tension between the two packs in the past, disputes over territory and resources that had sometimes escalated into brief skirmishes. But this was different. This was a blatant act of aggression, a direct challenge to the Wolfheart pack's strength and unity.

Luca couldn't shake the feeling that there was more to this than met the eye. The Silverfang pack's actions seemed too deliberate, too well-planned to be a mere coincidence. It was as if they had been waiting for this moment, biding their time until the perfect opportunity presented itself.

But why? What could they possibly hope to gain by attacking now, when the Wolfheart pack was at its strongest? And why were they so intent on capturing the man in Luca's arms?

Luca's gaze drifted down to the man's face, taking in his peaceful, almost serene expression. Despite the chaos and danger that surrounded them, the man looked as if he were merely sleeping, lost in a dream world far away from the troubles of the waking world.

"Who are you?" Luca whispered, his voice barely audible over the pounding of his own heart. "What secrets do you hold?"

As he ran, Luca's thoughts drifted to the vision he had seen in the silver tree, the image of the man's face that had been burned into his mind. He had looked so peaceful then, so content in Luca's arms.

As he neared the edge of the forest, Luca's keen ears picked up the sound of footsteps ahead of him. His heart leapt into his throat, and he instinctively tightened his grip on the man in his arms.

"Luca!" a familiar voice called out, and Luca felt a wave of relief wash over him as he recognized the sound of his packmate's voice.

He slowed his pace, coming to a stop as two of his fellow betas emerged from the trees, their faces etched with worry and concern.

"Thank the moon you're safe," one of them said, his eyes widening as he caught sight of the man in Luca's arms. "We heard the howls and came as quickly as we could."

Luca nodded, his heart swelling with gratitude for his packmates' support. He knew that the Wolfheart pack would do whatever it took to protect their own, to stand together in the face of any threat.

"The Silverfang pack, they attacked us," Luca explained, his voice hoarse with exhaustion. "Gareth and the others stayed behind to fight them off."

The betas exchanged a worried glance, their eyes filled with a mix of fear and determination. "We have to go back," one of them said, his hand already reaching for the sword at his hip. "We can't leave them to face the Silverfang pack alone."

But Luca shook his head, his grip tightening on the man in his arms. "No," he said, his voice firm and unyielding. "Gareth and the others are buying us time. We have to get back to the village and regroup, figure out our next move."

The betas hesitated, their loyalty to their packmates warring with their sense of duty to their pack as a whole. But finally, they nodded, their faces set with grim determination.

"You're right," one of them said, his eyes fixed on the man in Luca's arms. "We have to prioritize his safety, figure out what the Silverfang pack wants with him."

Luca nodded, his heart swelling with pride at his packmates' unwavering support. He knew that the road ahead would be long and treacherous, filled with dangers and challenges they could scarcely imagine.

As Luca approached his house, his steps heavy with exhaustion and worry, he was surprised to find the Elder waiting for him at the doorstep. The old wolf's face was etched with concern, his eyes filled with a wisdom and understanding that seemed to pierce straight through to Luca's soul.

"Elder," Luca said, his voice hoarse with emotion. "I didn't expect to see you here."

The Elder's gaze drifted to the man in Luca's arms, and his expression grew even more somber. "I sensed that something was amiss," he said, his voice low and urgent. "Come, we must get him inside quickly."

Luca nodded, his heart pounding with a mixture of relief and trepidation. He had always trusted the Elder's judgment, but the old wolf's presence here, now, suggested that the situation was even more serious than he had initially realized.

As they stepped inside the house, Luca was immediately struck by the heavy scent of herbs and incense that hung in the air. It was clear that the Elder had been preparing for this moment, warding the space with protective spells and charms.

"Take him to your bedroom," the Elder instructed, his movements swift and purposeful. "I have already warded it with the strongest protections I know."

Luca obeyed without question, carefully navigating the narrow hallways and steep stairs that led to his private quarters. As he laid the man gently on the bed, he couldn't help but take a moment to study his peaceful features, the steady rise and fall of his chest.

Even in sleep, the man was breathtakingly beautiful, his golden hair fanned out across the pillow like a halo of light. Luca felt a surge of protectiveness and affection wash over him, a deep and primal need to keep this man safe from harm.

Almost without thinking, he reached out and brushed a stray lock of hair from the man's forehead, his touch lingering for a moment longer than necessary. The man's skin was soft and warm beneath his fingertips, and Luca felt a shiver of something he couldn't quite name run down his spine.

"Luca," the Elder's voice broke through his reverie, and Luca turned to face the old wolf, his eyes filled with questions and worry.

"What's wrong with him, Elder?" he asked, his voice tight with emotion. "Why won't he wake up?"

The Elder's expression was grave, his eyes filled with a deep and ancient sadness. "I can sense a powerful curse within him," he said, his voice low and solemn. "One that has trapped him in a deep, unnatural sleep."

Luca's heart sank at the news, his worst fears confirmed. "Can you break it?" he asked, his voice barely above a whisper.

The Elder shook his head, his expression apologetic. "I'm afraid not," he said, his voice heavy with regret. "This curse is ancient and complex, woven with dark magic that I have never encountered before. It will require knowledge and power far beyond my own to break its hold."

Luca felt a wave of desperation and determination wash over him, a fierce and unyielding need to do whatever it took to save the man from the curse's grasp. "Then I'll find a way," he said, his voice ringing with conviction.

The Elder studied him for a long moment, his eyes searching Luca's face for something only he could see. "You care for him," he said, his voice soft with understanding. "More than you even realize."

Luca felt a flush of heat rise to his cheeks, but he didn't deny the Elder's words. "I don't know how to explain it," he said, his voice rough with emotion. "But from the moment I saw him, I felt a connection, a pull towards him that I can't ignore. It's like he's a part of me, a piece of my soul that I never even knew was missing."

The Elder's eyes softened with understanding, a small smile tugging at the corners of his mouth. "That connection you feel, Luca," he said, his voice low and gentle, "it's not just a fleeting emotion or a passing attraction. It's the bond of fated mates, the sacred tie that binds two souls together for all eternity."

Luca's eyes widened, his breath catching in his throat as the weight of the Elder's words sank in. "Fated mates?" he repeated, his voice barely above a whisper. "You mean, he and I... we're meant to be together?"

The Elder nodded, his expression solemn but filled with a quiet joy. "Yes, Luca," he said, his voice ringing with certainty. "The intense feelings and connection you've been experiencing are the result of the sacred bond you share. Fated mates are rare and cherished among our kind, and their love is said to be unbreakable, transcending even death itself."

Luca felt a wave of emotion wash over him, a mix of shock, wonder, and overwhelming love. He looked down at the man on the bed, seeing him in a new light, with a newfound understanding and adoration. This wasn't just a mysterious stranger he had stumbled upon in the forest. This was his soulmate, the one he was destined to be with for all eternity.

"I can't believe it," Luca murmured, his voice rough with emotion. "All my life, I've felt like something was missing, like there was a part of me that I couldn't quite reach. And now, knowing that he's been out there all along, waiting for me..."

He trailed off, his heart swelling with a fierce protectiveness and determination. If this man was truly his fated mate, then Luca knew he would stop at nothing to save him, to break the curse that held him in its thrall and bring him back to the world of the living.

The Elder watched him closely, his eyes glinting with a mixture of pride and understanding. "I know it's a lot to take in, Luca," he said, his voice gentle but firm. "But you must understand the gravity of the situation. Your mate is in danger, trapped by a curse that even I cannot fully comprehend. It will take all of your strength, all of your courage, to find a way to break its hold and bring him back to you."

Luca nodded, his jaw clenching with resolve. "I understand, Elder," he said, his voice steady and strong. "And I'm ready to do whatever it takes. I won't let him suffer like this, not when I have the power to help him."

The Elder smiled, his eyes crinkling with a mixture of affection and respect. "I have no doubt that you will succeed, Luca," he said, his voice filled with quiet conviction. "But before you embark on this journey, there is something else you must know, a story that may shed some light on the mystery surrounding your mate."

Luca leaned forward, his eyes wide with curiosity and apprehension.

"What is it, Elder?" he asked, his voice barely above a whisper.

The Elder settled back in his chair, his eyes taking on a faraway look as he began to weave the tale. "In a realm far beyond our own, there once lived a fae prince, beloved by all who knew him. He was kind and just, with a heart full of compassion and a soul that shone with the light of a thousand stars."

Luca leaned forward, his eyes wide with wonder as he listened to the Elder's words. He had always been fascinated by the stories of the fae, the mysterious and powerful beings who lived in the shadows of the world, hidden from mortal eyes.

"The prince was gifted with extraordinary magic," the Elder continued, his voice low and reverent. "He could heal the sick with a touch, bring life to barren lands, and even bend the elements to his will. His people adored him, and his kingdom prospered under his wise and benevolent rule."

Luca nodded, his heart swelling with admiration for the fae prince. He could almost picture him in his mind's eye, a figure of grace and beauty, with eyes that sparkled like stars and a smile that could light up the darkest of nights.

"But then, one day, the prince vanished without a trace," the Elder said, his voice growing somber. "He disappeared from his castle in the middle of the night, leaving no clues as to his whereabouts. His family was devastated, and his kingdom fell into turmoil as they searched for their beloved ruler."

Luca's brow furrowed with concern, his heart aching for the prince and his people. "What happened to him?" he asked, his voice barely above a whisper.

The Elder shook his head, his eyes filled with a deep and ancient sadness. "No one knows for certain," he said, his voice heavy with the weight of centuries. "Many searched for him, scouring every corner of the realm and beyond. But no one could find any trace of the prince, no clue as to where he might have gone or why he had left."

Luca's mind raced with possibilities, his thoughts turning to the man lying on the bed beside him. Could it be possible? Could this sleeping stranger, this fated mate of his, be the missing fae prince?

"Elder," he said, his voice trembling with a mixture of hope and fear. "Do you think… could it be? Could my mate be the lost prince?"

The Elder's expression grew thoughtful, his eyes searching Luca's face with a piercing intensity. "It's possible," he said, his voice low and measured. "The prince was said to possess a beauty beyond compare, a grace and elegance that could only be described as otherworldly. And the magic that surrounds your mate, the curse that holds him in its thrall… it reeks of fae influence."

Luca's heart skipped a beat, his breath catching in his throat as he considered the implications. If his mate truly was the missing fae prince, then what did that mean for their future, for their love? Would he even want to be with a mortal wolf, once he was freed from the curse's hold?

"But Elder," he said, his voice rough with emotion. "If he is the prince, shouldn't we be able to sense his magic, his power? I feel nothing from him, no hint of the extraordinary abilities you described."

The Elder nodded, his expression grave. "The curse may be suppressing his magic," he said, his voice low and thoughtful. "It's possible that the prince's true nature, his very essence, has been locked away by the dark magic that binds him. Until we can break the curse and free him from its grasp, we may never know the truth of his identity."

Luca's jaw clenched with determination, his eyes blazing with a fierce and unshakable resolve. "Then that's what we need to focus on," he said, his voice ringing with conviction. "Breaking the curse, freeing my mate from its hold. Everything else can wait until he's safe and awake again."

The Elder smiled, his eyes crinkling with a mixture of pride and affection. "You're right, Luca," he said, his voice warm and reassuring. "The curse is the key to unlocking the mysteries surrounding your mate, and it must be our top priority. But I warn you, the path ahead will not be easy."

Luca nodded, his heart swelling with a fierce and unshakable determination. "I'm ready, Elder," he said, his voice steady and strong. "I won't let anything stand in my way, not even my own doubts and fears. I will save him, no matter what it takes."

The Elder placed a hand on Luca's shoulder, his touch warm and comforting. "I have faith in you, Luca," he said, his voice filled with quiet encouragement.

8

Protective Instincts

Luca

Luca could feel the pull of their bond, even from a distance. It was like a physical ache in his chest, a yearning that grew stronger with every passing moment. He wanted nothing more than to abandon his tools and rush to his mate's side, to hold him close and never let go. But he knew that he couldn't, not yet.

There was still too much to be done, too many mysteries to unravel before he could allow himself the luxury of rest and comfort.

With a sigh, Luca set down the clockwork toy and ran a hand through his hair, his fingers snagging on the tangles and knots that had formed during his restless night. He couldn't stop thinking about the Elder's words.

He shook his head, trying to banish the dark thoughts that threatened to overwhelm him. His mate needed him, and he would be damned if he let his own insecurities and fears stand in the way of saving him.

But just as Luca was beginning to lose himself in his work, his heightened senses suddenly picked up on the sound of footsteps approaching the house. He froze, his body going tense as he listened intently, trying to gauge the intentions of the intruder

Luca's protective instincts kicked into overdrive, his mind racing with possibilities as he set down his tools and made his way out of the workshop. He couldn't take any chances, not with his mate lying helpless and vulnerable in the next room.

Luca entered the main living area, his senses on high alert and his body coiled with tension, he was surprised to find his mother and Gareth standing there. Their faces were etched with concern, their eyes filled with a mixture of curiosity and worry that radiated off of them in palpable waves.

For a moment, Luca simply stared at them, his mind racing with a thousand different thoughts and emotions. He had been so focused on protecting his mate, on keeping him safe from any potential threats, that he hadn't even considered the possibility of his family coming to check on him.

Luca let out a low, warning growl, his eyes flashing with a fierce protectiveness as he positioned himself between his family and the bedroom where his mate lay. It was an instinctive reaction, a primal need to keep his loved one safe from any potential harm.

Gareth, taken aback by Luca's uncharacteristic behavior, raised his hands in a gesture of peace and surrender. "Whoa, easy there, brother," he said, his voice low and soothing. "It's just us. We're not here to hurt anyone."

Luca blinked, his mind slowly catching up with his body as he realized how he must have looked to his family. He shook his head, trying to clear the fog of adrenaline and protectiveness that had clouded his thoughts.

"I'm sorry," he said, his voice rough with emotion. "I didn't mean to scare you. It's just... there's a lot of things going on."

His mother stepped forward and placed a gentle hand on his arm.

"Luca, my love," she said, her voice soft and filled with understanding. "You know that you can tell us anything, right? No matter what it is, we will always love and support you."

Luca took a deep breath, his heart pounding in his chest as he looked at his mother and brother. "The man that I found a man in the forest," he began, his voice low and hesitant. "He was unconscious, trapped in some kind of enchanted slumber."

Gareth's eyes widened, his brow furrowing with concern. "What do you mean?"

Luca ran a hand through his hair, his eyes distant as he remembered the moment he first laid eyes on his mate. "The Elder said that It's a curse," he said, his voice growing stronger and more confident with every word. "A powerful, ancient magic that's keeping him locked in a deep, unnatural sleep."

His mother gasped, her hand flying to her mouth. "A curse? But who would do such a thing?"

Luca shook his head, his expression grim. "I don't know," he admitted. "But the Elder thinks… he thinks that the man might be the missing fae prince, the one who disappeared all those years ago."

Gareth's jaw dropped, his eyes wide with shock and disbelief. "The missing fae prince? Are you serious?"

Luca nodded, his heart swelling with a fierce, protective love for the man who lay sleeping in the next room. "I know it sounds crazy," he said, his voice rough with emotion. "But from the moment I saw him, I felt this connection, this pull towards him that I can't explain. The Elder said that he's my fated mate."

His mother's eyes softened, a small smile tugging at the corners of her mouth. "Oh, Luca," she breathed, her voice filled with wonder and joy. "A fated mate? That's incredible."

Gareth stepped forward, placing a hand on Luca's shoulder in a gesture of support and understanding. "We're with you, brother," he said, his voice low and filled with conviction. "Whatever it takes, we'll help you break this curse and bring your mate back to the world of the living."

Luca looked at his brother, surprise and confusion evident in his eyes. "Why are you being so nice to me all of a sudden?" he asked, his voice tinged with suspicion. "I thought you'd be angry or jealous that I found my fated mate before you."

Gareth's expression softened, a small smile tugging at the corners of his mouth. "I'm not going to lie, Luca," he said, his voice low and filled with emotion. "A part of me is jealous. I've always dreamed of finding my own fated mate, of experiencing that kind of love and connection."

He paused, his eyes distant as he gazed out the window at the forest beyond. "But more than that," he continued, his voice growing stronger and more confident with every word, "I'm happy for you. And seeing you find your mate, seeing the joy and love that it brings you… it gives me hope that maybe, someday, I'll find my own fated mate too."

Luca didn't know what to feel about this side of his brother but he took it anyway. "Thank you, Gareth," he said, his voice rough with emotion. "That means more to me than you can ever know."

His mother wrapped them both in a tight, fierce hug, her arms holding them close as if she could protect them from all the dangers and uncertainties that lay ahead. "My boys," she whispered, her voice soft and filled with a fierce, protective love. "I'm so proud of you both, and I know that whatever challenges or dangers we may face, we will face them together, as a family."

As Luca basked in the warmth of his mother's embrace, he felt a sudden pang of fear and uncertainty wash over him. He pulled back, his eyes searching his mother's face with a desperate intensity.

"Mother, Gareth," he said, his voice low and urgent. "You can't tell anyone about this, especially not Father. Not until we know more."

Gareth frowned, his brow furrowing with confusion. "Why not?" he asked, his voice tinged with concern. "Father's the alpha, Luca. He needs to know what's going on in his own pack."

Luca shook his head, his jaw clenching with a stubborn determination. "You know how he feels about the fae," he said, his voice rough with emotion. "He's never trusted them, not since the war. If he finds out that my mate is a fae prince, he might…"

He trailed off, unable to finish the thought. The idea of his father rejecting his mate, of turning his back on Luca when he needed him most, was too painful to even contemplate.

But Gareth seemed to understand, his expression softening with a quiet empathy. "Okay," he said, his voice low and reassuring. "We won't say anything, not until you're ready."

As his mother wiped away her tears, her expression suddenly brightened, a glimmer of hope and excitement shining in her eyes. "Luca," she said, her voice low and urgent. "I just remembered something. There's someone in Willowbrook who might be able to help us, someone who knows more about curses and fae magic than anyone else I know."

Luca's heart skipped a beat, his breath catching in his throat. "Who?" he asked, his voice barely above a whisper.

His mother smiled, a small, secretive smile that made Luca's heart race with anticipation. She quickly scribbled a name and address on a piece of paper, her hand shaking with excitement as she pressed it into Luca's palm.

"Go to this address," she said, her voice low and urgent. "He's powerful that one. If anyone can help you break this curse and save your mate, it's him."

Luca stared down at the paper, his heart pounding with a fierce, unshakable hope.

"Thank you, Mother," he said, his voice rough with emotion. "Thank you for everything."

His mother smiled, her eyes shining with a fierce, unwavering love. "You're welcome, my darling boy,"

Gareth stepped forward, his expression serious and determined. "Do you want us to stay and help?" he asked, his voice low and urgent. "We can take shifts watching over your mate, make sure he's safe."

Luca felt a surge of gratitude and love for his brother, for the unwavering support and loyalty that he had always shown him. But he shook his head, his jaw clenching with a stubborn determination.

"No," he said, his voice rough with emotion. "I appreciate the offer, but I need to do this on my own. I need to focus all of my energy on finding a way to break this curse and save my mate."

His mother nodded, her eyes shining with understanding. "Of course," she said, her voice soft and filled with pride. "We understand, Luca. But promise me that you'll keep us updated, that you'll let us know if there's anything we can do to help."

Luca swallowed hard, his throat tight with emotion. "I will," he said, his voice barely above a whisper. "I promise."

9

The Missing Child

Luca

Luca swung his axe, the blade biting deep into the trunk of the tree with a satisfying thunk. The forest was alive with the sounds of his labors, the crack of splintering wood and the rustling of fallen leaves underfoot.

He could feel that there was a tension in the air, a sense of unease that prickled at the back of his neck like a warning.

And then, as he paused to catch his breath and wipe the sweat from his eyes, Luca's sharp werewolf hearing picked up on a conversation in the distance. His ears perked up, his senses straining to make out the words over the sound of his own labored breathing and the rustling of leaves in the wind.

"Did you hear about the missing child?" one of the betas asked, his voice low and urgent.

Luca's heart skipped a beat, his breath catching in his throat as he listened intently.

"Yeah, I heard," the other beta replied, his tone grave and somber. "It's the third one this month. The pack is starting to get worried."

With a heavy sigh, Luca pushed himself off the tree and retrieved his axe from the ground. He would finish his work here, would gather enough wood to last the pack through the long, cold months ahead. And then, he would return to the village and offer his help in any way that he could.

As he swung his axe once more, Luca's mind was already racing with plans and possibilities. His first instinct was to drop everything and join the search for the missing child. Every fiber of his being screamed at him to take action, to use his strength and skills to bring the little one home safe and sound.

He couldn't leave his mate alone, not now, not when he was defenseless, unable to protect himself from the dangers that lurked in the shadows.

As he approached his house, Luca was surprised to see a thin wisp of smoke curling up from the chimney, a sure sign that someone was inside. His heart leapt with a sudden, irrational hope, a fleeting thought that maybe, just maybe, his mate had awakened, that the curse had been broken by some miracle of fate or chance.

He found his mother sitting at the kitchen table with a steaming cup of tea cradled in her hands, was his mother, her face etched with lines of worry and concern.

"Mother," Luca said, his voice rough with surprise and emotion. "What are you doing here?"

His mother looked up at him, her eyes soft and filled with a quiet understanding. "I came to check on you," she said simply, her voice warm and gentle.

He sighed. "I don't know what I would do without you."

His mother smiled, her eyes crinkling with a hint of mischief. "Well, for starters, you'd probably forget to eat and sleep and take care of yourself," she teased, her voice light and playful. "Speaking of which, when was the last time you had a proper meal?"

Luca laughed, the sound startling in the heavy, somber atmosphere of the room. "I honestly can't remember," he admitted, his hand rubbing the back of his neck in a sheepish gesture. "I've been so focused on everything else that I guess I just forgot."

His mother tutted, her expression stern but filled with a fond exasperation. "Well, that simply won't do," she declared, rising from her chair with a determined air. "You sit down and rest for a moment, and I'll whip up something to fill your belly and give you strength for the journey ahead."

Luca opened his mouth to protest, to insist that he didn't have time for rest or food, that he needed to get back out there and keep searching for answers. But something in his mother's eyes, in the set of her jaw and the strength of her stance, made him pause.

"Okay" he said, his voice soft and filled with a quiet gratitude.

As his mother busied herself in the kitchen, Luca took a moment to check on his mate, his heart heavy with worry and concern. He made his way to the bedroom, his steps slow and hesitant, as if he were afraid of what he might find.

He was relieved to see that nothing had changed. His mate lay on the bed, his face peaceful and untroubled, his chest rising and falling with the steady rhythm of his breath.

With a gentle touch, Luca brushed a stray lock of hair from his mate's forehead, his fingers lingering on the soft, warm skin. "I will find a way to save you," he whispered, his voice low and fervent. "I swear it on my life."

He pressed a soft, reverent kiss to his mate's forehead, his lips whispering a silent prayer to the moon goddess for strength and guidance. And then, with a final, lingering glance, he turned and made his way back to the kitchen, his heart heavy but filled with a newfound sense of purpose and resolve.

Luca was greeted by the rich, savory scent of his mother's cooking, the warm, familiar aroma filling the air with the promise of comfort and nourishment. He felt a pang of nostalgia wash over him, memories of countless meals shared around this very table, of laughter and love and the unshakable bond of family and pack.

"It smells amazing," he said, his voice rough with emotion. "Just like when I was a pup."

His mother turned to him, her face breaking into a warm, loving smile. "Well, someone has to keep you fed and healthy, you big, strong wolf," she teased, her eyes twinkling with mirth.

Luca felt a flicker of warmth and amusement at his mother's playful words, a momentary respite from the heavy thoughts that weighed on his mind. But even as he savored the comfort of her presence, he couldn't shake the nagging sense of unease that had settled deep in his gut.

"I overheard something in the forest today, something about a missing child. Is it true?" He said, his voice low and hesitant.

His mother's expression grew somber, her eyes clouding with a mix of sorrow and concern. "Yes, Luca," she said, her voice heavy with emotion. "A young pup, barely old enough to shift, was discovered missing from his bed just last night. The whole pack is in an uproar, searching the forest and the surrounding areas for any sign of him."

Luca felt his heart clench at the news, a sickening sense of dread washing over him. He knew all too well the dangers that lurked in the shadows of the forest, the vicious predators and treacherous terrain that could spell doom for even the most experienced of wolves. The thought of a innocent child facing those perils alone, without the protection of his pack, was almost too much to bear.

"I have to do something," he said, his voice rough with emotion. "I can't just sit here and do nothing while a pup is out there, lost and afraid."

His mother reached across the table, her hand warm and comforting as she clasped his own. "I know, Luca," she said, her voice soft and understanding. "But you have to think about your mate, too. He needs you now more than ever, and you can't leave him unprotected, not in his current state."

Luca closed his eyes, his jaw clenching with the effort of holding back the howl of frustration that threatened to tear from his throat. He knew that his mother was right, that he had a duty to his mate that he could not ignore. But the thought of doing nothing, of sitting idly by while a child suffered, went against everything he believed in, everything he had been raised to value.

"How's Father handling this?" he asked, his voice tight with barely suppressed emotion. "Let me guess, he's barking orders and throwing his weight around, as usual."

His mother sighed, her eyes filled with a weary sadness. "Luca," she said, her voice gentle but firm. "Your father is doing the best he can. He's under a lot of pressure right now, and he needs our support, not our judgment."

Luca snorted, his lips curling into a bitter smile. "Support? Where was his support when I needed it? Where was his understanding, his compassion, when I was struggling to find my place in the pack?"

He shook his head, his eyes hard and filled with pain. "No, he's never been there for me, not really. All he cares about is his own power, his own authority. And now, with this missing pup… I guarantee he's more worried about how it makes him look than he is about actually finding the poor kid."

His mother's eyes flashed with anger, her voice sharp and filled with reproach. "That's not fair, Luca," she said, her words clipped and precise. "Your father loves this pack, loves every wolf under his care. And he would do anything, sacrifice anything, to keep them safe."

Luca felt a twinge of guilt at the hurt in his mother's voice, the pain that he had caused with his thoughtless words. But he couldn't bring himself to take them back, couldn't ignore the years of neglect and dismissal that had left their mark on his heart.

"I'm sorry," he said, his voice low and filled with regret. "I know you love him, and I know he's doing his best. But I can't pretend that everything is okay between us, can't act like the past doesn't matter."

His mother's expression softened. "I know, Luca," she said, her voice heavy with understanding. "And I'm not asking you to forget, or to forgive, if you're not ready. But I am asking you to try, to give him a chance to make things right."

Luca closed his eyes, his jaw clenching with the effort of holding back the howl of frustration that threatened to tear from his throat. He knew that his mother was right, that holding onto his anger and resentment would only poison his own heart, his own soul. But the thought of letting go, of opening himself up to more pain and disappointment… it was almost more than he could bear.

"I don't know if I can," he said, his voice barely above a whisper. "I don't know if I have it in me, to give him another chance."

His mother reached across the table, her hand warm and comforting as she clasped his own. "You do, Luca," she said, her voice soft but filled with conviction. "You have a strength and a resilience that even you don't fully understand. And I know that, in time, you'll find a way to heal, to forgive, and to move forward."

He had always known that his mother believed in him, that she saw the best in him even when he couldn't see it himself. But to hear her say it out loud, to feel the strength of her love and support in every word… it meant more to him than he could ever express.

"I'll try," he said, his voice rough and choked with emotion. "For you, and for the pack. But I can't make any promises, can't guarantee that things will ever be right between me and Father."

"I know, Luca," she said, her voice soft and filled with understanding. "And that's okay. All I ask is that you keep an open heart, and that you never forget the love that binds us all together, no matter how strained or broken our relationships may seem."

Luca felt a surge of emotion wash over him, a wave of love and gratitude so strong that it threatened to bring him to his knees. He had always known that his mother was his rock, his anchor in the storm of life. But to feel the depth of her wisdom, the strength of her compassion, in moments like these… it was a gift beyond measure.

"I won't forget," he said, his voice rough and filled with promise. "I swear it, on my life and on my honor."

His mother smiled, her eyes bright with pride and love. "That's my boy," she said, her voice warm and filled with encouragement. "That's the wolf I raised, the warrior I always knew you could be."

10

A Fracturing Pack

Luca

As Luca stepped out into the bright, unforgiving light of day, his enhanced senses were immediately assaulted by the sound of raised voices, the tension in the air so thick he could almost taste it on his tongue. His heart raced with a sudden, sickening sense of dread, his instincts screaming at him that something was wrong, that the situation was escalating rapidly.

Without even realizing what he was doing, Luca found himself quickening his pace, his feet pounding against the hard-packed earth as he raced towards the pack house. He could feel the eyes of his packmates on him as he passed, could sense their fear and uncertainty like a physical weight pressing down on his shoulders.

But he didn't have time to stop, didn't have time to offer words of comfort or reassurance. Because he knew that every second counted, that the lives of innocent children hung in the balance.

As he burst through the doors of his father's office, Luca was greeted by a scene of chaos and confusion. His brother and father were locked in a heated argument, their faces flushed with anger and frustration as they hurled accusations and insults at each other like weapons.

"You're not doing enough!" Gareth shouted, his voice raw with emotion. "You're supposed to be our alpha, our protector, and yet you sit here in your office while our children are being stolen from their beds!"

The alpha's eyes flashed with a dangerous light, his lips curling into a snarl of rage. "Watch your tongue, boy," he growled, his voice low and menacing. "I am still your father, and your alpha. And I will not be spoken to with such disrespect."

Luca felt a surge of anger and frustration well up inside him, his jaw clenching with the effort of holding back the biting retort that danced on the tip of his tongue. He had always known that his father was a stubborn and proud man, that he clung to his power and authority like a drowning man to a life raft.

But to see him like this, to watch him prioritize his own ego over the safety and well-being of their pack... it was almost more than Luca could bear.

"Enough!" he shouted, his voice cutting through the din like a knife through butter. "Both of you, just... enough."

He stepped between his father and brother, his presence a calming force that seemed to diffuse the volatile situation like a cool breeze on a hot summer day. He could feel the eyes of both men on him, could sense their surprise and confusion at his sudden interruption.

But Luca didn't have time for their petty squabbles, didn't have time for their bruised egos and wounded pride. Because he knew that the longer they spent bickering and arguing, the more time they wasted, the more innocent lives were put at risk.

"Father," he said, his voice low and filled with a quiet intensity. "We need to talk about the missing children. We need to come up with a plan, a strategy for finding them and bringing them home safe."

The alpha's eyes narrowed, his lips twisting into a sneer of contempt.

"And what would you know about strategy, boy?" he scoffed, his voice dripping with disdain. "You, who have never led a pack, never borne the weight of leadership on your shoulders?"

Luca felt a flicker of anger and resentment spark to life in his chest, his hands clenching into fists at his sides. He had always known that his father saw him as weak, as unworthy of the power and responsibility that came with being an alpha.

But to hear him say it out loud, to feel the sting of his dismissal and his scorn... it was like a knife to the heart, a reminder of all the ways in which he had failed, all the ways in which he had fallen short.

"I may not be an alpha," Luca said, his voice low and filled with a quiet intensity. "But I am a member of this pack, a protector of the innocent. And I will not stand by and watch as our children are stolen from their beds, as our people live in fear and terror."

Luca stood his ground, his eyes blazing with a fierce determination as he faced down his father's dismissive attitude. He could feel the weight of the alpha's gaze on him, could sense the disdain and the disappointment that radiated from him like a physical force.

But he refused to be cowed, refused to back down in the face of his father's scorn and contempt. Because he knew that this was bigger than their own personal grievances, bigger than the years of hurt and resentment that stretched between them like an unbridgeable chasm.

"Father, Alpha" he said, his voice low and filled with a quiet intensity, "I know that we have our differences, that we have never seen eye to eye on many things. But this is not about you or me. This is about our pack, about the innocent lives that are at stake."

He could see the flicker of surprise in his father's eyes, the momentary flash of something that might have been respect or admiration. But it was gone as quickly as it had appeared, replaced by the cold, hard mask of the alpha, the unyielding facade of power and authority.

"And what would you know about the needs of the pack?" the alpha sneered, his lips curling into a mocking smile.

Luca felt a surge of anger and resentment well up inside him, his hands clenching into fists at his sides. He had always known that his father saw him as weak, as unworthy of the power and responsibility that came with being an alpha.

But to hear him say it out loud, to feel the sting of his dismissal and his scorn… it was like a knife to the heart, a reminder of all the ways in which he had failed, all the ways in which he had fallen short.

"I may not be perfect," Luca said, his voice rough and choked with emotion, "but I have always done my best to serve this pack, to protect and defend those who cannot protect themselves. And I will not stand by and watch as our people suffer, as our children are stolen from their beds and our territory is breached by unknown intruders."

He could see the flicker of surprise in his father's eyes, the momentary flash of something that might have been respect or admiration. But it was gone as quickly as it had appeared, replaced by the cold, hard mask of the alpha, the unyielding facade of power and authority.

"And what would you have me do, boy?" the alpha growled, his voice low and menacing. "Would you have me send out search parties, risk the lives of our warriors on a wild goose chase? Would you have me abandon my duties as alpha, neglect the needs of the pack in favor of chasing after ghosts and shadows?"

Luca shook his head, his jaw clenching with the effort of holding back the biting retort that danced on the tip of his tongue. He knew that his father was stubborn, that he clung to his pride and his authority like a drowning man to a life raft.

But he also knew that there was a kernel of truth in his words, a reminder that they needed to be smart, to be strategic in their approach to this crisis.

"No," he said, his voice soft but filled with a steely determination. "I would have you listen to your sons, to the members of this pack who have sworn to serve and protect it with their lives. I would have you put aside your pride and your ego, and work with us to find a solution, to bring our people back together and keep them safe."

For a long moment, the alpha simply stared at him, his eyes hard and unreadable as he weighed the sincerity of Luca's words. And then, with a heavy sigh, he nodded, his shoulders slumping with the weight of his own weariness and frustration.

"Very well," he said, his voice clipped and filled with a reluctant acceptance. "What would you have us do, then? How would you propose we go about finding these missing children and dealing with this unknown intruder?"

"We need to organize scouting parties," he said, his mind racing with possibilities and plans. "We need to establish a rotation of shifts, ensure that our territory is constantly monitored and patrolled. And we need to work together, to put aside our differences and our grievances, and focus on the task at hand."

He could see the flicker of surprise in his father's eyes, the momentary flash of something that might have been respect or admiration. And for a moment, Luca allowed himself to hope, to believe that maybe, just maybe, they could find a way to bridge the gap that had grown between them, to heal the wounds that had festered for so long.

But before he could say anything more, before he could even begin to formulate his next thought, the door to the alpha's office burst open, and a frantic beta stumbled inside, his face pale and drawn with fear.

"Alpha!" he gasped, his voice high and tight with panic. "We have a problem. An unknown intruder has breached our perimeter, leaving several scouts injured and unconscious in their wake."

Luca felt a chill run down his spine, his heart clenching with a sudden, sickening sense of dread. He exchanged a worried glance with his brother, both of them realizing in that moment that the situation had just become even more dire, even more dangerous than they had ever imagined.

"What do you mean, an unknown intruder?" the alpha demanded, his voice low and filled with a quiet menace. "How could someone have gotten past our defenses, past our warriors?"

The beta shook his head, his eyes wide and filled with a helpless confusion. "I don't know, Alpha," he said, his voice trembling with fear and uncertainty. "But whoever they are, they are powerful, and they are not here for a friendly visit."

Luca felt a surge of anger and determination well up inside him, his hands clenching into fists at his sides. He knew that he couldn't let this stand, couldn't allow some unknown enemy to threaten his pack, to put the lives of his people at risk.

"Father," he said, his voice low and filled with a quiet intensity, "we need to act now. We need to send out a team to track down this intruder, to find out who they are and what they want."

He could see the flicker of hesitation in his father's eyes, the momentary flash of something that might have been fear or uncertainty. But it was gone as quickly as it had appeared, replaced by the cold, hard mask of the alpha, the unyielding facade of power and authority.

"Very well," the alpha said, his voice clipped and filled with a reluctant acceptance. "Gareth, you will lead the team. Take our best trackers and scouts, and find out whatever you can about this intruder."

Gareth nodded, his eyes flashing with a fierce determination. "Yes, Father," he said, his voice low and filled with a quiet intensity. "I will not fail you, or the pack."

Luca felt a flicker of pride and admiration kindle in his chest, his heart swelling with love and respect for his brother. He knew that Gareth was strong, that he was brave and loyal and true. And he knew that together, they could face whatever challenges lay ahead, could overcome whatever obstacles stood in their way.

Without a word, they turned and raced out of the alpha's office, their feet pounding against the hard-packed earth as they made their way towards the heart of the confrontation. Luca could feel the blood rushing in his ears, the thrum of his own heartbeat drowning out the sounds of the forest around him.

11

Serpent's Smile

Luca

Luca's heart pounded in his chest as he and Gareth raced towards the pack's perimeter, their feet flying over the uneven ground with a speed and agility that only a wolf could possess. The scent of blood and pain hung heavy in the air, a sickening mixture that made Luca's stomach churn and his hackles rise with a primal sense of urgency.

He could hear the sounds of battle growing louder as they approached the gates, the snarls and howls of his packmates mingling with the strange, unsettling laughter of their unknown attacker. Luca's mind raced with possibilities and fears, his imagination conjuring up a thousand different scenarios, each one more terrifying than the last.

But he pushed those thoughts aside, focusing instead on the task at hand, on the need to protect his pack and his people from whatever threat lay waiting for them beyond those gates.

As they rounded the final bend in the path, Luca's heart nearly stopped in his chest at the sight that greeted them. There, just outside the gates, lay one of their scouts, his body writhing and contorting on the ground in a sickening display of agony. Luca could hear the wolf's whimpers and moans, could see the way his eyes rolled back in his head as he fought against the pain that consumed him.

Without a second thought, Luca raced to the fallen scout's side, his hands running over the wolf's body in a desperate search for injuries or wounds. But even as he looked, even as he prayed to the moon goddess for guidance and strength, he knew that this was no ordinary attack, no simple case of violence or aggression.

There was something else at work here, something dark and twisted and evil that made Luca's skin crawl and his heart clench with a fear that he had never known before.

Suddenly, a chilling laugh cut through the tension, drawing Luca's attention away from the fallen scout and towards the figure standing just beyond the gates. Luca's eyes narrowed as he took in the man's appearance, his hackles rising with a sense of unease and suspicion that he couldn't quite explain.

The man was impeccably dressed, his suit a deep, rich black that seemed to absorb the light around him. His fingers were wrapped around the handle of a sleek, black cane, the polished wood gleaming in the dappled sunlight that filtered through the trees. But it was his eyes that really caught Luca's attention, those cold, calculating orbs that seemed to drill straight into his soul, stripping away all of his defenses and leaving him feeling exposed and vulnerable.

"Well, well, well," the man said, his voice a low, mocking drawl that made Luca's skin crawl with revulsion. "What do we have here? A couple of little wolves, come to play hero and save the day?"

Luca felt a growl building in his throat, his lips pulling back in a snarl of pure, unadulterated rage. He could feel Gareth tensing beside him, could sense the barely contained fury that radiated off of his brother in waves.

With a fierce, guttural growl that seemed to rise up from the very depths of his soul, Luca stepped forward, his eyes blazing with a fury that he could barely contain. "Who the hell are you?" he demanded, his voice a low, menacing snarl that made even Gareth flinch beside him. "And what gives you the right to come into our territory and attack our people?"

The stranger merely chuckled, his smirk widening into a cruel, mocking grin that made Luca's blood boil with rage. "Names are unnecessary, little wolf," he said, his voice a silky purr that dripped with false sincerity.

Luca felt a shiver run down his spine at the man's words, a sense of dread and foreboding that he couldn't quite shake. There was something about this man, something dark and malevolent that made Luca's instincts scream with warning.

"I don't care what you call yourself," Luca growled, his voice a low, steady rumble that seemed to echo through the clearing. "What I want to know is what you want with our pack, and why you thought it was a good idea to come here and start trouble."

The stranger's smirk widened, his eyes glinting with a malevolent amusement that made Luca's skin crawl with revulsion. "Oh, but I think you do care, little wolf," he said, his voice a low, seductive purr that made Luca's heart race with a mixture of fear and anticipation. "Because you see, you possess something that belongs to me, something that you value above all else in this world."

Luca felt a flicker of confusion and dread wash over him, his mind racing with possibilities and fears.

"I don't know what you're talking about," he said, his voice tight with barely contained frustration and anger. "I have nothing that belongs to you, and even if I did, I sure as hell wouldn't give it to someone like you."

The stranger chuckled, his eyes glinting with a cruel, calculating light that made Luca's blood run cold. "Oh, but you do, little wolf," he said, his voice a low, menacing whisper that seemed to drill straight into Luca's soul. "You have something that is very, very precious to me, something that you took from me."

And then, with a sudden, sickening clarity, Luca understood.

"No," he whispered, his voice a hoarse, broken rasp that seemed to tear at his very soul. "No, you can't have him. He's not yours to take, not now, not ever."

The stranger's smile widened, his teeth flashing in a predatory grin that made Luca's stomach twist with unease. "Oh, but he is, little wolf," he said, his voice a low, seductive purr that made Luca's skin crawl with revulsion. "He belongs to me, body and soul, and I will not rest until I have claimed what is rightfully mine."

Luca felt a surge of anger and defiance well up inside him, his hands clenching into fists at his sides. He knew that he couldn't let this man take his mate, knew that he would fight to his last breath to keep him safe and protected from the darkness that sought to claim him.

"Over my dead body," he growled, his voice a low, menacing rumble that seemed to echo through the clearing. "I won't let you take him, not now, not ever. He's my mate, my love, and I will die before I let you lay a single finger on him."

The stranger chuckled, his eyes glinting with a malevolent amusement that made Luca's blood run cold. "Mate, you say? This has gotten more interesting by the day. Such bravado," he said, his voice a mocking drawl that dripped with false sincerity. "But I'm afraid that your little threats are meaningless to me, little wolf. I have powers that you can scarcely imagine, abilities that would make even the strongest and bravest of your kind tremble with fear."

Luca felt a shiver run down his spine at the man's words, a sense of dread and foreboding that he couldn't quite shake. He knew that this was a dangerous game they were playing, a game with stakes that were far too high to even contemplate.

But he also knew that he had no choice, that he had to find a way to protect his mate and his pack, no matter what the cost.

"I don't care what powers you have," he said, his voice a low, steady growl that seemed to echo through the clearing. "I won't let you take him, not without a fight. And if that means going up against you and all of your dark magic, then so be it."

The stranger's smile widened, his teeth flashing in a predatory grin that made Luca's stomach twist with unease. "We shall see, little wolf," he said, his voice a low, seductive purr that made Luca's skin crawl with revulsion. "We shall see."

"Luca," his father said, his voice low and filled with a quiet intensity that made Luca's heart race with a mixture of fear and anticipation. "What is this man talking about? What does he want with you, and why does he seem to think that you have something that belongs to him?"

Luca felt a flicker of panic and uncertainty wash over him, his mind racing with possibilities and fears. He knew that he couldn't tell his father the truth, couldn't reveal the existence of his sleeping mate and the curse that held him in its thrall. But he also knew that he couldn't lie, couldn't betray the trust and the love that his father had always shown him, even in the darkest of times.

And so, with a heavy heart and a sense of dread that seemed to settle deep in his bones, Luca remained silent, his jaw clenched with barely contained rage as he stared down the stranger with a fierce, unyielding intensity.

"Answer me, Luca," his father demanded, his voice rising with a hint of anger and frustration. "What is going on here, and why are you keeping secrets from your own pack, your own family?"

Luca felt a surge of guilt and shame wash over him, his heart aching with the weight of his own deception and betrayal. He knew that his father deserved the truth, deserved to know about the man who had captured his heart and his soul, the man who now lay sleeping in his bed, trapped in an endless slumber by a curse that Luca could not begin to understand.

But he also knew that he could not risk his mate's safety, could not expose him to the dangers and the uncertainties of a world that sought to tear them apart at every turn.

"I can't tell you, Father," he said, his voice low and filled with a quiet intensity that made even the stranger pause in his tracks. "I'm sorry, but there are some things that I must keep to myself."

His father's eyes flashed with anger and disappointment, his lips twisting into a scowl of disapproval that made Luca's heart ache with a deep, unrelenting pain.

"You would defy me, Luca?" he growled, his voice low and filled with a quiet menace that made even Gareth flinch beside him. "You would keep secrets from your own alpha, your own father?"

Luca felt a surge of anger and defiance well up inside him, his hands clenching into fists at his sides as he met his father's gaze with a fierce, unyielding intensity.

"My mate is not a possession to be claimed or bartered," he snarled, his voice rising with a hint of desperation and fear. "He is a living, breathing person, with thoughts and feelings and desires of his own. And I will not let anyone, not even you, Father, treat him like a piece of property to be bought and sold at will."

His father's eyes widened with shock and disbelief, his mouth falling open in a moment of stunned silence. But before he could even begin to formulate a response, Luca felt a sudden, overwhelming surge of energy coursing through his veins, a primal, animalistic urge that seemed to consume him from the inside out.

With a fierce, guttural growl that seemed to rise up from the very depths of his soul, Luca shifted into his wolf form, his powerful muscles rippling beneath his fur as he lunged towards the stranger, intent on ending the threat once and for all.

But even as his jaws closed around the man's throat, even as he felt the satisfying crunch of bone and sinew beneath his teeth, Luca knew that something was wrong, that this was not the end of their confrontation, but merely the beginning.

For in a flash of dark energy that seemed to split the very fabric of reality itself, the stranger vanished from beneath Luca's paws, his body dissolving into a shimmering mist that drifted away on the wind like smoke.

Luca whirled around, his eyes searching the clearing for any sign of the man, his heart pounding with a mixture of fear and anticipation. But there was nothing, no trace of the stranger or his dark magic, only the faint, lingering scent of brimstone and decay that hung heavy in the air like a shroud.

And then, just as Luca was about to turn away, just as he was about to shift back into his human form and face the consequences of his actions, he heard a voice whispering through the air, a chilling promise that made his blood run cold with dread.

"We're not done, little wolf," the voice said, its tone low and filled with a quiet menace that made Luca's skin crawl with revulsion. "You may have won this battle, but the war is far from over. And I will not rest until I have claimed what is rightfully mine, until I have taken back who belongs to me, body and soul."

12

Bound and Torn

Luca

Without a second thought, Luca shifted back into his human form, his muscles aching from the sudden transformation.

He didn't pause to catch his breath or to acknowledge the concerned faces of his pack mates. Instead, he took off running, his feet pounding against the earth as he raced towards his house. The need to ensure his mate's safety consumed him, driving him forward with a desperate urgency that he had never known before.

Behind him, he could hear his father's voice, calling out his name, demanding answers and explanations. But Luca couldn't focus on that now. He couldn't let himself be distracted by the weight of his father's disapproval or the growing unease that seemed to settle over the pack like a dark cloud.

All that mattered was his mate.

Luca pushed himself harder, his lungs burning with the effort as he tore through the familiar paths that led to his home. He could feel the eyes of his packmates on him as he passed, could sense their confusion and concern. But he didn't stop, didn't slow down, not even when his legs began to tremble with exhaustion and his vision blurred with unshed tears.

Finally, after what felt like an eternity, Luca burst through the door of his house, his chest heaving with exertion. He scanned the room frantically, his eyes searching for any sign of danger or intrusion.

And then he saw her, his mother, sitting near the window with a book in her hands. She looked up at him, startled by his sudden entrance, her brow furrowed with worry.

"Luca?" she said, her voice laced with concern. "What's wrong? What's happened?"

For a moment, Luca couldn't speak. The words stuck in his throat, choking him with the weight of his own fear and desperation. He wanted to tell her everything, to pour out the secrets that he had kept hidden for so long. But he knew that he couldn't, not yet, not until he had made sure that his mate was safe.

Without a word, Luca rushed past his mother, his feet carrying him swiftly towards the bedroom where his mate lay. He could feel his heart pounding in his chest, his blood rushing in his ears as he pushed open the door and stepped inside.

And there he was, his beautiful mate, still and peaceful amidst the chaos that threatened to engulf them. Luca's eyes roamed over his features, drinking in the sight of him like a man lost in the desert. He looked so vulnerable, so fragile, lying there on the bed with his eyes closed and his chest rising and falling with each shallow breath.

With a deep, shuddering breath, Luca reached out and took his mate's hand in his own, his fingers trembling as they brushed against the soft, warm skin. He could feel the steady pulse of his mate's heartbeat, the gentle rise and fall of his chest, and it gave him a flicker of hope, a glimmer of light in the darkness that surrounded them.

"I'm here," he whispered, his voice hoarse with emotion. "I won't let anything happen to you. I swear it on my life, on my honor, on everything that I am and ever will be."

He knew that his words were a promise, a vow that he would do whatever it took to keep his mate safe, to break the curse that held him in its thrall and bring him back to the world of the living.

The sound of approaching footsteps caught his attention. Luca tensed, his muscles coiling with anticipation as he positioned himself between his mate and the door, ready to defend him against any threat that might come their way.

But when the door swung open, it was not an enemy that stood before him, but his brother Gareth and his father, their faces etched with worry and confusion.

"Luca," Gareth said, his voice low and urgent. "I tried to stop him, but Father insisted on coming. He wants to know what's going on."

Luca felt a flicker of anger and frustration well up inside him, his jaw clenching with the effort of holding back the biting retort that danced on the tip of his tongue. He had hoped to have more time, to find a way to explain the situation to his father on his own terms. But it seemed that fate had other plans.

"Luca," his father said, his voice tight with barely contained anger. "What is the meaning of this? Who is this man, and why did that stranger at the perimeter speak of him as if he were some kind of prize to be won?"

Luca took a deep breath, his eyes never leaving his mate's face as he gathered his thoughts and his courage. He knew that the time for secrets and half-truths was over, that he owed his father the full story, no matter how difficult or painful it might be.

"Father," he said, his voice low and steady despite the pounding of his heart. "This man... he is my fated mate. The one I am destined to be with, the one I will stop at nothing to protect from those who seek to take him away."

For a long moment, the room was silent, the only sound the soft, steady breathing of the sleeping man on the bed. And then, with a heavy sigh, Luca's father spoke, his voice softer and more gentle than Luca had ever heard it before.

"Your fated mate?" he said, his eyes widening with surprise and concern. "Luca, I had no idea. Why did you not tell me sooner?"

Luca felt a lump rising in his throat, his eyes stinging with sudden, unexpected tears. He had always known that his relationship with his father was strained, that there was a chasm of hurt and resentment that stretched between them like an unbridgeable gap.

But to hear the genuine concern and care in his father's voice, to see the softening of his usually stern and unyielding features… it was almost more than Luca could bear.

"I was afraid," he admitted, his voice barely above a whisper. "Afraid of what you might think, of what you might do. I know that our pack has always been wary of outsiders, of those who are different from us. And I didn't want to risk losing him, not when I had just found him."

Luca's father sighed, his eyes filling with a deep, aching sadness. "Oh, Luca," he said, his voice heavy with regret. "I know that I have not always been the best father to you, that I have been hard and unyielding in my ways. But please, never doubt that I love you, that I want nothing more than for you to be happy and safe."

He paused, his gaze drifting to the sleeping man on the bed. "And if this man is truly your fated mate, then I will do everything in my power to help you protect him, to keep him safe from those who would seek to harm him."

Luca felt a surge of emotion wash over him, a wave of gratitude and love so strong that it threatened to bring him to his knees. He had always known that his father loved him, but to hear him say it out loud, to feel the strength of his conviction in every word… it was a gift beyond measure.

"Then you will have to show it because for the past couple of years I feel like I've been trashed around like I am nothing.," he said, his voice rough and choked with emotion.

His father nodded, his eyes shining with a quiet and After a beat he asked."The stranger at the perimeter… who was he? What did he want with your mate?"

"I don't know," he admitted, his voice barely above a whisper. "All I know is that he wants my mate, that he sees him as something to be claimed and possessed."

Luca's father nodded, his jaw clenching with a fierce, protective anger. "Then we must be vigilant," he said, his voice ringing with conviction. "We must watch over your mate, keep him safe from those who would seek to take him away. And we must find out more about this stranger, about the dangers that he poses to our pack and our way of life."

"What about the curse?" Gareth asked, his voice low and filled with concern. "How do we break it, how do we bring Luca's mate back to the world of the living?"

Luca felt a flicker of uncertainty wash over him, his mind racing with the countless questions and doubts that had plagued him since he first laid eyes on his sleeping mate.

"Luca," his father said, his voice low and urgent, "this curse that holds your mate… what do you know of it? How can we break it and bring him back to the world of the living?"

He opened his mouth to speak, to give voice to the fears and uncertainties that swirled within him, but before he could utter a word, the door to the room swung open once more, and a familiar figure stepped inside.

It was the Elder, his weathered face etched with lines of wisdom and concern. He moved with a quiet grace, his presence a calming force amidst the tension that hung heavy in the air.

"Alpha," he said, his voice low and respectful as he addressed Luca's father. "I apologize for the intrusion, but I sensed that my presence was needed here."

Luca's father nodded, his expression a mix of surprise and relief. "Elder," he said, his voice tight with barely contained emotion. "Please, if you have any knowledge or insight into the curse that holds Luca's mate, we would be grateful for your guidance."

The Elder nodded, his eyes drifting to the sleeping man on the bed. For a long moment, he simply stood there, his gaze distant and unfocused, as if he were seeing something that the rest of them could not.

And then, with a heavy sigh, he spoke, his voice low and filled with a quiet intensity. "The curse that holds this man… it is ancient and powerful, woven with a magic that even I cannot fully comprehend. But one thing is clear: only Luca has the power to break it, to bring his mate back to the world of the living."

Luca felt a weight settle on his shoulders, a sense of responsibility and destiny that made his heart race with a mixture of fear and anticipation. He had always known that his connection to his mate was special, that there was a bond between them that went beyond the physical and the mundane.

But to hear it spoken aloud, to have the Elder confirm what he had always suspected… it was both thrilling and terrifying, a reminder of the challenges and obstacles that lay ahead.

"How?" he asked, his voice barely above a whisper. "How do I break the curse, how do I bring him back to me?"

The Elder's expression grew somber, his eyes filled with a deep, aching sadness. "That, I cannot say," he admitted, his voice heavy with regret. "The path ahead is shrouded in mystery and shadow, and even I cannot see where it will lead. But I do know this: time is of the essence, and the stranger at the perimeter is no ordinary man. Your mate holds the key to unlocking the secrets that surround us, and there are those who would stop at nothing to claim him for their own."

Luca felt a chill run down his spine, a sense of dread and foreboding that made his blood run cold. He had always known that there was something special about his mate, something that set him apart from all others.

But to hear the Elder speak of him as a key, as a prize to be won… it made Luca's heart clench with a fierce, protective anger, a determination to keep his mate safe from all who would seek to harm him.

"What must I do?" he asked, his voice low and filled with a quiet intensity. "How can I keep him safe, how can I protect him from those who would take him away?"

The Elder's expression softened, his eyes filled with a quiet, unwavering faith. "You must trust in yourself, Luca," he said, his voice low and filled with a quiet conviction. "Trust in the bond that ties you to your mate, in the love and the strength that flows between you. It is that love, that unbreakable connection, that will guide you through the darkness and into the light beyond."

Luca nodded, his heart swelling with a fierce, unshakable resolve. He knew that the Elder was right, that he had to believe in himself and in the love that he shared with his mate.

His father turned to Gareth, his eyes hard and filled with a fierce, protective anger. "Gareth," he said, his voice ringing with command. "I need you to take charge of the investigations into the disappearances that have plagued our pack. We cannot afford to let this threat go unchallenged, not when the safety and well-being of our people hang in the balance."

Gareth nodded, his expression grim and filled with a quiet determination. "Of course, Father," he said, his voice low and filled with a quiet intensity. "I will not rest until we have uncovered the truth, until we have brought those responsible to justice."

Luca's father nodded, his expression softening with a hint of pride and affection. And then, with a final, lingering glance at Luca and his sleeping mate, he turned and strode from the room, his shoulders squared and his head held high, ready to face the challenges and burdens of leadership that awaited him beyond the door.

Luca felt a weight settle on his shoulders, a sense of responsibility and destiny that made his heart race with a mixture of fear and anticipation. He knew that the road ahead would be long and treacherous, filled with dangers and uncertainties that he could scarcely imagine.

His gaze drifting to his mate, his expression softening with a hint of tenderness and longing. "I must go to Willowbrook," he said, his voice barely above a whisper.

13

Journey to Willowbrook

Luca

Luca took a deep breath as he stepped out onto the path that would lead him to Willowbrook. The sun was just beginning to peek over the horizon, painting the sky in shades of pink and gold, but Luca hardly noticed the beauty of the morning. His mind was too full of thoughts of his mate.

His feet crunching on the fallen leaves and twigs that littered the forest floor, Luca couldn't help but think back to the promises that his brother Gareth had made before he left. Gareth had sworn to keep him updated on the pack's situation, to send word if anything changed or if his assistance was needed. And Luca knew that he could count on his brother to keep his word, to stand by his side even when they were miles apart.

The hours seemed to slip by like water through his fingers. The sun climbed higher in the sky, its warm rays filtering through the canopy of leaves above him, and the sounds of the forest filled the air around him - the chirping of birds, the rustling of small animals in the underbrush, the distant babble of a brook.

And then, just as Luca was beginning to wonder if he would ever reach his destination, he saw it - the towering stone archway that marked the entrance to Willowbrook, its weathered surface covered in intricate carvings and runes that seemed to pulse with an ancient, mysterious power.

Luca's heart skipped a beat as he approached the arch, his hand instinctively reaching for the paper that his mother had given him before he left. He unfolded it carefully, his eyes scanning the words that were written there in his mother's neat, precise handwriting.

"Benjamin," the note read, followed by a brief description of where he could be found - "works around the library."

And so, with a deep breath and a determined nod, Luca stepped through the arch and into the heart of Willowbrook.

As he walked through the town's narrow, winding streets, Luca couldn't help but marvel at the sights and sounds that surrounded him. The buildings here were unlike anything he had ever seen before - tall and narrow, with pointed roofs and intricate carvings that seemed to dance and shimmer in the sunlight. The air was filled with the scent of exotic spices and the chatter of voices in a dozen different languages, and everywhere he looked, Luca saw people going about their daily lives - merchants hawking their wares, children playing in the streets, lovers strolling arm in arm.

It was a world that was so different from the one he had known, a world that was full of mystery and magic and endless possibilities. And yet, even as he drank it all in, even as he felt a sense of excitement and wonder stirring in his chest, Luca couldn't shake the feeling of unease that had settled deep in his gut.

Luca's eyes fell upon a small, cozy-looking inn nestled between two towering buildings. The sign above the door read "The Dreamery," and something about the name made Luca's heart skip a beat, made him feel like he had found the perfect place to rest his head and gather his thoughts.

With a smile tugging at the corners of his mouth, Luca pushed open the door and stepped inside, his eyes adjusting to the dim, flickering light of the candles that lined the walls. The air inside was warm and inviting, filled with the scent of cinnamon and cloves and the soft murmur of conversation from the patrons who sat at the tables scattered throughout the room.

Luca made his way to the bar, his eyes scanning the faces of the people around him as he walked. He couldn't help but feel a sense of curiosity, a desire to know more about these strangers who had chosen to make their home in this strange and wonderful town.

"What can I get for you, love?" the bartender asked as Luca approached, her voice warm and friendly despite the hint of mischief that sparkled in her eyes.

Luca smiled, feeling a sense of ease and comfort wash over him as he settled onto one of the stools at the bar. "A room for the night, if you have one available," he said, his voice low and slightly rough from disuse. "And maybe a bite to eat, if it's not too much trouble."

The bartender grinned, her eyes crinkling at the corners as she nodded her head. "Of course, love," she said, her voice filled with a hint of laughter. "We've always got room for a handsome wolf like yourself. And as for food, well, let's just say that the Dreamery is known for more than just its comfortable beds and friendly service."

Luca chuckled, feeling a sense of warmth and camaraderie wash over him as he listened to the bartender's playful banter. He knew that he had made the right choice in coming here, that this was exactly the kind of place he needed.

He settled into his room, his pack slung carelessly in the corner and his boots kicked off by the door, Luca couldn't help but feel a sense of peace wash over him, a sense of rightness and belonging that he had never known before.

With a soft, contented sigh, Luca let himself drift off to sleep, his mind full of dreams of his mate and the future that they would build together. And as he slept, the world around him seemed to shimmer and dance with a magic all its own, a magic that whispered of love and destiny and the endless possibilities that lay ahead.

* * *

It was early in the morning and the streets of Willowbrook were already bustling,. Luca couldn't help but feel a sense of wonder and excitement wash over him. Everywhere he looked, he saw signs of the supernatural, of a world that was so different from the one he had known back home.

There were witches and warlocks, their eyes glinting with mischief and magic as they wove their spells and charms. There were faeries and nymphs, their laughter tinkling like bells on the wind as they danced and played in the dappled sunlight. And there were creatures that Luca had never even heard of before, beings that seemed to defy description and explanation, that made his head spin with the sheer scope and scale of the world he had stumbled into.

At first, Luca felt a flicker of unease, a sense of being out of place and out of his depth in this strange and wondrous town. He knew that he needed to be careful, to avoid drawing too much attention to himself or giving away his true nature as a wolf. The last thing he wanted was to stir up trouble or make enemies in a place where he was already at a disadvantage.

Luca's mind began to wander, to drift back to the life he had left behind and the responsibilities that had once seemed so heavy on his shoulders. He thought of his pack, of the bonds of love and loyalty that had tied him to his family and his people for as long as he could remember. And he thought of the dreams he had once had, the hopes and aspirations that had been pushed aside in the face of duty and obligation.

For a moment, Luca felt a flicker of regret, a sense of longing for the life he had never had the chance to live. He had always been the responsible one, the one who put his pack first and his own desires second. And while he didn't regret the choices he had made, while he knew that he would make them again in a heartbeat, he couldn't help but wonder what might have been, what adventures and experiences he might have had if he had been free to follow his own path.

But even as that thought crossed his mind, even as he felt a pang of wistfulness and longing, Luca knew that he couldn't dwell on the past, couldn't let himself get lost in the what-ifs and might-have-beens. He had a job to do, a mission to complete. And he knew that he needed to stay focused, to keep his eyes on the prize and his mind on the task at hand.

His stomach began to rumble, reminding him that he hadn't eaten since the night before. And so, with a quick glance around, Luca spotted a small, cozy-looking coffee shop nestled between two towering buildings, its sign reading "Glimmer" in swirling, iridescent letters.

With a smile tugging at the corners of his mouth, Luca pushed open the door and stepped inside, his senses immediately assaulted by the rich, heady scent of coffee and baked goods. The air inside was warm and inviting, filled with the soft murmur of conversation and the gentle clink of cups and plates.

As he approached the counter, Luca was greeted by a man with dark, tousled hair and bright, mischievous eyes. The man's gaze swept over him, taking in his appearance with a practiced, assessing look that made Luca feel suddenly self-conscious and exposed.

"What do we have here? A wolf in Willowbrook, and not just any wolf, but a newcomer at that." The man said, his voice low and playful

Luca felt a flicker of unease at the man's words, a sense of wariness and suspicion that made his hackles rise and his muscles tense. He knew that he needed to be careful, to choose his words and his actions wisely in a place where he was already at a disadvantage.

"I'm just passing through," he said, his voice low and guarded. "Here on business, nothing more."

The man's eyes narrowed, his smile turning sly and knowing. "Of course you are."

Luca's jaw clenched, his eyes flashing with a hint of anger and frustration. He didn't like being mocked, didn't like the feeling of being looked down upon or underestimated. But he knew that he needed to keep his cool, to avoid making a scene or drawing too much attention to himself.

"Look," he said, his voice low and steady. "I don't want any trouble. I just want a cup of coffee and a bite to eat, and then I'll be on my way."

The man's smile widened, his eyes glinting with a hint of mischief and amusement. "Well, why didn't you say so?" he said, his voice suddenly warm and friendly. "I'm Dominic, by the way."

Luca felt a flicker of surprise at the man's sudden change in demeanor, a sense of confusion and uncertainty that made him hesitate for a moment. But then, with a mental shrug, he decided to play along, to see where this strange and unexpected encounter might lead.

"I'm Luca," he said, his voice still guarded but not quite as hostile as before. "And I'll have a large black coffee and a blueberry muffin, if you've got them."

Dominic's smile widened, his eyes crinkling at the corners as he nodded his head. "Coming right up," he said, his voice filled with a hint of laughter.

Luca couldn't help but chuckle at that, feeling a sense of warmth and camaraderie wash over him despite his earlier reservations. He knew that he needed to be careful, that he couldn't afford to let his guard down or trust too easily in a place like this. But there was something about Dominic, something about his easy, playful manner that made Luca feel strangely at ease, like he had found a kindred spirit in the midst of all the chaos and uncertainty.

As he waited for his order, Luca's eyes drifted around the coffee shop, taking in the eclectic mix of patrons and decor. There were witches and warlocks, their eyes glinting with mischief and magic as they sipped their lattes and chatted quietly amongst themselves. There were faeries and nymphs, their laughter tinkling like bells on the wind as they nibbled on pastries and flitted about the room. And there were creatures that Luca had never even heard of before, beings that seemed to defy description and explanation, that made his head spin with the sheer scope and scale of the world he had stumbled into.

But as his gaze swept over the room, Luca's attention was suddenly caught by a figure that made his heart skip a beat, that made his breath catch in his throat with a mixture of shock and disbelief.

There, standing in the doorway of the coffee shop, was a vampire, his pale, ethereal features glowing in the soft, diffused light of the room. Luca's eyes widened, his mind racing with questions and possibilities. He had always thought that vampires avoided sunlight, that they were creatures of the night who shunned the daylight hours. But here was one, bold as brass and brazen as could be, striding into the coffee shop like he owned the place.

As Luca watched, the vampire made his way over to the counter, his movements graceful and fluid despite the heavy, cumbersome cloak that draped over his shoulders. And then, to Luca's utter shock and amazement, the vampire leaned in and pressed a soft, lingering kiss to Dominic's lips, his fingers tangling in the barista's dark, tousled hair with a familiarity and intimacy that made Luca's heart ache with longing and envy.

For a moment, Luca couldn't breathe, couldn't think, couldn't do anything but stare at the two men, his mind reeling with the implications of what he was seeing. He had never thought of himself as the jealous type, had never begrudged others their happiness or their love. But seeing Dominic and the vampire together, seeing the easy, natural way they interacted and the obvious affection that flowed between them, made something twist and churn in Luca's gut, made him feel suddenly and acutely alone in a way he had never felt before.

Because he knew that he wanted that, wanted the kind of love and connection that Dominic and the vampire shared. He wanted to hold his mate in his arms, to feel the warmth of his skin and the beat of his heart against his own. He wanted to wake up every morning to the sight of his face, to fall asleep every night wrapped in the comfort and safety of his embrace.

But he also knew that he couldn't have that, not yet, not until he had broken the curse that held his mate in its thrall and brought him back to the world of the living. And so, with a heavy heart and a renewed sense of determination, Luca forced himself to look away, to turn his attention back to his coffee and his muffin and the task that lay ahead.

He knew that he had a long road ahead of him, that there were challenges and obstacles waiting for him at every turn. But he also knew that he was ready, that he had the strength and the courage to face whatever lay ahead, to fight for the love and the life that he knew was waiting for him, just beyond the horizon.

And so, with a deep breath and a silent vow, Luca picked up his coffee and his muffin and made his way over to a quiet corner of the shop, his mind already racing with thoughts of the future and the destiny that awaited him, just out of reach but tantalizingly close, like a dream that he could almost touch if he just stretched out his hand and grasped it with all his might.

14

The Librarian

Luca

Luca stood before the library, his heart pounding with a mix of anticipation and trepidation. Taking a deep breath, he steeled himself and pushed open the heavy wooden doors, stepping into the grand foyer of the library.

Luca couldn't help but marvel at the grandeur of the building. Towering bookshelves lined the walls, filled with countless tomes and manuscripts, while intricate stained-glass windows cast a kaleidoscope of colors across the polished marble floor. It was a sight that took his breath away, a testament to the knowledge and history that lay within these walls.

As he approached the desk, Luca was greeted by a warm, friendly face. The woman behind the counter, whom he later learned was named Mrs. Ethel, had a soft, inviting smile that seemed to light up the room. Her eyes sparkled with a hint of mischief, as if she knew secrets that Luca had yet to uncover.

"Hello there, my dear," Mrs. Ethel said, her voice as sweet as honey. "How can I assist you today?"

Luca couldn't quite put his finger on it, but there was something about Mrs. Ethel that made him wonder about her true nature. Was she a witch, like Dominic? Or perhaps some other supernatural being, hiding in plain sight? But he knew it would be rude to pry, and so he pushed those thoughts aside and focused on the task at hand.

"Good afternoon, ma'am," Luca replied, his voice polite and respectful. "I'm looking for a man named Benjamin. I was told he might be able to help me with a... personal matter."

Mrs. Ethel's smile widened, her eyes twinkling with a knowing look that made Luca feel as if she could see right through him. "Ah, yes. Benjamin. Such a lovely young man, always so helpful and kind. You'll find him in the children's section, dear. He's reading to the little ones, along with his companion, Peter."

Luca's eyebrows shot up in surprise. "His companion?"

Mrs. Ethel chuckled, a soft, musical sound that filled the air. "Oh, yes. Those two are quite the pair. Always bringing joy and laughter to the children. It's a sight to behold, truly."

"Thank you, Mrs. Ethel," Luca said, his voice sincere and grateful. "I appreciate your help."

With a nod and a smile, Luca turned and made his way towards the children's section, following the sound of laughter and excited chatter that echoed through the halls. As he walked, he couldn't help but feel a sense of hope blossoming in his chest, a glimmer of possibility that perhaps, just perhaps, Benjamin might hold the key to unlocking the mysteries that surrounded his mate's curse.

As Luca stepped into the children's section, he was immediately struck by the vibrant colors and whimsical decorations that adorned the walls and shelves. It was a world apart from the rest of the library, a magical space where imagination and wonder reigned supreme.

Scanning the area, Luca spotted a quiet corner, partially hidden from view by a towering bookshelf. He made his way over and settled into a cozy armchair, his eyes drawn to the sight of Benjamin, surrounded by a gaggle of eager children.

Benjamin was a charismatic figure, his presence commanding the room with an effortless charm. He had a mop of unruly curls, the color of burnished copper, and eyes that sparkled with mirth and mischief. His smile was infectious, and his laughter, warm and rich, seemed to fill the air with a joyous melody.

As Luca watched Benjamin interact with the children, he couldn't help but feel a pang of longing in his heart. He imagined a future where he and his mate might have little ones of their own, a family to love and cherish. It was a dream that seemed so far out of reach, a happiness that hinged upon breaking the curse that held his love captive.

Lost in his thoughts, Luca almost missed the moment when Benjamin reached for the pendant that hung around his neck. It was a small, unassuming thing, a simple quill carved from some unknown material. But as Benjamin's fingers closed around it, Luca felt a sudden surge of power, an immense energy that radiated from the object like a beacon in the night.

Luca's eyes widened as the pendant began to glow, its form shifting and changing until it had transformed into a full-sized quill, its nib gleaming with an otherworldly light. He could sense the magic that thrummed through it, a power that was ancient and wild, barely contained within the fragile shell of its physical form.

As Benjamin began to read, his voice rich and melodious, the magic of the quill seemed to come to life. The words that flowed from his lips took on a tangible presence, weaving themselves into the very fabric of reality. The children gasped and giggled as the stories unfolded before their eyes, fantastical scenes of dragons and fairies, knights and princesses, all brought to vivid life by the power of Benjamin's enchanted quill.

Luca watched, transfixed, his mind struggling to comprehend the incredible display of magic that was unfolding before him. He had always known that the supernatural world was full of wonders, but this… this was something else entirely. It was a magic that was pure and joyous, a celebration of the power of stories and the imagination.

So engrossed was Luca in the spectacle before him that he almost didn't notice when someone settled into the chair beside him. It was only when the newcomer spoke that Luca startled, his heart leaping into his throat as he turned to face the intruder.

"Amazing, isn't it?" the man said, his voice low and conspiratorial. "The way he brings the stories to life, the magic that he weaves with nothing more than his words and his quill."

Luca blinked, taking in the man's appearance with a wary eye. He was handsome, with dark hair and piercing blue eyes, his features sharp and angular. There was something about him that set Luca's senses on edge, a power that simmered beneath the surface of his skin, not unlike the magic that emanated from Benjamin's quill.

"Who are you?" Luca asked, his voice low and guarded. "And how do you know about Benjamin's magic?"

The man chuckled, his eyes sparkling with amusement. "Forgive me," he said, his tone light and teasing. "I forget my manners sometimes. My name is Peter, and I'm a friend of Benjamin's. Mrs. Ethel mentioned that you were looking for him, and I thought I'd come and introduce myself."

Luca's eyes narrowed, his suspicion warring with his curiosity. "A friend?" he repeated, his tone skeptical. "And what kind of friend might that be, exactly?"

Peter's grin widened, his eyes dancing with mischief. "Oh, you know," he said, his voice dripping with innuendo. "The kind of friend who appreciates the finer things in life. Good food, good drink, and of course, good magic."

Despite himself, Luca felt a smile tugging at the corners of his mouth. There was something about Peter's easy charm and irreverent humor that was impossible to resist, even for a stoic warrior like himself.

"Is that so?" he said, his voice dry and amused. "And I suppose you're quite the expert on magic yourself, then?"

Peter laughed, the sound rich and warm. "Oh, I dabble here and there," he said, his tone self-deprecating. "But Benjamin… he's the real deal. The kind of magic he wields, the stories he brings to life… it's like nothing I've ever seen before."

Luca nodded, his gaze drifting back to where Benjamin sat, still weaving his enchanted tales for the enraptured children. "It's incredible," he murmured, his voice soft and reverent. "The way he captures their imaginations, the joy and wonder he brings to their lives."

Peter hummed in agreement, his eyes soft and fond as he watched his friend work his magic. "It's a gift," he said, his voice quiet and sincere. "A rare and precious thing, to be able to bring such happiness to others."

For a moment, the two men sat in silence, each lost in their own thoughts as they watched the scene before them. Luca couldn't help but feel a sense of kinship with Peter, a recognition of the longing and admiration that shone in his eyes when he looked at Benjamin.

As the final words of the story faded into the air, the children erupted into a chorus of cheers and applause, their faces alight with joy and wonder. Benjamin grinned, his eyes sparkling with a warm, infectious happiness as he took a bow, the enchanted quill still glowing softly in his hand.

Luca watched the scene with a smile, his heart swelling with a bittersweet ache. It was a beautiful thing, to see such pure, unbridled joy on the faces of the little ones, to witness the magic and the wonder that Benjamin had brought into their lives.

The children began to disperse, running to their waiting parents with excited chatter and laughter, Luca saw Peter approach Benjamin, a soft, tender smile on his face.

And then, to Luca's surprise, Benjamin turned and caught his eye, a warm, welcoming smile spreading across his face. He said something to Peter, who nodded and gave Luca a friendly wave, before making his way over to where Luca sat, his steps easy and unhurried.

"Ah, you must be Luca," Benjamin said, his voice rich and melodious, with a hint of mischief dancing in his eyes. "Peter told me you were looking for me. I hope you enjoyed the story?"

Luca felt a flush of heat rising to his cheeks, a sudden, awkward shyness that he couldn't quite explain. "I did," he said, his voice rough and hesitant. "It was… it was amazing, the way you brought the tale to life, the magic that you wove with your words and your quill."

Benjamin's smile widened, his eyes crinkling with pleasure. "Thank you," he said, his tone sincere and warm. "It's a joy and a privilege, to be able to share these stories with the children, to bring a little bit of magic and wonder into their lives."

He paused, his expression growing more serious, a hint of concern creeping into his voice. "But I sense that you didn't come here just to listen to my tales," he said, his gaze searching and intent. "Peter mentioned that you had a… a personal matter, something that you hoped I might be able to help with?"

Luca swallowed hard, his throat suddenly dry and tight. He knew that this was the moment he had been waiting for, the chance to share his story and his struggles with someone who might be able to help him, to offer guidance and support in his quest to save his mate.

But now that the moment had arrived, he found himself hesitating, a sudden, irrational fear gripping his heart. What if Benjamin couldn't help him? What if there was no way to break the curse, no hope of bringing his love back to the world of the living?

"I… I don't want to impose," he said at last, his voice rough and uncertain. "I know that you must be busy, that you have your own life and your own responsibilities to attend to."

Benjamin shook his head, his expression kind and understanding. "Nonsense," he said, his tone firm and reassuring. "If there's anything I can do to help, anything at all, I'll gladly do it. That's what friends are for, after all."

He glanced around, taking in the bustling activity of the library, the curious glances and whispered conversations of the patrons who had witnessed his magical storytelling session. "But perhaps we should continue this conversation somewhere a bit more private," he said, his voice lowering conspiratorially. "My office is just down the hall, and it's much more comfortable than these hard library chairs."

Luca hesitated for a moment, a flicker of uncertainty and doubt crossing his face. But then he nodded, a small, grateful smile tugging at the corners of his mouth. "That would be… that would be wonderful," he said, his voice soft and sincere. "Thank you, Benjamin. Thank you for your kindness, and your willingness to help."

Benjamin grinned, his eyes sparkling with warmth and mischief. "Think nothing of it," he said, his tone light and teasing. "It's not every day that a handsome wolf like yourself comes seeking my aid. I'd be a fool to turn down such an opportunity."

Despite himself, Luca felt a laugh bubbling up in his throat, a sudden, unexpected moment of levity in the midst of his pain and uncertainty. "Well, I'll do my best not to disappoint," he said, his voice dry and amused.

And with that, the two men made their way out of the children's section, Benjamin leading the way with a confident, easy stride, Luca following close behind, his heart pounding with a mixture of hope and trepidation.

As they entered Benjamin's office, a cozy, cluttered space filled with books and oddities, Luca felt a sense of warmth and comfort washing over him, a sudden, inexplicable feeling of safety and belonging.

He settled himself onto a plush, overstuffed couch, his muscles slowly unwinding as he took in the eclectic decor, the shelves filled with ancient tomes and mysterious artifacts, the walls covered in vibrant, abstract paintings that seemed to dance and shimmer in the soft, golden light.

He took a deep breath, his hands clenching and unclenching in his lap as he tried to find the words, to give voice to the pain and the desperation that had driven him to seek out Benjamin's help.

"I… I don't know where to begin," he said at last, his voice rough and hesitant, his eyes fixed on some distant point as he struggled to gather his thoughts. "My mother… she told me to come to you, to seek your aid in a matter that is… that is very close to my heart."

Benjamin leaned forward, his expression open and understanding, his eyes filled with a quiet, unwavering support. "Take your time, Luca," he said, his voice low and gentle, a hint of encouragement in his tone. "We're here to listen, to help in any way that we can."

Luca nodded, his throat tight with emotion as he forced himself to continue, to give voice to the words that had been burning in his heart for so long.

"My mate," he said, his voice barely above a whisper, his eyes stinging with sudden, unexpected tears. "He's… he's trapped, under a sleeping curse that no one seems to know how to break."

He paused, his breath catching in his throat as he remembered the last time he had seen his love, the way his face had been so still and peaceful, as if he were merely dreaming, lost in some distant, unreachable place.

For a long moment, the room was silent, the only sound the soft, steady ticking of the clock on the wall, the distant murmur of voices from the library beyond.

And then, with a quiet, compassionate sigh, Benjamin spoke, his voice low and gentle, his eyes filled with a deep, aching sympathy.

"Oh, Luca," he said, his tone soft and understanding, his hand reaching out to rest on Luca's arm in a gesture of comfort and support. "I can only imagine the pain you must be feeling, the desperation and the fear that have brought you to my door."

He paused, his expression growing thoughtful, his brow furrowing with concentration as he seemed to search for the right words, the right way to offer his aid and his guidance.

"I… I don't know if I have the answers you seek," he said at last, his voice hesitant and uncertain, his eyes filled with a quiet, apologetic regret. "The magic of curses and enchantments is a tricky thing, a web of secrets and mysteries that even the wisest among us struggle to unravel."

Luca felt his heart sinking, a sudden, sickening sense of despair washing over him at Benjamin's words. If even the great mage himself couldn't help him, couldn't offer him some glimmer of hope or guidance, then what chance did he have of ever breaking the curse, of ever bringing his love back to the world of the living?

But before he could give voice to his fears, before he could let the darkness consume him once more, Peter spoke up, his voice low and earnest, his eyes shining with a fierce, unwavering determination.

"We may not have all the answers, Luca," he said, his tone firm and resolute, his hand reaching out to clasp Luca's shoulder in a gesture of solidarity and support. "But we will do everything in our power to help you, to stand by your side and fight for the love that you hold so dear."

He glanced over at Benjamin, a silent question in his eyes, a wordless plea for his friend to join him in his vow of aid and assistance.

And Benjamin, his expression softening with a quiet, gentle smile, nodded his head, his hand reaching out to join Peter's on Luca's shoulder, a silent promise of support and understanding.

"Peter is right," he said, his voice low and sincere, his eyes shining with a quiet, unwavering conviction. "We may not have all the answers, but we will stand with you, Luca, through whatever trials and challenges may lie ahead."

He paused, his expression growing thoughtful once more, his brow furrowing with concentration as he seemed to search for the right words, the right way to offer his guidance and his wisdom.

"You would… you would help me, work with me to find a way to break the curse?"

Benjamin smiled, his eyes crinkling with warmth and compassion, his hand reaching out to clasp Luca's shoulder in a gesture of support and encouragement.

"Of course," he said, his voice low and sincere, his tone filled with a quiet, unwavering conviction. "I would be honored to help you, Luca. In fact, why don't you come to our house?"

He paused, his expression growing thoughtful, his brow furrowing with concentration as he seemed to search for the right words, the right way to offer his guidance and his wisdom.

"Our house is not hard to find," he said at last, his voice low and cryptic, his eyes distant and unfocused, as if he were seeing something that Luca could not. "Just follow the northern road out of Willowbrook, and you'll know it when you see it. Trust in your heart, Luca, and let it guide you to where you need to be."

Luca nodded, his throat tight with emotion, his eyes stinging with sudden, unexpected tears. He knew that Benjamin was right, that he had to trust in himself, in the love that burned bright and unending within his heart.

"Thank you," he said, his voice rough and choked, his hand reaching out to clasp Benjamin's in a gesture of gratitude and friendship. "Thank you for your help, for your guidance, for… for everything."

Benjamin smiled, his eyes shining with a warm, infectious joy, his hand squeezing Luca's in a silent promise of support and camaraderie.

"Think nothing of it," he said, his voice light and teasing, his eyes sparkling with mischief and warmth. "That's what friends are for, after all."

And Luca, his heart swelling with a sudden, fierce surge of love and gratitude, couldn't help but laugh, a soft, joyful sound that seemed to fill the room with a warm, golden light.

"Friends," he said, his voice soft and wondering, his eyes shining with a quiet, unshakable conviction. "I like the sound of that."

15

Whispers of Hope

Luca

As Luca stepped into the cozy warmth of his room at the inn, he felt a wave of exhaustion wash over him, the events of the day finally catching up to his weary body and mind. But even as he longed to collapse onto the soft, inviting bed and let sleep claim him, he knew that there was one more thing he needed to do, one more connection he needed to make before he could rest.

Luca reached for his phone, his fingers trembling slightly as he dialed the familiar number. The call connected after a few rings, and he felt a surge of relief and comfort wash over him at the sound of his mother's warm, loving voice.

"Luca, my darling boy," she said, her tone filled with equal parts affection and concern. "How are you holding up? Is everything alright?"

Something about his mother's gentle, understanding presence always seemed to break through his defenses, to strip away the layers of bravado and reveal the vulnerable, aching heart beneath.

"I'm… I'm okay," he said, his voice rough and choked, his free hand clenching into a fist at his side. "I just… I needed to hear your voice, to know that everything is alright back home."

There was a moment of silence on the other end of the line, a pause that seemed to stretch on for an eternity. And then, with a soft, knowing chuckle, his mother spoke again, her tone light and teasing.

"You're becoming quite the worry wart, aren't you? I never thought I'd see the day when my brave, fearless son would be fretting like a mother hen."

Despite himself, Luca felt a smile tugging at the corners of his mouth, a flicker of warmth and humor chasing away the shadows of his worry and fear. His mother had always had a way of doing that, of finding the light in even the darkest of moments, of reminding him that there was still joy and laughter to be found in the world, even in the midst of the most trying of times.

"I can't help it," he said, his voice softening with a quiet, rueful affection. "I just… I need to know that he's okay, that he's safe and protected, even when I'm not there to watch over him."

"I know, my love," his mother said, her voice filled with a deep, aching understanding. "And I promise you, he is. He's resting peacefully, just as he was when you left. And you'll never guess who's been here to check on him…"

Luca felt a flicker of surprise and curiosity, his brow furrowing as he tried to imagine who could have come to visit his sleeping mate in his absence. "Who?" he asked, his voice low and urgent, his heart pounding with a sudden, irrational fear.

"Your father and brother," his mother said, her tone filled with a quiet, knowing amusement. "They've been here every day, sitting by his bedside and talking to him, telling him stories of the pack and the life that awaits him when he wakes."

Luca felt a surge of emotion wash over him, a mix of gratitude and disbelief and a deep, aching love for the family that he had always taken for granted, the bonds of blood and loyalty that had always seemed so strained and tenuous, but that now shone with a fierce, unbreakable strength.

"I never thought… I never imagined that they would…"

"Oh, Luca," his mother said, her voice filled with a gentle, loving understanding. "They love you, and they love him, too. They may not always know how to show it, but it's there, in every word and every action, in every moment that they spend by his side."

Luca felt a lump rising in his throat, his heart swelling with a fierce, overwhelming love for the family that had always been his anchor, his guiding light in the darkness. He had spent so long pushing them away, so long trying to prove that he was strong enough, brave enough, to stand on his own. But now, in this moment of vulnerability and need, he realized that he had never been alone, that he had always had the love and support of his pack, his family, to guide him through even the darkest of times.

"Thank you," he said, his voice rough and choked, his hand trembling as he wiped away the tears that streaked his face. "Thank you for telling me, for… for everything."

"Of course, my darling boy," his mother said, her voice filled with a deep, unshakable love. "Now, tell me about your journey. Did you make it to Willowbrook safely? Have you found the answers you seek?"

Luca felt a flicker of excitement and anticipation, his heart leaping in his chest as he thought of the incredible people he had met, the wonders and mysteries that he had only just begun to unravel. "I did, Mom," he said, his voice filled with a quiet, bubbling enthusiasm. "And you won't believe the things I've seen, the people I've met. It's like… it's like a whole new world, one that I never even knew existed."

He paused, his expression growing thoughtful, his brow furrowing with a quiet, aching regret. "I just… I wish I had explored more, when I was younger. I feel like I've missed out on so much, like I've been so focused on my duties and my responsibilities that I've forgotten to live, to experience all the incredible things that the world has to offer."

"It's never too late to start exploring, to start discovering the wonders and the joys that life has to offer. And just think… when your mate wakes up, when you finally have the chance to be together, you'll be able to share all of those incredible experiences with him, to create new memories and new adventures that will last a lifetime."

Luca felt a surge of emotion wash over him, a mix of longing and hope and a deep, aching love for the man who held his heart, his soul, in the palm of his hand. He knew that his mother was right, that there was still so much to look forward to, so much to discover and explore and experience, once his mate was back by his side.

"You're right," he said, his voice filled with a quiet, unshakable determination. "And I promise you, I won't waste a single moment, a single opportunity to make the most of this incredible life that we've been given."

"I know you won't, my darling boy," his mother said, her voice filled with a deep, unshakable pride. "Now, get some rest. You have a big day ahead of you tomorrow, and you'll need all your strength and courage to face whatever challenges may come."

Luca felt a flicker of fear and uncertainty, his heart clenching with the weight of the task that lay before him. But he pushed it aside, focusing instead on the love and the hope that burned bright within him, the unshakable faith that he would find a way to break the curse, to bring his mate back to the world of the living.

"I will," he said, his voice filled with a quiet, unwavering resolve. "I love you."

"I love you too, Luca," his mother said, her voice soft and tender, filled with a deep, unending love. "Always and forever."

And with those words, the call ended, leaving Luca alone in the quiet, shadowed room, his heart filled with a mix of emotions that he could scarcely begin to untangle. But even in the midst of his fear and his uncertainty, he felt a flicker of hope, a glimmer of light in the darkness that seemed to grow brighter with every passing moment.

* * *

Luca squared his shoulders and began to walk, his strides long and purposeful as he made his way towards the outskirts of the town, towards the rolling hills and the dense, verdant forests that lay beyond. It was a habit that he had learned from his life in the pack, a way of moving through the world that was as natural to him as breathing or eating or sleeping, and he knew that he could not abandon it now, not even in the face of the most daunting of challenges.

He quickened his pace, his eyes fixed on the distant horizon and the secrets that lay waiting for him, just beyond the next bend in the road.

As he approached the manor, Luca felt his breath catch in his throat, his eyes widening with awe and wonder at the sight that greeted him. The house was massive, a towering, imposing structure of stone and glass and wrought iron that seemed to loom over the surrounding landscape like a sentinel, like a guardian of the secrets and the mysteries that lay within.

For a moment, Luca found himself hesitating, his hand hovering over the ornate, gilded knocker that adorned the front door. He had never seen a place like this before, had never even imagined that such grandeur and opulence could exist in the world that he knew, and he felt a flicker of uncertainty, a sense of being out of his depth and out of his element.

He raised his hand, his knuckles rapping against the heavy, polished wood with a sharp, decisive sound. He knew that he could not turn back now, that he had come too far and risked too much to let his own fears and insecurities hold him back, and he was determined to see this through, no matter what challenges or obstacles might lie ahead.

Almost immediately, the door swung open, revealing a tall, impeccably dressed man with a serene, unflappable expression. "Ah, you must be Mr. Luca," he said, his voice smooth and cultured, his accent hinting at a life lived in the highest echelons of society. "Master Benjamin and Master Adrian are expecting you in the kitchen. Please, follow me."

He stepped over the threshold and into the gleaming, marble-floored foyer of the manor, his heart pounding with a mix of excitement and trepidation as he followed the butler deeper into the house.

As they made their way through the winding, labyrinthine halls of the manor, Luca found himself marveling at the sheer opulence of his surroundings, at the priceless works of art and the gleaming, polished surfaces that seemed to stretch out before him like a never-ending sea of luxury and refinement. He had always known that there was a world beyond the borders of his pack, a realm of wealth and power that he could scarcely begin to imagine, but to see it firsthand, to walk among the trappings of a life that he had never even dreamed of… it was almost more than he could bear.

They emerged into a spacious, sun-drenched kitchen, a room that was filled with the tantalizing scents of fresh-baked bread and sizzling bacon, of rich, dark coffee and sweet, ripe fruit. And there, seated at a long, wooden table that seemed to gleam with the patina of age and use, were Benjamin and another man, their heads bent together in quiet, intimate conversation.

As Luca stepped into the room, Benjamin looked up, his eyes widening with surprise and delight as he caught sight of his guest. "Luca!" he exclaimed, his voice warm and effusive as he rose from his seat and hurried over to greet him. "You made it! I'm so glad you could come."

And then, before Luca could even begin to respond, Benjamin was pulling him into a tight, fierce hug, his arms wrapping around him with a strength and a tenderness that made Luca's heart ache with a sudden, fierce longing.

"Thank you for inviting me," he said, his voice low and sincere, his gaze filled with a quiet, unspoken gratitude. "I know that you're taking a risk, letting me into your home and your life like this. And I want you to know that I appreciate it, more than I can say."

Benjamin's smile softened, his eyes crinkling with a hint of mischief and warmth. "Think nothing of it," he said, his voice light and teasing, his hand reaching out to squeeze Luca's shoulder with a reassuring, steady pressure. "What are friends for, if not to take risks and share secrets and embark on grand, life-changing adventures together?"

Despite himself, Luca felt a smile tugging at the corners of his mouth, a flicker of amusement and affection chasing away the shadows of his own doubts and fears. Benjamin had a way of doing that, he realized, of finding the light in even the darkest of moments, of reminding him that there was still joy and laughter to be found in the world, even in the midst of the most trying of times.

"And speaking of friends," Benjamin continued, his voice growing more serious, his gaze drifting over to the man who still sat at the table, watching their exchange with a quiet, curious intensity, "I'd like you to meet my husband, Adrian. He's the one who's been helping me to research the curse that's been placed on your mate, and I think you'll find that he has some valuable insights and ideas to share."

Luca stepped forward and extended his hand, his voice low and sincere as he met Adrian's gaze with a quiet, unwavering intensity. "It's a pleasure to meet you, Adrian," he said, his words filled with a quiet, unspoken gratitude. "And thank you, for everything that you've done to help me and my mate. I know that I can never repay you for your kindness and your generosity, but I want you to know that I will never forget it, not as long as I live."

Adrian's smile was warm and genuine, his hand clasping Luca's with a firm, steady pressure. "The pleasure is all mine, Luca," he said, his voice low and sincere, his gaze filled with a quiet, unwavering support. "So, Luca," he began, his voice warm and engaging, "tell us a bit about your pack. The Wolfheart pack, right? I believe I've had the pleasure of meeting your father before."

Luca's eyebrows shot up in surprise, a flicker of excitement and apprehension coursing through him. "You know my father?" he asked, his voice laced with a mix of awe and trepidation.

Adrian chuckled, his eyes crinkling at the corners. "Our paths have crossed a few times over the years. He's a remarkable wolf, your father. Strong, wise, and fiercely protective of his pack."

Luca nodded, a small smile tugging at the corners of his mouth. "He is," he agreed, his voice softening with a hint of pride and affection. "Though, I must admit, we haven't always seen eye to eye. The pack has faced its fair share of challenges lately, and sometimes it feels like we're all just trying to keep our heads above water."

Benjamin leaned forward, his expression filled with empathy and understanding. "I can only imagine the weight you must carry, Luca," he said gently. "But you don't have to shoulder this burden alone. We're here to help, in any way we can."

"Thank you," he managed, his voice rough with emotion. "That means more to me than you can possibly know."

Benjamin exchanged a glance with Adrian, a silent conversation passing between them. "Actually," Benjamin began, his voice tentative, "your mother called ahead and filled us in on some of the details. About your mate, and the curse that holds him."

Luca's heart skipped a beat, a wave of gratitude and relief washing over him. His mother's foresight never ceased to amaze him. "She did?" he asked, his voice barely above a whisper.

Benjamin nodded, his eyes filled with compassion. "She did. And we want you to know that we'll do everything in our power to help you break this curse and bring your mate back to you."

Luca felt a weight lifting from his shoulders, a glimmer of hope piercing through the darkness that had shrouded his heart for so long. "I don't even know where to begin," he admitted, his voice trembling slightly. "The curse is powerful, and I've searched everywhere for answers, but I keep coming up empty-handed."

Adrian reached across the table, his hand resting on Luca's arm in a comforting gesture. "That's where we come in," he said, his voice filled with determination. "Between Benjamin's magical knowledge and the resources we have at our disposal, I'm confident we can find a way to break this curse."

As the meal drew to a close, Benjamin rose from his seat, his eyes sparkling with excitement. "Come with me, Luca," he said, his voice filled with anticipation. "There's something I want to show you."

Luca followed Benjamin through the winding hallways of the manor, his heart pounding with a mix of nerves and curiosity. When they finally reached their destination, Luca's breath caught in his throat, his eyes widening in awe.

Before him stood the most magnificent library he had ever seen, its walls lined with countless books and tomes, the scent of aged paper and leather filling the air. Luca felt as though he had stepped into another world, a realm of knowledge and secrets just waiting to be unlocked.

"This is incredible," he breathed, his voice filled with reverence.

Benjamin grinned, his eyes twinkling with pride. "It is, isn't it? And somewhere in here, I believe we'll find the key to helping your mate."

He led Luca to a large table, where a stack of books lay waiting, their covers worn and faded with age. "I've already taken the liberty of pulling some texts that I think may be relevant," Benjamin explained, his fingers tracing over the spines. "But there's still so much more to explore."

Luca felt a surge of gratitude and determination, his heart swelling with the knowledge that he was no longer alone in this fight. "Thank you," he said, his voice thick with emotion. "For everything."

Benjamin placed a comforting hand on Luca's shoulder, his smile warm and reassuring. "We're in this together, Luca. We'll find a way to break this curse, I promise you that."

16

Troubles Beyond Comprehension

Luca rubbed his eyes, the words on the ancient pages blurring together as fatigue and frustration settled in his bones. He had been poring over the tomes for hours, desperately searching for any clue that might lead him to a way to break his mate's curse. But with each passing minute, he felt the weight of time pressing down on him, a constant reminder that every second spent in this library was another second his love remained trapped in an enchanted slumber.

He slammed the book shut, a growl of impatience rumbling in his throat. He knew he had to stay focused, to keep pushing forward no matter how daunting the task seemed. But the restlessness that coursed through his veins was becoming harder and harder to ignore, the urge to do something, anything, to save his mate growing stronger with each passing heartbeat.

"You look like you could use a break," Benjamin's voice cut through Luca's troubled thoughts, startling him from his reverie. He looked up to see the mage standing before him, a steaming cup of tea in his outstretched hand and a sympathetic smile on his face.

Luca accepted the cup gratefully, the warmth seeping into his fingers and easing some of the tension that had settled in his shoulders. "Thanks," he mumbled, taking a sip of the fragrant liquid. "I just feel like we're running out of time, like every moment I spend here is a moment lost."

Benjamin nodded, understanding etched in the lines of his face. "I know it's hard, Luca. But we can't rush this. The answers we seek are here, I'm sure of it. We just have to keep looking."

Luca sighed, setting the cup down on the table and leaning back in his chair. His gaze drifted to the bookshelves that surrounded them, the endless rows of leather-bound spines seeming to mock him with their secrets. "How do you and Adrian do it?" he asked suddenly, the question tumbling from his lips before he could stop it. "How do you keep going, day after day, when the world seems determined to tear you apart?"

Benjamin's smile softened, his eyes taking on a distant, almost dreamy quality. "Love," he said simply, as if it were the most obvious thing in the world. "Adrian and I, we've been through our share of trials and tribulations. But at the end of the day, we know that we have each other, and that's enough to keep us going, no matter what the world throws our way."

Luca felt a pang of longing in his chest, a fierce desire to have that kind of love, that kind of unwavering devotion, with his own mate. "Do you ever think about having children?" he asked, the words coming out in a rush. "Building a family together?"

Benjamin's eyes widened in surprise, but his smile never faltered. "We've talked about it," he admitted, his voice taking on a wistful note. "Adrian and I, we both come from big families, and the idea of creating our own little clan is definitely appealing. But we also know that it's not something to rush into, not when there's still so much work to be done in the world."

Luca nodded, understanding the sentiment all too well. As much as he longed for a future with his mate, for the chance to build a life and a family together, he knew that there were battles to be fought and challenges to overcome before that dream could become a reality.

Just as he was about to voice his thoughts, Benjamin let out a sudden gasp, his eyes flying wide with excitement. "Luca, come look at this!" he exclaimed, beckoning him over to the table where he had been working.

Luca jumped to his feet, his heart pounding with a mix of hope and trepidation as he rushed to Benjamin's side. There, spread out on the table before them, was an ancient, yellowed parchment, its edges frayed and its ink faded with age. But even through the wear and tear of centuries, Luca could make out the words that had captured Benjamin's attention, the legend that spoke of a fae prince trapped beneath a silver tree.

"It says here that the prince was cursed by his own father," Benjamin explained, his finger tracing over the faded lines of text. "A punishment for daring to seek more from life, for wanting to better himself and explore the world beyond the borders of his kingdom. The only way to break the curse is through a ritual that requires the presence of the prince's mate, a bond that even the most powerful of magics cannot hope to sever."

Luca's breath caught in his throat, his mind racing with the implications of Benjamin's words. If this legend was true, if his own mate was the key to breaking the curse that held him captive, then there was still hope, still a chance to bring him back to the world of the living.

But before he could voice his thoughts, before he could even begin to process the enormity of the revelation, the shrill ring of his phone cut through the air, startling them both. Luca fumbled for the device, his heart skipping a beat when he saw Gareth's name flashing on the screen.

"Gareth?" he answered, his voice tight with concern. "What's wrong? Is everything okay?"

There was a moment of silence on the other end of the line, a pause that seemed to stretch on for an eternity. And then, with a heavy sigh, Gareth spoke, his words hitting Luca like a physical blow.

Luca's heart raced as he pressed the phone to his ear, Gareth's frantic panting filling the silence. "Luca!" his brother gasped, his voice strained with urgency. "The pack... we're under attack! Shadow creatures... everywhere. We need you... now!"

The call ended abruptly, leaving Luca stunned and worried. He looked up at Benjamin, his eyes wide with fear and determination. "I have to go," he said, his voice rough with emotion. "My pack needs me."

Benjamin nodded, his expression grave but understanding. "Of course," he said, his hand reaching out to clasp Luca's shoulder. "But you're not going alone. Adrian and I will come with you. We can help."

Luca hesitated, his instinct to protect his pack warring with his desire for assistance. But as he looked into Benjamin's eyes, he saw a fierce, unwavering resolve, a determination to stand by his side no matter what challenges lay ahead.

"Thank you," he said, his voice rough with gratitude. "But how will we get there in time? It's too far to run, and we don't have a car."

Benjamin's lips curved into a knowing smirk, his eyes twinkling with mischief. "Oh, don't worry about that," he said, his voice light and teasing. "I have just the solution. Meet me in the backyard in five minutes."

Luca nodded, his heart pounding with anticipation as he followed Benjamin out of the library and into the sprawling grounds of the manor. He paced back and forth, his mind racing with possibilities and fears, until he heard the sound of footsteps approaching.

He turned to see Benjamin and Adrian walking towards him, a small, fluffy cat trailing at their heels. Luca raised an eyebrow, his confusion momentarily overriding his anxiety. "Uh, not to be rude," he said, his voice hesitant, "but how is a cat going to help us get to my pack?"

Adrian chuckled, his eyes sparkling with amusement. "The cat's not for transportation," he said, his voice warm and teasing. "But tell me, Luca, do you know how to ride?"

Luca blinked, his brow furrowing in confusion. "Ride? Like a horse? Yeah, I've done that before. But I don't see how that's going to help us either."

Adrian's smile widened, his eyes taking on a mysterious, other-worldly glow. "Oh, you'll see," he said, his voice low and cryptic. "Just watch."

And with that, he stepped forward, his body beginning to glow with an ethereal, shimmering light. Luca watched in awe as Adrian's form began to shift and change, growing larger and more imposing with each passing second.

Where once had stood a man, now loomed a magnificent dragon, its scales glistening like diamonds in the sun. Its wings stretched out behind it, casting shadows across the ground, and its eyes glowed with a fierce, icy intelligence that made Luca's heart skip a beat.

"Holy shit," he breathed, his voice barely above a whisper. "You're a… a dragon?"

Benjamin laughed, his eyes sparkling with delight at Luca's astonishment. "Indeed he is," he said, his voice filled with pride and affection. "And he's going to be our ride to your pack."

Luca swallowed hard, his mind reeling with the enormity of what he was seeing. Dragons were real. His friend's husband was a dragon. And now, he was going to ride that dragon into battle to save his pack from an army of shadow creatures.

It was almost too much to process, too much to believe. But as he looked into Adrian's eyes, as he felt the icy chill of his breath and the power that radiated from his massive form, Luca knew that it was all too real, all too true.

"Okay," he said, his voice rough with determination. "Let's do this."

Benjamin grinned, his eyes sparkling with excitement as he climbed onto Adrian's back, settling himself between the dragon's massive wings. "Hop on," he said, his voice light and teasing. "And hold on tight. It's going to be a wild ride."

Luca hesitated for a moment, his heart pounding with a mix of fear and anticipation. But then, with a deep, steadying breath, he stepped forward and swung himself onto Adrian's back, his hands gripping the dragon's scales with a white-knuckled intensity.

"Ready?" Benjamin asked, his voice barely audible over the roar of the wind that whipped around them.

Luca nodded, his jaw clenched with determination. "Ready," he said, his voice rough with emotion. "Let's go save my pack."

* * *

They soared through the skies, the wind whipping past them with a deafening roar, Luca felt his heart pounding in his chest, a mixture of fear and determination coursing through his veins. He could hear the sounds of battle growing louder with each passing second, the clashing of claws and the snarls of his packmates echoing through the air like a symphony of chaos and destruction.

"There!" he shouted, his voice straining to be heard over the howling wind. "Set us down over there, by the edge of the clearing!"

Adrian banked sharply, his massive wings flaring out to slow their descent as he angled towards the ground. Luca clung to his back, his knuckles white with the force of his grip, as they plummeted towards the earth, the trees and the grass rushing up to meet them with dizzying speed.

But just before they hit the ground, Adrian opened his jaws and let loose a blast of icy breath, the frigid air swirling around them in a glittering, crystalline cloud. Luca watched in awe as the shadow constructs that had been surging towards them suddenly froze in their tracks, their bodies encased in a thick layer of ice that glittered like diamonds in the sun.

"Hold on tight," Benjamin called out, his voice barely audible over the roar of the wind. "This is going to be a bumpy landing!"

Luca braced himself, his muscles tensing as Adrian's claws touched down on the ground, the impact sending shockwaves through his body. But even as he fought to keep his balance, even as he struggled to catch his breath in the aftermath of their wild ride, he couldn't help but feel a flicker of hope, a glimmer of determination that burned bright and fierce within his heart.

They had made it. They were here, in the heart of the battle, ready to fight for the ones they loved with every last breath in their bodies.

As they dismounted from Adrian's back, the dragon's form shimmering and shrinking until he stood before them once more in his human guise, Luca heard a familiar voice calling out his name.

"Luca!" Gareth shouted, his eyes wide with relief and amazement as he raced towards them. "You made it! And you brought… is that a dragon?"

Luca grinned, his heart swelling with pride and affection as he clapped his brother on the shoulder. "Long story," he said, his voice rough with emotion. "But yeah, that's Adrian. He's a friend. And this is Benjamin, another friend. They're here to help."

Gareth nodded, his expression grave but determined. "We need all the help we can get," he said, his voice low and urgent. "These shadow constructs… they just keep coming, no matter how many we take down. It's like they're being controlled by someone, some kind of dark magic that we can't even begin to understand."

Luca felt a flicker of unease, a sense of dread that made his stomach clench and his heart race. He had never heard of shadow constructs before, had never even imagined that such creatures could exist. But here they were, swarming over his pack's territory like a plague of locusts, threatening everything and everyone he held dear.

Luca found himself fighting side by side with Benjamin and Adrian, their powers combining in a dazzling display of magic and might. He watched in awe as Benjamin wielded his staff, the quill-shaped weapon glowing with an otherworldly light as he wove spells and enchantments that seemed to defy the very laws of reality itself.

With a flick of his wrist, Benjamin sent a wave of energy cascading towards the shadow constructs, the force of the blast sending them flying backwards like leaves caught in a gale. The air crackled with the power of his magic, the very fabric of space and time bending and warping around him as he fought to push back the enemy and protect the pack.

Beside him, Adrian was a force to be reckoned with, his ice magic freezing the shadow constructs in their tracks and shattering them into a thousand glittering shards. His eyes glowed with a fierce, frigid light as he summoned blizzards and ice storms out of thin air, the temperature around him dropping so low that even the bravest of warriors shivered and shook in his presence.

Together, they were a formidable team, their powers complementing each other in a way that was both beautiful and terrifying to behold. But even as they fought, even as they poured every ounce of their strength and their determination into the battle, Luca couldn't shake the feeling that something was wrong, that there was more to this attack than met the eye.

And then, just as he was about to launch himself back into the fray, he heard a voice that made his blood run cold, a voice that dripped with malice and cruelty and a darkness that seemed to seep into his very bones.

"Benjamin," the voice said, its tone mocking and cruel. "How lovely to see you again. And Adrian, too. What a delightful surprise."

Luca turned to see a figure emerging from the shadows, a figure that seemed to radiate an aura of pure, unadulterated evil. He was tall and gaunt, with skin as pale as moonlight and eyes that glittered like black diamonds in the depths of his skull. His robes were the color of midnight, and they swirled around him like a living thing, like tendrils of darkness that reached out to ensnare and consume everything in their path.

"Malachite," Benjamin said, his voice low and dangerous as he leveled his staff at the warlock's chest. "I should have known it was you behind this attack. What do you want with the Wolfheart pack? What could you possibly hope to gain from this senseless violence?"

Malachite laughed, the sound of it like the scraping of bone against stone. "Oh, Benjamin," he said, his voice dripping with false sympathy. "You always were so naive, so blind to the true nature of power. I want what I have always wanted: to claim what is rightfully mine, to take back the magic that was stolen from me so long ago."

His gaze shifted to Luca, his eyes boring into him with a intensity that made his skin crawl and his heart race with fear. "And as for you, little wolf," he said, his voice low and menacing. "I know what you seek, what you hope to find in the depths of your mate's enchanted slumber. But you will never have him, never claim him as your own. For he belongs to my master, body and soul, and I will not rest until I have taken back what is his."

Luca felt a surge of rage and defiance wash over him, his hands clenching into fists at his sides as he met the warlock's gaze with a fierce, unyielding determination. "You're wrong," he said, his voice rough with emotion. "My mate belongs to no one but himself, and I will fight to my last breath to protect him from the likes of you."

Malachite's lips curled into a sneer, his eyes flashing with a cruel, mocking light. "We shall see, little wolf," he said, his voice low and taunting. "We shall see."

And with that, he raised his hands and sent a blast of dark energy hurtling towards them, the force of it sending them flying backwards like ragdolls caught in a hurricane. Luca felt the breath being knocked from his lungs as he slammed into the ground, his body aching with the impact and his mind reeling with the shock of the warlock's power.

But even as he struggled to his feet, even as he fought to catch his breath and clear his vision, he saw Benjamin and Adrian standing tall and proud before him, their magic blazing like twin suns in the heart of the battlefield.

"Enough!" Benjamin shouted, his voice ringing out like a clarion call above the chaos of the battle. "You will not have him, Malachite. You will not have any of them. This ends now."

And with that, he raised his staff and unleashed a blast of pure, blinding light, the force of it so powerful that it seemed to shake the very foundations of the earth itself. Malachite screamed in agony as the light engulfed him, his body writhing and twisting as he fought to escape its searing, purifying touch.

But it was too late, too powerful for even his dark magic to withstand. With a final, agonized howl, he vanished in a burst of shadows and smoke, his body disintegrating into a thousand tiny fragments that drifted away on the wind like ashes from a funeral pyre.

For a moment, there was silence, a stillness that seemed to stretch out into eternity. And then, with a shuddering gasp, Luca collapsed to his knees, his body shaking with the aftershocks of the battle and his mind reeling with the implications of what he had just witnessed.

"Is he dead?" Luca asked.

Benjamin shook his head. "No, knowing Malachite, he definitely doesn't go away that easily though we have more things to worry about. His master."

"We have to go," he said, his voice rough and urgent as he struggled to his feet once more. "We have to get back to my mate, have to perform the ritual before it's too late."

Benjamin nodded, his expression grave but determined as he reached out to help Luca to his feet. "You're right," he said, his voice low and steady. "We can't waste any more time. Every second counts."

***

They raced towards Luca's house, the wind whipping past them and the adrenaline pumping through their veins, Luca couldn't help but feel a flicker of hope, a glimmer of light in the darkness that had consumed his world for so long. They had fought hard, had faced down the warlock and his shadow constructs with a courage and determination that had left him breathless and awed.

But even as he savored that small victory, even as he clung to the promise of the ritual and the chance to finally be reunited with his mate, Luca knew that the true test was still to come. Because he had seen the look in Malachite's eyes, had heard the malice and the cruelty in his voice when he spoke of claiming Luca's mate for his own.

And he knew, with a certainty that went beyond words or reason, that the warlock would not rest until he had taken what he believed to be his, until he had destroyed everything and everyone that Luca held dear.

As they approached the house, Luca's heart began to race, his palms sweating and his breath coming in short, sharp gasps. He could feel the weight of the moment pressing down on him, the enormity of what they were about to attempt and the consequences that would follow, no matter the outcome.

But before he could even begin to voice his fears, before he could let the doubts and the worries consume him, he saw his mother rushing out to meet them, her face etched with lines of worry and her eyes shining with unshed tears.

"Luca!" she cried, her voice breaking with emotion as she threw her arms around him, holding him close as if she would never let him go. "Thank the gods you're safe. I was so worried, so scared that something had happened to you."

Luca hugged her back, his own eyes stinging with tears as he breathed in the familiar scent of her, the warmth and comfort of her embrace. "I'm okay, Mom," he said, his voice rough and choked with emotion. "I'm here, and I'm not going anywhere."

She pulled back, her hands coming up to cup his face as she searched his eyes, as if looking for some sign of the boy he had once been, the son she had raised and loved with all her heart. "Your father," she said, her voice tight with worry. "Where is he? Is he safe?"

Luca felt a flicker of unease, a sense of dread that made his stomach clench and his heart race. He had been so focused on getting back to his mate, on performing the ritual and breaking the curse that held him in its thrall, that he had almost forgotten about his father, about the danger that he and the rest of the pack still faced.

But before he could answer, before he could find the words to reassure his mother and ease her fears, Gareth stepped forward, his expression grave but determined.

"He's okay," he said, his voice low and steady. "He's with the Jensen pack, coordinating our next move and making sure that everyone is safe. He'll be back as soon as he can, I promise."

Their mother nodded, her eyes shining with a fierce, unwavering love as she looked at her sons, at the men they had become and the warriors they had always been. "I know," she said, her voice soft but filled with a quiet strength. "I just worry, that's all. It's what mothers do."

Luca felt a lump rising in his throat, his heart swelling with love and gratitude for this woman who had always been his rock, his anchor in the storm of life. But before he could find the words to express what he felt, Benjamin stepped forward, his expression focused and intent.

"I'm sorry to interrupt," he said, his voice low and urgent. "But we need to move quickly. Every second counts, and we can't afford to waste any more time."

Luca nodded, his jaw clenching with determination as he met Benjamin's gaze. "You're right," he said, his voice rough and steady. "Let's do this."

He led them into the house, his steps quick and purposeful as he made his way to the room where his mate lay, his heart pounding with a fierce, desperate hope. And as he pushed open the door and stepped inside.

Behind him, he could hear Benjamin moving around the room, setting up the ritual circle and preparing the tools and ingredients that he would need. But Luca barely noticed, his attention focused solely on the man before him, on the face that he had dreamed of and longed for, every moment of every day since he had first laid eyes on him.

"What do I need to do?" he asked, his voice rough and uncertain as he glanced over his shoulder at Benjamin, at the man who held the key to his mate's salvation.

Benjamin looked up, his eyes meeting Luca's with a steady, unwavering gaze. "Just stay close to him," he said, his voice low and reassuring. "Hold his hand, talk to him, let him feel your presence and your love. And when the time comes, follow your instincts. Trust in the bond that you share, and let it guide you to where you need to be."

Luca nodded, his throat tight with emotion as he turned back to his mate, his fingers twining with his own and his heart racing with a wild, desperate hope. He watched as Benjamin retrieved his quill necklace, as he held it aloft and whispered words of power and magic that made the air around them crackle and hum with energy.

And then, with a blinding flash of light, the quill transformed into a staff, its surface glowing with an otherworldly radiance that made Luca's eyes water and his skin tingle with the force of its power.

"It's time," Benjamin said, his voice low and solemn as he raised the staff above his head, as he began to chant the words of the ritual that would break the curse and bring Luca's mate back to the world of the living.

Luca watched in awe as the circle began to glow, as the runes and symbols that Benjamin had drawn on the floor began to pulse and shimmer with a mystical energy that made the very air around them thrum with power. He could feel the magic washing over him, could feel it tugging at his heart and his soul, calling him to something that he couldn't quite understand.

And then, just as he was about to lose himself in the swirling vortex of light and sound, just as he was about to let the power of the ritual sweep him away, he heard a voice, a soft, gentle whisper that seemed to come from everywhere and nowhere all at once.

"Kiss him," the voice said, its tone warm and encouraging, like a mother soothing a frightened child. "Seal the bond between you, and let your bond be the key that unlocks the door to his mind and his soul."

And so, with a deep, steadying breath, he leaned down and pressed his lips to his mate's, his eyes fluttering closed as he poured every ounce of his love and his devotion into the kiss, into the bond that had brought them together and the destiny that awaited them both.

The moment their lips touched, Luca felt a surge of energy coursing through him, a wave of power and magic that made his skin tingle and his blood sing with the force of its intensity. He could feel the bond between them growing stronger, could feel the connection that had always been there, hidden beneath the surface of their lives, rising up to claim its rightful place in the world.

And as the glow of the ritual circle intensified, as the light and the sound and the power of the magic reached a fever pitch, Luca knew that they had done it, that they had broken the curse and brought his mate back to the world of the living.

When he finally broke the kiss and pulled back, his heart pounding with a wild, desperate hope, he saw that his mate's eyes were still closed, his face still slack and unmoving in the depths of his enchanted slumber.

"What's happening?" he asked, his voice rough and choked with emotion as he looked up at Benjamin, at the man who had promised him a miracle and delivered only heartache. "Why isn't he waking up?"

Benjamin's expression softened, his eyes filled with a deep, aching sympathy. "Curses like this, they take a toll on the body and the mind," he said, his voice low and gentle. "It will take time for him to recover, to come back to himself and to the world that he left behind."

17

Kiss of Life

Rowan

R owan was lost in an endless void of darkness, a place where time seemed to have no meaning. He couldn't remember how long he had been trapped in this abyss, his mind adrift in a sea of nothingness. But just as he was about to give in to despair, a melodic female voice called out to him, its gentle tones cutting through the oppressive silence.

"Rowan," the voice whispered, "open your eyes."

At first, Rowan wasn't sure if he had the strength to obey. The darkness had become a familiar companion, and the thought of facing the unknown filled him with trepidation. But there was something about the voice that compelled him, a soothing presence that urged him to trust in its guidance.

As he slowly blinked his eyes open, Rowan's thoughts immediately turned to his family. Were his siblings safe? How long had he been away from them? A wave of worry washed over him, threatening to pull him back into the depths of his own fears.

But as his vision cleared, Rowan found himself standing in a place that could only be described as paradise. A vast field stretched out before him, its expanse filled with tulips of every color imaginable. The sight took his breath away, and for a moment, he forgot about his worries, lost in the sheer beauty of the scene.

As he took a step forward, marveling at the way the tulips swayed gently in the breeze, Rowan noticed a figure in the distance. Even from afar, there was something about the man that made Rowan's heart race, a strange pull that he couldn't quite explain.

"Go to him, Rowan," the female voice encouraged, her words filled with warmth and understanding.

Rowan hesitated for a moment, uncertainty clouding his thoughts. But deep down, he knew that he couldn't ignore the inexplicable connection he felt to the mysterious figure. With a deep breath, he began to make his way through the field, his steps cautious but determined.

"Hello?" Rowan called out, his voice carried away by the gentle wind that rustled through the tulips. "Can you hear me?"

As he drew closer to the man, Rowan felt a strange sensation wash over him, as if his very life force was being drawn towards the figure. It was both exhilarating and terrifying, a feeling he had never experienced before.

And then, the man turned, and Rowan found himself gazing into the most captivating eyes he had ever seen. They were a striking shade of green, flecked with gold and filled with a depth of emotion that made Rowan's breath catch in his throat. He felt as though he could lose himself in those eyes, content to drown in their mesmerizing beauty.

The man extended his hand, a silent invitation that sent shivers down Rowan's spine. "Take it, Rowan," the female voice whispered, her tone filled with encouragement. "Trust in the connection you feel."

Without a second thought, Rowan reached out and grasped the man's hand, their fingers intertwining as if they were always meant to be together. The moment their skin touched, the world around them dissolved, the field of tulips vanishing in a blinding flash of white light.

Suddenly, they were suspended in a void of nothingness, just the two of them, their hands still clasped tightly together. Rowan knew he should have *been afraid, but somehow, with this man by his side, he felt an inexplicable sense of safety and belonging.*

He found himself gasping for air, his eyes snapping open to an unfamiliar wooden room. Disorientation washed over him like a tidal wave, leaving him feeling lost and unmoored in this strange new reality.

As his gaze darted around the room, taking in the rustic furnishings and the warm, golden light that streamed through the windows, Rowan's eyes landed on a woman seated beside him, her nose buried in a book. She seemed not to have noticed his sudden awakening, too engrossed in the pages before her to pay him any mind.

But then, as if sensing his gaze upon her, the woman looked up, her eyes widening in surprise as she took in Rowan's confused and disoriented expression. "Oh my goodness," she exclaimed, her voice filled with a mixture of joy and disbelief. "You're awake! Luca! Luca, come quickly!"

Before Rowan could even begin to wrap his head around the impossibility of it all, the door burst open, and there he was. The man from his dream, the one whose eyes had captivated him, whose touch had set his soul on fire. He was here, in the flesh, and the sight of him made Rowan's heart skip a beat, his breath catching in his throat as he tried to process the reality of what he was seeing.

"You're awake," the man breathed, his voice filled with a depth of emotion that made Rowan's chest ache. "I can't believe it."

And then, before Rowan could even begin to formulate a response, the man was crossing the room in two long strides, his arms wrapping around Rowan's shoulders and pulling him into a tight, desperate embrace. Rowan froze for a moment, his body stiff and unyielding in the man's arms. But then, as the man pressed a tender kiss to his forehead, Rowan felt himself melting into the embrace, his own arms coming up to wrap around the man's waist as he buried his face in the crook of his neck.

"I don't understand," Rowan whispered, his voice muffled against the man's skin. "How is this possible? Who are you?"

The man pulled back slightly, his hands coming up to cup Rowan's face as he gazed into his eyes with a look of pure, unadulterated affection. "My name is Luca," he said softly, his thumbs gently stroking Rowan's cheekbones. "And I've been waiting for you to wake up, to come back to me."

Rowan's brow furrowed in confusion, his mind racing as he tried to make sense of Luca's words. "Come back to you?" he repeated, his voice small and uncertain. "But I don't even know you. At least, I don't think I do."

Luca smiled, a soft, tender thing that made Rowan's heart flutter in his chest. "It's a long story."

"I'm Rowan. Rowan Elderwood." Rowan croaked.

Luca smiled at him sweetly. "And my name is Luca. Lovely to finally meet you, Rowan."

As if sensing the shift in the room, the woman who had been seated beside Rowan quietly rose from her chair, a small smile playing at the corners of her mouth as she took in the sight of the two men locked in each other's arms. "I'll give you two some privacy," she said softly, her voice filled with a quiet kind of understanding. "But if you need anything, just call for me, okay?"

Rowan nodded, his gaze never leaving Luca's face as he murmured a soft "thank you" in the woman's direction. And then, as the door clicked shut behind her, he turned his attention back to Luca, his heart racing as he tried to find the words to express the depth of his feelings, the overwhelming sense of connection and belonging that he felt in Luca's presence.

"Luca," he said softly, his voice hesitant and raspy from disuse. "Where am I? What is this place?"

Luca's response was immediate, his voice deep and soothing as he pulled Rowan closer, his arms tightening around his waist in a gesture of comfort and protection. "You're in the Wolfheart Pack, Rowan. This is my home, and the home of my people."

Rowan felt a shiver run down his spine at Luca's words, his mind racing with the implications of what he had just heard. The Wolfheart Pack. He had heard stories of wolf shifters before, had read about them in the ancient myths and legends that he had always been so fascinated by. But he had never imagined that they could be real, that he could be standing here, in the heart of their territory, wrapped in the arms of one of their own.

"Wolf shifters," he murmured, his voice filled with a mix of awe and disbelief. "I thought they were just stories, just tales that people told around the campfire to scare each other."

Luca chuckled, his breath warm against Rowan's ear as he nuzzled into his neck, inhaling deeply as if trying to memorize his scent. "We're very real."

Rowan's brow furrowed in confusion, his mind racing with questions as he tried to make sense of Luca's words. "How long have I been asleep?"

He could feel Luca stiffen slightly in his arms, could sense the hesitation and uncertainty in his voice as he pulled back to look Rowan in the eye. "I don't know. I wish I could give you a clear answer, but the truth is, we don't know how long you've been under the curse. It could have been days, or weeks, or even years."

Rowan felt a wave of panic wash over him at Luca's words, his heart clenching with fear and confusion as he tried to wrap his mind around the idea of losing so much time, of being separated from his family and his life for an unknown period. "But my family," he said, his voice small and afraid. "My siblings, my parents. They must be worried sick about me. I have to find them, Luca. I have to let them know that I'm okay."

Luca's expression softened, his hand coming up to cup Rowan's cheek as he gazed into his eyes with a look of pure, unadulterated understanding. "I know, Rowan. And we will find them, I promise you. But right now, the most important thing is figuring out what happened to you, and how we can keep you safe from whatever or whoever put you under that curse in the first place."

Rowan swallowed hard, his throat suddenly dry as he tried to process the enormity of what Luca was saying. He had so many questions, so many gaps in his memory that he didn't even know where to begin. But as he looked into Luca's eyes, as he saw the depth of concern and affection shining there, he knew that he had to trust him, had to believe that together, they could unravel the mysteries of his past and find a way forward.

As if sensing his distress, Luca reached out and took Rowan's hand in his own, his touch warm and comforting against Rowan's skin. "Hey," he said softly, his voice filled with a quiet kind of reassurance. "I know this is a lot to take in, Rowan. But I promise you, I will be here with you every step of the way. We will figure this out together, no matter how long it takes or how hard it gets."

Rowan felt a lump rising in his throat at Luca's words, his eyes stinging with sudden, unexpected tears. He had always been the strong one, the one who took care of others and shouldered their burdens without complaint. But now, in the face of so much uncertainty and confusion, he found himself leaning into Luca's support, drawing strength and comfort from the warmth of his presence.

"I just feel so lost, Luca," he admitted, his voice small and vulnerable in the quiet of the room. "Like I'm adrift in a sea of questions and doubts, with no idea which way to turn or where to begin."

Luca's expression softened, his hand tightening around Rowan's in a gesture of comfort and understanding. "I know, Rowan. And it's okay to feel that way. This is a lot for anyone to handle, let alone someone who's just woken up from a curse with no memory of how they got there."

He paused for a moment, his eyes searching Rowan's face as if trying to find the right words to say. "But you're not alone in this, Rowan. You have me, and you have the support of the entire Wolfheart Pack behind you. We will do whatever it takes to help you unravel the secrets of your past and find your way forward."

Rowan felt a flicker of warmth and gratitude kindling in his chest at Luca's words, a sense of hope and determination that helped to chase away some of the shadows that had been clinging to his heart. He knew that the road ahead would be long and difficult, that there would be challenges and obstacles at every turn. But with Luca by his side, he felt like maybe, just maybe, he could face whatever lay ahead with courage and strength.

"Thank you, Luca," he said softly, his voice filled with a quiet kind of awe. "I don't know what I did to deserve your kindness and support, but I am so grateful for it. I don't think I could do this without you."

Luca smiled, his eyes crinkling at the corners in a way that made Rowan's heart skip a beat. "You don't have to thank me, Rowan. This is what pack is for. We take care of each other, no matter what. And you're a part of that now, whether you realize it or not."

18

Fae Prince

Rowan

Rowan leaned into Luca's embrace, savoring the warmth and comfort that seemed to radiate from his very being. It was strange, he thought, how quickly he had come to trust this man, how easily he had allowed himself to be vulnerable in his presence. But there was something about Luca, something that made Rowan feel safe and cherished in a way he had never experienced before.

"Rowan," Luca said softly, his voice filled with a tenderness that made Rowan's heart skip a beat. "There's something I need to tell you."

Rowan pulled back slightly, his brow furrowing in confusion as he searched Luca's face for any hint of what was to come. "What is it?" he asked, his voice barely above a whisper.

Luca took a deep breath, his eyes never leaving Rowan's as he spoke. "We're fated mates, Rowan. Destined to be together, bonded by a connection that goes beyond anything either of us can fully understand."

Rowan felt his breath catch in his throat, his mind reeling with the implications of Luca's words. Fated mates? How was that even possible? He had heard stories of such things, of course, whispered tales of love and destiny that had always seemed too good to be true. But to hear Luca say it out loud, to feel the truth of it resonating in his very bones... it was almost too much to process.

"Fated mates," he repeated softly, his voice filled with a mix of awe and disbelief. "But how? How can you be so sure?"

Luca smiled, his hand coming up to cup Rowan's cheek in a gesture of tender affection. "I can feel it, Rowan. In my heart, in my soul. It's like a part of me that I never even knew was missing has suddenly fallen into place. And when I look at you, when I hold you in my arms... it's like coming home."

"I feel it too," he admitted softly, his voice filled with a quiet kind of wonder. "Like I've been searching for you my whole life, even if I didn't know it until now."

Luca's smile widened, his eyes shining with unshed tears as he leaned in to press a gentle kiss to Rowan's forehead. The intimate gesture caught Rowan off guard, his breath hitching in his throat as a wave of emotion washed over him. It was strange, he thought, to feel so connected to someone he had only just met, to allow himself to be so vulnerable and open with a man he barely knew.

But as he looked into Luca's eyes, as he saw the depth of love and commitment shining there, he knew that he couldn't deny the truth of what he felt. Fated mates or not, there was something special between them, something that went beyond mere attraction or infatuation.

"Luca," he said softly, his voice filled with a quiet kind of determination. "There's something I need to tell you too. Something about who I am, or at least, who I used to be."

Luca's expression grew serious, his hand tightening around Rowan's in a gesture of silent support. "You can tell me anything, Rowan."

Rowan took a deep breath, his heart pounding in his chest as he gathered his courage. "I'm the fae prince of the Seelie court," he said, his voice barely above a whisper. "Or at least, I was. Before all of this happened, before I ended up here."

He saw that Luca wasn't surprised by this news and he wondered why. "Our elder told me the story about the tree though he didn't know the specifics. Do you know what happened to you, Rowan?"

Rowan shook his head, his expression growing distant and pained as he tried to make sense of the fragmented memories that swirled through his mind. "I don't know," he admitted softly, his voice filled with a quiet kind of desperation. "I can't remember much of anything before I woke up here. Just bits and pieces, like shards of a broken mirror that I can't quite put back together."

Luca's expression softened, his hand coming up to brush a stray lock of hair from Rowan's forehead. "It's okay, Rowan. We'll figure it out together. I promise you, I won't rest until we unravel the truth of what happened to you and how you ended up here."

Rowan felt a lump rising in his throat, his eyes stinging with sudden, unexpected tears. He had never had someone care about him like this before, someone who was willing to stand by his side and fight for him, no matter what challenges lay ahead.

"Thank you, Luca," he whispered, his voice filled with a quiet kind of awe. "I don't know what I did to deserve you, but I'm so grateful to have you in my life."

Luca smiled, his eyes shining with a fierce kind of love and protectiveness that made Rowan's heart ache with longing. "You deserve everything, Rowan. And I'll spend the rest of my life making sure you know that."

Rowan felt a wave of emotion wash over him at Luca's words, his heart swelling with a love and gratitude that he couldn't quite put into words. He knew that there was still so much uncertainty ahead, so many questions that needed to be answered and challenges that needed to be faced.

But in that moment, none of it seemed to matter. All that mattered was the feeling of Luca's arms around him, the warmth of his skin against his own, and the promise of a future that they would face together, no matter what.

"I can't even begin to wrap my head around all of this," Rowan admitted, his voice soft and filled with a quiet kind of vulnerability. "The idea of having a fated mate, of being connected to someone in such a profound and unbreakable way... it's a lot to take in."

Luca nodded, his expression filled with understanding and compassion. "I know, Rowan. And I don't want to overwhelm you with too much too soon. We can take this at your pace, figure things out together as we go along."

Rowan felt a rush of gratitude and affection for Luca, for the way he seemed to instinctively understand what he needed, even when he couldn't put it into words himself. "Thank you, Luca. For being so patient with me, for giving me the space to process all of this."

Luca's smile softened, his hand coming up to brush a stray lock of hair from Rowan's forehead. "Of course, Rowan. I'll always be here for you, no matter what. That's what it means to be fated mates, to be connected in a way that goes beyond anything either of us can fully understand."

Rowan felt a shockwave of emotion ripple through his body, his mind reeling with the implications of Luca's words. Fated mates. Destined partners. It was a concept that he had only ever heard of in stories and legends, a fantasy that had always seemed too good to be true.

And yet, as he looked into Luca's eyes, as he felt the warmth and the strength of his presence washing over him like a balm, he couldn't deny the truth of what he felt. There was a connection between them, a bond that went beyond mere attraction or infatuation. It was like a piece of his soul that he hadn't even known was missing had suddenly clicked into place, making him feel whole and complete in a way he had never experienced before.

Rowan leaned into Luca's touch, savoring the warmth and comfort of his presence. He knew that he should be overjoyed, that he should be reveling in the discovery of his fated mate and the promise of a future filled with love and happiness.

But even as he tried to lose himself in the moment, he couldn't shake the nagging sense of uncertainty that lingered in the back of his mind. There were still so many questions left unanswered, so many pieces of the puzzle that he couldn't quite fit together.

"Rowan," Luca said softly, his voice cutting through the din of Rowan's thoughts. "I know there's a lot on your mind right now, but there are some people who have been waiting to meet you, ever since we brought you back from the forest."

Rowan felt a flicker of surprise and apprehension at Luca's words. "People?" he repeated, his brow furrowing in confusion. "What people?"

Luca smiled, his eyes crinkling at the corners in that way that made Rowan's heart skip a beat. "The rest of the pack, of course. They've been worried about you, Rowan. They want to make sure you're okay, and to welcome you into the fold."

Rowan swallowed hard, his throat suddenly dry at the thought of facing a whole group of strangers, especially in his current state. He was acutely aware of the fact that he hadn't bathed or changed his clothes since waking up, and he could only imagine how disheveled and unkempt he must look.

"I don't know, Luca," he said hesitantly, his gaze dropping to his lap. "I'm not sure I'm ready to face anyone else just yet. I mean, look at me. I'm a mess."

Luca's expression softened, his hand coming up to cup Rowan's cheek in a gesture of tender reassurance. "You're beautiful, Rowan. Inside and out. And the pack will see that too, I promise you."

But even as he spoke, Rowan could see the understanding dawning in Luca's eyes, the realization that he needed some time to himself, to collect his thoughts and prepare himself for the challenges that lay ahead.

"Tell you what," Luca said, his voice gentle and coaxing. "Why don't we get you cleaned up a bit first, before we go out there and face the world? I'm sure a nice, hot shower would do wonders for you right about now."

Rowan felt a rush of gratitude and affection for Luca, for the way he seemed to instinctively understand what he needed, even when he couldn't put it into words himself. "That sounds amazing," he admitted, his voice soft and filled with a quiet kind of vulnerability. "But I'm not sure I even know how to work one of those things. We didn't exactly have showers back in the Seelie court."

Luca chuckled, his eyes sparkling with amusement and tenderness. "Don't worry, I'll show you. It's not as complicated as it looks, I promise."

With that, he helped Rowan to his feet, his arm slipping around his waist to steady him as they made their way towards the small bathroom attached to the bedroom. Rowan couldn't help but lean into Luca's touch, savoring the warmth and strength of his presence, the way he seemed to anchor him in a world that felt like it was spinning out of control.

As they stepped into the bathroom, Rowan felt a flicker of self-consciousness wash over him, his gaze darting around the unfamiliar space with a mix of curiosity and apprehension. He had never seen anything like it before, with its gleaming white tiles and strange, metal fixtures.

"Here, let me help you," Luca said softly, his hands moving to the hem of Rowan's shirt, his fingers brushing against the bare skin of his stomach in a way that made him shiver.

Rowan swallowed hard, his heart pounding in his chest as he allowed Luca to undress him, to peel away the layers of clothing that had been his only armor against the world for longer than he could remember. He felt exposed, vulnerable in a way that he had never experienced before.

But as Luca's hands moved over his body, as he helped him step into the shower and under the warm, cascading water, Rowan felt a sense of peace and rightness wash over him, a feeling of belonging that he had never known before.

"Is this okay?" Luca asked softly, his voice barely audible over the sound of the water. "I don't want to make you uncomfortable, Rowan. If you'd rather do this alone, just say the word and I'll give you some privacy."

Rowan nodded his head, no ready for his mate to his him at this state yet.

Luca smiled, his eyes shining with a fierce kind of love and protectiveness that made Rowan's heart ache with longing. "That's okay, I understand. Take your time okay? Call me when you need me. I am just one shout away."

19

Blossoming Bond

Luca

Luca rummaged through his closet, his mind was a whirlwind of thoughts and emotions. He wanted everything to be perfect for Rowan, to make him feel as comfortable and cared for as possible in this strange new world he had woken up to.

With a critical eye, he selected a soft, worn pair of jeans and a cozy blue sweater that he thought would complement Rowan's stunning purple eyes. As he laid the clothes out on the bed, he couldn't help but let his mind wander to the breathtaking beauty of his mate, to the sweet, gentle demeanor that had captured his heart from the very first moment he had laid eyes on him.

"Get it together, Luca," he muttered to himself, shaking his head to clear the distracting thoughts. "The last thing Rowan needs right now is you drooling all over him like a lovesick puppy."

But even as he tried to focus on the task at hand, Luca couldn't ignore the powerful desire that thrummed through his veins, the primal urge to claim his mate and make him his own in every way possible. He wanted nothing more than to join Rowan in the shower, to feel the heat of his skin and the crush of his lips against his own.

With a groan of frustration, Luca forced himself to take a step back, to remember the confusion and uncertainty that still lingered in Rowan's eyes. He knew that he had to be patient, to give his mate the time and space he needed to adjust to this new reality, no matter how much it might kill him to do so.

"Patience, Luca," he reminded himself, his jaw clenching with the effort of holding back. "Rowan needs you to be strong for him right now, not a horny mess."

With that thought firmly in mind, Luca placed the clothes on the bed and made his way out of the room, his heart heavy with the weight of his own desires, but determined to put Rowan's needs first, no matter what.

As he entered the kitchen, he was immediately enveloped in a warm cloud of laughter and chatter, the sound of his pack mates enjoying each other's company a welcome balm to his frayed nerves. He couldn't help but smile at the sight of them all gathered together, a mismatched family of misfits and outcasts who had somehow found a way to make a home with each other.

"Luca!" Benjamin called out, his eyes sparkling with mischief as he waved him over to the table. "How's our sleeping beauty doing? Has he gotten his first taste of life in the modern century yet?"

Luca rolled his eyes, but he couldn't quite suppress the grin that tugged at the corners of his mouth. "He's fine, Ben. Just taking a shower and getting cleaned up a bit. It's a lot for him to take in all at once, you know?"

Benjamin nodded, his expression softening with understanding. "I can only imagine. Waking up in a strange place, with no memory of how you got there, and a mate you never even knew you had? That's got to be tough."

Luca sighed, running a hand through his hair as he sank down into the chair next to Benjamin. "You have no idea. He's so confused, so lost. I just want to wrap him up in my arms and never let him go, but I know that's not what he needs right now."

Adrian reached out and placed a comforting hand on Luca's shoulder, his eyes filled with a quiet kind of sympathy. "It's going to take time, Luca. He's been through a lot, and he's going to need your patience and understanding as he navigates this new world he's found himself in."

Luca nodded, his throat tight with emotion. He knew that Adrian was right, that he had to be the rock that Rowan could cling to in the midst of the storm. But it was hard, so hard, to keep his distance when every fiber of his being was screaming at him to claim his mate, to make him his in every way possible.

"I just don't want to overwhelm him," he admitted, his voice rough and low. "I know that he's my fated mate, that we're meant to be together. But I also know that he's not ready for that yet, that he needs time to process everything that's happened."

Luca's mother, who had been listening quietly from her place at the stove, turned to face him, her eyes filled with a warm kind of understanding. "What's his name, love? And how did he take the news about you being fated mates?"

Luca felt a flicker of pride and protectiveness wash over him at the mention of Rowan, a fierce desire to keep him safe and cherished burning in his chest. "His name is Rowan. And he's not just any fae. He's the prince of the Seelie Court."

A collective gasp went up from the gathered pack members, their eyes wide with shock and disbelief. Luca couldn't blame them. The Seelie Court was the stuff of legend, a mythical realm that few had ever seen or experienced firsthand.

"A fae prince?" Benjamin repeated, his voice filled with a mix of awe and apprehension. "Luca, do you have any idea what that means? The kind of power and influence he must wield?"

Luca shook his head, his jaw clenching with a stubborn kind of determination. "I don't care about any of that, Ben. All I care about is Rowan, and making sure that he's safe and happy and loved."

His mother smiled, her eyes shining with a fierce kind of pride. "And that's exactly as it should be, love. Rowan is your mate, your other half. And no matter what challenges or obstacles you may face, you will face them together, with the strength and courage of your bond to guide you." She smiled, reaching out to pull him into a tight, fierce hug.

As Luca melted into his mother's embrace, he couldn't help but feel a flicker of hope and determination kindling in his chest. He knew that the road ahead would be long and difficult, that there would be challenges and obstacles at every turn.

"So, tell us more about Rowan," Benjamin said, breaking the comfortable silence that had settled over the room. "What's he like? Aside from being drop-dead gorgeous, of course."

Luca felt a flicker of amusement and exasperation wash over him at Benjamin's teasing words, but he couldn't deny the truth of them. Rowan was beautiful, inside and out, with a kind and gentle soul that shone through in every word and gesture.

"He's amazing, Ben," he said, his voice filled with a quiet kind of awe. "He's sweet and kind and funny, with a heart so big and open that it takes my breath away. And he's been through so much, but he still has this light inside him, this hope and optimism that nothing seems to be able to dim."

Benjamin grinned, his eyes sparkling with mischief. "Sounds like someone's already head over heels in love," he teased, his voice filled with a warm kind of affection.

Luca felt his cheeks heat with a sudden, unexpected blush, but he couldn't bring himself to deny the truth of Benjamin's words.

As Luca was about to delve further into the mysteries surrounding Rowan's past, the door to the room opened, and Rowan emerged, looking adorably shy and uncertain. Luca's heart skipped a beat at the sight of his mate, his breath catching in his throat as he took in the way the soft, worn jeans and cozy blue sweater hugged Rowan's slender frame.

Without even realizing what he was doing, Luca found himself moving towards Rowan, his arms opening wide in a silent invitation. Rowan hesitated for a moment, his violet eyes flickering with a mix of uncertainty and longing. But then, with a soft, shuddering sigh, he stepped into Luca's embrace, his body melting against Luca's chest as if it had always belonged there.

Luca felt a wave of relief wash over him as he held Rowan close, his nose buried in the soft, golden strands of his mate's hair. He breathed in the sweet, intoxicating scent of him, a mix of wildflowers and sunshine that made his heart ache with a fierce, protective love.

"You okay?" he murmured, his voice low and rough with emotion.

Rowan nodded, his face still hidden in the crook of Luca's neck. "Yeah," he whispered, his breath warm and soft against Luca's skin. "Just... overwhelmed, I guess. It's a lot to take in all at once."

Luca tightened his arms around Rowan, a silent promise of comfort and support. "I know, baby. But I'm here for you, okay? We'll figure this out together, one step at a time."

Rowan pulled back slightly, his violet eyes shining with unshed tears as he gazed up at Luca. "Thank you," he said softly, his voice filled with a quiet kind of awe.

For a moment, they simply stood there, lost in each other's eyes, content to let the rest of the world fade away to nothing. But then, with a small, mischievous smile, Rowan pulled back, his gaze drifting to the gathered pack members who were watching them with a mix of amusement, curiosity, and downright mirth.

"Are you going to introduce me to your friends?" he asked, his voice light and teasing.

Luca felt his cheeks heat with a sudden, unexpected blush, but he grinned back at Rowan, his eyes sparkling with joy and affection. "Of course," he said, his hand finding Rowan's and twining their fingers together. "Everyone, this is Rowan, my mate."

A chorus of hellos and welcomes filled the air as the pack members crowded around them, eager to meet the man who had captured their fierce, stubborn alpha's heart. Luca watched with pride and joy as Rowan greeted each of them in turn, his smile growing wider and more genuine with each passing moment.

"It's so nice to meet all of you," Rowan said, his voice filled with a quiet kind of wonder. "I can't thank you enough for everything you've done for me, for taking me in and caring for me while I was… asleep."

Luca's mother stepped forward, her eyes shining with warmth and affection as she pulled Rowan into a tight, fierce hug. "You're family now, Rowan," she said softly, her voice filled with a quiet kind of conviction. "And we take care of our own, no matter what."

Rowan's eyes widened, his breath catching in his throat as he returned the hug, his slender frame trembling slightly in Luca's mother's embrace. Luca could see the emotion welling up in his mate's eyes, the gratitude and the love that he couldn't quite put into words.

"Speaking of taking care of our own," Benjamin chimed in, his voice light and teasing. "How about we get some food in you, Rowan? I don't know about you, but being cursed and unconscious for who knows how long would leave me absolutely ravenous."

Rowan laughed, the sound of it bright and joyful, filling the room with a warm, golden light. "Food sounds amazing," he admitted, his hand finding Luca's once again and squeezing tight. "I don't even remember the last time I ate."

A flicker of sadness and guilt washed over Luca at Rowan's words, a sharp reminder of how much his mate had suffered, how much he had lost to the curse that had held him captive for so long. But he pushed those feelings aside, determined to focus on the here and now, on the fact that Rowan was awake and alive and by his side, where he belonged.

"Well then, let's get you fed," he said, his voice rough with emotion as he led Rowan to the table, his hand never leaving his mate's. "And while we eat, we can start figuring out where we go from here, how we break this curse once and for all."

As they sat down at the table, Luca's mother placed a steaming mug of tea in front of Rowan, her eyes soft with understanding and compassion. "Here, love," she said gently. "This will help warm you up and give you some strength."

Rowan took a tentative sip, his eyes widening in amazement at the rich, fragrant flavor that burst across his tongue. "This is incredible," he said softly, his voice filled with a quiet kind of reverence. "I've never tasted anything like it before."

"There's so much more for you to experience, baby," he said softly, his hand finding Rowan's under the table and twining their fingers together. "And I can't wait to show you all of it, to watch you discover everything this world has to offer."

Rowan's smile was soft and sweet, his violet eyes shining with a love and trust that took Luca's breath away. "I can't wait either," he said, his voice filled with a quiet kind of excitement.

As the conversation lulled, Adrian leaned forward, his eyes filled with a gentle curiosity as he studied Rowan's face. "If you don't mind me asking," he said softly, his voice low and soothing, "do you remember anything about what happened to you? About how you ended up cursed and trapped in that eternal slumber?"

Luca felt Rowan stiffen beside him, his mate's hand tightening around his own as a flicker of pain and sorrow washed over his face.

"I don't remember everything," Rowan admitted, his voice small and uncertain. "But I do remember my father, and the way he changed in the months leading up to my curse."

Luca's heart clenched at the pain in Rowan's voice, the raw, aching vulnerability that he could hear in every word. He wanted nothing more than to gather his mate into his arms, to shield him from the memories that were clearly causing him so much distress.

But he knew that Rowan needed to talk about this, needed to unburden himself of the secrets and the sorrows that had weighed him down for so long. And so, with a deep, steadying breath, Luca forced himself to remain silent, to listen and to support his mate in whatever way he could.

"My father was a good man," Rowan continued, his voice soft and distant, as if he were lost in the depths of his own memories. "A kind and just ruler, beloved by all who knew him. But then, something changed. He became distant, paranoid, prone to fits of rage and violence that none of us could understand."

Adrian nodded, his expression thoughtful as he listened to Rowan's words. "And you think that this change in your father's behavior was somehow connected to your curse?" he asked, his voice gentle and probing.

Rowan shrugged, his shoulders slumping with a heavy, weary kind of defeat. "I don't know for sure," he admitted, his voice small and lost. "But I do know that my brother Aedan was trying to find a cure for our father's madness, trying to figure out what had caused this sudden shift in his personality."

"And did he find anything?" Luca asked, his voice low and urgent. "Any clues or leads that might help us figure out what happened to you?"

Rowan's expression grew troubled, his brow furrowing as he tried to piece together the fragmented memories that swirled through his mind. "I think so," he said slowly, his voice hesitant and unsure. "I remember Aedan telling me that he had discovered something,but I can't remember what it was."

Luca felt a surge of anger and protectiveness wash over him at the thought of someone trying to hurt his mate, trying to use him as a pawn in their twisted games of power and control. He tightened his arm around Rowan's shoulders, pulling him closer and pressing a soft, reassuring kiss to his temple.

Rowan shuddered in Luca's arms, his slender frame trembling with a mix of fear and relief. "I don't want anyone else to get hurt because of me," he whispered, his voice small and broken. "I can't bear the thought of anyone else suffering the way I have."

Luca's heart ached at the pain and the selflessness in Rowan's words, the way his mate was always thinking of others, even in the midst of his own struggles and sorrows. "You don't have to worry about that, baby," he said softly, his voice filled with a quiet kind of conviction. "We're in this together, all of us. And we'll do whatever it takes to keep you safe."

Benjamin, who had been listening to the conversation with a keen, assessing gaze, leaned forward, his expression thoughtful as he studied Rowan's face. "You know," he said slowly, his voice filled with a quiet kind of excitement, "We might know someone who can help us with that."

Luca's head snapped up, his eyes widening with surprise and hope. "What do you mean?" he asked, his voice low and urgent. "Who are you talking about?"

Benjamin grinned, his eyes sparkling with mischief and anticipation. "There's a fae that's a close friend of ours," he said, his voice filled with a quiet kind of reverence. "A wise and powerful fae who had helped us in various situations. He might know more about the history and the magic of the fae than anyone else alive."

Rowan's eyes widened, his breath catching in his throat as he stared at Benjamin with a mix of hope and disbelief. "You think this person could help me?" he asked, his voice small and uncertain.

Benjamin's smile softened, his eyes filled with a quiet kind of understanding and compassion. "I think it's worth a shot," he said gently, his hand reaching out to rest on Rowan's arm in a gesture of comfort and support. "At the very least, they might be able to give us some insight into the kind of magic that was used to trap you."

Luca felt a flicker of hope and determination kindle in his chest, a fierce, unwavering belief that they could do this, that they could find a way to save his mate and bring him back to the world of the living. "Then that's what we'll do," he said, his voice low and steady with resolve. "We'll go see this person, and we'll find out everything we can about what happened."

He turned to Rowan, his eyes searching his mate's face for any sign of hesitation or fear. "Is that okay with you, baby?" he asked softly, his hand coming up to cup Rowan's cheek in a gesture of tender affection. "I know this is a lot to take in, and I don't want to push you into anything you're not ready for."

Rowan leaned into Luca's touch, his eyes fluttering closed for a moment as he savored the warmth and the comfort of his mate's presence. "I'm ready," he said, his voice soft but filled with a quiet kind of determination. "I want to know the truth, Luca. I want to understand what happened to me, and why. And if this person can help me do that, then I'm willing to take the risk."

The door to the room burst open, and Gareth strode in, his expression grim and his jaw set with a tense kind of determination.

"Luca," he said, his voice low and urgent. "Father needs to see you. Now."

Luca felt a flicker of irritation and frustration wash over him at the interruption, a sudden, irrational anger at the way his duties and responsibilities always seemed to pull him away from Rowan's side. But he pushed those feelings down, knowing that he couldn't ignore his father's summons, no matter how much he might want to.

"Can't it wait?" he asked, his voice tight with barely suppressed impatience. "We're kind of in the middle of something here."

Gareth's expression softened, his eyes flickering to Rowan with a look of sympathy and understanding. "I know, brother. And I'm sorry to interrupt. But you know how Father gets when he's kept waiting. It's best not to test his patience, not now."

Luca sighed, his shoulders slumping with a heavy, weary kind of defeat. He knew that Gareth was right, that he couldn't afford to defy his father's wishes, not when there was so much at stake. But that didn't make it any easier to tear himself away from Rowan's side, to leave his mate alone and vulnerable in the midst of so much uncertainty and fear.

"I'm sorry, baby," he murmured, his voice low and rough with emotion as he turned to Rowan, his hand finding his mate's and twining their fingers together. "I have to go. But I won't be gone long, I promise. And I'll be thinking of you every second that we're apart."

Rowan's smile was soft and sad, his eyes shining with a mix of love and understanding. "I know, Luca. And it's okay. I know you have responsibilities, duties that you can't ignore. I would never ask you to choose between me and your pack."

Luca's heart clenched at the selflessness in Rowan's words, the way his mate was always putting others before himself, even in the midst of his own struggles and fears. "You are my pack, Rowan," he said fiercely, his free hand coming up to cup his mate's cheek in a gesture of tender possessiveness. "I'll be back soon," he promised, his voice low and rough with emotion as he glanced back at Rowan over his shoulder.

20

The Calm Before the Storm

Luca

"Do you have any idea what this is about? Why Father summoned us so suddenly?"

Gareth shook his head, his brow furrowed with a mix of concern and confusion. "I'm just as in the dark as you are, brother. All I know is that he's been holed up in his study all day, going over reports and maps like a man possessed."

Luca felt a flicker of unease at his brother's words, a sense of foreboding that made his stomach clench and his heart race with a sickening kind of dread. He knew that whatever had prompted this sudden summons, it couldn't be good news.

As they walked, Gareth turned to him, his expression curious. "So, that man back at your house… was he your mate?"

Luca felt a rush of warmth and affection at the mention of Rowan, a soft, dreamy smile tugging at the corners of his lips. "Yeah, he is. His name is Rowan."

"I've never seen you like this before. So… happy, so at peace with yourself."

Luca ducked his head, feeling a sudden, uncharacteristic flush of embarrassment at his brother's words. "I know it's sudden, and I know it's a lot to take in. But I can't help how I feel, Gareth."

Gareth nodded, a look of understanding and sympathy crossing his face.

Their father was seated at his desk, an imposing figure even in this bastion of his power. Maps, reports, and papers littered the surface in organized chaos, a testament to the weight of responsibility upon his shoulders - the burden of leading a pack in a troubling time.

Luca and Gareth entered the room, the air thick with tension. Their father glanced up, his expression unreadable as he motioned for them to take a seat.

Luca hesitated, his muscles tense, before slowly lowering himself into a chair. He searched his father's face for any clue about the purpose of this meeting but found none.

"Father," Luca began, his voice tight, "how was your trip to the Jensen pack?"

Their father leaned back in his chair, his eyes hardening. "The trip was enlightening, Luca. It's the reason I called you both here."

Luca and Gareth exchanged a glance, their curiosity piqued. Their father rarely discussed pack business with them, preferring to keep his own counsel.

"We've made a decision," their father continued, his voice grave. "We're going to confront the Silverfang pack."

Luca's eyes widened, shock and disbelief coursing through his veins. The Silverfang pack was known for their ruthlessness, their disregard for pack laws and borders. Confronting them was a dangerous move, one that could have far-reaching consequences.

Gareth leaned forward, his brow furrowed in concern. "Father, are you sure that's wise? Confronting the Silverfang pack could lead to an all-out war between the packs. We need to think this through carefully."

Their father slammed his hand down on the desk, the sudden noise making Luca flinch. "Don't you think I've considered that, Gareth?" he growled, his eyes flashing with anger. "But we have no choice. The Silverfang pack has been taking wolves from our allies, and we cannot stand by and do nothing."

Luca's heart raced, his mind reeling with the implications of his father's words. The thought of innocent wolves being taken, their fates unknown, made his stomach churn with a sickening sense of dread.

"When do we leave?" Luca asked, his voice low and steady, despite the fear that gripped his heart.

Their father leaned forward, his gaze intense. "We leave at midnight, under the cover of darkness. We'll need the element of surprise on our side."

Luca and Gareth nodded, their expressions grim. They understood the gravity of the situation, the duty they had to protect their own and their allies.

* * *

As he stepped through the door, Luca was greeted by the sight of Rowan, curled up on the couch, his chest rising and falling with the gentle rhythm of sleep. His mother sat nearby, her eyes fixed on the television, a moment of normalcy amidst the chaos that swirled around them.

He couldn't resist the pull of his mate, the need to be near him, to feel the warmth of his skin and the beat of his heart.

With a soft, reverent touch, Luca leaned down and placed a gentle kiss on Rowan's forehead, his lips lingering for a moment as he breathed in the sweet, intoxicating scent of his mate. It was a gesture of love and reassurance, a silent promise that he would always be there, always fight for the happiness and safety of the man he loved.

Rowan stirred at the touch, his eyes fluttering open to meet Luca's gaze. "Hey," he murmured, his voice rough with sleep. "You're back."

Luca smiled, his hand coming up to brush a stray lock of hair from Rowan's forehead. "Yeah, I am. I'm sorry if I woke you."

Rowan shook his head, a small, sleepy smile tugging at the corners of his mouth. "No, it's okay. I'm glad you're here."

Luca's mother, who had been watching the exchange with a knowing look in her eyes, chose that moment to speak up. "Luca, honey, is everything alright? What did your father want?"

Luca felt his stomach clench at the question, a sudden, sickening sense of dread washing over him. He didn't want to burden his loved ones with the weight of what he knew, didn't want to see the fear and worry in their eyes when they learned of the danger that lay ahead.

But he also knew that he couldn't keep this from them, couldn't bear the thought of leaving them in the dark, not knowing what he was facing or why.

With a heavy sigh, Luca sat down on the couch beside Rowan, his hand finding his mate's and twining their fingers together in a gesture of comfort and support. "Father called a meeting," he said, his voice low and rough with emotion. "He's decided that we're going to confront the Silverfang pack, tonight at midnight."

Rowan's eyes widened, his grip on Luca's hand tightening as he sat up straighter on the couch. "What? Why? What's happened?" His voice was filled with concern, a hint of fear lacing his words.

Luca sighed, his heart heavy with the weight of the truth he had to share. He didn't want to overwhelm Rowan, not when his mate had just emerged from the curse and was still adjusting to the world around him. But he also knew that he couldn't keep this from him, couldn't bear the thought of hiding the truth from the man.

"The Silverfang pack has been taking wolves from our allies," he said, his voice low and rough with emotion. "Innocent people, torn from their families and their homes. They're causing chaos and fear, and we can't let it continue."

Rowan's expression darkened, his violet eyes flashing with a mix of horror and anger. "That's awful," he whispered, his voice trembling with the force of his emotions. "How could they do something like that? How could anyone be so cruel, so heartless?"

Luca shook his head, his jaw clenching with barely suppressed rage. "I don't know, Rowan. But we can't let them get away with it. We have to stand up for what's right, no matter the cost."

For a long moment, Rowan was silent, his gaze distant and thoughtful as he processed the weight of Luca's words. And then, with a sudden, fierce determination, he turned to face his mate, his expression hardening with resolve.

"I want to help," he said, his voice steady and strong despite the fear that Luca could see lurking in the depths of his eyes. "I can't just sit here and do nothing while you and your pack risk your lives to protect the innocent."

Luca's heart clenched at the words, a sudden, fierce protectiveness surging through him like a tidal wave. "No," he said, his voice low and rough with emotion. "Absolutely not. You just woke up from the curse, Rowan. You're still recovering, still adjusting to everything that's happened. I can't bear the thought of you getting hurt again."

But Rowan was already shaking his head, his expression set with a stubborn, unyielding kind of determination. "Luca, I appreciate your concern, but I'm not some fragile flower that needs to be coddled and protected. I have magic, powerful magic that could help turn the tide of this battle in our favor."

He reached out, his hand finding Luca's and twining their fingers together in a gesture of comfort and support. "We're mates, Luca. That means we face everything together, no matter how hard or scary it might be. I can't let you go into this fight alone, not when I have the power to help you."

Luca's heart ached with the force of his love for this man, the fierce, unshakable bond that tied them together, now and forever. He knew that Rowan was right, that they were stronger together than they could ever be apart.

But he also knew that he would never forgive himself if something happened to his mate, if Rowan was hurt or worse because of his involvement in this battle.

"I don't know, Rowan," he said, his voice low and rough with emotion.

Rowan's expression softened, his eyes shining with a deep, aching understanding. "If you want this to work then I am going to need you to trust me."

For a long moment, Luca simply stared at his mate, his heart torn between his desire to keep Rowan safe and his understanding of his determination to help. And then, with a heavy sigh, he nodded, his expression hardening with a fierce, unyielding kind of resolve.

"Okay," he said, his voice low and rough with emotion. "Okay, you can come. But you have to promise me that you'll be careful, okay?"

Rowan's smile was soft and sweet. "I promise, Luca. I'll be careful."

They simply held each other, their hearts beating in perfect sync as they savored the warmth and comfort of each other's presence. And then, with a final, lingering kiss, Luca pulled away, his expression hardening with a fierce, unyielding determination.

"Mom," he said, his voice steady and strong despite the fear and uncertainty that swirled within him. "I need you to do something for me."

His mother looked up, her expression filled with a mix of love and concern. "Of course, honey. What is it?"

Luca took a deep breath, his hand finding Rowan's and holding on tight. "I need you to get in touch with Benjamin and Adrian. Let them know what's happening, and that we might need their help. They're powerful allies, and I have a feeling we're going to need all the support we can get."

His mother nodded, her eyes shining with a fierce, unwavering pride. "I'll do it, Luca. You can count on me."

"We should get some rest," he said, his voice low and rough with emotion.

Rowan nodded, his hand tightening around Luca's as he rose to his feet. "Lead the way,"

Together, they made their way to their room, their steps heavy but purposeful as they walked hand in hand. Luca knew that the road ahead would be long and treacherous, that there would be dangers and challenges waiting for them at every turn.

As they lay together, wrapped in each other's arms, Luca felt a sense of peace and rightness wash over him, a deep, unshakable belief that this was exactly where he was meant to be, with the man he loved more than life itself.

He could feel Rowan's heart beating in sync with his own, a steady, comforting rhythm that seemed to chase away all the fears and doubts that had plagued him since the moment he had learned of the Silverfang pack's treachery.

But here, in the safety and comfort of Rowan's embrace, he felt like he could finally let his guard down, could finally allow himself to be vulnerable and honest in a way that he had never been before.

"I just… I can't lose you, Rowan. Not again. Not after everything we've been through to find each other." His voice was rough and choked with emotion, his fingers clutching at Rowan's shirt like a lifeline.

Rowan pulled back slightly, his violet eyes shining with a fierce, unwavering love as he gazed down at Luca. "You won't lose me, Luca. I promise you that. No matter what happens, no matter what we have to face, I will always be by your side. Always."

He surged forward, capturing Rowan's lips in a desperate, hungry kiss that seemed to set his very soul on fire.

Rowan responded with equal fervor, his hands tangling in Luca's hair as he deepened the kiss, his tongue sliding hot and slick against Luca's own. They clung to each other like drowning men, their bodies moving together in a dance that was as old as time itself.

But even as Luca lost himself in the heat and passion of the moment, he couldn't shake the feeling of unease that lurked in the back of his mind, the nagging sense that something wasn't quite right.

With a supreme effort of will, he pulled back, his breathing ragged and his heart pounding in his chest. "Rowan, wait. We can't... we shouldn't..."

Rowan frowned, his eyes dark with confusion and desire. "What's wrong, Luca? Don't you want this?"

Luca swallowed hard, his throat suddenly dry and tight. "Of course I want this, Rowan. I want you more than I've ever wanted anything in my life. But..."

He hesitated, his gaze dropping to the bed as he tried to find the words to express the fears and doubts that swirled within him. "You just woke up from the curse, Rowan. You're still healing, still recovering from everything that's happened. I don't... I don't want to hurt you, or push you into something you're not ready for."

For a long moment, Rowan was silent, his expression unreadable as he stared down at Luca. And then, with a soft, gentle smile, he reached out and cupped Luca's face in his hands, his touch warm and tender against Luca's skin.

"Luca. You could never hurt me. Not now, not ever. And as for being ready…" He leaned in, his lips brushing against Luca's ear in a whisper that sent shivers down Luca's spine. "I've never been more ready for anything in my life."

Rowan's whispered words sent electric shivers racing down Luca's spine. His heart thundered in his chest as Rowan leaned in close, soft lips brushing the sensitive skin of Luca's ear.

"Fuck, Rowan," Luca breathed, barely recognizing his own voice, low and rough with desire. "You can't just say things like that…"

Rowan pulled back slightly, violet eyes dark and heated as they met Luca's gaze. A playful smirk tugged at the corner of his mouth. "And why not? Afraid you won't be able to handle it, wolf boy?"

Something snapped inside Luca at the challenge in Rowan's tone. A growl rumbled deep in his chest as he surged forward, capturing Rowan's mouth in a searing kiss. Rowan met him with equal intensity, lips parting eagerly as Luca licked into his mouth, chasing the intoxicating taste of his fated mate.

Rowan's fingers tangled in Luca's hair, blunt nails scraping deliciously against his scalp. Luca groaned into the kiss, pressing closer, desperate to feel every inch of Rowan's lithe body against his own.

Rational thought fled as Luca lost himself in the slide of Rowan's lips, the clever stroke of his tongue. His hands roamed greedily over the planes of Rowan's back, slipping under the hem of his shirt to stroke the smooth, heated skin beneath.

The small, needy sounds that Rowan made only spurred Luca on, inflaming his desire to a fever pitch. He wanted - no, needed - to hear more of those intoxicating noises, to wring every last gasp and moan of pleasure from Rowan's lips.

With a low growl, Luca tore his mouth away from Rowan's, trailing biting kisses along the column of his throat. He laved his tongue over the racing pulse point, savoring the salt-sweet taste of Rowan's skin.

"Luca, please…" Rowan panted, arching into Luca's touch like a man starved. His hands scrabbled at Luca's shoulders, tugging impatiently at his shirt. "Need you. Need to feel you."

"Fuck, baby," Luca groaned, nipping sharply at Rowan's collarbone. "Want you so bad. Want to make you fall apart."

In a tangle of limbs and frantic, groping hands, they managed to shed their clothes, not caring where the fabric landed. The first press of skin against skin dragged twin moans from their throats, the sensation almost overwhelming in its intensity.

Luca pulled back just enough to look at Rowan laid out beneath him, all smooth, pale skin and toned, slender muscles. His golden hair fanned out across the pillows like a halo, kiss-swollen lips parted invitingly.

"You're so fucking beautiful," Luca rasped, reverent fingers tracing the dips and planes of Rowan's chest, his stomach. "Can't believe you're mine."

Something flickered in Rowan's violet eyes at that, an emotion that Luca couldn't quite decipher. But before he could dwell on it, Rowan surged up to claim his mouth once more, kissing him with a desperation that bordered on feral.

Luca growled into the kiss, pressing Rowan back into the mattress with the weight of his body. Their hips aligned in a delicious slide, hardness pressing against hardness, dragging broken moans from their throats.

"Luca…fuck…need you inside me," Rowan panted, hitching his hips in a needy, wanton roll. "Please. Need to feel you."

Luca's heart stuttered at the raw plea in Rowan's voice, the blatant desire and need. The wolf inside him howled in approval, urging him to claim his mate, to sink into that welcoming heat and make Rowan his in every way possible.

But the rational part of his brain, the part not wholly consumed by the inferno of lust, held him back. He pulled away reluctantly, searching Rowan's lust-blown eyes.

"Are you sure, baby?" he asked, voice rough and unsteady. "I don't want to hurt you."

Rowan silenced him with a searing kiss, hands fisting in Luca's hair almost painfully. "If you don't get inside me right the fuck now," he growled against Luca's lips. "I swear to the moon goddess herself I will hex your furry ass into next week."

Luca couldn't help the breathless laugh that escaped him at that, even as his cock twitched eagerly at the demand in Rowan's voice. "Well, since you asked so nicely…"

They came together in a heated rush of desperate touches and filthy, open-mouthed kisses. Luca worked Rowan open with slick fingers, reveling in every gasp and moan he drew from his mate's lips. By the time he finally pushed inside, Rowan's slim legs wrapped around his hips, they were both trembling with need.

"Fuck, you feel so good," Luca gritted out, bottoming out in one long, slow glide. He paused for a moment, muscles quivering with the effort of holding himself still, allowing Rowan time to adjust.

Rowan clung to him like a drowning man, short nails digging delicious furrows into Luca's shoulders. "Move," he demanded breathlessly. "Fuck me, Luca. Make me feel it."

With a low, rumbling growl, Luca obeyed, setting a deep, driving rhythm that had the headboard slamming against the wall and the bed frame creaking ominously. Rowan met him thrust for thrust, heels digging into Luca's ass as he urged him on.

The slick, obscene sound of Luca's hips smacking against Rowan's ass, the broken moans and growled curses, filled the room, drowning out the distant crash of thunder overhead.

Luca angled his hips, searching for that spot inside Rowan that would make him see stars. He knew he found it when Rowan cried out, back arching almost painfully as his head thrashed against the pillows.

"There! Fuck…right there," Rowan babbled, nails scrabbling at Luca's sweat-slick back. "Don't stop…gonna…fuck, Luca!"

The sight of Rowan coming undone, the way his velvet heat clenched rhythmically around Luca's cock as he climaxed untouched, was almost too much to bear. Luca pistoned his hips savagely, chasing his own release with single-minded determination.

He came with Rowan's name on his lips, a broken, worshipful prayer as he spilled himself deep inside his mate's willing body. For a timeless moment, he swore he could feel the earth move beneath them, the air around them crackling with ancient, primal magic.

21

A Moment of Connection

Rowan

Luca gently caressed his cheek, Rowan leaned into the touch, savoring the warmth and tenderness of his mate's fingers. "That was incredible," he murmured, his voice soft and filled with wonder. "I never knew it could be like that, so intense and overwhelming."

Luca's eyes softened, a small smile tugging at the corners of his mouth. "It was amazing for me too, Rowan. But I don't want you to feel like we have to rush into anything else. We can take our time, explore our bond at our own pace."

Rowan bit his lip, a sudden shyness washing over him. He knew that Luca was being considerate, giving him the space to adjust to their new relationship. But the truth was, Rowan didn't want space. He wanted to be as close to Luca as possible, to feel that connection again and again.

"I appreciate that, Luca," he said, his voice soft but filled with conviction. "But I don't want to take things slow. I want to experience everything with you, to taste and touch and feel you in every way possible."

Luca's eyes darkened, a heated look passing between them. "Are you sure, Rowan? I don't want you to feel pressured or uncomfortable."

Rowan shook his head, a small smile playing on his lips. "I'm sure, Luca. I've never been more certain of anything in my life."

With a soft growl, Luca leaned in and captured Rowan's lips in a searing kiss. Rowan melted into the embrace, his arms winding around Luca's neck as he parted his lips, inviting his mate to deepen the kiss.

They lost themselves in each other, hands roaming and breaths mingling as they explored and tasted and claimed. It was only when the need for air became too great that they reluctantly parted, their foreheads resting together as they panted softly.

"We should get some rest," Luca murmured, his voice rough with desire. "Tomorrow is going to be a big day, and we both need to be at our best."

"Luca, I… Can I kiss you again?"

Luca's smile widened, his eyes crinkling at the corners. "You never have to ask, Rowan. My lips are yours, whenever you want them."

With a soft, shy smile, Rowan leaned in and pressed his lips to Luca's, the kiss tender and sweet and filled with all the love and devotion he felt for his mate. They lost themselves in the moment, the world around them fading away until there was nothing but the two of them, wrapped in each other's arms.

But as Luca reluctantly pulled away and stood up, Rowan felt a sudden pang of confusion and concern. "Luca? Where are you going?"

Luca hesitated, his expression uncertain. "I thought I would grab a spare blanket and sleep on the floor tonight. Give you some space to adjust and get comfortable."

Rowan's heart sank, a flicker of doubt and insecurity washing over him. "Do you not want to sleep beside me? Are you… ashamed of what we did?"

Luca's eyes widened, a look of alarm crossing his face. "No, Rowan, of course not! I could never be ashamed of being with you. I just wanted to be a gentleman, to give you the choice and not assume anything."

He sat back down on the bed, his hand finding Rowan's and twining their fingers together. "But if you want me to stay, if you want me to hold you tonight, then there's nowhere else I'd rather be."

Rowan's doubts melted away, a warm, contented feeling spreading through his chest. "I do want that, Luca. More than anything."

With a soft, tender smile, Luca lay down beside Rowan, his strong arms wrapping around him and pulling him close. Rowan nestled into the embrace, his head resting on Luca's chest as he listened to the steady, comforting beat of his mate's heart.

* * *

"It's time to wake up. We need to get ready." Luca said, waking him up. He still couldn't believe that he can now wake up if he wanted to. It was a scary thought of not being able to wake up again.

Rowan sighed, pressing a kiss to Luca's chest before reluctantly pulling away. "I know," he said, stretching languidly. "As much as I'd love to stay in bed with you all day, we have a pack to protect and some Silverfang butt to kick."

Luca chuckled, his eyes sparkling with affection and amusement. "That's the spirit, baby. And don't worry, once this is all over, we'll have plenty of time for lazy mornings in bed."

The promise in Luca's voice sent a shiver of anticipation down Rowan's spine. He grinned, leaning in to steal a quick, heated kiss. "I'm holding you to that, wolf boy. Now, let's get dressed before I change my mind and drag you back to bed."

Luca groaned, nipping playfully at Rowan's bottom lip before pulling away. "You're going to be the death of me, you know that?"

Rowan just winked, sauntering over to where Luca had laid out some clothes for him. As he pulled on the slightly oversized shirt and pants, Rowan was enveloped in Luca's scent, a comforting blend of pine and musk that made him feel safe and cherished.

As he dressed, Rowan took a moment to look inward, seeking the familiar pulse of his magic. To his relief, he could still feel it thrumming through his veins, a gentle but insistent hum that filled him with a sense of power and purpose.

"I can feel my magic," he said softly, almost to himself. "It's still there, still a part of me."

Luca came up behind him, wrapping his arms around Rowan's waist and resting his chin on his shoulder. "Of course it is, love. It's who you are, a fundamental part of your being. And it's going to be a huge asset in the fight ahead."

Rowan leaned back into Luca's embrace, drawing strength and comfort from his mate's unwavering support. "I hope so," he murmured.

Luca pressed a kiss to Rowan's temple, his voice fierce and filled with conviction. "You will, Rowan. You are strong and brave and capable of so much more than you realize. And no matter what happens out there, I will be right by your side, fighting with you every step of the way."

Hand in hand, they made their way out of the house and towards the perimeter of the packlands. As they walked, Rowan could feel the tension thrumming through Luca's body, the coiled readiness of a warrior prepared for battle.

It made Rowan's heart swell with pride and admiration, knowing that this brave, strong, loyal man had chosen him, had claimed him as his mate and his equal.

As they approached the meeting point, Rowan could see a small group of men gathered, their postures tense and their expressions grim. Among them, he immediately recognized Gareth, Luca's brother and the pack's beta. The resemblance between the two was striking, the same chiseled features and piercing green eyes.

But it was the man standing beside Gareth that really caught Rowan's attention. He was older, his hair more silver than black, but there was no mistaking the regal bearing, the aura of power and authority that clung to him like a second skin.

"That's your father, isn't it?" Rowan murmured to Luca, his grip on his mate's hand tightening slightly. "The pack alpha."

Luca nodded, his jaw clenching almost imperceptibly. "Yeah, that's him. Don't worry, I'll make sure he doesn't give you any trouble."

Rowan could sense the tension between Luca and his father, the years of strain and unspoken grievances. It made his heart ache, knowing how much Luca had struggled to find his place, to earn his father's approval and respect.

As they drew closer to the group, Rowan could feel the weight of the alpha's gaze on him, assessing, judging. He met the older man's eyes squarely, refusing to be cowed or intimidated.

"Father," Luca said, his voice cool and formal. "This is Rowan, my mate. He's here to fight beside us, to help defend our pack and our allies."

The alpha's gaze flicked over Rowan, his expression unreadable. "A fae prince," he said, his voice flat and devoid of inflection. "And you think he can be trusted, Luca? You think he has a place here, among wolves?"

Rowan bristled at the implication, a hot surge of anger and indignation rising in his chest. But before he could speak, Luca stepped forward, his posture defensive and his eyes flashing with barely restrained fury.

"Rowan is my mate," he growled, his voice low and dangerous. "He is a part of this pack, a part of our family. And he has more courage and loyalty in his little finger than most wolves have in their entire bodies."

The alpha's eyes narrowed, a flicker of irritation crossing his face. "Watch your tone, boy," he warned, his voice cold and unyielding. "I am still your alpha, and I will not tolerate disrespect, even from my own son."

Luca's jaw clenched, his hands curling into fists at his sides. But before he could retort, Rowan placed a gentle hand on his arm, drawing his attention.

"It's okay, Luca," he murmured, his voice soft but filled with quiet strength. "I understand your father's concerns. I am an outsider, and I know I have to prove myself, to earn my place within the pack."

He turned to face the alpha, his chin lifted and his eyes clear and unwavering. "I may be a fae prince," he said, his voice ringing with conviction, "but my loyalty is to Luca, and to the Wolfheart pack. I will fight beside you, bleed beside you, and if necessary, die beside you to protect our people and our way of life."

For a long moment, the alpha simply stared at Rowan, his expression inscrutable. Then, slowly, almost grudgingly, he nodded, a glimmer of respect flickering in his eyes.

"Very well," he said, his voice gruff but not unkind. "We shall see if your actions match your words, fae prince. But for now, we have a battle to fight, and a pack to defend."

With that, he turned away, striding towards the gathered warriors with a purposeful gait. Gareth followed close behind, but not before shooting Rowan a small, approving smile over his shoulder.

Luca let out a shaky breath, his hand finding Rowan's and twining their fingers together. "I'm sorry about that," he murmured, his voice tight with anger and frustration. "My father can be a real ass sometimes."

Rowan just smiled, leaning up to press a soft, reassuring kiss to Luca's cheek. "It's okay, love. I can handle a little tough love from the big bad alpha. And besides, I meant what I said. I will do whatever it takes to prove myself worthy of you, and of this pack."

Luca's eyes softened, a warm glow of love and pride shining in their depths. "You already are worthy, Rowan. More than worthy. And I will spend the rest of my life making sure you never doubt that."

Rowan felt his heart swell with emotion at Luca's words, a warm glow of love and gratitude spreading through his chest. He still couldn't quite believe that this amazing, incredible man had chosen him, had claimed him as his mate and his equal.

The alpha's voice rang out across the clearing, commanding the attention of every wolf present. Rowan turned to face him, his hand still clasped tightly in Luca's, ready to hear what the older man had to say.

"My fellow wolves," the alpha began, his voice filled with authority and determination. "We stand here tonight on the brink of a confrontation that will determine the future of our pack, and of all the packs who call themselves our allies."

A murmur of agreement rippled through the crowd, heads nodding and eyes flashing with resolve. The alpha continued, his gaze sweeping over the gathered warriors with a fierce, unwavering intensity.

"The Silverfang pack has broken the most sacred laws of our kind, has taken our people and our allies as if they were nothing more than chattel to be bought and sold. This cannot stand, and it will not stand."

A growl of anger and determination rose from the throats of the assembled wolves, a primal sound that sent a shiver down Rowan's spine. He could feel the tension in the air, the coiled readiness of a pack prepared to fight for their own.

"But," the alpha held up a hand, his voice growing more measured and controlled. "We must remember that violence is not our first resort. We will go to the Silverfang pack and demand the return of our people, will offer them a chance to make amends and avoid the bloodshed of an all-out war."

Rowan nodded along with the others, a sense of pride and respect welling up in his chest. He had always believed in the power of diplomacy, in the idea that even the most bitter of enemies could find common ground if they were willing to listen and compromise.

"However," the alpha's voice hardened, his eyes flashing with a steely resolve. "If they refuse our demands, if they choose to fight rather than negotiate, then we will meet them on the field of battle. We will show them the true strength and unity of the Wolfheart pack, and we will not rest until our people are safe and our enemies are defeated."

A roar of approval went up from the gathered wolves, fists pumping in the air and voices raised in a chorus of defiance and determination. Rowan felt a thrill of excitement and purpose wash over him, a sense that he was part of something greater than himself, something worth fighting for.

22

Darkness Unveiled

Rowan

As the group made their way towards the Silverfang pack's territory, Rowan found himself walking alongside Luca's father, while Luca and his brother took the lead. The silence between Rowan and the alpha stretched on, heavy and awkward, until finally, the older man cleared his throat and spoke.

"So, you're Rowan, right?" he asked, his voice gruff but not unkind. "The fae prince who stole my son's heart?"

Rowan felt a flicker of nervousness at the alpha's words, unsure of how to respond. "Yes, sir," he said, his voice soft but steady. "But I didn't steal anything. Luca and I... we're fated mates. We belong together."

To his surprise, the alpha chuckled, a low, rumbling sound that seemed to come from deep within his chest. "Relax, kid. I'm not accusing you of anything. I just want to get to know the person who's captured my boy's heart so completely And I just want to apologize back there. My track record with the faes was not the greatest. Hopefully you can forgive me."

Rowan felt a warmth bloom in his chest at the alpha's words, a sense of relief and gratitude washing over him. "I understand, and there's not need to apologize sir. And I want you to know that I would do anything to make him happy, to keep him safe."

The alpha nodded, his expression thoughtful as he studied Rowan's face. "I can see that. And I appreciate it, more than you know." He sighed, his eyes growing distant as he gazed out into the dark, silent forest. "I know I can be hard on my boys sometimes. Tough, unyielding, even harsh. But it's only because I care about them so damn much."

Rowan felt a pang of sympathy for the older man, a sense of understanding and compassion welling up in his heart. "I know, sir. And I'm sure Luca and Gareth know it too, even if they don't always show it."

The alpha snorted, a wry smile tugging at the corners of his mouth. "Those two, they're stubborn as hell. Get it from their mother, I suppose. But they're good boys, strong and brave and loyal to a fault."

He paused, his expression growing serious as he turned to face Rowan fully. "I worry about them constantly, you know? Even though they're grown men now, warriors in their own right. I can't help but see them as the little pups they once were, all big eyes and wagging tails and endless energy."

Rowan felt a lump rising in his throat, his heart aching with a bittersweet mixture of love and loss. He thought of his own family, of the parents and siblings he had left behind in the fae realm, and he felt a sudden, fierce surge of empathy for the alpha and his sons.

"I understand, sir," he said softly, his voice thick with emotion. "And I want you to know that I will do everything in my power to keep Luca safe, to stand by his side and fight with him, no matter what comes our way."

The alpha's eyes shone with a warmth and gratitude that made

Rowan's heart swell with pride and affection. "Thank you, Rowan. That means more to me than you can possibly know."

He smiled, a real, genuine smile that transformed his face and made him look years younger. "And please, call me Gary. None of this 'sir' nonsense. We're family now, after all."

Rowan felt a grin tugging at the corners of his mouth, a sense of happiness and belonging washing over him like a warm, comforting blanket. "Thank you, Gary. I'm honored to be a part of your family."

The alpha - Gary - clapped him on the shoulder, his hand warm and solid and reassuring. "The honor is all mine, kid. Now, what do you say we catch up to those two knuckleheads up ahead and make sure they're not getting into too much trouble?"

Rowan laughed, the sound bright and joyful in the stillness of the night. "Lead the way, Gary. I'm right behind you."

As they quickened their pace, drawing level with Luca and Gareth at the head of the group, Rowan felt a sense of purpose and determination wash over him. He knew that the confrontation with the Silverfang pack would be a test of their strength and their resolve, a battle that would push them all to their limits.

But just as he was about to voice his thoughts, a sudden, sickening wave of wrongness washed over him, making his stomach churn and his skin crawl with revulsion. He stumbled, his hand reaching out to grip Luca's arm as he fought to keep his balance.

"Rowan?" Luca's voice was sharp with concern, his eyes searching Rowan's face for any sign of distress. "What's wrong, baby? Are you okay?"

Rowan shook his head, his breath coming in short, sharp gasps as he tried to find the words to describe the feeling that had overcome him. "No, Luca. Something's not right. I can feel it, a darkness, a wrongness that's permeating the very air around us."

Luca's brow furrowed, his hand tightening around Rowan's as he scanned the dark, silent trees with wary, suspicious eyes. "What do you mean, Rowan? What kind of darkness?"

Rowan swallowed hard, his heart racing as he tried to put the sensation into words. "It's like nothing I've ever felt before, Luca. A dark magic that feels twisted and corrupted, like it's been tainted by something truly evil." He shivered, his own magic humming within him like a warning, a clear sign of the danger that lay ahead. "We need to be careful, Luca. Whatever's waiting for us out there, it's not going to be pretty."

Luca's father, Gary, stepped forward, his expression grim and his eyes hard with determination. "The boy's right," he said, his voice low and gruff. "We can't afford to take any chances. Everyone, stay on high alert and proceed with caution."

He turned to face the group, his gaze sweeping over them with a fierce, unwavering intensity. "If anyone senses any immediate danger, howl. It'll be our signal to rally to each other's aid."

Rowan nodded, his jaw clenching with a stubborn, unyielding resolve. He knew that he was young, that he was still learning the ways of this world and the magic that flowed through his veins. But he also knew that he had a role to play, a purpose to fulfill, and he would not let his own fears and doubts hold him back.

As they cautiously entered the Silverfang pack's territory, Rowan and Luca were immediately struck by the eerie silence that hung heavy in the air. There were no sounds of life, no signs of the bustling community they had expected to encounter.

"Where is everyone?" Luca murmured, his voice low and tense as he scanned the empty, abandoned buildings with wary, suspicious eyes. "It's like they've all just vanished into thin air."

Rowan shook his head, a sense of dread and unease settling in the pit of his stomach. And then, as if on cue, the metallic scent of blood filled the air, a grim confirmation of their worst fears. Rowan and

Luca exchanged a knowing look, their expressions grim and their hearts heavy with the weight of what they both knew to be true.

"They're dead, aren't they?" Rowan whispered, his voice small and broken in the stillness of the night. "Or they've fled, trying to escape whatever darkness has taken hold of this place."

Luca nodded, his jaw clenching with a fierce, unyielding determination. "We have to find out what happened here."

He turned to face the group, his voice ringing out with a clear, commanding authority. "We split up and search the area. Look for any survivors, any clues that might tell us what happened to the Silverfang pack."

Rowan followed Luca as they made their way towards the pack house, the heart of the Silverfang pack's territory. With each step, the sense of unease that had been growing in the pit of Rowan's stomach intensified, a sickening feeling of wrongness that made his skin crawl and his magic hum with warning.

As they approached the entrance, Luca paused, his hand resting on the heavy wooden door. He glanced back at Rowan, his brow furrowed with concern. "Are you ready for this, baby? We don't know what we're going to find in there."

Rowan swallowed hard, his heart pounding in his chest. He knew that Luca was right, that they had to be prepared for the worst. But he also knew that they couldn't turn back now, not when there might still be people in need of their help.

"I'm ready," he said, his voice steady despite the fear that thrummed through his veins. "Let's do this."

With a nod, Luca pushed open the door, and they stepped inside. The darkness that greeted them was thick and oppressive, a physical weight that seemed to press down on Rowan's chest, making it hard to breathe.

"Luca, I can't see a thing," he whispered, his hand reaching out to find his mate's in the gloom. "Can you?"

Luca shook his head, his voice tight with tension. "No, it's too dark. We need some light."

Rowan nodded, his magic already gathering at his fingertips. With a soft murmur of incantation, he conjured a small, glowing orb of light, its soft radiance illuminating the room around them.

And that's when they saw it. The bodies of the Alpha's Betas, strewn across the floor like broken dolls, their eyes staring sightlessly up at the ceiling. The air was thick with the coppery scent of blood, a sickening tang that made Rowan's stomach heave with nausea.

"Oh gods," he whispered, his eyes wide with horror. "Luca, what happened here?"

Luca shook his head, his expression grim and his eyes hard with a fierce, protective anger. "I don't know, baby. But we're going to find out."

He turned to Rowan, his hand finding his mate's and holding on tight. "Can you sense any other signs of life, Rowan? Any heartbeats or auras that might lead us to survivors?"

Rowan nodded, his eyes fluttering closed as he focused his magic inward, letting it expand outwards like ripples in a still pond. At first, there was nothing, just a yawning void where life should have been, a silence that made his heart ache with a deep, profound sense of loss.

But then, just as he was about to give up hope, he felt it. A faint, flickering pulse of life, so weak and thready that he almost missed it. His eyes snapped open, his breath catching in his throat as he turned to Luca with a wild, desperate hope.

"There's someone alive, Luca. Below us, in what feels like a hidden room or cell."

Luca's eyes widened, his hand tightening around Rowan's. "Lead the way, baby. We have to get to them, fast."

They raced through the pack house, their footsteps echoing off the walls as they followed the faint, pulsing thread of life that Rowan's magic had detected. It led them to a small, nondescript door, hidden away in a corner of the basement.

"This is it," Rowan said, his voice tight with tension. "They're in here, Luca. I can feel it."

Luca nodded, his jaw clenching with determination as he reached out and wrenched the door open. The sight that greeted them made Rowan's heart stop in his chest, his breath catching in his throat as he stared in horror at the scene before him.

There, huddled together in the darkness, were a group of children and older shifters, their faces pale and drawn with fear and exhaustion. Most of them were unconscious, their breathing shallow and labored, but one, a young girl with wide, haunted eyes, was still clinging to awareness.

"Please," she whispered, her voice thin and reedy with pain. "Help us. We don't know what happened, we don't know why they did this to us."

Rowan felt tears prickling at the corners of his eyes, his heart breaking at the raw, aching vulnerability in the girl's voice. He knelt down beside her, his hand reaching out to brush a strand of matted, sweat-soaked hair from her face.

"It's okay," he murmured, his voice soft and soothing. "We're here to help you, to get you out of here and to safety."

He glanced up at Luca, his expression grim and his eyes hard with a fierce, protective anger. "We have to get them out of here, Luca. They need medical attention, and they need it now."

Luca nodded, his hand finding Rowan's and holding on tight. "You're right, baby. But we can't do this alone. We need help."

He turned towards the door, his head tilting back as he let out a long, powerful howl that seemed to shake the very foundations of the pack house. It was a call for aid, a signal to their packmates that they needed assistance, and fast.

Within moments, Gareth and their father came rushing into the room, their eyes wide with shock and horror as they took in the scene before them.

"What happened here?" Gary demanded, his voice low and gruff with anger. "Who did this to these people?"

Luca shook his head, his expression grim. "We don't know. But we have to get them out of here, get them to safety and medical care."

Rowan nodded, his magic already reaching out to assess the condition of the shifters. To his relief, he could sense that they were all still alive, though some were in much worse shape than others.

"We need to move quickly," he said, his voice tight with urgency. "Some of them are in critical condition, and they won't last much longer without help."

Gareth and Gary sprang into action, their hands reaching out to scoop up the unconscious shifters and carry them towards the door. Luca and Rowan followed close behind, the young girl cradled gently in Rowan's arms.

Then Rowan felt a sudden chill run down his spine, a sense of wrongness that made his magic flare in warning. He whirled around, his eyes widening in horror as he saw a blast of dark energy hurtling towards them, its twisted tendrils reaching out to ensnare and destroy.

"Look out!" he cried, his hands already moving in a complex pattern as he summoned a shield of shimmering light. The dark magic slammed into the barrier with a sickening crackle, its force nearly knocking Rowan off his feet.

"Luca, get them out of here!" he yelled, his voice strained with the effort of maintaining the shield. "I'll hold them off, buy you some time!"

Luca's eyes widened, his expression torn between fear and determination. "No way, Rowan. I'm not leaving you behind!"

Rowan shook his head, his jaw clenching with stubborn resolve. "You have to, Luca. These people need you, need all of you. I can handle this, I promise."

He could see the conflict in Luca's eyes, the desperate need to stay by his side warring with the duty to protect the innocent. But in the end, Luca nodded, his hand reaching out to squeeze Rowan's briefly before he turned to lead the survivors to safety.

"Be careful, baby," he whispered, his voice rough with emotion. "Come back to me, you hear?"

Rowan managed a small, tight smile, his heart aching with love and fear. "I will, Luca. I promise."

As the last of the survivors disappeared from view, Rowan turned to face the attackers, his magic humming with power and determination. Two figures emerged from the shadows, a man and a woman, their auras pulsing with the same sickening darkness that he had sensed earlier.

"Well, well, well," the woman purred, her voice like silk sliding over steel. "What do we have here? A little fae prince, all alone and out of his depth?"

Rowan's eyes narrowed, his hands clenching into fists at his sides. "Who are you?" he demanded, his voice hard and unyielding. "What do you want with these people?"

The man chuckled, a low, sinister sound that made Rowan's skin crawl. "We want what our master wants, little prince."

Rowan felt a surge of anger and revulsion wash over him, his magic sparking at his fingertips. "You're monsters," he spat, his voice trembling with rage. "Nothing but puppets, dancing on the strings of a greater evil."

The woman's eyes flashed with a cruel, mocking light. "Oh, you have no idea, little prince. Our master's power is beyond anything you can imagine, and soon, it will be beyond anything anyone can stop."

With those words, the dark mages launched their attack, their tainted magic crashing against Rowan's shield like a tidal wave of darkness. He gritted his teeth, his muscles straining with the effort of holding them back, but he could feel his strength waning with every passing second.

"Luca, hurry," he whispered, his voice barely audible over the roar of the battle. "I don't know how much longer I can hold them."

But even as the words left his lips, he saw a flash of movement out of the corner of his eye. Luca, Gareth, and their father were racing towards him, their faces set with grim determination as they joined the fray.

"I thought I told you to go!" Rowan yelled, his voice strained with equal parts relief and frustration. "I had it under control!"

Luca just grinned, his eyes flashing with a fierce, protective light. "Like hell you did, baby. We're in this together, remember?"

even with their combined efforts, the dark mages proved to be formidable opponents. Their magic was fueled by a malevolent force that seemed to have no end, a twisted, corrupted energy that sapped the strength and the will of those who faced it.

"We can't keep this up much longer!" Gareth yelled, his voice strained with the effort of fending off a particularly vicious attack. "They're too strong, too powerful!"

Rowan felt a surge of fear and desperation wash over him, his heart pounding in his chest as he struggled to maintain the shield that was the only thing standing between them and the dark mages' twisted magic. He could feel his strength waning with every passing second, his muscles burning with the effort of holding back the onslaught.

"Luca," he gasped, his voice hoarse and strained. "I don't know how much longer I can hold them off. We need a miracle, and we need it now."

Luca's eyes flashed with a fierce, protective determination, his hand tightening around Rowan's. "Just hold on, baby. We'll find a way, I promise."

But even as the words left his mate's lips, Rowan could see the doubt and the fear creeping into Luca's eyes, the realization that they were outnumbered and outmatched, that their chances of survival were growing slimmer by the moment.

And then, just as all hope seemed lost, a sound filled the air that made Rowan's heart leap with a wild, desperate joy. It was the sound of wings, great, powerful wings that seemed to shake the very foundations of the earth as they drew closer and closer.

"Luca, look!" Rowan cried, his voice rising above the din of the battle. "Up there, in the sky!"

Rowan watched as Luca's head snapped up, his mate's eyes widening in awe and disbelief as he saw the magnificent creature soaring above them. It was a dragon, its scales glistening like diamonds in the sunlight, its wings stretching out like great, billowing sails.

"Is that…" Gary breathed, his voice filled with a mixture of fear and wonder. "Is that a dragon?"

Rowan nodded, a fierce, joyful grin spreading across his face. "It is. And I think I know who's riding it."

As if in answer to his words, the dragon let out a great, thunderous roar, its jaws opening wide to unleash a blast of icy breath that engulfed the dark mages in a frigid embrace. They screamed in agony, their tainted magic shattering like glass under the onslaught of the dragon's power.

And then, with a grace and precision that seemed almost other-worldly, the dragon landed, its great, clawed feet touching down on the ground with a soft, almost gentle thud. Its rider dismounted, his cloak billowing out behind him as he strode towards them with a confident, purposeful gait.

"Benjamin!" Rowan cried, his heart swelling with relief and

gratitude at the sight of his friend and ally. "How did you find us? How did you know we needed help?"

Benjamin just grinned, his eyes sparkling with a mischievous, knowing light. "I had a feeling," he said, his voice warm with affection. "Call it a hunch, or maybe just a bit of magical intuition." He turned to face the dark mages, his expression hardening with a fierce, unyielding determination. "But enough talk. It's time to show these bastards what happens when they mess with the wrong people."

With those words, Benjamin raised his staff, the quill-shaped weapon glowing with a brilliant, reality-warping light. The dragon beside him shimmered and shifted, its form blurring and changing until it resolved into the familiar, beloved shape of Adrian, Benjamin's husband and partner in all things.

Together, they launched themselves at the dark mages, their magic and their strength combining in a dazzling display of power and skill. Benjamin's staff flashed and whirled, its enchanted light piercing through the darkness like a beacon of hope, while Adrian's icy breath froze the mages in their tracks, rendering them helpless and immobile.

Rowan watched in awe as his friends fought, their movements fluid and graceful, their power and their purpose unwavering in the face of the enemy. He could feel his own magic rising up to join them, his love and his determination fueling his strength and his resolve.

And then, with a final, shattering burst of light and ice, the dark mages fell, their tainted magic dissipating like smoke on the wind. They lay still and silent on the ground, their faces twisted in expressions of agony and defeat.

"It's over," Luca breathed, his voice filled with a quiet, disbelieving relief. "We won."

Rowan felt a lump rising in his throat, his eyes stinging with sudden, unexpected tears. He had been so afraid, so certain that they were all going to die, that their love and their bond would be snuffed out like a candle in the wind.

But they had survived, had triumphed against all odds, and the knowledge of that filled him with a fierce, unshakable joy.

"We did it," he whispered, his voice choked with emotion. "Together, we did it."

Luca smiled, his hand finding Rowan's and twining their fingers together in a silent promise. "Of course we did, baby. We're unstoppable, remember?"

Rowan laughed, a bright, joyful sound that seemed to chase away the last lingering shadows of the battle. "Damn right we are."

But even as they savored their victory, even as they reveled in the relief and the happiness of the moment, a chill ran down Rowan's spine, a sense of foreboding that made his magic hum with warning.

And then, from the depths of the shadows, a voice rang out, cold and cruel and filled with a malevolent, twisted glee.

"You may have won this battle, little prince," the voice hissed, its tone dripping with venom and hatred. "But the war is far from over. We will return, and when we do, we will claim you for our own, body and soul."

Rowan felt his blood run cold, his heart clenching with a sickening mixture of fear and revulsion. He knew that voice, knew the twisted, corrupted energy that pulsed behind it like a living thing.

It was the same energy he had felt in the dark mages, the same tainted, malevolent force that had sought to destroy them all. And he knew, with a certainty that went beyond words or reason, that this was only the beginning, that the true battle was still to come.

"Let them come," Luca growled, his voice low and dangerous, his eyes flashing with a fierce, protective anger. "We'll be ready for them, no matter what they throw at us."

Rowan nodded, his jaw clenching with a stubborn, unyielding resolve. "Damn right we will. We're not going to let them win, not now, not ever."

23

Unraveling the Threads

Rowan

Rowan felt a wave of exhaustion wash over him as they approached the Wolfheart Pack house, the weight of the battle and the rescue mission finally catching up to him. But beneath the weariness, there was a sense of relief and accomplishment, a quiet pride in knowing that they had saved lives.

As they stepped through the door, Luca's mother rushed forward, her arms outstretched and her face etched with concern and love. "Oh, thank the moon you're all safe!" she exclaimed, pulling them each into a warm, comforting hug.

When she reached Rowan, he melted into her embrace, his eyes fluttering closed as he savored the feeling of her arms around him. It reminded him of his own mother, of the love and comfort he had once known in the fae realm.

For a moment, he felt a pang of bittersweet longing, a sharp ache in his chest for the family he had lost. But as he pulled back and saw the warmth and acceptance shining in Luca's mother's eyes, he felt a flicker of hope and belonging kindle in his heart.

"Thank you," he murmured, his voice soft and filled with gratitude. "For everything."

She smiled, her hand reaching up to cup his cheek in a gesture of maternal affection. "You're part of our family now, Rowan. Never forget that."

As they made their way into the living room, Rowan couldn't help but marvel at the strange and wondrous devices that filled the space. Sleek, glowing screens and gleaming metal contraptions that he had never seen before, all humming with a quiet, mysterious energy.

"Gareth," Alpha Wolfheart said, his voice cutting through Rowan's thoughts. "I need you to contact Alpha Jensen, let him know what we've discovered."

Rowan frowned, the name unfamiliar to him. "Who's Alpha Jensen?" he asked, his brow furrowing in confusion.

Luca smiled, his hand finding Rowan's and giving it a reassuring squeeze. "He's the leader of another pack, one of our allies. We need to let him know what's going on, so we can coordinate our efforts and keep everyone safe."

Rowan nodded, trying to wrap his mind around the concept. In his time, communication between packs had been limited to messengers and face-to-face meetings, a slow and cumbersome process that often led to misunderstandings and conflicts.

"But how will Gareth contact him?" he asked, his voice hesitant. "It's not like he can just send a messenger owl or something."

Luca chuckled, his eyes sparkling with amusement and affection. "No, baby. We have something called phones now. They let us talk to people instantly, no matter how far away they are."

Rowan's eyes widened, his mind reeling with the implications. "Really? That's amazing!"

He thought of all the times he had wished for a way to talk to his family, to hear their voices and know that they were safe. The idea that such a thing was possible now, that he could connect with his loved ones with just the touch of a button… it was almost too much to comprehend.

"I have so much to learn," he murmured, his voice filled with a quiet, awed wonder. "So many things have changed since I was cursed."

Luca's expression softened, his hand tightening around Rowan's. "I know, baby. And I'll be with you every step of the way, helping you navigate this new world and discover all the incredible things it has to offer."

Their conversation was interrupted by Gareth's return, his face grim and his eyes shadowed with concern. "I just got off the phone with Alpha Jensen," he said, his voice tight with tension. "He's on his way here now, along with his top advisors. He wants to hear everything we've learned, and figure out our next move."

Luca's father nodded, his expression serious. "Good. We need all the help we can get, if we're going to stop this darkness before it consumes us all."

Rowan felt a flicker of fear and uncertainty wash over him, his mind flashing back to the grim discovery they had made at the Silverfang pack house. The sight of those lifeless bodies, the knowledge that even the strongest and bravest among them had fallen to the dark forces that threatened their world… it was enough to make his blood run cold.

"I still can't believe it," Gareth said, his voice soft and filled with a quiet, aching sorrow. "Alpha Silverfang's betas, dead. And the rest of the pack, vanished without a trace."

Luca sighed, his hand running through his hair in a gesture of frustration and concern.

He paused, his expression growing thoughtful. "And the truth is, we were wrong about the Silverfang pack. We thought they were responsible for the disappearances, that they were the ones behind all of this. But now… now it seems like they were just as much victims as anyone else."

Rowan nodded, his mind racing with the implications of Luca's words. If the Silverfang pack wasn't responsible for the disappearances, then who was? What dark and terrible force was at work, pulling the strings and manipulating events from behind the scenes?

"We have to find out who's really behind this," he said, his voice filled with a quiet, unwavering determination. "We have to stop them, before they can hurt anyone else."

Luca's father nodded, his expression grim. "Agreed."

Rowan watched as Gareth approached the rescued shifters, his expression gentle and his voice soft as he knelt down beside them. "I know you've been through a lot," he said, his hand reaching out to rest on the shoulder of a young woman who seemed to be the most coherent of the group. "But if you can, we need to know what happened. What did you see? Who did this to you?"

The woman shuddered, her eyes filling with tears as she clutched at the blanket wrapped around her shoulders. "It was horrible," she whispered, her voice hoarse and broken. "They came out of nowhere, like shadows in the night. They tore through our defenses like they were nothing, like we were just lambs to the slaughter."

Rowan felt a chill run down his spine at her words, his mind flashing back to the horrific scene they had stumbled upon in the Silverfang pack house. The bodies of the betas, the eerie silence that had hung heavy in the air… it was like something out of a nightmare.

"What did they want?" Gareth pressed, his voice still soft but insistent. "Did they say anything about why they were doing this?"

The woman shook her head, her eyes distant and haunted. "They didn't say much. Just that we were weak, that we didn't deserve to live. That their master would remake the world in his image, and we were just pawns in his game."

Rowan felt a flicker of anger and revulsion wash over him at her words, his hands clenching into fists at his sides. The idea that someone could be so cruel, so callous with the lives of innocent people… it made his blood boil and his magic spark with a fierce, protective fury.

"We need more information. Anything you can tell us, anything at all… it could be the key to stopping this before it's too late." Alpha Wolfheart said.

The shifters exchanged nervous glances, their faces pale and drawn with fear and exhaustion. But finally, a young man spoke up, his voice hesitant and unsure. "I don't know if this means anything," he said, his eyes darting around the room as if seeking reassurance. "But when they were attacking us… it was like they weren't entirely in control of their actions. Like they were puppets on a string, dancing to someone else's tune."

Rowan's eyes widened, a sudden, sickening realization washing over him. He had felt it too, in the heat of battle… the sense that the Silverfang pack members were not acting entirely of their own volition, that there was something else at work, pulling the strings and manipulating events from behind the scenes.

"It's dark magic," he said, his voice soft but filled with a quiet, unwavering certainty. "I could feel it, in the air and in their auras. Someone's controlling them, using them as pawns in their twisted game."

The room fell silent at his words, the weight of the revelation hanging heavy in the air. Rowan could see the fear and the uncertainty in their eyes, the unspoken question that lingered on everyone's lips… if the Silverfang pack was being controlled by dark magic, then who else might be under its sway? And how could they hope to fight an enemy that could turn their own people against them?

"Benjamin, Adrian," Luca said, his voice tight with tension as he turned to their allies. "Have you ever seen anything like this before? Do you have any idea who could be behind it?"

The two men exchanged a grim, knowing look, their expressions darkening with a quiet, simmering anger. "We might," Adrian said, his voice low and filled with a quiet, deadly intensity. "There are a few names that come to mind... old enemies we thought we had defeated long ago."

Benjamin nodded, his hand tightening around the staff at his side. "Malachite and Lina," he said, his voice heavy with the weight of old memories and past battles. "They were powerful dark magic users and we fought them before."

Rowan felt a shiver run down his spine at the names, a sense of foreboding that made his magic hum with warning. He had never heard of Malachite or Lina before, but something about them... something about the way Benjamin and Adrian spoke of them... it made his blood run cold and his heart clench with fear.

"I thought you said you defeated them," Luca said, his brow furrowing in confusion. "How could they be behind this now?"

Adrian shook his head, his expression grim. "We thought we had. But it seems that they've found a way to cheat death... or perhaps they've been resurrected by someone even more powerful than they were."

Rowan's mind raced with the implications of Adrian's words, his hand finding Luca's and holding on tight. If Malachite and Lina had been brought back from the dead... if they were now serving a master even more terrible than they had been in life... then what hope did any of them have of stopping the darkness that threatened to consume their world?

"The Deal Maker," Benjamin said, his voice soft but filled with a quiet, ominous certainty. "It has to be. Only he would have the power to bring back the dead, to gather an army of darkness to do his bidding."

"Hold on," Luca's father said, his voice sharp with alarm. "This Deal Maker. Who is he, exactly? And what does he have to do with all of this?"

Benjamin sighed, his expression grim. "The Deal Maker is a shadowy figure, a being of immense power and unknown motives. We've only found out his involvement not that long ago. Always lurking in the background, pulling strings and manipulating events to suit his own twisted ends."

Rowan felt a chill run down his spine at Benjamin's words, a sense of foreboding that made his magic hum with warning. "But why?" he asked, his voice small and unsure. "Why would he want to destroy the packs, to turn us against each other?"

Adrian shook his head, his expression bleak. "We don't know. The Deal Maker's motives have always been a mystery, even to those who have tangled with him before. All we know is that he's cunning, elusive, and utterly ruthless in his pursuit of power."

Luca's father frowned, his brow furrowing with concern. "So what you're saying is, we're up against an enemy we don't understand, with powers we can't even begin to fathom?"

Benjamin nodded, his jaw clenching with a quiet, simmering anger. "I'm afraid so. But we can't let that stop us. We have to find a way to unravel his plans, to stop him before it's too late."

The meeting concluded on a somber note, the weight of the revelations hanging heavy in the air. Rowan could feel the tension and the fear that thrummed through the room, the unspoken dread that they were all facing a threat unlike anything they had ever encountered before.

But as he looked at Luca, at the fierce, unwavering love and determination that shone in his mate's eyes, he felt a flicker of hope and strength kindle in his heart. They were in this together, bound by a love that was stronger than any darkness, any evil that the world could throw at them.

"Let's go home," Luca murmured, his hand finding Rowan's and twining their fingers together. "I think we could both use a little quiet time, just the two of us."

Rowan nodded, a small, grateful smile tugging at his lips. "That sounds perfect."

As they made their way back to Luca's house, Rowan could feel the weight of the day's events settling on his shoulders, the exhaustion and the fear and the uncertainty that had been building up inside him for hours.

But as soon as they stepped through the door, as soon as he felt the warm, comforting presence of his mate surrounding him, all of that seemed to melt away, replaced by a deep, aching need to be close, to feel the reassuring beat of Luca's heart against his own.

"Luca," he whispered, his voice rough with emotion as he pulled his mate into his arms. "I need you. I need to feel you, to know that you're here with me."

Luca's eyes softened, his hand coming up to cup Rowan's cheek with a tenderness that made his heart ache. "I'm here, baby. I'm not going anywhere. Not now, not ever."

Their lips met in a kiss that was soft and sweet and filled with all the love and devotion that words could never express. Rowan lost himself in the warmth of Luca's embrace, in the gentle, reverent touch of his hands as they mapped the contours of his body.

They made love slowly, tenderly, their bodies moving together in a dance that was as old as time itself. Rowan savored every gasp and sigh, every whispered word of love and praise that fell from Luca's lips, committing them to memory like precious gems to be treasured and cherished forever.

And when it was over, when they lay tangled together in the afterglow, their skin slick with sweat and their hearts full to bursting,

Rowan felt a sense of peace and belonging wash over him, a deep, unshakable certainty that this was exactly where he was meant to be.

204

24

Eye of the Storm

Rowan

With no immediate threats on the horizon, Rowan found himself with a rare moment of respite, a chance to catch his breath and enjoy the simple pleasures of life among his newfound family. And as he woke that morning, wrapped in the warmth of Luca's embrace, an idea began to take shape in his mind.

"Morning, sleepyhead," Luca murmured, his voice rough with sleep as he pressed a soft kiss to Rowan's forehead. "What's got you up so early?"

Rowan grinned, a mischievous glint in his eye. "It's a surprise. But I need you to promise me something first."

Luca raised an eyebrow, curiosity and amusement warring in his expression. "Oh? And what might that be?"

"I need you to stay out of the kitchen today. No peeking, no sneaking tastes, nothing. Can you do that for me?"

Luca's eyes widened, a slow, delighted smile spreading across his face. "Are you planning on cooking for me, my love?"

Rowan ducked his head, a faint blush staining his cheeks. "Maybe.

But it won't be a surprise if you go snooping, now will it?"

Luca chuckled, his arms tightening around Rowan's waist. "Alright, alright. I promise to stay out of your way."

With a final, lingering kiss, Rowan slipped out of bed, his mind already racing with plans and possibilities. He knew that he wanted to make something special for Luca, something that would show him just how much he meant to him.

But as he rummaged through the cupboards and pantry, Rowan quickly realized that he was missing some key ingredients. He frowned, his brow furrowing in thought. He couldn't very well surprise Luca with a half-finished meal, now could he?

And then, like a bolt of lightning, an idea struck him. The omegas. They had taken him under their wing from the moment he arrived, offering him a sense of belonging and support that he had never known before.

With a determined nod, Rowan set off towards the houses of the omegas, a spring in his step and a smile on his face. As he walked, he couldn't help but marvel at the sense of peace and contentment that had settled over him in recent days.

It was a far cry from the fear and uncertainty that had plagued him when he first woke from his cursed slumber, lost and alone in a world he barely recognized. But now, with Luca by his side and the support of the pack around him, Rowan felt like he had finally found his place in the world.

As he approached the houses of the omegas, Rowan was struck by the warm, inviting atmosphere that seemed to radiate from every doorway. The sound of laughter and chatter filled the air, mingling with the delicious scents of baking bread and simmering stews.

"Rowan!" a voice called out, and he turned to see a familiar face beaming at him from a nearby porch. It was Sarah, one of the first omegas he had met upon his arrival, her belly round with the promise of new life.

"Hey, Sarah," he said, his own smile widening as he took in the glow of happiness that seemed to surround her. "You look positively radiant today."

Sarah laughed, her hand coming to rest on the swell of her stomach. "I feel like a beached whale, but thank you for saying so. What brings you to our neck of the woods?"

Rowan ducked his head, suddenly feeling a bit sheepish. "Actually, I was hoping to borrow some ingredients. I wanted to surprise Luca with a home-cooked meal, but I'm missing a few things."

Sarah's eyes softened, a knowing look passing over her face. "Ah, young love. There's nothing quite like it, is there?"

Rowan felt his cheeks heat, but he couldn't deny the truth of her words. "No, there really isn't. I never thought I could feel this way about anyone, but Luca… he's my everything."

Sarah reached out, her hand finding Rowan's and giving it a gentle squeeze. "I know exactly how you feel. When I met my mate, it was like the whole world just clicked into place. Like I had finally found the missing piece of my soul."

Rowan nodded, his throat suddenly tight with emotion. "That's exactly it. Like everything I went through, all the pain and the heartache, was worth it because it led me to him."

Sarah smiled, her eyes shining with understanding. "Hold onto that feeling, Rowan. Cherish it, nurture it, and never let it go. It's the most precious thing in the world."

With those words ringing in his ears, Rowan followed Sarah into her house, his heart full to bursting with love and gratitude. Together, they gathered the ingredients he needed, chatting and laughing like old friends.

And as he made his way back to Luca's house, his arms laden with supplies and his mind buzzing with ideas, Rowan felt a sense of excitement and anticipation wash over him.

He couldn't wait to see the look on Luca's face when he tasted the meal he had prepared, couldn't wait to share this small but meaningful gesture of his love and devotion.

As he stepped into the kitchen, Rowan felt a rush of memories wash over him, bittersweet and tinged with a hint of melancholy. He remembered his own mother, her face warm and smiling as she moved around their small kitchen, her hands deft and sure as she chopped and stirred and seasoned.

She had always been happiest when she was cooking, pouring her love and care into every dish she made. And now, as Rowan set about preparing his own meal, he felt a sense of connection to her, a thread of continuity that stretched across the years and the realms.

The hours passed and the meal began to take shape, Rowan felt a sense of pride and accomplishment wash over him. The kitchen was filled with the rich, savory scents of roasting meat and simmering sauces, the air thick with the promise of a delicious feast.

Just as Rowan was putting the finishing touches on their dinner, the front door swung open, revealing a thoroughly exhausted and mud-covered Luca. Despite his disheveled appearance, Luca's face lit up with a brilliant smile the moment his eyes landed on Rowan.

"Hey, baby," he said, his voice warm and affectionate as he crossed the room to gather Rowan in his arms. "Something smells amazing in here."

Rowan grinned, leaning into Luca's embrace despite the mud and grime. "Welcome home, love. I thought you might be hungry after a long day of working on the new homes for the pack."

Luca's eyes softened, his hand coming up to cup Rowan's cheek with a tenderness that made his heart skip a beat. "You cooked for me? Rowan, that's... I don't even know what to say."

Rowan felt a flush of pleasure at the clear appreciation in Luca's voice. "You don't have to say anything. Just go get cleaned up, and then we can sit down and enjoy the meal together."

Luca pressed a quick, grateful kiss to Rowan's lips before hurrying off to the bathroom, leaving a trail of muddy footprints in his wake. Rowan couldn't help but chuckle at the sight, his heart swelling with a deep, abiding love for his mate and all his endearing quirks.

By the time Luca emerged, fresh-faced and dressed in clean clothes, Rowan had set the table and was just placing the last steaming dish in the center. Luca's eyes widened as he took in the spread, a look of pure wonder and appreciation crossing his face.

"Rowan, this is incredible," he breathed, his voice filled with awe. "You did all this for me?"

Rowan felt a lump form in his throat, his eyes stinging with sudden, unexpected tears. "Of course I did, Luca. You're my mate, my partner in all things. I wanted to do something special for you, to show you how much you mean to me."

They sat down to eat, their hands still clasped together as they savored each bite and sip. The food was delicious, but it was the company that made the meal truly special. They talked and laughed and simply basked in each other's presence, the troubles of the outside world fading away until it was just the two of them, wrapped in a bubble of love and contentment.

After dinner, they retired to the couch, snuggling close as Luca reached for the remote control. Rowan watched with a mix of fascination and bemusement as the television flickered to life, still not quite used to the modern technology that seemed so commonplace to everyone else.

"I don't think I'll ever get used to this," he murmured, his head resting on Luca's shoulder as he watched the images dance across the screen. "It's like magic, but different from anything I've ever known."

Luca chuckled, his arm tightening around Rowan's waist. "It's just electricity and science, baby. But I can see how it might seem like magic to someone who's never seen it before."

Rowan hummed, content to simply bask in the warmth and comfort of Luca's embrace. But just as he was about to drift off, lulled by the steady beat of his mate's heart, a sudden, sharp disturbance in his magic jolted him back to full alertness.

"Luca," he said, his voice tight with tension as he sat up straight. "Something's coming. I can feel it."

Luca was on his feet in an instant, his body coiled and ready for action. "What is it, Rowan? What do you sense?"

Before Rowan could answer, a swirling vortex of energy materialized in the center of the room, the air crackling with the force of the magic that powered it. Luca pushed Rowan behind him, a low, warning growl rumbling in his chest as he faced the unknown threat.

But as the portal stabilized and a figure emerged from its depths, Rowan felt a flicker of recognition wash over him. The man was tall and broad-shouldered, with piercing blue eyes and a shock of silver hair that seemed to glow in the dim light of the room.

"Peace, wolf," the man said, his voice deep and resonant as he held up his hands in a gesture of non-aggression. "I mean you no harm. I am Roman, a friend and ally of Benjamin's. The name is Roman."

Luca's stance relaxed slightly, but Rowan could still feel the tension thrumming through his mate's body. "Benjamin sent you?" he asked, his voice wary but not outright hostile.

Rowan stepped forward, his hand finding Luca's and giving it a reassuring squeeze. "Please, come in," he said, his voice soft but filled with a quiet, cautious welcome. "If Benjamin trusts you, then so do we."

Roman inclined his head, a small, grateful smile tugging at the corners of his mouth as he stepped into the warmth and comfort of their home. "Thank you, little prince. I know my arrival was unexpected, but I come bearing news that I think you will want to hear."

Rowan felt a flicker of curiosity and apprehension wash over him, his mind racing with the possibilities of what Roman might have to say. He gestured for their guest to take a seat, his hand never leaving Luca's as they settled onto the couch beside him.

"What news?" he asked, his voice tight with a mixture of hope and fear. "Is it about my family? The Seelie Court?"

Roman nodded, his expression growing serious as he leaned forward, his elbows resting on his knees. "I'm afraid so, Rowan. The Seelie Court has been in turmoil since your disappearance, torn apart by power struggles and infighting as different factions vie for control."

Rowan felt his heart clench at the words, a wave of guilt and sorrow washing over him. He had never wanted to abandon his people, to leave them vulnerable and leaderless in the face of such chaos.

"And my family?" he asked, his voice barely above a whisper. "Are they...?"

"They're alive," Roman said, his voice gentle but filled with a quiet, aching sympathy. "Your siblings have been doing their best to hold things together in your absence, but it hasn't been easy. And your father..." He trailed off, his eyes growing distant and troubled. "I'm afraid his whereabouts are still unknown, Rowan. He disappeared around the same time you did, and no one has been able to find any trace of him since."

Rowan felt like he had been punched in the gut, the air rushing out of his lungs in a sharp, painful gasp. His father, missing? It was like history repeating itself, a cruel echo of his own unexplained absence.

"I don't understand," he said, his voice rough with emotion. "How could this happen? How could my father just vanish like that?"

Roman shook his head, his expression grim. "I wish I had more answers for you, Rowan. But the truth is, we're all still trying to piece together what happened, to make sense of the chaos and confusion that has engulfed the Seelie Court."

Rowan felt Luca's arm tighten around his shoulders, a silent show of support and understanding. He leaned into the warmth of his mate's embrace, drawing strength and comfort from the solid, steady presence beside him.

"What do we do now?" he asked, his voice small and lost in the heavy silence of the room. "How can we help, when we're so far away and caught up in our own battles?"

Roman's expression softened, a look of quiet, aching sympathy crossing his face. "For now, little prince, you focus on the task at hand. On protecting your pack and your mate, and unraveling the mysteries that surround you. The Seelie Court will endure, as it always has. And when the time is right, you will find your way back to your people, to take your rightful place as their leader and guide."

Rowan felt a lump rising in his throat, his eyes stinging with sudden, unshed tears. He wanted to believe Roman's words, wanted to have faith that everything would work out in the end.

But the weight of his responsibilities, of the challenges and dangers that lay ahead, seemed to press down on him like a physical force, threatening to crush him under their unbearable weight.

"I don't know if I can do this," he whispered, his voice choked with emotion. "I don't know if I'm strong enough, wise enough, to be the leader they need."

Luca's hand found his, their fingers twining together in a silent promise of love and support. "You are, Rowan," he said, his voice fierce with conviction. "You're the strongest, bravest, most compassionate person I know. And you won't be doing this alone. I'll be by your side, every step of the way."

Roman nodded, a small, approving smile tugging at his lips. "Your mate is right, Rowan. You have the strength and the courage within you to face whatever lies ahead. And you have the love and support of those who believe in you, who will fight by your side until the very end."

Rowan felt a warmth blossoming in his chest, a flicker of hope and determination chasing away the shadows of his doubt and fear. He knew that Roman and Luca were right, that he wasn't alone in this fight.

He had his mate, his pack, and the unwavering support of his friends and allies. Together, they would find a way to overcome the challenges that lay ahead, to unravel the mysteries and defeat the enemies that sought to destroy them.

"Thank you," he said, his voice soft but filled with a quiet, unshakable conviction. "Thank you for believing in me, for standing by my side through all of this."

Roman's smile widened, his eyes crinkling at the corners with a look of warm, affectionate pride. "Always, little prince. Now, I'm afraid I must take my leave. There are matters that require my attention, and I have tarried here long enough."

He rose to his feet, his form shimmering and blurring around the edges as he prepared to step back through the portal. But just as he was about to disappear, his eyes suddenly flashed with an intense, almost maddened light, a look of urgency and fear crossing his face.

"Rowan, Luca," he said, his voice tight with tension. "Willowbrook is under attack. Malachite has returned, and he brings with him an army of darkness that threatens to overwhelm the town's defenses."

Rowan felt a chill run down his spine, his heart clenching with a sickening sense of dread. Malachite, the dark mage who had been one of their most formidable foes, allied once again with the malevolent forces that sought to destroy them.

Rowan felt a chill run down his spine, his heart clenching with a sickening sense of dread. Malachite, the dark mage who had been one of their most formidable foes, allied once again with the malevolent forces that sought to destroy them.

Without hesitation, Rowan turned to Luca, his eyes blazing with a fierce, unyielding determination. "Luca, we have to go. We can't just sit here while our friends, our allies, face this danger alone."

Luca's jaw clenched, his own sense of duty and loyalty surging to the surface like a tidal wave. "I know, baby. I'm with you, no matter what."

Rowan felt a surge of love and gratitude wash over him, his heart swelling with the knowledge that he had such an incredible, unwavering partner by his side. "Thank you, Luca. I don't know what I'd do without you."

Luca's expression softened, his hand reaching out to cup Rowan's cheek with a tenderness that made his knees go weak. "You'll never have to find out, Rowan. I'm yours, always and forever."

They sprang into action, their minds racing as they gathered their belongings and prepared for the unexpected journey ahead. Rowan could feel the adrenaline pumping through his veins, the urgency of the situation lending speed and purpose to his every move.

"What do you think we'll find when we get there?" he asked, his voice tight with a mix of fear and anticipation. "Do you think we'll be able to make a difference, to turn the tide of the battle in our favor?"

Luca paused, his expression growing serious as he considered the question. "I don't know, baby. But what I do know is that we have to try."

25

Darkest Hour

Rowan

As the shimmering portal winked out of existence behind them, Rowan, Luca, and Roman found themselves standing in the heart of Willowbrook, the once-peaceful city center transformed into a chaotic battleground. The air was thick with the metallic scent of blood and the acrid stench of dark magic, a suffocating miasma that made Rowan's stomach churn and his heart race with a primal, instinctive fear.

Everywhere he looked, he saw battle and destruction, the forces of good and evil clashing in a desperate, brutal struggle for survival. People and supernaturals alike fought side by side, their powers and abilities pushing back against the tide of dark constructs that threatened to overwhelm them.

"This is insane," Luca growled, his eyes flashing with a fierce, protective anger. "We have to do something, Rowan. We can't let Malachite and his goons destroy this place."

Luca shifted into his wolf form, his powerful muscles rippling beneath his sleek, silver fur. Rowan felt a surge of love and pride wash over him at the sight of his mate, so strong and brave and beautiful in the face of such overwhelming darkness.

But before they could leap into the fray, a blood-curdling roar split the air, and Rowan whirled around to see Roman shifting into a massive, towering bear, his form rippling with raw, elemental power.

Rowan breathed, his eyes wide with shock and amazement. "I didn't know you could do that, Roman."

The bear let out a rumbling chuckle, his eyes glinting with amusement. "There's a lot you don't know about me, little prince," he said, his voice a deep, growling bass. "But now's not the time for stories. We have a city to save."

Rowan felt a surge of determination and purpose wash over him, his magic crackling at his fingertips as he stepped forward, ready to join the fray. But before he could take more than a few steps, a blood-curdling shriek rent the air, and he whirled around to see a monstrous creature charging towards them, its grotesque form radiating an aura of pure, unadulterated malice.

"Look out!" Roman shouted, his hand shooting out to erect a shimmering barrier of energy between them and the attacking construct. "Rowan, Luca, stay behind me! I'll handle this!"

Rowan caught sight of Luca out of the corner of his eye, his mate locked in a desperate struggle with another construct that had managed to slip past their defenses.

"Luca!" Rowan cried out, his heart in his throat as he broke away from Roman's protection, his magic surging forth in a blinding flash of power. He knew he wasn't at full strength, that the curse that had held him captive for so long had taken its toll on his body and his mind. But in that moment, none of that mattered. All that mattered was protecting his mate, keeping Luca safe from harm no matter the cost.

With a wordless cry of rage and defiance, Rowan unleashed a blast of pure, radiant energy at the construct that threatened Luca, his magic slamming into the creature with the force of a thunderbolt. The construct staggered backwards, its form wavering and distorting as Rowan's power tore through it like a hot knife through butter. And then, with a final, agonized shriek, it burst into a cloud of ash and shadow, its essence scattered to the winds like so much dust in the breeze.

"Rowan," Luca gasped, his eyes wide with shock and amazement as he turned to face his mate. "That was incredible. How did you…?"

But before he could finish his thought, another wave of constructs crashed over them, their numbers seemingly endless as they poured forth from the shadows like a tide of living darkness. Roman was there in an instant, his own magic flaring to life as he fought to hold back the horde, but Rowan could see the strain on his face, the toll that the endless battle was taking on even his vast reserves of power.

"We can't keep this up forever," Roman gritted out, his voice strained with the effort of maintaining his defenses. "We need to find a way to end this, and fast."

Rowan's mind raced, his thoughts turning to the vast, untapped wellspring of power that lay dormant within him. He was a child of two worlds, born of both fae and undine blood, and he knew that if he could just find a way to harness that power, to unleash the full might of his heritage upon their enemies, he could end this battle in a heartbeat.

He closed his eyes, reaching deep within himself to touch the swirling vortex of magic that pulsed at his core. He could feel the icy chill of his undine blood, the raw, elemental fury of the storm that raged within him. If he could just find a way to unleash that power, to call forth a devastating hailstorm that would tear through the constructs like a scythe through wheat…

But even as the thought crossed his mind, Rowan felt a flicker of doubt, a nagging sense of unease that made him hesitate. He knew that his power was vast, that he could level entire city blocks with a single thought if he so chose. But he also knew that such destruction came with a price, that the innocent and the guilty alike would be caught in the crossfire of his rage.

He thought of the people fighting alongside them, the brave souls who had taken up arms to defend their homes and their loved ones against the darkness that threatened to consume them all. How could he unleash such devastation upon them, knowing that they would be caught in the midst of the maelstrom, their lives snuffed out like candles in the wind?

Suddenly, a chorus of howls pierced through the cacophony of battle, a sound that made Rowan's heart leap with a wild, desperate hope. He whirled around, his eyes widening as he saw a familiar group of figures emerging from the fray, their forms shifting and blurring as they moved between wolf and human shape.

"The pack!" Luca cried out, his voice ringing with joy and relief. "They've come to help us!"

And there, at the head of the pack, was Luca's father, his human form tall and proud as he strode towards them with a fierce, determined expression on his face.

"Luca, Rowan, Roman," he called out, his voice carrying over the din of the battle. "You need to make your way now. We'll handle things here on the front lines."

Luca hesitated, his eyes flickering between his father and the ongoing battle with a look of torn indecision. "We can't just leave you here. We have to help, we have to-"

"No, son," his father interrupted, his voice firm but filled with a quiet, unwavering love. "Your place is with your mate and your allies. Trust in your pack, Luca. We'll hold the line here."

Luca's father shifted back into his wolf form and bounded off into the fray with a howl of defiance and rage. Rowan watched him go, his heart aching with a mix of fear and admiration for the brave, and selfless wolf.

"Come on," Roman growled, his bear form looming over them like a protective shadow. "We need to get to the manor, now."

They set off at a run, their feet pounding against the cobblestone streets as they raced towards the heart of the city, towards the place where they knew their allies would be making their final stand. Rowan could feel his magic thrumming through his veins, a pulsing, electric current that seemed to grow stronger with every step he took.

As they rounded the final corner and the manor came into view, Rowan felt his breath catch in his throat, his eyes widening with a mix of awe and horror at the sight that greeted them. The once-peaceful grounds had been transformed into a war zone, the lush gardens and manicured lawns now a churning sea of dark constructs and battling supernaturals.

And there, in the midst of it all, were their friends and allies, their powers and abilities blazing like beacons in the darkness. Rowan saw Benjamin wielding his reality-warping magic like a conductor directing an orchestra, his quill-shaped staff flashing and whirling as he tore through the ranks of the enemy with a fierce, unyielding determination.

Beside him, Adrian was a force of nature, his ice magic freezing the dark constructs in their tracks and shattering them into a thousand glittering shards with every blast of his power. His eyes glowed with an eerie, otherworldly light, his face set in a mask of grim concentration as he fought to hold the line against the relentless onslaught.

And all around them, Rowan could see the other members of their unlikely alliance - a man with hair the color of storm clouds who wielded lightning like a whip, a vampire with eyes like molten gold who moved with a lethal, inhuman grace, a figure cloaked in shadows who seemed to melt in and out of the darkness at will, and a towering warrior with a face like carved granite and a wicked-looking hook in each hand.

Rowan lost himself in the rhythm of the battle, his magic flowing through him like a raging river as he unleashed blast after blast of icy power against the constructs that swarmed towards them. He could feel Luca at his back, could sense the raw, primal strength of his wolf form as they moved together in perfect sync, their every breath and heartbeat aligned in a dance of deadly precision.

All around them, their allies fought with a fierce, unyielding determination, their powers and abilities blazing like stars in the darkness. Adrian's ice magic was a thing of terrible beauty, the air around him shimmering with a thousand glittering shards as he froze the constructs in their tracks and shattered them into oblivion.

Benjamin's reality-warping magic was a dizzying, mind-bending spectacle, the very fabric of the world seeming to warp and twist around him as he tore through the ranks of the enemy like a force of nature. The weather witch's lightning crackled and sizzled through the air, leaving smoking, charred husks in its wake, while the vampire and the shadow magic user darted and danced through the fray like wraiths, their every move a study in lethal grace.

And the warrior with the hooks… Rowan had never seen anything like him before, a mountain of muscle and sinew who moved with a speed and agility that belied his size. His hooks flashed and whirled in a dizzying blur of silver, each blow sending dark constructs flying like ragdolls through the air.

But even as they fought, even as they pushed back against the tide of darkness with everything they had, Rowan could feel a flicker of doubt, a nagging sense of unease that made his heart clench with a sickening sense of dread. Because no matter how many constructs they destroyed, no matter how many blows they landed or enemies they felled, there always seemed to be more, an endless sea of shadow and malice that threatened to drown them all.

Rowan heard Adrian's voice ringing out over the din of battle, his words filled with a desperate, urgent hope.

"The source!" he shouted, his ice magic crackling and sizzling as he fought to make himself heard. "The dark energy powering these constructs, it's coming from the peak of the Willowbrook mountains! That's where the ancient leylines converge, where the enemy's power is strongest!"

Rowan felt a surge of determination wash over him, his heart pounding with a fierce, unyielding resolve. If they could just make it to the mountaintop, if they could strike at the heart of the enemy's power, then maybe, just maybe, they could put an end to this nightmare once and for all.

"We have to get up there," he said, his voice rough with exhaustion and determination as he turned to Luca and Roman. "We have to stop this at the source, before it's too late."

Luca nodded, his wolf form shimmering and blurring as he shifted back into his human shape.

Benjamin's voice cut through the chaos, his tone filled with a fierce, unyielding determination.

"I can clear you a path," he shouted, his staff glowing with a blinding, radiant light. "But you'll have to move fast, before the constructs have a chance to regroup."

Rowan nodded, his jaw clenching with a stubborn, unyielding resolve. "We'll be ready," he said, his voice ringing with conviction. "Just give us the signal, and we'll make a run for it."

Benjamin's eyes flashed with a fierce, feral light, and then he was moving, his staff whirling and spinning in a dizzying blur of motion. A massive blast of energy erupted from the tip of the quill, a shockwave of pure, reality-warping power that tore through the ranks of the dark constructs like a hot knife through butter.

"Now!" he shouted, his voice cracking with the strain of his exertion. "Go, now!"

Rowan didn't hesitate, his heart pounding with a wild, desperate hope as he leaped onto Roman's back, his hands tangling in the thick, shaggy fur of the enormous bear. Luca shifted into his wolf form once more, his sleek, silver shape a blur of motion as he raced alongside them, his paws pounding against the blood-soaked earth.

Together, they charged forward, the wind whipping through Rowan's hair and Roman's fur as they plunged into the gap in the enemy's lines. Dark constructs lunged and slashed at them from every side, their shadowy forms warping and twisting in the eerie, unnatural light of the mage's power.

But Rowan and Luca fought back with everything they had, their magic and their claws tearing through the monsters like they were nothing more than paper dolls. Rowan's water magic surged and swirled around him, freezing the constructs in their tracks or shattering them into a thousand glittering shards with every blast of his power.

Beside him, Luca was a whirlwind of tooth and claw, his wolf form a sleek, deadly blur as he lunged and snapped at the enemies that dared to come too close. And Roman, his bear form radiating an aura of pure, unyielding strength, simply plowed through the constructs like they were nothing more than blades of grass, his massive paws crushing them into the dirt with every thundering step.

Higher and higher they climbed, the treacherous, winding path of the mountain growing steeper and more perilous with every passing moment. The air grew thin and cold, the wind howling like a living thing as it tore at their clothes and their fur.

Finally, after what felt like an eternity of blood and sweat and tears, they reached the summit of the Willowbrook mountains, their chests heaving and their limbs trembling with exhaustion. But even as they paused to catch their breath, even as they allowed themselves a moment of rest and reprieve, Rowan felt a chill run down his spine, a sudden, sickening sense of dread that made his stomach churn and his blood run cold.

Because there, at the center of the mountaintop, stood a figure cloaked in shadow, their form writhing and twisting like a living thing. Dark magic pulsed and throbbed around them, a swirling vortex of malevolent energy that seemed to suck the very light and warmth from the air.

And flanking the mage on either side, their eyes glowing with a cruel, hungry light, were two figures that Rowan had hoped never to see again. The man and woman who had attacked them in the Silverpack Lands, who had sought to capture Rowan and bring him before their dark master.

"You," he whispered, his voice shaking with a mix of fear and rage as he gazed upon their twisted, leering faces. "I should have known you'd be here, should have known you were behind this."

The woman laughed, a cold, mocking sound that made Rowan's skin crawl with revulsion. "Oh, little prince," she cooed, her voice dripping with false sympathy. "Did you really think you could escape us so easily? Did you think we would let you slip through our fingers, when our master has such grand plans for you?"

Rowan's eyes narrowed, his hand tightening around Luca's as he glared at the woman with a fierce, defiant light. "I don't care about your master, or his plans," he spat, his voice ringing with conviction. "I won't let you hurt anyone else, won't let you destroy this town."

The man chuckled, a low, sinister sound that made the hairs on the back of Rowan's neck stand up. "You have spirit, I'll give you that," he said, his eyes glinting with a cruel, predatory light. "But spirit alone won't save you, little prince. Not when the power of the dark mage is on our side."

Rowan felt a flicker of fear and doubt wash over him, his heart clenching with a sudden, sickening sense of dread. But he pushed it down, his jaw clenching with a stubborn, unyielding resolve as he glared at the man with a fierce, defiant light.

"Why do you want me?" he demanded, his voice ringing out with a clear, unwavering conviction. "What could your master possibly hope to gain by targeting me, by attacking innocent people and destroying everything in your path?"

The woman laughed, a cold, mocking sound that made Rowan's skin crawl with revulsion. "Our master has had his eye on you for a long time, longer than you could possibly imagine. He sees the power that lies dormant within you, the untapped potential that could reshape the very fabric of reality itself."

Rowan felt a wave of confusion and dread wash over him, his mind reeling with the implications of the woman's words. He had always known that he was different, that the mix of fae and undine blood that flowed through his veins granted him abilities beyond those of ordinary wolves.

But to hear it spoken of so plainly, to know that his power had drawn the attention of a being so dark and terrible that even the bravest of warriors quailed before him… it was almost too much to bear.

"I won't let you take me," he said, his voice shaking with a mix of fear and determination. "I won't let you use me as a pawn in your twisted games, won't let you destroy everything I hold dear."

The man's eyes flashed with a cruel, hungry light, and then he was moving, his hands weaving in a complex pattern as he summoned forth a blast of pure, malevolent energy. Rowan barely had time to react before the wave of dark magic slammed into him, his body flying backwards like a ragdoll as he crashed to the ground in a crumpled heap.

Dimly, he heard Luca and Roman crying out his name, their voices raw and ragged with desperation as they fought to reach his side. But the dark mage was relentless, his barrage of blood magic and shadow magic tearing through their defenses like they were nothing more than paper dolls.

Rowan struggled to his feet, his head spinning and his vision blurring as he tried to focus on the enemies before him. He could feel his own magic rising up within him, a churning maelstrom of water and wind that begged to be unleashed upon his foes.

But even as he gathered his power, even as he prepared to strike back with everything he had, he heard a sound that made his blood run cold, a scream of agony and despair that tore through the air like a knife through flesh.

Rowan's heart shattered as he heard Luca's scream of agony, the sound tearing through his very soul. Despite the dire situation, Luca's voice rang out, fierce and desperate. "Rowan, don't do it! Don't give in to them, no matter what!"

Rowan's eyes met Luca's, seeing the determination and love burning within them, even as his mate stood on the brink of death. "I can't lose you, Luca," he choked out, tears streaming down his face. "I won't let them take you from me."

Luca's expression softened, a sad smile gracing his lips. "And I can't bear the thought of you in their clutches, my love. I would gladly give my life to keep you safe."

Rowan's heart clenched, a wave of despair washing over him. How could he choose between his own freedom and the life of his fated mate? The mere idea of living without Luca by his side was unthinkable, a void of endless sorrow and pain.

The shadow mage's cruel laughter echoed through the air, cutting through their moment of heartache. "Tick tock, little prince. The longer you hesitate, the more your precious mate will suffer."

Rowan's fists clenched, his nails digging into his palms as he fought back the urge to lash out. He knew that any act of defiance would only put Luca in greater peril. With a heavy heart and a sense of resignation, he made his decision.

"I'll do it," he whispered, his voice barely audible over the howling wind. "I'll surrender myself to you, just… just don't hurt him anymore. Please."

Luca's eyes widened, a look of anguish and horror etched across his face. "Rowan, no! You can't-"

But before he could finish his plea, the shadow mage waved a hand, silencing him with a brutal burst of magic. Luca crumpled to the ground, his body convulsing in pain as the dark tendrils tightened their grip.

Rowan's heart shattered, a scream of despair tearing from his throat as he lunged forward, desperate to reach his fallen mate. But the shadow mage was faster, a sinister smile twisting his lips as he cast a powerful spell, engulfing Rowan in a suffocating shroud of darkness.

As the world around him began to blur and distort, Rowan's gaze remained fixed on Luca, their eyes locking in a final, desperate moment of connection. The anguish and despair etched across Luca's face burned itself into Rowan's memory, a silent scream frozen on his mate's lips as the enchantment dragged him down into the abyss.

Rowan fought against the spell with every ounce of his strength, his magic surging and crackling as he struggled to break free. But it was no use, the shadow mage's power too strong, too all-consuming.

As his consciousness began to fade, Rowan's thoughts raced with fear and uncertainty. What fate awaited him in the clutches of his captors? What horrors would he be forced to endure, and would he ever see Luca again?

But even as the darkness closed in around him, even as the last remnants of hope slipped from his grasp, Rowan clung to one final, desperate thought.

"I love you, Luca," he whispered, his voice lost in the swirling void of the enchantment. "No matter what happens, no matter what they do to me, I will always love you. And I will find my way back to you, I swear it."

26

Feeling Helpless

Luca

Luca watched in horror as the shadows engulfed Rowan, his mate's form disappearing into the swirling vortex of darkness. He struggled against his captors, his wolf snarling and snapping with a desperate, feral rage, but it was no use. The dark magic that held him was too strong, too all-consuming, and he could only watch helplessly as Rowan was taken away, his heart shattering into a million jagged pieces with every passing second.

As the portal winked out of existence, taking Rowan with it, Luca felt a wave of despair and self-loathing wash over him, his knees buckling under the weight of his failure. He had sworn to protect his mate, to keep him safe from harm no matter the cost, and yet here he was, helpless and broken, while Rowan suffered gods only knew what torments at the hands of their enemies.

"I'm sorry, Rowan," he whispered, his voice raw and choked with emotion as he stared at the spot where his mate had disappeared. "I'm so sorry, baby. I failed you. I wasn't strong enough, wasn't fast enough, and now you're gone, and it's all my fault."

He could feel the hot sting of tears in his eyes, the ache of his fangs as they elongated in response to his rage and his grief. He wanted to howl, to let loose the agony that was tearing him apart from the inside out, but he couldn't find the strength, couldn't summon the will to do anything but kneel there in the dirt, his head bowed and his heart shattered beyond repair.

He was aware of Roman's presence beside him, the bear shifter's hand resting on his shoulder in a gesture of silent support. But even that small comfort felt like too much, like a weight that he didn't deserve, a kindness that he had no right to accept.

"Luca," Roman's voice was low and urgent, cutting through the haze of Luca's despair like a blade through fog. "Luca, listen to me. This isn't your fault. You did everything you could, everything anyone could have done in that situation."

Luca shook his head, his lips curling back in a snarl of self-loathing. "No, I didn't. I should have been stronger, should have fought harder. I should have found a way to save him, to keep him safe. But I failed, and now he's gone, and it's all because of me."

Roman's grip on his shoulder tightened, his fingers digging into Luca's flesh with a fierce, unyielding pressure. "Stop it, Luca. Stop blaming yourself for something that was beyond your control. Rowan made his choice, and he did it out of love, out of a desire to protect you and everyone else he cares about."

Luca's head snapped up, his eyes blazing with a wild, desperate light. "But it should have been me, Roman! It should have been me who made that sacrifice, not him. He's the one who matters, the one who deserves to be safe and happy and loved. I'm just a fucking failure, a pathetic excuse for a mate who couldn't even keep the man he loves from being taken away."

Roman's eyes flashed with a fierce, unyielding determination, his hand moving to grip Luca's chin, forcing him to meet his gaze. "Listen to me, Luca. Rowan loves you, more than anything in this world or the next. He made that sacrifice because he couldn't bear the thought of losing you, of watching you suffer and die while he stood by helpless. And he did it because he knows that you're strong enough to survive this, to keep fighting even when all hope seems lost."

Luca felt a flicker of something stir in his chest at Roman's words, a tiny spark of light in the overwhelming darkness that threatened to consume him. He wanted to believe, wanted to cling to that glimmer of hope like a drowning man to a life raft, but the weight of his guilt and his grief was too heavy, too all-consuming.

"I don't know if I can, Roman," he whispered, his voice barely audible over the howling of the wind and the pounding of his own heart. "I don't know if I have the strength, the courage, to keep going without him by my side."

Roman's smile was soft and sad, his eyes filled with a deep, aching understanding. "You do, Luca. You have more strength and courage than you even realize. And you won't be doing this alone. I'll be with you every step of the way, fighting by your side until we bring Rowan back home where he belongs."

Luca felt a lump rising in his throat, his eyes stinging with sudden, unshed tears. He had always known that Roman was a loyal friend, a fierce and unshakable ally, but to hear him say those words, to know that he would stand by him even in the darkest of moments... it meant more than he could ever express.

"Thank you, Roman," he said, his voice rough with emotion. "I don't know what I would do without you."

Roman grinned, his eyes sparkling with a hint of their old mischief. "Probably get yourself killed within a week, if we're being honest."

Despite himself, Luca felt a small, reluctant smile tugging at the corners of his mouth. "Asshole," he muttered, but there was no heat in his words, only a fond, exasperated affection.

Roman clapped him on the shoulder, his touch warm and solid and grounding. "Come on, Luca. We need to get back to the manor, regroup with the others and figure out our next move."

Luca nodded, his jaw clenching with a renewed sense of determination. Roman was right. They couldn't afford to wallow in their grief and their guilt, not when Rowan needed them, not when the fate of the world hung in the balance.

As they made their way back through the ruined streets of Willowbrook, Luca couldn't help but notice the eerie stillness that had settled over the town. The dark constructs that had swarmed the streets only moments before were gone, vanished like smoke on the wind, as if they had never existed at all.

But Luca knew better than to let his guard down, knew that the danger was far from over. The enemies they faced were cunning and ruthless, and they would stop at nothing to achieve their twisted goals.

"We'll find him, Luca," Roman said, his voice low and fierce as they approached the manor, the once-grand building now battered and scarred from the battle that had raged around it. "We'll bring Rowan back, no matter what it takes."

Luca nodded, his heart heavy but unbroken, his spirit battered but undefeated. He knew that the road ahead would be long and treacherous, filled with dangers and challenges that would test him to his very limits.

But he also knew that he had no choice, that he would fight and bleed and die a thousand times over if it meant saving the man he loved, the mate who held his heart and his soul in the palm of his hand.

As Luca and Roman approached the manor, Luca's heart felt like a lead weight in his chest, each step a monumental effort. The thought of facing the others, of seeing the pain and disappointment in their eyes when they realized that Rowan was gone… it was almost more than he could bear.

But he knew that he had no choice, that he owed it to his friends and his allies to be strong, to keep fighting even in the face of overwhelming grief and despair.

Luca was immediately greeted by the sight of Benjamin rushing towards them, his face alight with excitement and relief.

"Luca, Roman, thank the gods you're alright!" he exclaimed, his arms outstretched as if to embrace them both. "We were so worried, we didn't know what had happened to you out there."

But as he drew closer, as he took in the haunted look in Luca's eyes and the grim set of Roman's jaw, his smile faltered, his brow furrowing with a sudden, sickening realization.

"Where's Rowan?" he asked, his voice barely above a whisper, as if he already knew the answer but couldn't bring himself to say it out loud.

Luca felt his throat tighten, his eyes stinging with the hot press of tears. He opened his mouth to speak, but no words came out, only a choked, broken sound that was halfway between a sob and a growl.

Roman placed a hand on his shoulder, his touch warm and grounding, a silent reminder that he wasn't alone. "Rowan sacrificed himself," he said, his voice low and heavy with emotion. "He gave himself up to save us, to save everyone. And there was nothing we could do to stop him."

A collective gasp went up from the gathered allies, their faces etched with shock and disbelief. Luca could see the pain and the sorrow in their eyes, the unspoken question that hung heavy in the air.

'How could this happen?' their expressions seemed to say. 'How could we have let one of our own be taken, be lost to the darkness that threatened to consume us all?'

"There's something else," Roman continued, his voice cutting through the heavy silence that had fallen over the room. "The enemies we faced out there, Malachite and Lina and Wanda… their powers have grown, far beyond anything we've seen before. And they mentioned the Deal Maker, someone who seems to be pulling the strings behind the scenes."

A ripple of unease went through the gathered allies, their faces growing pale and drawn with worry. Luca could see the fear in their eyes, the unspoken dread of what this new threat might mean for their world, for their very survival.

Peter, one of the newer members of their alliance, stepped forward, his brow furrowed with concern. "The Deal Maker?" he repeated, his voice low and troubled. He trailed off, his expression growing distant and haunted, as if he were remembering something he'd rather forget. "If the Deal Maker is involved in this, if they're the ones behind Malachite and Lina and Wanda's newfound power... then we're in for a fight like none we've ever faced before."

Suddenly, the air in the room began to shimmer and ripple, a pulse of energy that made the hairs on the back of Luca's neck stand up. He whirled around, his claws extending and his fangs bared, ready to face whatever new threat had come to challenge them.

But as the portal stabilized and the figures within began to take shape, Luca felt his heart skip a beat, his breath catching in his throat with a sudden, overwhelming surge of emotion.

For there, standing before him, were three people he had never seen before, but whose faces were as familiar to him as his own reflection. A regal woman with hair the color of spun gold and eyes that glittered like amethysts, flanked by two men who bore a striking resemblance to Rowan, their features sharp and angular and filled with a quiet, undeniable strength.

"Rowan's family," Luca breathed, his voice barely above a whisper as he stared at the newcomers in awe and disbelief. "But how... how did you find us? How did you even know where to look?"

The woman stepped forward, her movements graceful and fluid, her presence seeming to fill the room with a calm, commanding authority. "I am Queen Elara of the Seelie Court," she said, her voice rich and melodious, like the ringing of silver bells. "And these are my sons, Princes Aedan and Kieran."

Luca stared in awe at the regal figures before him, his heart pounding with a mixture of hope and trepidation. The revelation of their identities sent a shockwave through the room, and he could feel the eyes of his allies upon him, waiting for his reaction.

"Queen Elara," he said, his voice rough with emotion as he bowed his head in respect. "I… I don't know what to say."

The Queen's eyes softened, a flicker of understanding and compassion passing over her face. "I know, Luca. And I wish we had come to you sooner, with better news and brighter tidings. But the truth we bring is a heavy one, and it will not be easy to hear."

Luca swallowed hard, his jaw clenching with a stubborn determination. "Whatever it is, we can handle it. We have to, for Rowan's sake."

Roman stepped forward, his massive form dwarfing even the towering figures of the fae princes. He knelt before the Queen, his head bowed in a gesture of humility and respect. "Your Majesty," he said, his voice low and solemn. "Please, if you know anything about the Deal Maker, about who he really is and what he wants with Rowan… we need to know. We can't fight this battle blind."

The Queen nodded, her expression growing somber. "You are right, Roman. And it is time for the truth to be told, no matter how painful it may be."

She took a deep breath, her eyes distant and haunted. "For years, we believed that my husband was alive because he was there in the flesh but things got complicated as soon as Rowan disappeared. We thought that he was just distant because of Rowan but we were wrong. The real Oberon, my beloved mate and the father of my children… he was slain by his own brother, Riordan, shortly after Rowan's birth. He took Rowan's trust when he was a kid and used that to his advantage."

Luca felt like he had been punched in the gut, the air rushing out of his lungs in a sharp, painful gasp. "But why? Why would he do such a thing?"

Aedan stepped forward, his eyes blazing with a fierce, unyielding light. "For power," he said, his voice low and filled with a quiet, simmering anger. "Riordan was always jealous of our father, of the love and devotion he commanded from his people. He wanted that power for himself, and he was willing to do anything to get it."

Kieran nodded, his expression grim. "It was Aedan who first suspected the truth," he said, his voice filled with a quiet pride. "He noticed the changes in our father's behavior, the way he seemed to grow colder and more distant with each passing day. And when we confronted him, when we demanded to know the truth… that's when we learned of Riordan's treachery."

Luca's mind was reeling, his thoughts spinning with the implications of what he was hearing. This Riordan, he was the Deal Maker, the one who held Rowan in his clutches and sought to control the mortal realm.

"But why?" he asked, his voice barely above a whisper. "Why does he want Rowan? Why does he care about the mortal realm at all?"

"Because Rowan poses a threat to him," Aedan replied, his voice heavy with sorrow and concern. "Riordan knows that Rowan is special, that he's the successor to the Seelie Court and a child of two worlds, just like you are a wolf but can also shift into human form. Rowan is so much more than just an ordinary fae and his magic is much more potent. And that kind of power terrifies him. But it also tempts him."

Queen Elara nodded, her voice unwavering. "Riordan seeks to harness Rowan's power for himself, to bend the mortal realm to his will. He wants a weapon, a tool that he could use to expand his control over all Realms. If he succeeds, the consequences would be catastrophic."

The weight of Aedan's revelation hit Luca like a tidal wave, the enormity of the challenge ahead crashing down on him. If Riordan was behind everything, then they were up against an enemy far more powerful and cunning than they had ever imagined.

"What do we do?" Luca asked, his hands clenching at his sides. "How do we stop him?"

"It won't be easy," The Queen warned. "Riordan is powerful, and his dark magic runs deep. But he underestimates the strength of the love and loyalty that binds you and your allies together."

Luca took a deep breath, squaring his shoulders with a newfound determination. The revelation of Riordan's true identity had only served to ignite the fire of his resolve. "The Queen's right. He may be powerful, but he doesn't know the first thing about the strength of the love I have for Rowan or the bonds I share with my friends and allies. That's one thing we have that Riordan will never understand or overpower."

Roman gave Luca an encouraging pat on the back. "Luca's right, guys! We have something that Riordan underestimates; each other. We are a team, a family, and we will never stop fighting for one of our own!"

Peter, the newest member, couldn't help but smile. "Yeah, and with Luca leading us, the Deal Maker's about to learn what it really means to mess with the Wolfheart Pack!"

"We also have the support of the Seelie Court," Kieran added. "We came here to fight alongside you. Rowan is our brother, and we will do whatever it takes to bring him home."

27

Betrayal

Rowan

Rowan stirred, his mind struggling to break free from the hazy veil of unconsciousness that enveloped him. The last fragmented memories of his capture and Luca's anguished cries pierced through the fog, sending a jolt of panic through his body. His eyes snapped open, only to be met with an all-consuming darkness that seemed to stretch endlessly in every direction.

"Luca?" he called out, his voice cracking with desperation. "Where am I? What's going on?"

Silence was his only answer, the deafening absence of sound amplifying the sense of isolation that threatened to overwhelm him. Rowan's heart raced as he tried to make sense of his surroundings, his thoughts consumed with worry for his mate and their loved ones.

"Where's Luca?" Rowan demanded, his voice rising with a growing anger. "If you've hurt him, I swear I'll-"

His words were cut short by a sound that sent a chill down his spine - the slow, deliberate clapping of hands. The echo reverberated through the darkness, each hollow applause a mocking reminder of his helplessness.

"Congratulations Rowan, my son. Finally, you managed to discover the truth," a familiar voice drawled, the words dripping with malice. "You should be proud of yourself."

Rowan froze, his breath catching in his throat as a figure emerged from the shadows. The face that greeted him was one he knew all too well - the face of his father. But something was wrong, a twisted perversion of the man he once loved and admired.

"You... you can't be," Rowan whispered, his voice trembling with disbelief. "But my father... this is not right."

The impostor grinned, a grotesque stretching of lips that held no warmth or affection. "Right? No, Rowan. This is the truth that you've been too naive to see. The truth that I've been trying to show you all along."

Rowan's mind raced, trying to make sense of the situation. He knew he had to be careful, to play along until he could uncover the true nature of this deception.

"Father," he said, forcing a calmness into his voice that he didn't feel. "I don't understand. What truth are you talking about?"

The impostor chuckled, a sound that sent shivers down Rowan's spine. "The truth about who you are, my dear boy. The truth about the power that lies dormant within you."

Rowan shook his head, confusion and anger warring within him. "What power? I don't know what you're talking about."

The impostor tsked, his eyes glinting with a malevolent amusement. "Oh, but you do, Rowan. You've always known, deep down."

Rowan's heart pounded, his mind reeling with the implications of the impostor's words. "No," he whispered, his voice barely audible over the roaring in his ears. "That's not possible. I'm just... I'm just me."

"Oh, you are so much more than that, Rowan," the impostor crooned, his voice sickly sweet. "You are a child of two worlds, fae and undine. You are the key to unlocking a power beyond imagining."

Rowan swallowed hard, his throat suddenly dry and tight. "And what do you want with this power?" he asked, dreading the answer even as he spoke the words.

The impostor's grin widened, a predatory flash of teeth in the darkness. "Why to seize control of the mortal realm of course! And you, my dear boy, will be the instrument of my triumph."

"No!" Rowan's voice rang out, filled with defiance. "I won't help you. I won't be a part of your twisted schemes."

The impostor laughed, a cold, cruel sound that echoed through the darkness. "Oh, but you will, Rowan. You won't have a choice."

Rowan's mind raced as he struggled to comprehend the impostor's words. A cold, sinking feeling settled in the pit of his stomach, a sense of dread that he couldn't shake.

"But why?" he asked, his voice trembling despite his efforts to keep it steady. "Why did you curse me? What could you possibly gain from removing me from the world?"

The impostor's eyes glinted with a malevolent satisfaction, a twisted pleasure in the pain and confusion that played across Rowan's face.

"Oh, my dear boy," he purred, his voice dripping with false sympathy. "Don't you see? You were a threat to my grand design, a potential obstacle in my path to power and dominion."

He began to pace, his form moving through the darkness like a shark through the depths of the ocean.

"I have ambitions, Rowan, ambitions that extend far beyond the petty squabbles of the fae courts. I seek to conquer the mortal plane, to harness its energy and bend it to my will."

Rowan felt a surge of disgust and anger rising within him, a hot, sickening wave of emotion that threatened to overwhelm him.

"You're insane," he spat, his voice shaking with barely contained rage. "The mortal realm is not yours to conquer, not yours to control."

The impostor threw back his head and laughed, a cold, cruel sound that echoed through the darkness.

"Oh, but it will be, Rowan. With the power I will gain, I will create a world steeped in fear and perpetual war, a world where I am the undisputed master of all I survey."

Rowan's patience snapped, his disgust and anger boiling over into a white-hot fury.

"Enough!" he shouted, his voice ringing out with a power and authority that surprised even him. "I don't know who or what you are, but I know one thing for certain. You are not my father."

The impostor's grin widened, a grotesque stretching of lips that held no warmth or affection.

"No," he agreed, his voice filled with a smug, self-satisfied tone. "I am not. Took you long enough."

Rowan's heart raced, his mind reeling as he tried to make sense of the situation.

"Then who are you?" he demanded, his voice shaking with a mix of fear and anger. "Show me your true face, you coward!"

The impostor's form shimmered and shifted, the illusion of Rowan's father melting away to reveal a figure that was at once familiar and utterly alien.

"Uncle Riordan?" Rowan whispered, his voice barely audible over the roaring in his ears.

The figure before him was a twisted mockery of the man he had once known, his features warped and distorted by the dark magic that pulsed through his veins.

"Surprised, nephew?" Riordan asked, his voice filled with a cruel, mocking amusement. "You shouldn't be. After all, who else would have the power and the cunning to orchestrate such a grand deception?"

Rowan's mind raced, trying to make sense of the revelation. Riordan, his father's brother, a man he had once looked up to and admired… now a twisted, malevolent creature of the Unseelie Court.

"My father," he whispered, his voice shaking with dread. "What have you done with him?"

Riordan's cruel smile widened, a sadistic gleam in his eyes as he relished the pain and confusion etched upon Rowan's face.

"Oh, you poor, naive child," he sneered, his voice dripping with mock sympathy. "Did you really believe that the man who raised you, who pretended to love you, was your true father?"

Rowan's heart clenched, a cold, sickening dread settling in the pit of his stomach. "What are you talking about?" he whispered, his voice trembling despite his efforts to keep it steady.

Riordan threw back his head and laughed, a harsh, grating sound that sent shivers down Rowan's spine.

"Your father, the real Oberon, has been gone since the day you were born," he said, his tone filled with a perverse joy. "I killed him, consumed his life force to fuel my own power and ambition. And then, I took his place, wearing his face like a mask as I manipulated you and everyone around you."

Rowan's world spun, the revelation hitting him like a physical blow. His entire life, his entire existence… all of it had been a lie, a cruel deception orchestrated by the monster that stood before him.

"No…" he whispered, his voice barely audible over the roaring in his ears. "No, it can't be true. It can't be…"

But even as the words left his lips, Rowan knew in his heart that they were a lie. He could see the truth in Riordan's eyes, could feel the twisted, malevolent energy that radiated from his very being.

"Why?" he asked, his voice breaking with the weight of his despair. "Why would you do this? Why would you deceive me, deceive everyone, for all these years?"

Riordan's grin widened, a grotesque stretching of lips that held no warmth or affection.

"Power, Rowan. It's always been about power. With your father gone and his form at my command, I could move through the world undetected, manipulating events to suit my own ends. I could gain the trust of those around me, all the while working to further my own dark agenda."

He leaned in close, his breath hot and fetid against Rowan's face.

"And you, my dear nephew… you were the key to it all. The child of prophecy, the one destined to inherit the power of the Seelie Court. With you under my control, with your magic bound to my will… I would be unstoppable, the undisputed master of all I surveyed."

Rowan's heart raced, his mind reeling as he tried to make sense of the twisted, malevolent scheme that Riordan had laid out before him. All his life, he had been nothing more than a pawn, a tool to be used and manipulated in service of his uncle's dark ambitions.

But even as despair threatened to overwhelm him, even as the weight of Riordan's betrayal threatened to crush his very soul… a tiny spark of defiance began to flicker to life within him, a small but unshakable flame that refused to be extinguished.

"You may have killed my father," he whispered, his voice trembling with a mix of grief and rage. "You may have stolen his face and his form. But you will never be him, never possess the love and the light that he brought into this world."

Riordan's eyes flashed with a dark, dangerous light, a look of cruel amusement playing across his twisted features.

"Love? Light?" he scoffed, his voice filled with a mocking disdain. "Such pretty words, Rowan. Such naive, foolish sentiments. In the end, they mean nothing, nothing at all in the face of true power and ambition."

But Rowan was not listening, his focus turned inward as he reached for the well of strength and courage that he could feel burning within him. His father may have been gone, stolen from him by the monster that wore his face… but his spirit, his love, his light… those things could never be extinguished, never be consumed by the darkness that sought to swallow them whole.

"You're wrong, Uncle," he said, his voice filled with a quiet, unshakable conviction. "Love and light… they are everything. They are the very essence of what makes us who we are, the foundation upon which all true power and strength are built."

He lifted his chin, his eyes blazing with a fierce, unyielding determination.

"And I will never stop fighting for them, never stop believing in the goodness and the beauty that they represent. I will find a way to break free of this nightmare, to return to the world and stand against you with every fiber of my being."

Riordan threw back his head and laughed, a cold, mocking sound that echoed through the darkness.

"Such brave words, nephew. Such foolish, empty bravado. But in the end, they will avail you nothing. You are mine now, now and forever. And I will use you, use your power, to bring my grand design to fruition."

Grief and rage warred within him, a storm of emotion that threatened to consume him whole. But beneath it all, a fierce, unyielding determination began to take root, a fire that burned bright and hot in the depths of his soul.

"You…" he whispered, his voice shaking with the force of his emotion. "You monster. You vile, despicable creature. I swear, on my life, on all that I hold dear, that I will stop you."

Riordan threw back his head and laughed, a harsh, grating sound that set Rowan's teeth on edge.

"You? Stop me? Oh, Rowan, you naive little fool. You have no idea of the power I wield, of the forces I command. You are nothing more than a pawn in my game, a piece to be moved and manipulated as I see fit."

But Rowan was not listening, his focus turned inward as he reached for the well of power that he could feel thrumming through his veins. His magic, so long dormant, began to stir and awaken, a tingling, electric sensation that filled him with a sense of strength and purpose.

Rowan reached deep within himself, desperately grasping for the familiar warmth of his magic. He could feel it stirring, a faint glimmer of power that had lain dormant for so long. A tingling sensation began to spread through his body, and for a brief, exhilarating moment, Rowan felt a surge of strength and purpose.

But as he tried to channel his magic, to gather it into a force that could strike back against Riordan, Rowan's elation quickly turned to horror. His power felt strained and weak, as if an invisible force was draining it away, siphoning off his energy like a leech.

"What's happening?" Rowan gasped, his eyes widening in confusion and fear. "Why can't I…?"

Riordan's cruel laughter filled the air, echoing off the unseen walls of the void that surrounded them. "Did you really think it would be that easy? That I would allow you to access your full power here, in this realm of my own making?"

Rowan's heart sank, a cold realization settling in the pit of his stomach. "What have you done to me?" he whispered, his voice trembling with a mix of anger and dread.

Riordan's smile was a twisted, malevolent thing, filled with a perverse delight at Rowan's helplessness. "I've bound your magic, dear nephew. A simple siphoning spell, designed to keep you weak and compliant. After all, we can't have you causing any trouble, can we?"

Rowan's mind raced, desperately searching for a way out, a loophole in Riordan's scheme. "There has to be a way to break it," he said, his voice filled with a stubborn determination. "Every spell has a counter, every curse a cure."

But even as the words left his lips, Rowan could see the truth in Riordan's eyes, could feel the iron-clad certainty of his uncle's power.

"Oh, there is a way, Rowan. But it's not one that you can access on your own." Riordan's voice was a silken purr, filled with a mocking, malevolent amusement. "Only your mate, your beloved Luca, has the power to break the siphon that binds you. And something tells me that he's far too busy fighting for his life and the lives of your pathetic allies to come to your rescue."

Rowan's heart clenched at the mention of Luca, a desperate, aching need to be with his mate overwhelming him. "Luca will come for me," he said, his voice filled with a fierce, unwavering conviction. "He won't rest until he finds me, until he frees me from your twisted games."

Riordan's laughter was a harsh, grating sound, filled with a cruel, mocking disdain. "Oh, I'm sure he will, Rowan. But by the time he does, it will be too late. You'll be nothing more than a shell, a broken husk of the man you once were."

He leaned in close, his breath hot and fetid against Rowan's face. "And do you know why, dear nephew? Because you and your precious mate have not yet fully accepted your bond. You've danced around each other, playing at love and devotion, but you've never truly given yourselves over to the power that lies between you."

Rowan's mind reeled, a sickening sense of realization washing over him. He knew that Riordan was right, that he and Luca had never taken that final step, never fully consummated their bond in the way that fate had intended.

And now, that hesitation, that fear of the unknown, had left him vulnerable, exposed to the machinations of his twisted, malevolent uncle.

"Luca and I…" he whispered, his voice barely audible over the roaring in his ears. "We were waiting for the right moment, the perfect time to…"

"To what?" Riordan sneered, his voice dripping with a cruel, mocking disdain. "To pledge your love, your devotion, your very souls to each other? How touching. How naive."

He straightened up, his eyes flashing with a dark, malevolent light. "But it matters not, Rowan. For now, you are mine. And I have very special plans for you."

He snapped his fingers, and suddenly, the void around them was filled with a swirling, writhing mass of shadow and darkness. Three figures emerged from the maelstrom, their forms twisted and grotesque, their eyes gleaming with a malevolent anticipation.

"Keep watch over him," Riordan commanded, his voice filled with a cold, imperious authority. "Make sure he doesn't try anything foolish. I have work to do, and I can't afford any distractions."

The minions bowed low, their motions jerky and unnatural, like puppets on invisible strings. "Yes, master," they hissed, their voices filled with a sycophantic, groveling obedience.

And then Riordan was gone, disappearing into the shadows as if he had never been there at all, leaving Rowan alone with his twisted, malevolent guardians.

Rowan's mind raced, a desperate, frantic energy coursing through him. He knew that he had to find a way out, a way to warn Luca and their allies of the true nature of the threat they faced. But how could he do that, when his own magic had been stripped away, when he was nothing more than a helpless prisoner in his uncle's twisted game?

"Luca," he whispered, his voice filled with a quiet, aching desperation. "I don't know if you can hear me, if you can feel me through our bond. But I need you, my love. I need you to find me, to save me from this nightmare."

The minions cackled and jeered, their eyes filled with a cruel, mocking delight. "Poor little prince," one of them hissed, its voice like the scraping of nails against stone. "Crying out for his mate, like a lost little lamb bleating for its mother."

But Rowan ignored them, his focus turned inward as he reached for the tiny, flickering spark of hope that still burned within him. He knew that Luca would come for him, that their love was stronger than any darkness, any evil that sought to tear them apart.

28

The Fated Bond

Luca

Luca paced the room, his mind racing with a desperate need to find Rowan, to bring his mate back safe and sound. He couldn't shake the feeling of helplessness that had been growing inside him since the moment Rowan disappeared. It was like a part of his soul had been ripped away, leaving a gaping hole that nothing could fill.

He turned to Queen Elara, his eyes pleading. "Your Majesty, there has to be a way to locate Rowan. I can't just sit here and do nothing while he's out there, trapped and alone."

The Queen's expression softened, a look of understanding and sympathy crossing her face. "I know, Luca. And I promise you, we will do everything in our power to bring my son home."

Luca's mind latched onto an idea, a glimmer of hope in the darkness that had consumed him. "What about our mate bond?" he asked, his voice trembling with a mix of excitement and fear. "Could we use it to find him, to track him down no matter where he is?"

Queen Elara's eyes widened, a flicker of surprise and uncertainty passing over her face. "The mate bond? I… I don't know, Luca. It's never been attempted before, not like this."

But Luca was undeterred, his jaw set with a stubborn determination. "I have to try," he said, his voice filled with a quiet, unwavering conviction. "I can't leave any stone unturned, not when Rowan's life is at stake."

Roman stepped forward, his expression thoughtful as he tapped his chin with one large, clawed finger. "It's a long shot," he said, his voice low and measured. "But it might just work. I've heard stories of ancient magic, spells that could strengthen the bond between mates and allow them to find each other across great distances."

Luca's heart leaped with hope, a burning fire igniting in his chest. "Tell me what I need to do," he said, his voice rough with emotion. "I'll do anything, face any challenge, if it means bringing Rowan back to me."

Roman nodded, a small smile tugging at the corners of his mouth. "Very well," he said, his voice filled with a quiet, solemn authority. "Stand before me, Luca. And focus your thoughts solely on Rowan. Pour every ounce of your love and longing into the bond that connects your hearts and souls."

Luca took a deep breath, his eyes fluttering closed as he let his mind fill with images of his beautiful mate. He thought of Rowan's smile, the way it lit up his entire face and made Luca's heart skip a beat. He remembered the sound of Rowan's laughter, the way it rang out like a melody in the air, filling Luca with a warmth and joy that he had never known before.

He let himself get lost in the memories, in the cherished moments that he and Rowan had shared. He could almost feel the softness of Rowan's skin beneath his fingertips, could almost taste the sweetness of his kiss on his lips.

As Luca poured his heart and soul into the bond, he felt something stirring within him, a fragile but growing connection that seemed to span the distance between them. It was like a gossamer thread, delicate and shimmering, but filled with a power and a purpose that took his breath away.

"That's it," Roman murmured, his voice soft and encouraging. "Keep going, Luca. The magic is taking hold."

Luca's brow furrowed with concentration, his mind delving deeper into the well of his love for Rowan. He pictured their future together, the life they would build side by side. He saw them standing hand in hand, their hearts and souls entwined in a bond that could never be broken.

He imagined lazy mornings spent in bed, their bodies tangled together as they watched the sun rise through the window. He saw them walking through the forest, the dappled sunlight filtering through the leaves and casting a golden glow on their skin.

And he saw them standing before their family and friends, their hands clasped and their eyes filled with love and devotion, as they pledged their lives and their hearts to each other forever.

As Luca lost himself in these visions, in these dreams of a future that he longed for with every fiber of his being, he could feel the bond between them growing stronger, more vibrant and alive with each passing moment.

"It's working," Roman said, his voice filled with a quiet, earnest amazement. "I can feel the connection between you and Rowan, the love that binds you together across any distance."

Luca's heart swelled with hope and joy, a feeling of elation that made him want to laugh and cry all at once. "I knew it," he whispered, his voice choked with emotion. "I knew our love was stronger than any curse, any darkness that tried to keep us apart."

But even as he savored the moment, even as he let himself bask in the warmth and the light of their bond, he couldn't shake the feeling that something was still missing, that their connection was not yet complete.

As if sensing his thoughts, Roman's expression grew serious, his eyes filled with a quiet, solemn intensity. "The spell is complete," he said, his voice low and measured. "Your bond with Rowan is established, a fragile but unbreakable link that will guide you to him no matter where he may be."

Luca's heart leaped with excitement, his mind already racing with plans and possibilities. But before he could speak, Queen Elara stepped forward, her face etched with a deep, aching wisdom.

"But the bond is still raw," she said, her voice soft and filled with a quiet, unwavering certainty. "Unfinished, like a tapestry with threads left dangling. To truly seal your connection, to make it strong enough to withstand any challenge or trial, there is one more step that must be taken."

Luca's brow furrowed with confusion, his mind struggling to make sense of the Queen's cryptic words. "What step?" he asked, his voice tight with a mix of anticipation and fear. "What do I need to do?"

Queen Elara's smile was soft and sad, her eyes filled with a deep, aching love for her son and the man who held his heart. "To fully bond with a fae," she said, her voice low and reverent, "a wedding ceremony must take place in the sacred halls of the Seelie Court. It is a rite of passage, a joining of two souls that can never be undone."

Luca's breath caught in his throat, his heart pounding with a sudden, overwhelming surge of emotion. A wedding ceremony. A chance to pledge his love and devotion to Rowan in front of the entire world, to make their bond official and unbreakable in the eyes of the gods and all who knew them.

It was a dream that he had never dared to voice, a hope that he had kept buried deep within his heart. But now, with the Queen's words ringing in his ears and the power of their bond thrumming through his veins, he knew that it was a dream that could finally become a reality.

"A wedding," he whispered, his voice filled with a quiet, awed reverence. "A chance to make Rowan mine, now and forever."

Queen Elara nodded, her eyes shining with a fierce, unwavering love. "Yes, Luca. A chance to seal your bond and your love in the most sacred and unbreakable of ways."

Luca's heart swelled with a fierce, overwhelming joy, the promise of a future alongside Rowan filling him with a hope and determination that he had never known before. He turned to Roman, his eyes shining with a desperate, eager need for confirmation.

"Did it work?" he asked, his voice trembling with a mix of excitement and fear. "Can we find Rowan now, bring him back to us?"

Roman's smile was small but filled with a quiet, unwavering confidence. "There's only one way to find out," he said, his voice low and filled with a hint of mischief.

With a flourish of his hand, he released the essence of Luca and Rowan's bond into the air, where it hung suspended like a shimmering, ethereal thread. It glowed with an inner light, pulsing and thrumming with the power of their love and connection.

Luca's breath caught in his throat, his eyes widening with awe and wonder as he watched the bond take shape before him. It was like nothing he had ever seen before, a tangible manifestation of the unbreakable tie that bound his heart to Rowan's.

"What is that?" he whispered, his voice filled with a quiet, reverent amazement.

Roman grinned, his eyes sparkling with a hint of pride and satisfaction. "That, my friend, is the key to finding your mate. It's a tracing device, a modern manifestation of the ancient tether that binds your souls together."

He gestured to the glowing thread, which had begun to drift lazily through the air, leaving a shimmering trail in its wake. "All we have to do is follow it, and it will lead us straight to Rowan, no matter where he may be."

Luca's heart leaped with excitement, his mind already racing with the possibilities and the challenges that lay ahead. He knew that they had a long way to go, that they would have to fight and struggle and sacrifice to bring Rowan back and stop Riordan's twisted schemes.

But he also knew that they would face those trials together, hand in hand and heart to heart. Because their love was a force that could not be denied, a power that could overcome any darkness or evil that dared to stand in their way.

"Then what are we waiting for?" he said, his voice filled with a fierce, unwavering determination. "Let's go get our boy back."

Without another word, he set off after the glowing thread, his steps quick and purposeful as he followed the shimmering trail through the winding halls of the castle. The others fell into step behind him, their faces set with the same grim determination and the same fierce, unyielding love.

As they walked, Luca couldn't help but marvel at the strange and wondrous world that Rowan had come from, at the beauty and the magic that seemed to suffuse every corner of the fae realm. He had always known that his mate was special, that he was a creature of light and wonder and mystery.

But seeing it firsthand, walking in the footsteps of the ancient fae and feeling the power of their magic thrumming through the very air around him... it was almost more than he could comprehend, more than he could ever have imagined in his wildest dreams.

And yet, even in the midst of all this beauty and wonder, Luca's thoughts were never far from Rowan, from the man who held his heart and his soul in the palm of his hand. He could feel their bond growing stronger with every step he took, could feel the love and the longing that pulsed between them like a living, breathing thing.

"Hold on, baby," he whispered, his voice soft and filled with a quiet, aching desperation. "I'm coming for you. Just hold on a little longer."

As they followed the trail deeper into the woods, Luca felt a growing sense of unease, a prickling at the back of his neck that made him feel like they were being watched. He scanned the trees around them, his eyes searching for any sign of danger or threat.

But there was nothing, only the rustling of leaves in the wind and the soft, muted sounds of the forest around them. And yet, he couldn't shake the feeling that something was off, that they were walking into a trap of some kind.

Suddenly, Rowan's mother stopped, her eyes widening with a sudden, dawning realization. "Wait," she said, her voice low and urgent. "Something's not right. I can feel it, a concealing force at work."

Luca's heart clenched with fear and dread, his mind racing with the possibilities of what that might mean. But before he could say anything, Queen Elara raised her hand, her eyes flashing with a fierce, unwavering determination.

With a wave of her hand, she cast a powerful spell, her magic pulsing and thrumming through the air like a living, breathing thing. The clearing around them began to glow with a brilliant blue light, the trees and the grass and the very earth itself seeming to shimmer and ripple like the surface of a pond.

And then, as quickly as it had begun, the light faded, and Luca's breath caught in his throat at the sight that greeted them. There, rising from the depths of the earth like a great, slumbering beast, was a castle, its walls gleaming in the sunlight like polished ivory.

It was a sight that took Luca's breath away, a testament to the power and the beauty of the fae realm. And yet, even as he stared at the magnificent structure before him, he couldn't shake the feeling of dread that had settled in the pit of his stomach, the sense that they were walking into a trap of some kind.

"Rowan's in there," he said, his voice low and filled with a quiet, unwavering determination. "I can feel it, like a pull in my chest that won't let go."

Queen Elara nodded, her expression grim but filled with a fierce, unyielding love. "He is," she said, her voice soft but filled with a quiet, unwavering conviction. "And we're going to get him back, no matter what it takes."

Luca's heart swelled with gratitude and love, a fierce, overwhelming emotion that made him want to laugh and cry all at once. He had always known that he was lucky, that he had been blessed with a family and a pack that would stand by his side through even the darkest of times.

But to hear the Queen say those words, to feel the strength of her conviction and her love for her son and the man who held his heart… it was a gift beyond measure, a balm to the aching wound that had festered in his heart for so long.

"Riordan won't give up his prize so easily," Roman warned, his brow furrowed with concern. "He'll have traps and tricks set up every step of the way."

Luca nodded, his jaw set with a stubborn determination. "He's kept Rowan from me long enough. I don't care what obstacles he puts in our path. I'll tear them all down with my bare hands if I have to."

Aedan and Kieran exchanged a look, a silent conversation passing between them in an instant. "Count us in," Kieran said, a small smile playing at the corner of his lips. "We're not going to let our little brother face this alone."

Luca felt a rush of warmth and affection for Rowan's siblings, a sense of camaraderie and unity that filled him with a quiet, unwavering strength. "Thank you," he said, his voice rough with emotion. "Thank you for being here, for standing with us."

Kieran grinned, his eyes sparkling with a hint of mischief. "Hey, what's family for?" he said, his voice light and teasing. "Besides, I've been itching to give that Riordan a piece of my mind. He's long overdue for a good ass-kicking."

Despite the gravity of the situation, Luca couldn't help but chuckle, a small, fleeting moment of levity in the midst of the darkness that surrounded them. "I'll be sure to save a piece for you," he said, his voice dry and filled with a hint of amusement.

And then, with a final, determined nod, they set off towards the castle, their steps quick and purposeful as they made their way up the winding path that led to the great, arched entrance. Luca could feel his heart pounding in his chest, his blood singing with the thrill of the hunt and the fierce, unyielding love that drove him onwards.

As they crossed the threshold, Luca's heart nearly stopped at the scene that greeted them. The castle was in utter chaos, a maelstrom of dark magic and fierce battle that seemed to consume every inch of the once-grand halls.

Shadow creatures, born of the same malevolent power that had stolen Rowan away, swarmed the corridors like a plague, their inky forms twisting and writhing with a hunger that knew no bounds. And there, in the midst of it all, were Malachite and Lina, their faces contorted with a hatred and a madness that made Luca's blood run cold.

"Fuck," he breathed, his eyes wide with horror and disbelief. "This is bad, guys. Really bad."

Roman nodded, his expression grim as he surveyed the carnage before them. "Riordan's been busy," he said, his voice low and filled with a quiet, simmering anger. "He's not just content with taking Rowan anymore. He wants to destroy everything and everyone that stands in his way."

Luca's heart clenched at the thought, a sickening sense of dread washing over him. He knew that Riordan was powerful, that he had the ability to manipulate and control the very fabric of reality itself. But to see the extent of his cruelty, the depths of his depravity laid bare before them… it was almost more than he could bear.

And yet, even in the midst of the chaos and the destruction, there was a glimmer of hope, a flicker of light that refused to be extinguished. For there, fighting alongside the shadow creatures and the twisted mages, were the fae, their armor gleaming and their weapons flashing as they clashed with the forces of darkness.

"The fae army," Queen Elara breathed, her eyes wide with wonder and pride. "They've come to defend their prince, to fight for the light and the love that Riordan seeks to destroy."

Luca felt a surge of gratitude and awe wash over him, a fierce, overwhelming love for the brave and loyal warriors who had come to stand by their side. He knew that they were risking everything, that they were putting their very lives on the line to protect Rowan and the future that he and Luca had dreamed of building together.

But he also knew that they didn't have time to dwell on the sacrifices that were being made, on the blood that was being spilled in the name of their love. Because somewhere in the depths of this castle, Rowan was waiting for him, trapped and helpless and in desperate need of his help.

"We have to find Rowan," he said, his voice rough and urgent as he turned to Roman. "Can you sense him, feel his presence in this place?"

Roman closed his eyes, his brow furrowing with concentration as he reached out with his senses, seeking the familiar pulse of Rowan's magic in the chaos that surrounded them. For a long, tense moment, there was nothing, only the clashing of steel and the cries of the wounded and the dying.

But then, just as Luca was about to give in to despair, Roman's eyes flew open, a triumphant grin spreading across his face. "I've got him," he said, his voice filled with a fierce, unwavering confidence. "He's deep in the castle, down in the dungeons where the dark magic is strongest."

Luca's heart leaped with relief and determination, a fire igniting in his veins as he turned to the others. "Then that's where we're going," he said, his voice filled with a stubborn, unyielding resolve. "We're not leaving this place without Rowan, no matter what it takes."

And with that, he shifted into his wolf form, his body rippling and changing as he let the primal, animalistic power of his nature take over. He could feel the strength and the speed of the wolf flowing through him, could feel the sharpness of his claws and the power of his jaws as he raced down the winding corridors of the castle.

The others followed close behind, their own magic and skills brought to bear as they battled their way through the hordes of shadow creatures that sought to bar their way. Roman's fire magic blazed like a beacon in the darkness, incinerating the monsters with a heat and a fury that was almost palpable. Queen Elara's fae magic shimmered and danced, creating barriers and shields that protected them from the worst of the onslaught.

But it was Luca who led the charge, his wolf form a blur of speed and power as he tore through the ranks of the enemy like a hot knife through butter. He could feel Rowan's presence growing stronger with every step he took, could feel the pull of their bond guiding him onwards like a lodestone.

At last, they reached a dark and foreboding door, the wood scarred and pitted with the marks of countless battles. Luca shifted back into his human form, his chest heaving with exertion and his heart pounding with a desperate, aching need.

"He's in there," he said, his voice raw and choked with emotion. "I can feel him, sense his presence like a physical ache in my chest."

With a fierce, desperate cry, he summoned all his strength and charged forward, his shoulder slamming into the door with a force that sent splinters flying in every direction. The wood buckled and groaned under the impact, but held fast, refusing to yield.

Luca growled with frustration and fear, his mind racing with the knowledge that every second they wasted out here was another second that Rowan was suffering, another chance for Riordan to steal him away forever.

But before he could try again, Roman stepped forward, his eyes flashing with a determined fire. "Allow me," he said, his voice low and filled with a quiet, simmering rage.

He closed his eyes, his hands weaving in a complex pattern as he called forth the very essence of his magic, the raw, elemental power of the dragon that dwelled within him. The air around him began to shimmer and warp, the temperature rising to an almost unbearable degree.

And then, with a roar that shook the very foundations of the castle, Roman unleashed his magic, a blast of pure, white-hot flame that slammed into the door with the force of a thousand suns. The wood disintegrated instantly, reduced to nothing more than ash and smoke in the face of such overwhelming power.

Luca didn't hesitate, didn't stop to marvel at the incredible display of magic that he had just witnessed. He charged forward, his heart in his throat as he burst into the room beyond, his eyes frantically searching for any sign of his mate.

And there, lying on a cold, stone altar, was Rowan, his face pale and still and his breathing shallow and labored. The air around him was thick with the tang of dark magic, a cloying, oppressive force that made Luca's skin crawl and his stomach churn.

"Rowan," he breathed, his voice barely more than a whisper as he raced to his mate's side, his hands trembling as he reached out to touch the cool, clammy skin of his face. "Baby, I'm here. I'm here, and I'm going to get you out of this, I swear it."

But before he could even begin to process the horror of what he was seeing, before he could start to formulate a plan to break the curse and save his mate, a chilling laugh filled the air, a sound that made Luca's blood run cold and his heart seize with dread.

"Well, well, well," a voice drawled, the words dripping with malice and contempt. "What have we here? A lovesick wolf, come to save his precious mate?"

Luca spun around, his eyes widening with shock and horror as he took in the figure that had materialized out of the shadows like a specter of death and decay. It was Riordan, his face twisted into a grotesque mask of cruelty and malevolence, his eyes glittering with a sick, perverse delight.

"You," Luca growled, his voice low and filled with a hatred that burned like a physical fire in his veins. "What have you done to him? What have you done to my mate?"

Riordan laughed, a cold, mocking sound that echoed off the walls of the chamber like the tolling of a funeral bell. "Oh, nothing much," he said, his voice filled with a false, sickening sweetness. "Just a little spell, a little curse to keep him nice and docile while I siphon away his magic, his very life force."

He grinned, a cruel, twisted expression that made Luca's stomach turn with revulsion. "And you, my dear wolf, are powerless to stop it. Powerless to save him from the fate that I have planned for him."

Luca's heart clenched with a sickening sense of despair, a over-whelming feeling of helplessness and hopelessness that threatened to bring him to his knees. He looked down at Rowan's still, silent form, at the man he loved more than life itself, and felt a rage and a determination build within him like a physical force.

"No," he said, his voice low and filled with a conviction that burned like a fire in his soul. "You're wrong, Riordan. You're wrong about everything."

He straightened up, his eyes flashing with a fierce, unyielding light as he met the man's gaze with a defiance and a strength that he had never known before. "I am not powerless," he said, his voice ringing out like a clarion call in the stillness of the chamber. "I have the strength of my love for Rowan, the unbreakable bond that we share. And that is a power that you can never take away, never destroy."

With a fierce, primal growl, Luca shifted back into his wolf form, his body rippling and changing as he let the animal within him take control. He could feel the power of his love for Rowan flowing through him, a white-hot flame that burned away the fear and the doubt and the despair that had threatened to consume him.

He lunged at Riordan, his teeth bared and his claws flashing as he sought to tear the man apart, to destroy the evil that had dared to threaten the one he loved most in all the world. The two of them crashed together in a whirlwind of fur and fangs and magic, a desperate, brutal struggle for dominance and control.

Luca could feel Riordan's dark magic battering at him, seeking to overwhelm him and crush his will. But he refused to yield, refused to give in to the despair and the hopelessness that the man sought to plant in his heart.

29

Awakened

Rowan

Rowan lay on the cold, hard floor, his body feeling like a lead weight, drained of all energy and strength. The sounds of battle raged around him, a cacophony of snarls, growls, and the clash of magic against magic. Despite the chaos, he could sense Luca's presence, a warm, comforting beacon in the darkness that threatened to consume him.

"Luca," he whispered, his voice barely audible even to his own ears. "I'm here, my love. I'm here."

With a herculean effort, Rowan struggled to open his eyes, his lids feeling like they were weighed down with stones. As his vision slowly came into focus, he caught a glimpse of Luca in his wolf form, a magnificent silver beast locked in a deadly dance with Riordan.

Pride and love swelled in Rowan's chest as he watched his mate fight with a fierce determination, his powerful jaws snapping and his claws tearing at the malevolent figure that had caused them so much pain.

With a grunt of effort, Rowan tried to push himself up, his arms trembling with the strain. "Come on, body," he muttered, his teeth gritted with determination. "Work with me here. Luca needs me."

But his limbs refused to cooperate, his muscles feeling like they were made of jelly. Tears of frustration and despair pricked at the corners of his eyes, and he blinked them away angrily.

"Luca!" he called out, his voice cracking with emotion.

For a brief moment, Luca's wolf form turned towards him, his eyes meeting Rowan's with a flash of recognition and love. Rowan felt his heart swell with hope and relief, the connection between them flaring to life like a flame in the darkness.

But then, Riordan saw his opportunity. With a cruel smirk twisting his lips, he unleashed a blast of dark magic straight at Luca's exposed flank. The sound of the impact was like a thunderclap, and Rowan watched in horror as his mate's wolf form was sent flying through the air, crashing into a nearby wall with a sickening thud.

"No!" Rowan screamed, his voice raw and ragged with anguish. "Luca, no!"

Riordan's cold, malevolent laughter filled the air, a sound that made Rowan's blood run cold. "Foolish wolf," he sneered, his eyes glittering with a sadistic glee. "Did you really think you could defeat me? I am the master of darkness, the lord of all that is evil and corrupt. And now, I will destroy you and your precious mate, and claim my rightful place as the ruler of this world."

Rowan felt hot tears streaming down his face, a raw, desperate anguish tearing at his heart. He couldn't bear the thought of losing Luca, of watching helplessly as his mate was destroyed by the evil that threatened to consume them all.

"Luca!" he screamed, his voice raw and ragged with emotion.

In that instant, the world around him seemed to dissolve, the sounds of battle fading into a distant echo as a blinding white light engulfed him. Rowan felt a strange, weightless sensation, as if he were floating in a realm beyond the physical plane.

"What's happening?" he whispered, his voice trembling with fear and confusion. "Where am I?"

He spun around, his eyes searching desperately for any sign of Luca, for any hint of the familiar and the beloved. But there was nothing, only an endless expanse of white that stretched out in every direction.

"Luca!" he called out, his voice echoing in the vast, empty space. "Please, I need to get back to him! I need to save him!"

Tears continued to stream down his face, his heart aching with a desperate, all-consuming need to be by his mate's side. He couldn't lose Luca, not now, not after everything they had been through together.

As if in answer to his prayers, a figure emerged from the light, a woman whose skin shimmered like glass and whose long hair flowed in an unseen breeze. Rowan's eyes widened, his breath catching in his throat as he took in the otherworldly beauty of the stranger.

"Who are you?" he asked, his voice hushed with awe and wonder.

The woman smiled, her eyes filled with an ancient wisdom that seemed to reach into the very depths of Rowan's soul. "I am the guardian of this realm," she said, her voice soft and melodic, like the whispering of wind through the trees. "And I have been watching you, Rowan Elderwood, prince of the Seelie Court and mate to Luca Wolfheart."

Rowan's heart leaped at the mention of his mate's name, a fierce, desperate hope rising up within him. "Please," he begged, his voice raw with emotion. "Please, I need to get back to Luca. He needs me. I can't let him face this evil alone."

The guardian's expression softened, a look of gentle understanding crossing her face. "I know, young prince," she said, her voice filled with compassion. "Your love for your mate is strong, a bond that transcends the boundaries of time and space."

She stepped closer, her hand reaching out to brush a stray lock of hair from Rowan's forehead. "But before you can fulfill your destiny and save Luca, you must first accept yourself for who you truly are. You must awaken the true potential that lies dormant within you."

Rowan frowned, his brow furrowing with confusion. "I don't understand," he said, his voice hesitant and unsure. "What do you mean, accept myself? What potential are you talking about?"

The guardian smiled, a mysterious, enigmatic expression that made Rowan's heart race with a strange, inexplicable anticipation. "You are more than just a fae prince, Rowan," she said, her voice filled with a quiet, unwavering certainty. "You are a child of two worlds, a being of immense power and potential."

She waved her hand, and suddenly, images began to appear in the air around them, memories and visions that Rowan had never seen before. He saw himself as a child, playing in the gardens of the Seelie Court, his laughter ringing out like a bell in the warm, golden light.

He saw his mother, her face filled with love and pride as she watched him grow and learn, as she nurtured the spark of magic that glowed within him. And he saw his father, strong and wise and kind.

But there was more, other memories that seemed to flicker and dance just beyond the edge of his understanding. He saw himself standing on a rocky shore, the waves crashing against his feet as he stared out at the vast, endless expanse of the sea.

He saw himself diving beneath the surface, his body moving with a grace and fluidity that seemed almost inhuman. And he saw himself rising from the depths, his skin shimmering with a strange, otherworldly light, as if he were made of the very water itself.

"What does it mean?" he whispered, his voice filled with a quiet, awed wonder.

The guardian's smile widened, a look of gentle encouragement crossing her face. "It means that you are more than just a fae, Rowan," she said, her voice filled with a quiet, unwavering conviction. "You are also a child of the sea, a being of water and air and wind and fire.

And it is time for you to embrace that heritage, to awaken the true power that lies within you."

Rowan's heart raced, a strange, exhilarating sense of possibility and destiny washing over him. He had always known that he was different, that there was something within him that set him apart from the other fae.

But to hear it spoken aloud, to see the truth of his own nature laid bare before him… it was almost more than he could comprehend, more than he could ever have imagined.

"What must I do?" he asked, his voice trembling with a mix of fear and determination. "How can I awaken this power within me?"

The guardian's expression grew serious, a look of quiet, solemn intensity crossing her face. "You must trust in yourself, Rowan," she said, her voice filled with a quiet, unwavering conviction. "You must let go of your doubts and your fears, and embrace the truth of who you are."

She reached out, her hand resting gently on Rowan's chest, just above his heart. "Close your eyes," she murmured, her voice soft and soothing. "And feel the power that flows within you, the ancient magic that is your birthright."

Rowan's eyes fluttered closed, his breath catching in his throat as he focused on the steady beat of his own heart. At first, there was nothing, only the familiar rhythm of his own pulse and the soft, distant sound of the guardian's voice.

But then, slowly, he began to feel it, a strange, tingling sensation that seemed to spread out from his chest and into every corner of his being. It was like a fire, a glowing ember that had been smoldering within him all his life, waiting for the moment when it could burst into flame.

"That's it," the guardian whispered, her voice filled with a quiet, encouraging pride. "Let it fill you, Rowan. Let it become a part of you."

Rowan felt the power growing stronger, a swirling, pulsing energy that seemed to dance and crackle beneath his skin. It was like nothing he had ever felt before, a raw, primal force that made him feel alive in a way he had never known.

And with each passing moment, he could feel himself changing, his body and his mind and his very soul becoming something new and different and wonderful. It was as if he were being reborn, his true self emerging from the cocoon of his old life like a butterfly from its chrysalis.

Rowan's eyes snapped open, the ethereal realm dissolving around him as he found himself once again in the midst of the chaotic battle. The air crackled with energy, the clashing of magic against magic creating a dizzying display of light and color.

His gaze swept across the room, taking in the sight of his loved ones fighting with every ounce of their strength. His mother and siblings, their faces etched with determination and exhaustion, stood side by side, their powers intertwined as they fought to hold back Riordan's dark onslaught.

"Mom, Aedan, Kieran!" Rowan called out, his voice rising above the din of battle.

Their eyes widened, a flicker of relief and joy flashing across their faces as they caught sight of him. But there was no time for reunions, no moment to spare for heartfelt embraces or words of love.

Because Riordan was still there, his dark magic swirling around him like a living, breathing thing. His eyes burned with a malevolent fire, a twisted grin spreading across his face as he caught sight of Rowan.

"Well, well, well," he sneered, his voice dripping with malice and contempt. "Look who's decided to join the party. The little fae prince, back from his little nap."

Rowan felt a surge of anger and defiance wash over him, his hands clenching into fists at his sides. He stepped forward, his chin lifted and his eyes blazing with a fierce, unyielding light.

"Enough, Riordan," he said, his voice ringing out like a clarion call across the battlefield. "This ends now. You will never again bring harm to those I love, to those who fight for light and love and all that is good in this world."

Riordan threw back his head and laughed, a cold, mocking sound that sent shivers down Rowan's spine. "And who's going to stop me, little prince? You? With your pretty words and your flimsy magic?"

But Rowan was not listening, his focus turned inward as he reached for the well of power that he could feel thrumming through his veins. It was like a symphony, a crescendo of elemental forces that sang in his blood and his bones and his very soul.

He closed his eyes, his breath coming in deep, steady pulls as he let the power wash over him, filling him with a strength and a clarity that he had never known before. When he opened his eyes again, they were glowing with an otherworldly light, a swirling vortex of blue and green and gold that seemed to hold the very essence of the world itself.

"You have no idea what I am capable of, Riordan," Rowan said, his voice low and thrumming with power. "But you're about to find out."

With a gesture of his hand, Rowan unleashed a blast of pure, elemental energy, a swirling maelstrom of wind and water and fire that slammed into Riordan with the force of a thousand hurricanes. The dark mage staggered back, his eyes widening with shock and disbelief as he struggled to hold his ground against the onslaught.

But Rowan was relentless, his attacks coming faster and harder with each passing moment. He could feel the elements bending to his will, could feel the very fabric of reality shifting and warping around him as he poured every ounce of his newfound power into the battle.

The air crackled with electricity, the ground shaking beneath their feet as Rowan and Riordan clashed again and again, their magic intertwining in a deadly dance of light and shadow. Rowan's body was alive with sensation, every nerve and synapse firing with an intensity that bordered on painful.

He could feel the wind whipping through his hair, the water flowing through his veins, the fire burning in his heart. It was exhilarating, terrifying, a rush of power and adrenaline that made him feel invincible, untouchable.

But even as he reveled in the thrill of the battle, even as he let himself get lost in the heady rush of his own magic, Rowan never lost sight of what was truly important. His family, his friends, his mate… they were the reason he fought, the reason he would never give up or give in, no matter how hard the struggle might become.

And so he pressed on, his attacks growing more focused, more precise with each passing moment. He could see the strain on Riordan's face, could sense the dark mage's power beginning to falter and fade under the relentless onslaught of Rowan's elemental might.

But even as victory seemed within his grasp, even as he dared to hope that the battle might finally be won, Riordan rallied, his eyes flashing with a desperate, manic light. With a roar of fury and defiance, he unleashed a final, devastating blast of dark magic, a seething, writhing mass of shadows and corruption that barreled towards Rowan with terrifying speed.

Rowan braced himself, his teeth gritted and his muscles tensed as he prepared to meet the attack head-on. But before he could unleash his own counterstrike, a blur of silver and gold flashed in front of him, a lithe, powerful form that seemed to materialize out of thin air.

It was Luca, his mate, his love, his everything. The wolf shifter stood tall and proud, his body positioned between Rowan and the oncoming attack, his eyes blazing with a fierce, protective light.

"I won't let you hurt him," Luca growled, his voice low and menacing as he glared at Riordan with unmitigated hatred. "Not now, not ever."

With a roar of challenge, Luca leaped forward, his body shifting and changing in midair as he let the wolf within him take over. He landed on all fours, his teeth bared and his hackles raised as he launched himself at Riordan with a fury and a savagery that took Rowan's breath away.

The two titans clashed, dark magic against raw, primal power, in a battle that shook the very foundations of the castle. Rowan watched in awe and terror, his heart in his throat as he saw his mate fighting with every ounce of strength and determination he possessed.

But even as Luca fought, even as he poured every last drop of his own power into the battle, Rowan could see that he was weakening, that the wounds he had sustained earlier were beginning to take their toll. His movements grew slower, more labored, his breathing coming in ragged gasps as he struggled to hold his ground against Riordan's relentless onslaught.

"Luca!" Rowan cried out, his voice raw and desperate as he watched his mate falter, watched him stumble and fall to one knee. "Hold on, my love! I'm coming!"

With a burst of speed and agility, Rowan raced forward, his own magic flaring to life around him as he threw himself into the fray. He could feel the elements responding to his call, could feel the wind and the water and the fire rising up to aid him as he landed blow after blow against Riordan's weakening defenses.

Together, he and Luca fought, their powers and their spirits intertwined in a bond that was unbreakable, unstoppable. They moved as one, anticipating each other's every move, each other's every thought, as they pushed Riordan back, step by step and inch by inch.

And then, with a final, desperate roar of fury and defiance, Riordan unleashed a blast of dark magic that sent Luca flying backwards, his body slamming against the far wall with a sickening crack. Rowan felt his heart seize in his chest, a scream of horror and despair tearing from his throat as he watched his mate crumple to the ground, unmoving and still.

"No!" he howled, his voice raw and ragged with grief and rage. "Luca, no!"

He turned to Riordan, his eyes blazing with a fire that seemed to consume him from the inside out. "You," he snarled, his voice low and deadly. "You will pay for what you've done, for all the pain and suffering you've caused."

Riordan laughed, a cold, mocking sound that only fueled the inferno of Rowan's rage. "And who's going to make me pay, little prince?" he sneered, his eyes glinting with malevolent glee. "You? With your pitiful magic and your weak, broken mate?"

Rowan felt something snap inside him, a dam bursting open as a flood of raw, primal power surged through his veins. He closed his eyes, his breath coming in deep, shuddering gasps as he reached deep within himself, tapping into a well of strength and determination that he had never known existed.

And then, with a scream of rage and agony and love, he unleashed everything he had, a maelstrom of elemental fury that tore through the air like a thousand lightning bolts. It slammed into Riordan with the force of a thousand tsunamis, the dark mage's body convulsing and spasming as the raw, unfiltered power of the elements ripped through him like a hot knife through butter.

For a long, tense moment, there was nothing but the sound of Rowan's labored breathing and the crackling of residual magic in the air. And then, with a final, shuddering gasp, Riordan crumpled to the ground, his body broken and battered and barely clinging to life.

"This isn't over," he hissed, his voice weak and thready as he glared up at Rowan with eyes full of hatred and malice. "I will return, and I will finish what I started. You and your precious mate, and all those you hold dear… I will destroy you all."

And then he was gone, his body disappearing in a swirl of shadows and dark magic, leaving nothing but an empty, echoing silence in his wake.

Rowan didn't hesitate, didn't stop to savor his victory or catch his breath. He raced to Luca's side, his heart in his throat as he gathered his mate into his arms, cradling him close as he searched desperately for any sign of life, any hint of the spark and the fire that had always burned so brightly within him.

"Luca," he whispered, his voice choked with tears and desperation. "Luca, please. Please wake up. Please come back to me."

He could feel his own magic pulsing and throbbing within him, could feel the elements responding to his silent plea as he poured every ounce of his love and his hope and his faith into the still, silent form of his mate.

And then, just as he was about to give in to despair, just as he was about to let the darkness consume him once and for all, he felt a flicker of life, a faint, thready pulse that grew stronger with each passing moment.

"Rowan," Luca murmured, his voice weak and hoarse as his eyelids fluttered open, his gaze locking onto Rowan's with a love and a devotion that stole the breath from his lungs. "You saved me. You saved us all."

Rowan felt a sob of relief and joy tear from his throat, his arms tightening around Luca as he buried his face in the crook of his mate's neck, breathing in the scent of him like a drowning man gulping down air.

"I thought I'd lost you," he whispered, his voice muffled against Luca's skin. "I thought… I thought…"

But Luca just shook his head, a small, tired smile tugging at the corners of his lips. "You could never lose me, Rowan," he murmured, his hand coming up to stroke the soft, silken strands of Rowan's hair. "I will always be here, always be yours. No matter what."

30

New Beginnings

Luca

Luca's eyes fluttered open, the first rays of sunlight filtering through the curtains and casting a warm, golden glow over the room. For a moment, he simply lay there, his mind still hazy with the remnants of sleep, his body aching with the dull, persistent throb of healing wounds.

But then, as his gaze drifted to the side, all thoughts of pain and discomfort vanished, replaced by a rush of love and contentment so strong that it stole the breath from his lungs.

There, lying beside him, was Rowan, his mate, his love, his everything. The fae prince's face was peaceful in slumber, his long lashes casting delicate shadows against his cheeks, his lips parted slightly as he breathed in and out in a slow, steady rhythm.

Luca felt his heart swell with emotion, a lump rising in his throat as he drank in the sight of his beloved. It had been two days since the attack at Willowbrook, two days since they had faced down the forces of darkness and emerged victorious, if not unscathed.

But even now, with the memories of that terrible battle still fresh in his mind, Luca couldn't help but feel a sense of gratitude and wonder, a deep and abiding thankfulness for the precious moments he and Rowan shared.

Unable to resist the urge to express his affection, Luca leaned in, his lips brushing against Rowan's in a gentle, feather-light kiss. "Good morning, my love," he whispered, his voice rough with sleep and emotion.

Rowan stirred, his eyelids fluttering open to reveal those stunning violet eyes that never failed to take Luca's breath away. A sleepy smile tugged at the corners of his mouth, his hand coming up to cup Luca's cheek in a tender caress.

"Mmm, good morning to you too," he murmured, his voice soft and warm with affection. "I could get used to waking up like this every day."

Luca felt a grin tugging at his own lips, a playful spark kindling in his chest. "Oh, really?" he teased, his fingers dancing along Rowan's side in a mischievous tickle. "Even if I do this?"

Rowan let out a yelp of laughter, his body squirming and wriggling as he tried to escape Luca's relentless attack. "Luca!" he gasped, his eyes sparkling with mirth and joy. "Stop it, you brute!"

But Luca was merciless, his own laughter mingling with Rowan's as he continued his playful assault. The sound of their shared joy filled the room, chasing away the lingering shadows of the past few days and replacing them with a warmth and light that seemed to suffuse every corner of their little haven.

Finally, breathless and giddy, Luca relented, his arms wrapping around Rowan's waist and pulling him close. He buried his face in the crook of his mate's neck, breathing in the sweet, familiar scent of him.

"I love you," he whispered, his voice muffled against Rowan's skin. "I love you so much, Rowan. I don't know what I would do without you."

Rowan's arms tightened around him, his hand coming up to stroke the short, silky strands of Luca's hair. "I love you too, Luca," he murmured, his voice soft and filled with a quiet, unwavering conviction. "More than anything in this world or the next."

They lay like that for a long moment, their bodies entwined and their hearts beating in perfect sync. Luca could feel the steady thrum of Rowan's pulse against his own, could feel the warmth and strength of his mate's embrace seeping into his very bones.

But even as he savored the peaceful, perfect moment, Luca couldn't ignore the nagging sense of unease that lurked at the back of his mind, the knowledge that their battle was far from over.

"Now, what do you say we get up and face the day? I don't know about you, but I'm starving."

Luca chuckled, the somber mood broken by Rowan's playful, irreverent tone. "You're always starving," he teased, his own lips twitching with a hint of a smirk. "But yeah, let's get some food in you before you waste away to nothing."

Together, they rose from the bed, their movements perfectly synchronized as they went about their morning routine. Luca couldn't help but marvel at the easy, natural way they moved around each other, the way they seemed to anticipate each other's needs and desires without even having to speak.

It was a testament to the strength of their bond, to the depth of the love and understanding that flowed between them like a never-ending river.

As they stepped into the shower, the hot water cascading over their bodies and washing away the last lingering traces of sleep and fatigue, Luca felt a sense of peace and contentment settle over him, a feeling of rightness and belonging that he had never known before.

Here, in this moment, with Rowan by his side and the promise of a future together stretching out before them like an endless, shining road, he knew that he was exactly where he was meant to be, doing exactly what he was meant to do.

As Luca and Rowan entered the kitchen, their laughter and playful banter filling the air, Luca stopped short, his eyes widening in surprise at the sight that greeted him. There, sitting at the table and engaged in warm, animated conversation, were his mother and Rowan's mother, Queen Elara.

"Mom?" he said, his voice filled with a mix of confusion and delight. "What are you doing here? And with Queen Elara, no less?"

His mother looked up, her eyes sparkling with joy and affection as she rose from her seat to pull him into a tight, fierce hug. "Oh, Luca," she murmured, her voice soft and filled with emotion. "Can't a mother come and visit her son and his mate without an ulterior motive?"

Luca chuckled, his arms tightening around his mother's waist as he breathed in the familiar, comforting scent of her. "Of course," he said, his voice muffled against her shoulder. "But it's not every day that I find you chatting with the Queen of the Seelie Court like you're old friends."

His mother pulled back, her hands coming up to cup his face as she gazed at him with a look of pure, unbridled love. "Well, we have a lot in common, Elara and I," she said, her voice filled with a quiet, knowing amusement. "We're both mothers who love our sons more than anything in this world or the next."

Luca felt his heart swell with emotion, a lump rising in his throat as he saw the truth of his mother's words shining in her eyes. He had always known that she loved him, that she would do anything to protect him and keep him safe. But to hear her say it out loud, to feel the depth of her devotion and care... it was almost more than he could bear.

Beside him, Rowan let out a delighted cry, his face lighting up with joy as he caught sight of his own mother. "Mama!" he exclaimed, rushing forward to throw his arms around the Queen in a tight, exuberant hug. "What are you doing here? Is everything okay back home?"

Queen Elara laughed, her arms wrapping around her son's waist as she held him close. "Everything is fine, my darling," she said, her voice filled with a warm, reassuring affection. "But I have some news that I think will make you very happy."

Rowan pulled back, his eyes wide and curious as he searched his mother's face for any hint of what she might be talking about. "What is it?" he asked, his voice filled with a mix of excitement and trepidation. "What's going on?"

The Queen's smile widened, her eyes shining with a fierce, unbridled joy. "I've come to discuss the completion of your bond with Luca," she said, her voice filled with a quiet, reverent awe. "And to start planning your wedding ceremony in the Seelie Court."

Luca felt his breath catch in his throat, his heart pounding with a sudden, overwhelming surge of emotion. A wedding ceremony. A chance to pledge his eternal love and devotion to Rowan in front of their families and friends, to make their bond official and unbreakable in the eyes of the gods and all who knew them.

It was a dream that he had never dared to voice, a hope that he had kept buried deep within his heart. But now, with the Queen's words ringing in his ears and the love of his life by his side... it felt like anything was possible, like the future he had always longed for was finally within his grasp.

"A wedding," he whispered, his voice rough and choked with emotion as he turned to Rowan, his hand finding his mate's and twining their fingers together. "I... I don't know what to say. It's everything I've ever wanted, everything I never even knew I could have."

Rowan's eyes were shining with unshed tears, his smile so wide and bright that it seemed to light up the entire room. "Me too," he said, his voice soft and filled with a quiet, unwavering conviction. "I want nothing more than to be yours forever, Luca. To pledge my heart and my soul to you in front of the whole world."

Luca felt a lump rising in his throat, his eyes stinging with sudden, unexpected tears. He had always known that Rowan loved him, that their bond was strong and true and unbreakable. But to hear him say those words, to feel the depth of his devotion and commitment… it was almost more than he could bear.

"I love you," he whispered, his voice rough and choked with emotion as he leaned in to press his forehead against Rowan's, breathing in the sweet, familiar scent of his mate. "I love you so much, Rowan. And I can't wait to marry you, to spend the rest of my life by your side."

Rowan's smile was soft and sweet, his eyes shining with a fierce, unwavering love. "I love you too, Luca," he murmured, his hand coming up to cup Luca's cheek in a tender, reverent caress. "More than anything in this world or the next."

For a long moment, they simply stood there, lost in each other's eyes and in the quiet, perfect intimacy of the moment. But then, with a small, contented sigh, Rowan turned back to his mother, his expression curious and eager.

"So, what do we need to do?" he asked, his voice filled with a quiet, thrumming excitement. "How do we make this official in the eyes of the Seelie Court?"

Queen Elara's smile was warm and knowing, her eyes crinkling at the corners with a hint of mischief. "Well, first things first," she said, her voice filled with a quiet, playful amusement. "We need to start planning the ceremony itself. The guest list, the decorations, the food…"

She trailed off, her expression growing thoughtful as she tapped a finger against her chin. "And of course, we'll need to invite all of your friends and loved ones from Willowbrook. They've been through so much with you, and I know they'll want to be there to celebrate your special day."

Luca felt his heart swell with gratitude and love, a warm, glowing feeling spreading through his chest at the thought of all the people who had stood by their side through the darkest of times. Benjamin and Adrian, Roman and Peter, Gareth and his father… they were more than just friends, more than just allies. They were family, bound by a love and a loyalty that could never be broken.

"That would be amazing," he said, his voice rough with emotion as he met the Queen's gaze with a look of quiet, sincere gratitude. "I can't imagine getting married without them there, without having the chance to share our joy and our love with the people who mean the most to us."

His mother nodded, her eyes shining with a fierce, proud light. "And of course, the entire Wolfheart pack will be there as well," she said, her voice filled with a quiet, unwavering conviction. "We wouldn't miss it for the world, Luca. Not when it means so much to you and Rowan."

Luca felt a lump rising in his throat, his eyes stinging with sudden, unshed tears. He had always known that his pack loved him, that they would stand by his side through thick and thin. But to hear his mother say it out loud, to know that they would be there to witness the most important moment of his life… it meant more than he could ever put into words.

"Thank you," he whispered, his voice rough and choked with emotion as he reached out to take his mother's hand, squeezing it tight in a gesture of silent, heartfelt gratitude. "Thank you for everything, Mom. For being here, for supporting us, for loving us… it means more than you could ever know."

His mother's smile was soft and tender, her eyes shining with a fierce, unwavering love. "Oh, Luca," she murmured, her voice filled with a quiet, aching affection. "You never have to thank me for that. You're my son, and I will always love you, no matter what."

Luca felt his heart swell with emotion, a warmth and a love so fierce and so overwhelming that it stole the breath from his lungs. He had always known that he was lucky, that he had been blessed with a family and a pack that loved him unconditionally, that would stand by his side through even the darkest of times.

But even as Luca savored the warmth and joy of the moment, he couldn't help but notice the flicker of concern that passed over Queen Elara's face, the way her smile faltered ever so slightly as she glanced at Rowan with a look of quiet, solemn intensity.

"What is it, Mother?" Rowan asked, his brow furrowing with worry as he caught the change in his mother's expression. "What's wrong?"

The Queen sighed, her eyes filled with a deep, aching sadness as she reached out to take her son's hand, squeezing it tight in a gesture of comfort and support. "It's Riordan," she said, her voice low and heavy with emotion. "He survived the battle, Rowan. And though he has been severely weakened, I fear that he will stop at nothing to regain his power and seek his revenge."

Luca felt a chill run down his spine at the mention of Riordan's name, a cold, creeping dread that made his stomach clench and his heart race with fear. He had seen firsthand the cruelty and malevolence of the dark mage, had watched as he sought to destroy everything and everyone that Luca held dear.

And the thought of facing him again, of putting Rowan and their loved ones in danger once more… it was almost more than he could bear.

But even as the fear and the doubt threatened to overwhelm him, Luca felt a flicker of something else stirring within him, a quiet, stubborn determination that refused to be extinguished. He was a warrior, a protector, a champion of the light. And he would not let

Riordan or anyone else stand in the way of the happiness and the future that he and Rowan had fought so hard to build.

"We'll be ready for him," he said, his voice low and filled with a quiet, unwavering conviction. "We've beaten him before, and we'll beat him again. Together."

Rowan turned to him, his eyes shining with a fierce, unshakable love. "Luca's right," he said, his hand tightening around his mate's in a gesture of solidarity and support. "We're stronger than Riordan, stronger than anything he can throw at us. And we won't let him take away the life and the love that we've worked so hard to create."

Queen Elara's smile was soft and proud, her eyes filled with a quiet, aching affection. "I know you won't," she said, her voice filled with a deep, abiding faith in her son and his mate. "And you won't be facing him alone, either. The Seelie Court stands with you, Rowan. And we will do everything in our power to ensure that Riordan and his minions are brought to justice once and for all."

Luca's brow furrowed, a flicker of confusion and concern passing over his face. "His minions?" he asked, his voice low and filled with a quiet, simmering anger. "You mean the three dark magic users who caused so much pain and suffering? The ones who helped him to take Rowan in the first place?"

The Queen nodded, her expression grim and filled with a quiet, righteous fury. "Yes," she said, her voice low and filled with a deep, unwavering conviction. "But you needn't worry about them any longer, Luca. They have been imprisoned in a place from which they can never escape, their ability to harm others forever stripped away."

Luca felt a wave of relief wash over him, a weight lifting from his shoulders at the knowledge that at least some of the evil that had threatened their world had been vanquished for good. But even as he savored the small victory, he couldn't help but feel a flicker of unease, a sense that the battle was far from over.

Beside him, Rowan seemed to sense his disquiet, his hand tightening around Luca's in a gesture of comfort and support. "Hey," he said softly, his voice low and filled with a quiet, aching tenderness. "It's okay, Luca. We're going to get through this, I promise."

Luca felt a lump rising in his throat, his eyes stinging with sudden, unshed tears. He knew that Rowan was right, that they had faced worse odds and come out stronger on the other side. But the thought of losing his mate, of watching helplessly as Riordan tore away the happiness and the love that they had fought so hard to build… it was almost more than he could bear.

"I know," he whispered, his voice rough and choked with emotion as he leaned in to rest his forehead against Rowan's, breathing in the sweet, familiar scent of his mate. "I just… I can't lose you again, Rowan. I can't go through that, not now, not ever."

Rowan's smile was soft and tender, his hand coming up to cup Luca's cheek in a gesture of quiet, perfect intimacy. "You won't," he murmured, his voice filled with a deep, unwavering conviction. "I'm not going anywhere, Luca. I'm yours, now and forever. And nothing, not Riordan or anyone else, is ever going to change that."

Luca felt his heart swell with emotion, a fierce, unshakable love burning bright and strong within his chest. He knew that Rowan was right, that their bond was stronger than any darkness or evil that sought to tear them apart. And with his mate by his side, he knew that he could face anything, could overcome any obstacle and emerge victorious on the other side.

"I love you," he whispered, his voice rough and filled with a quiet, aching intensity. "I love you so much, Rowan. And I promise, I will always be there to protect you, to keep you safe from harm, no matter what."

Rowan's smile was soft and sweet, his eyes shining with a fierce, unwavering love. "I know you will, Luca," he murmured, his hand tightening around his mate's in a gesture of quiet, perfect trust. "And I will always be there to do the same for you. Because that's what love is, isn't it? Being there for each other, no matter what."

Luca felt a warmth and a joy so fierce and so overwhelming that it stole the breath from his lungs, a love that seemed to fill every corner of his heart and soul until there was no room for anything else. And in that moment, he knew that Rowan was right, that their love was a force that could overcome any darkness, any evil that sought to tear them apart.

"You're right," he said softly, his voice filled with a quiet, unwavering conviction. "And that's why we can't let Riordan or anyone else dim the brightness of our future together. We have to keep moving forward, keep fighting for the life and the love that we know we deserve."

Queen Elara smiled, her eyes shining with a fierce, proud light. "Spoken like a true king," she said, her voice filled with a quiet, knowing amusement. "And speaking of which… I believe we have a wedding to plan, do we not?"

Luca felt a grin tugging at his lips, a flicker of excitement and anticipation chasing away the lingering shadows of fear and doubt. "We do indeed," he said, his voice filled with a quiet, thrumming joy. "And I don't know about you, but I can't wait to get started."

Rowan laughed, the sound bright and joyful and filled with a fierce, unbridled happiness. "Me neither," he said, his hand tightening around Luca's in a gesture of quiet, perfect unity. "So, where do we begin?"

Epilogue

Rowan

Rowan stood before the full-length mirror, his hands trembling slightly as he fiddled with the intricate fastenings of his traditional fae wedding attire. The soft, shimmering fabric felt like liquid moonlight against his skin, but despite its ethereal beauty, Rowan couldn't seem to quell the nerves that fluttered in his stomach like a kaleidoscope of butterflies.

"Come on, Rowan," he muttered to himself, his brow furrowing in frustration as he struggled with a particularly stubborn clasp. "You've faced down dark mages and shadow beasts. Surely you can handle a little bit of formal wear."

But even as he spoke the words, Rowan knew that his anxiety had little to do with the clothes themselves. It was the weight of the moment, the significance of the day that loomed before him like a towering mountain, both thrilling and terrifying in its immensity.

A knock at the door startled him from his reverie, and Rowan turned to see Benjamin poking his head into the room, a warm smile on his face. "Hey there, groom-to-be," he said, his voice filled with a gentle, teasing affection. "How are you holding up?"

Rowan let out a shaky laugh, his hands falling to his sides as he turned to face his friend. "Honestly? I'm a nervous wreck," he admitted, his voice raw with emotion. "I know it's silly, but I can't help feeling like something's going to go wrong, like I'm going to trip over my own feet or forget my vows or…"

He trailed off, his throat tightening with a sudden, overwhelming surge of emotion. Benjamin's smile softened, his eyes filled with a deep, understanding sympathy as he stepped fully into the room, closing the door behind him with a quiet click.

"Oh, Rowan," he said, his voice low and soothing as he crossed the space between them, pulling the younger man into a warm, comforting embrace. "It's not silly at all. What you're feeling is completely normal, I promise."

Rowan let out a shuddering breath, his arms coming up to wrap around Benjamin's waist as he leaned into the hug, drawing strength and comfort from the solid, steady presence of his friend. "Really?" he asked, his voice small and uncertain. "Because right now, I feel like I'm about to vibrate out of my own skin."

Benjamin chuckled, the sound warm and rich and filled with a quiet, knowing amusement. "Trust me, I've been there," he said, pulling back to look Rowan in the eye, his hands resting on the younger man's shoulders in a gesture of comfort and support. "When I married Adrian, I was so nervous I thought I was going to pass out right there at the altar."

Rowan's eyes widened, a flicker of surprise and disbelief washing over his face. "You?" he asked, his voice filled with a quiet, awed incredulity. "But you always seem so calm and collected, so sure of yourself and your love."

Benjamin's smile was soft and tender, his eyes filled with a deep, abiding affection. "That's because I had Adrian by my side," he said, his voice low and filled with a quiet, unwavering conviction. "And I knew that no matter what happened, no matter how nervous or unsure I felt in that moment, he would always be there to catch me if I fell."

Rowan felt a lump rising in his throat, his eyes stinging with sudden, unshed tears. He knew exactly what Benjamin meant, knew the depth of love and devotion that flowed between him and Luca like a never-ending river. It was a bond that went beyond words, beyond reason, a connection that could weather any storm and emerge stronger and more radiant than ever before.

"I feel the same way about Luca," he said softly, his voice rough with emotion. "Like he's my rock, my anchor in the storm. And I know that as long as we're together, as long as we have each other… everything will be okay."

Benjamin nodded, his eyes shining with a fierce, proud light. "Exactly," he said, his voice filled with a quiet, unwavering certainty. "And that's why you have nothing to worry about, Rowan. Because at the end of the day, all that matters is the love that you and Luca share. Everything else is just details."

Rowan felt a warmth and a joy so fierce and so overwhelming that it stole the breath from his lungs, a love that seemed to fill every corner of his heart and soul until there was no room for anything else. He knew that Benjamin was right, that the nerves and the doubts and the fears that plagued him were nothing compared to the incredible, unshakable bond that he and Luca had forged through all their trials and tribulations.

"You're right," he said softly, a small, grateful smile tugging at the corners of his lips. "Thank you, Benjamin. For being here, for talking me down from the ledge. I don't know what I would do without you."

Benjamin grinned, his eyes sparkling with a hint of mischief. "Well, for starters, you'd be walking down the aisle with your tunic on backwards," he teased, his hand reaching out to adjust a stray fold of fabric at Rowan's shoulder. "Here, let me help you with that."

Rowan laughed, the sound bright and joyful as he relaxed into Benjamin's expert ministrations. The older man's hands were deft and sure as they smoothed out the wrinkles and straightened the seams, his touch gentle and reassuring.

"There," Benjamin said at last, stepping back to admire his handiwork with a critical eye. "Now you look like a true prince of the Seelie Court. Luca won't know what hit him."

Rowan turned back to the mirror, his breath catching in his throat as he took in his own reflection. The person staring back at him was almost unrecognizable, a vision of ethereal beauty and regal grace that seemed to glow with an inner light. The soft, shimmering fabric of his tunic and trousers clung to his lithe frame like a second skin, the delicate embroidery and intricate bead work catching the light and casting a kaleidoscope of colors across his skin.

But it was the look in his eyes that truly took Rowan's breath away, the fierce, unwavering love and joy that seemed to radiate from every pore. It was a look that spoke of hope and promise, of a future filled with endless possibilities and unbreakable bonds.

"I almost don't recognize myself," he whispered, his voice filled with a quiet, awed wonder. "I never thought… I never dreamed that I would ever have this, that I would ever find a love like the one Luca and I share."

Benjamin smiled, his hand coming to rest on Rowan's shoulder in a gesture of quiet, understanding support. "But you did," he said softly, his voice filled with a deep, abiding affection. "And now, you get to spend the rest of your life celebrating that love, nurturing it and watching it grow stronger with each passing day."

Rowan felt a lump rising in his throat, his eyes stinging with sudden, unshed tears. He knew that Benjamin was right, that the incredible, unshakable bond that he and Luca shared was a gift beyond measure, a blessing that he would cherish and protect with every fiber of his being.

And in that moment, standing there in his wedding finery with his dearest friend by his side, Rowan felt a sudden, overwhelming surge of gratitude and love, a fierce, unshakable conviction that he was exactly where he was meant to be, doing exactly what he was meant to do.

"Speaking of celebrating love," he said softly, his voice filled with a quiet, hesitant excitement as he turned to face Benjamin fully, his eyes searching the older man's face for any hint of reaction. "I have something for you, Benjamin. A gift, to thank you for everything you've done for me and Luca."

Benjamin's eyes widened, a flicker of surprise and curiosity washing over his face. "Rowan, you didn't have to do that," he said, his voice filled with a quiet, touched wonder. "Being here, getting to share in your special day… that's gift enough for me."

But Rowan just shook his head, a small, secretive smile tugging at the corners of his lips. "I know," he said softly, his hand reaching into the folds of his tunic to retrieve a small, intricately carved wooden box. "But I wanted to. Because you and Adrian… you've been more than just friends to us. You've been family, in every sense of the word."

He held out the box to Benjamin, his hand trembling slightly with a mix of nerves and anticipation. "I know that you and Adrian have been talking about starting a family of your own," he said softly, his voice filled with a quiet, understanding sympathy. "And I wanted to do something to help make that dream a reality."

Benjamin's eyes widened, his hand reaching out to take the box with a reverent, almost awestruck gentleness. "Rowan," he breathed, his voice filled with a quiet, disbelieving wonder. "What… what is this?"

Rowan smiled, his eyes shining with a fierce, proud light. "It's a sacred apple from the grove of Cernunnos," he said softly, his voice filled with a quiet, unwavering conviction. "A gift from the gods themselves, imbued with the power to grant life and fertility to those who partake of its flesh."

Benjamin's breath caught in his throat, his eyes filling with sudden, unshed tears. "Rowan," he whispered, his voice choked with emotion. "I don't… I don't know what to say. This is… it's too much, too generous."

But Rowan just shook his head, his smile soft and tender as he reached out to clasp Benjamin's hand in his own. "It's not," he said softly, his voice filled with a quiet, unwavering certainty. "After everything you and Adrian have done for us, for the countless times you've risked your own lives to keep us safe… this is the least I could do to repay that kindness."

He paused, his expression growing serious as he fixed Benjamin with a steady, unwavering gaze. "There are instructions inside the box," he said softly, his voice filled with a quiet, solemn intensity. "A ritual that must be performed to unlock the apple's power. But Benjamin, I need you to promise me something."

Benjamin nodded, his eyes wide and filled with a quiet, awed wonder. "Anything," he breathed, his voice barely above a whisper.

Rowan's hand tightened around Benjamin's, his expression filled with a fierce, protective urgency. "Don't open the box until you and Adrian are absolutely certain that you're ready," he said softly, his voice filled with a quiet, unwavering conviction. "Having a child… it's not a decision to be made lightly, and I don't want you to feel pressured or obligated just because I've given you this gift."

Benjamin's eyes softened, a small, grateful smile tugging at the corners of his lips. "I understand, Rowan," he said softly, his voice filled with a quiet, unwavering certainty. "And I promise, Adrian and I will think long and hard before we take this step. But knowing that we have your support, your blessing… it means more than I can ever say."

Rowan felt a lump rising in his throat, his eyes stinging with sudden, unshed tears. He had always known that Benjamin and Adrian would make incredible parents, that any child would be lucky to be born into a family so full of love and light and laughter.

And now, knowing that he had played a small part in making that dream a reality, that he had given his dearest friends a gift that would change their lives in ways they could scarcely imagine… it filled him with a joy and a sense of purpose that he had never known before.

"I love you, Benjamin," he said softly, his voice rough with emotion as he pulled the older man into a tight, fierce hug. "I love you and Adrian both, more than I can ever say. And I know that you're going to be the most incredible parents any child could ever ask for."

Benjamin's arms tightened around him, a soft, shuddering sob escaping his lips as he buried his face in Rowan's shoulder. "Thank you, Rowan," he whispered, his voice choked with emotion. "Thank you for being my friend, my brother in all but blood. I don't know what I would do without you."

Rowan felt a warmth and a love so fierce and so overwhelming that it stole the breath from his lungs, a bond of friendship and family that could weather any storm and emerge stronger and more radiant than ever before.

And as they stood there in the quiet, sunlit room, their hearts full to bursting with joy and gratitude and the promise of a future filled with endless possibilities, Rowan knew that he had finally found his place in the world, his purpose and his destiny.

Luca

Luca stood before the mirror, his hands smoothing down the front of his suit in a nervous, repetitive motion. He could hardly believe that this day had finally arrived, that in just a few short hours, he would be standing before his friends and family, pledging his heart and his soul to the love of his life.

A knock at the door startled him from his thoughts, and Luca turned to see his brother Gareth poking his head into the room, a small, knowing smile on his face.

"Hey, little bro," Gareth said, his voice warm with affection. "Father wants to see you. Says it's important."

Luca felt a flicker of surprise and apprehension wash over him, his brow furrowing in confusion. "He's here?" he asked, his voice filled with a quiet, hesitant disbelief. "I didn't think he was going to make it."

Gareth just shrugged, his smile widening into a playful grin. "You know Father," he said, his voice filled with a fond, exasperated amusement. "He's always full of surprises."

With a final, reassuring nod, Gareth slipped back out of the room, leaving Luca alone with his thoughts and his mounting nerves. He took a deep breath, his hands clenching and unclenching at his sides as he tried to steady himself, to prepare for whatever conversation lay ahead.

But before he could fully collect himself, the door opened once more, and Luca found himself face to face with his father, the man who had been both his mentor and his tormentor for so many years.

"Father," he said, his voice rough with emotion as he took in the sight of his father, dressed to the nines in a perfectly tailored suit, his usually stern face softened by a small, almost sheepish smile.

"Luca," his father said, his voice warm and filled with a quiet, hesitant affection. "You look… you look good, son. Really good."

Luca felt a lump rising in his throat, his eyes stinging with sudden, unshed tears. It had been so long since he had heard his father speak to him with anything resembling warmth or approval, so long since he had felt like anything more than a disappointment, a failure in his father's eyes.

"Thanks, Father," he said softly, his voice filled with a quiet, awed gratitude. "You look pretty sharp yourself. Did Mom have to wrestle you into that suit?"

His father chuckled, a low, rumbling sound that filled the room with a warmth and a levity that Luca had never heard before. "You know your mother," he said, his eyes crinkling at the corners with a fond, exasperated amusement. "She's always been the one to keep me in line, to make sure I'm presentable for the important occasions."

Luca felt a small, hesitant smile tugging at the corners of his lips, a flicker of hope and possibility kindling in his chest. Maybe, just maybe, this was a sign that things could be different between them, that they could find a way to mend the broken bridges and heal the old, festering wounds that had kept them apart for so long.

But even as he savored the warmth and the joy of the moment, Luca couldn't help but feel a flicker of concern, a nagging sense of unease that made his stomach clench and his heart race with sudden, irrational fear.

"Is everything okay?" he asked, his voice low and filled with a quiet, hesitant trepidation. "Is Rowan alright? Did something happen?"

His father's smile softened, his eyes filling with a deep, aching understanding. "Everything's fine, son," he said, his voice low and soothing, like a balm to Luca's frayed nerves. "Rowan's fine, the wedding's still on track. I just... I wanted to talk to you, before everything gets started."

Luca felt a flicker of surprise and curiosity wash over him, his brow furrowing in confusion. "Talk to me?" he repeated, his voice filled with a quiet, hesitant wonder. "About what?"

His father sighed, a heavy, weary sound that seemed to carry the weight of a thousand unsaid words, a thousand unspoken regrets. "About... about everything, Luca," he said softly, his voice filled with a quiet, aching sincerity. "About the way I've treated you, the way I've pushed you and challenged you and made you feel like you were never good enough."

Luca felt his breath catch in his throat, his eyes widening with shock and disbelief. In all his years, he had never once heard his father apologize, never once heard him admit to any fault or flaw or weakness.

And yet here he was, standing before him with tears in his eyes and a tremor in his voice, laying his soul bare in a way that Luca had never thought possible.

"Father," he said softly, his own voice choked with emotion as he took a step forward, his hand reaching out to rest on his father's shoulder in a gesture of comfort and support. "You don't have to… you don't have to apologize. I know that everything you did, every challenge you put me through… it was all to make me stronger, to prepare me for the battles that lay ahead."

But his father just shook his head, a small, sad smile tugging at the corners of his lips. "No, Luca," he said softly, his voice filled with a quiet, aching regret. "It wasn't just about making you stronger, about preparing you for the future. It was about my own fear, my own insecurity. I was so afraid of losing you, of watching you get hurt or disappointed or heartbroken… that I pushed you away, that I made you feel like you had to earn my love and my approval."

Luca felt a lump rising in his throat, his eyes stinging with sudden, unshed tears. He had always known that his father loved him, that beneath the gruff exterior and the stern demeanor, there was a heart that beat with a fierce, unwavering devotion to his family.

But to hear him say it out loud, to hear the raw, aching vulnerability in his voice… it was almost more than Luca could bear.

"Father," he whispered, his voice choked with emotion as he pulled his father into a tight, fierce hug, his arms wrapping around the older man's broad shoulders like a lifeline, like an anchor in the storm. "I forgive you. I forgive you for everything, for every harsh word and every cold shoulder. Because I know that beneath it all, you were just trying to keep me safe, to protect me from the world and all its dangers."

His father's arms tightened around him, a soft, shuddering sob escaping his lips as he buried his face in Luca's shoulder. "I'm so proud of you, Luca," he whispered, his voice muffled and thick with tears. "I'm so proud of the man you've become, of the strength and the courage and the love that you bring to everything you do."

A knock at the door startled them both, and they pulled apart to see Luca's mother standing in the doorway, her eyes shining with tears and her lips curved in a soft, tender smile.

"It's time, my loves," she said softly, her voice filled with a quiet, aching joy. "The guests are all seated, and Rowan is waiting for you at the altar."

Luca felt his heart skip a beat, a sudden, overwhelming surge of love and excitement and anticipation washing over him like a tidal wave. This was it, the moment he had been waiting for, the moment he had dreamed of for longer than he could remember.

His father's hand clasped his shoulder, his grip strong and steady and filled with a quiet, unwavering support. "You've got this, Luca," he said softly, his voice filled with a fierce, proud conviction. "You and Rowan… you were meant to be together, meant to build a life and a love that will stand the test of time."

With a final, tearful nod and a whispered word of thanks, Luca stepped forward, his mother's arm linked through his own as they made their way towards the altar, towards the man who held his heart and his soul in the palm of his hand.

As he stepped into the main hall, Luca felt his breath catch in his throat, his eyes widening with awe and wonder at the sight that greeted him. The room was filled with flowers and candlelight, their friends and family gathered together in a sea of smiling faces and shining eyes.

And there, at the end of the aisle, stood Rowan, his face radiant with joy and his eyes filled with a love so fierce and so pure that it stole the breath from Luca's lungs.

He looked like a vision, an angel sent from the heavens to bless Luca with his love and his light. His hair was a halo of spun gold, his skin luminous in the soft, warm glow of the candles. And the smile that curved his lips, the way his eyes shone with unshed tears… it was the most beautiful thing Luca had ever seen, a sight that he knew he would carry with him for the rest of his days.

As he walked down the aisle, his steps slow and measured, Luca felt a sense of peace and rightness wash over him, a bone-deep certainty that this was exactly where he was meant to be, doing exactly what he was meant to do.

And when he reached the altar, when he took Rowan's hands in his own and gazed into those endless, violet eyes… he knew that he had found his home, his haven, his forever.

"Rowan," he said softly, his voice rough with emotion as he squeezed his mate's hands in a gesture of love and devotion. "From the moment I first saw you, I knew that you were the one, the missing piece of my heart that I had been searching for all my life."

Rowan's eyes shone with tears, his smile trembling with the force of his love and his joy. "Luca," he whispered, his voice soft and filled with a quiet, aching tenderness. "You are my everything, my sun and my moon and my stars. Without you, I am lost, adrift in a sea of darkness and despair."

Luca felt his own tears spilling over, his heart swelling with a love so fierce and so overwhelming that it threatened to consume him whole. "I promise to love you, Rowan," he said softly, his voice filled with a quiet, unwavering conviction. "To cherish you and protect you and stand by your side through every trial and every triumph. I promise to be your shelter in the storm, your light in the darkness, your home and your haven for all the days of our lives."

Rowan's smile was blinding, his eyes shining with a joy that seemed to light up the entire room. "And I promise to love you, Luca," he said softly, his voice filled with a quiet, aching sincerity. "To be your strength when you are weak, your comfort when you are hurting, your partner and your equal in all things. I promise to walk beside you on this journey, to build a life and a love with you that will endure through every challenge and every change."

And with those words, with those vows of love and devotion and eternal commitment, they sealed their bond with a kiss, their lips meeting in a sweet, perfect moment of unity and bliss.

Around them, their friends and family cheered and wept and laughed, their voices rising in a joyful cacophony of love and celebration. But Luca and Rowan barely heard them, lost as they were in the perfect, shining wonder of each other's eyes.

They were married now, bound together by the unbreakable ties of love and fate and destiny. And as they turned to face the world, hand in hand and heart to heart, they knew that they could face anything, could overcome any obstacle and emerge stronger and more united than ever before.

For they were Luca and Rowan, mates and partners and soulmates in every sense of the word. And together, they would build a life and a love that would stand the test of time, that would endure through every trial and every triumph.

And nothing, not the darkness of their pasts or the uncertainty of their futures, could ever tear them apart. For their love was a force that could move mountains, a light that could chase away even the deepest of shadows.

And with that love burning bright within them, with the strength and the courage of their bond to guide them through... they knew that they could achieve anything, could make any dream a reality.

And so, with hearts full of joy and eyes shining with the promise of a future more beautiful than they could ever have imagined… Luca and Rowan stepped forward into the world, ready to face whatever lay ahead.

Together, always and forever.

Thank you and Please Leave a Review!

Dear Readers,

As we come to the end of this wild and whimsical journey with the maybe Final book of the Willowbrook Series, I want to take a moment to express my deepest gratitude. Thank you for joining us on this adventure filled with laughter, love, and a touch of the supernatural.

It's been an absolute joy to share this story with you, and I hope their antics brought a smile to your face and warmth to your heart. Writing their tale has been an incredible experience, and I'm so grateful for the opportunity to share it with all of you.

If you enjoyed our story, please consider leaving a review. Your feedback means the world to me, and it helps other readers discover our book and join in on the fun.

Thank you again for your support, your laughter, and your love. Here's to many more adventures together!

With heartfelt appreciation,
Ken Sanchez

About the Author

Ken Sanchez, the visionary behind spellbinding M/M romance-fantasy worlds where love and magic entwine in a mesmerizing dance. With a heart devoted to the art of LGBTQ+ romance and an unbounded imagination,

Please sign up for my newsletter to get my new releases and get some freebies! And join my Facebook group for more updates! Linktree link is below!

You can connect with me on:

🔗 https://linktr.ee/kensanchezbooks

Also by Ken Sanchez

Enchanted (Willowbrook Book One)
In the enchanting town of Willowbrook, a young man named Benjamin discovers a remarkable power—the ability to bring stories to life. When he encounters a reclusive Beast named Adrian, cursed to shift between a fearsome ice dragon and a human form that freezes everything he touches, their destinies entwine.

As Benjamin and Adrian navigate a treacherous journey filled with love, friendship, and the transformative power of stories, they must break Adrian's curse to save Willowbrook from an eternal winter. With the town's magical essence slowly fading, time is running out.

Stormweaver (Willowbrook Book Two)

In the enchanted town of Willowbrook, where supernatural forces intertwine, a storm is brewing, threatening to shatter the delicate balance between magic and reality. Weather witch Dominic Reed seeks solace in his bakery, Glimmer, but his haunted past and tumultuous family dynamics refuse to fade.

Enter Christian Belgrade, heir to a vampire coven, whose scarred history and possessive nature are eclipsed only by his mysterious powers. When their worlds collide at Christian's club, a revelation unfolds, setting off a chain of events that will test their strengths, unravel their vulnerabilities, and force them to confront the shadows that lurk in the magical underbelly of Willowbrook.

As the connection deepens between Dominic and Christian, they must navigate the treacherous waters of Elder Eros Grim's vendetta and Dominic's malevolent stepfamily. Will love be enough to weather the storm that threatens to consume them, or will the secrets of their pasts tear them apart?

Shadowplay (Willowbrook Book Three)

When Peter Naps arrives in the enchanting town of Willowbrook, he's hoping to find answers to the questions that have haunted him for years. Plagued by mysterious gaps in his memory and a sense of otherness he can't quite shake, Peter is drawn to the town's strange energy and the whispers of magic that seem to call to him from every corner.

But as he delves deeper into the secrets of Willowbrook and his own forgotten past, Peter finds himself entangled in a web of danger and intrigue. Guided by cryptic clues and the enigmatic James Crane, a man with his own hidden agenda, Peter begins to uncover the truth about his powers and the forces that seek to control them.

With the help of a quirky cast of characters, including his fiercely loyal best friend Lyra and the mysterious librarian who seems to know more than she's letting on, Peter must navigate a treacherous landscape of shadows and secrets, where nothing is quite as it seems and the line between friend and foe is blurred. As he races to unravel the mystery of his own identity and the dark forces that threaten to tear Willowbrook apart, Peter will be forced to confront his deepest fears and most painful truths, to embrace the power that lies within him and the love that refuses to let him go.

Echoes of Destiny (Shadowguards Book One)
Eryx, a gifted musician, channels haunting melodies that echo his forgotten godly lineage. When a sinister encounter alters his reality, he finds solace in an enigmatic guardian named Alex, whose alluring presence sparks an inexplicable connection.

Unbeknownst to Eryx, Alex is Hades, sentinel of the Underworld. As he guides Eryx through their intertwined destinies, an undeniable attraction forms, challenging the fabric of their worlds.

Amidst mysticism in contemporary New York, ancient prophecies resurge with encroaching darkness. Their bond becomes a beacon of hope as Eryx's ancestry awakens and their love deepens. The duo embarks on a quest that will test their resolve, unravel hidden truths, and decide humanity's fate.

Light Redeemed (Shadowguards Book Two)
The line between mortal and divine blurs as an ancient threat resurfaces, determined to plunge New York into chaos. Eryx Ross, now fully embracing his destiny as Apollo's vessel, must navigate his burgeoning powers and deepening bond with the enigmatic Alexander Knight, the mortal embodiment of Hades. Together, they face an unconventional challenge that will test their love and the very fabric of their world.

Amidst the gathering darkness, Eryx and Alex's souls entwine on a cosmic scale, their love a beacon of hope against the sinister machinations of the Order. They rally allies both old and new, gods and mortals alike, to stand against the rising tide of evil. But the Order holds a terrifying trump card – a mimic with the power to steal magic – threatening to unravel all they hold dear.

Twisted Fate (Major Arcana Book One)
In a world where mutants are feared and hunted, one man stands as a beacon of hope and justice. Ethan Hawke, a successful businessman by day and a vigilante known as "The Arcana" by night, wields the power of the tarot to protect the innocent and uncover a sinister conspiracy that threatens the very fabric of society.

But when a chance encounter with Liam Quinn, a heroic firefighter with pyrokinetic abilities, sparks a bitter rivalry, Ethan must confront not only the forces of evil that lurk in the shadows but also his own deepest fears and desires.

As the two men clash and the mystery deepens, they find themselves drawn into a web of secrets, lies, and forbidden passion. With danger lurking around every corner and the fate of the world hanging in the balance, Ethan and Liam must put aside their differences and forge an unlikely alliance to unravel the truth before it's too late.

But in a city where nothing is as it seems and power comes at a price, can they learn to trust each other—and themselves—in time to save everything they hold dear?

No Matter What

David Miller's world is turned upside down when a brutal hate crime leaves him battered, broken, and robbed of his memories. As he struggles to piece together the fragments of his past, there's one constant he can always count on: his best friend, Ryan Evans.

Ryan has been by David's side since their teenage years, his unwavering support a beacon of hope in the darkness. But as David begins the long road to recovery, Ryan realizes that his feelings run deeper than friendship. He's in love with his best friend, and he'll do anything to help David heal.

Through tender moments, heartfelt confessions, and the unbreakable bond of their friendship, David and Ryan embark on a journey of rediscovery and newfound love. Together, they'll face the challenges of the past and present, fighting for a future where their love can flourish.

No Matter What is a poignant, emotional tale of resilience, hope, and the transformative power of love. It's a reminder that even in our darkest hours, the unbreakable bonds of friendship and love have the power to heal, to mend, and to make us whole again.